Her Miracle

She's having his baby!

By Request

Praise for three bestselling authors – Barbara Hannay, Cathy Williams and Marion Lennox

About Barbara Hannay:
'…Barbara Hannay pens a wonderful romance with two vulnerable yet strong characters.'
—*Romantic Times*

About THE BABY SCANDAL:
'Cathy Williams pens an emotional tale with a layered conflict and great character development.'
—*Romantic Times*

About Marion Lennox:
'Marion Lennox's latest is a dynamic read with outstanding characters, a fabulous conflict and wonderful development.'
—*Romantic Times*

Her Nine Month Miracle

THE PREGNANCY
DISCOVERY
by
Barbara Hannay

THE BABY SCANDAL
by
Cathy Williams

EMERGENCY WEDDING
by
Marion Lennox

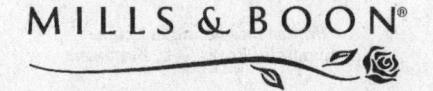

MILLS & BOON®

DID YOU PURCHASE THIS BOOK WITHOUT A COVER?
If you did, you should be aware it is **stolen property** as it was reported *unsold and destroyed* by a retailer. Neither the author nor the publisher has received any payment for this book.

All the characters in this book have no existence outside the imagination of the author, and have no relation whatsoever to anyone bearing the same name or names. They are not even distantly inspired by any individual known or unknown to the author, and all the incidents are pure invention.

All Rights Reserved including the right of reproduction in whole or in part in any form. This edition is published by arrangement with Harlequin Enterprises II B.V. The text of this publication or any part thereof may not be reproduced or transmitted in any form or by any means, electronic or mechanical, including photocopying, recording, storage in an information retrieval system, or otherwise, without the written permission of the publisher.

This book is sold subject to the condition that it shall not, by way of trade or otherwise, be lent, resold, hired out or otherwise circulated without the prior consent of the publisher in any form of binding or cover other than that in which it is published and without a similar condition including this condition being imposed on the subsequent purchaser.

MILLS & BOON and MILLS & BOON with the Rose Device are registered trademarks of the publisher.
Harlequin Mills & Boon Limited,
Eton House, 18-24 Paradise Road, Richmond, Surrey, TW9 1SR

PLAIN JANE MAKEOVER
© by Harlequin Enterprises II B.V., 2005

The Pregnancy Discovery, The Baby Scandal and *Emergency Wedding* were first published in Great Britain by Harlequin Mills & Boon Limited in separate, single volumes.

The Pregnancy Discovery © Barbara Hannay 2001
The Baby Scandal © Cathy Williams 2000
Emergency Wedding © Marion Lennox 2001

ISBN 0 263 84480 3

05-1005

Printed and bound in Spain
by Litografia Rosés S.A., Barcelona

Barbara Hannay was born in Sydney, educated in Brisbane, and has spent most of her adult life living in tropical North Queensland, where she and her husband have raised four children. While she has enjoyed many happy times camping and canoeing in the bush, she also delights in an urban lifestyle—chamber music, contemporary dance, movies and dining out. An English teacher, she has always loved writing, and now, by having her stories published, she is living her most cherished fantasy. Visit www.barbarahannay.com

Don't miss Barbara Hannay's latest emotional story: CHRISTMAS GIFT: A FAMILY On sale in November 2005, in Tender Romance™!

THE PREGNANCY DISCOVERY

by

Barbara Hannay

For Magnetic Island and my fortunate
friends who live there.

PROLOGUE

MEG almost missed seeing the old bottle lying half in, half out of the damp sand.

Most evenings, on her solitary walks along the beach on Magnetic Island, she found a trail of shells, broken coral and driftwood. She often came across fishing floats, pieces of timber from wrecks on the Great Barrier Reef...and bottles.

But this evening, just as she passed this particular bottle, a ray from the setting sun struck its glass. It glinted and winked at her. Meg paused and bent closer. It was then she noticed that the neck was sealed and a little stirring of curiosity, a prickle of anticipation, prompted her to reach down and tug the bottle out of its sandy bed.

At first she thought it was empty. But when she held it up to the fading light, she saw a shadowy cylinder of paper inside and her breath snagged on a sudden gasp.

A letter.

A letter in a bottle.

Her first reaction was excitement, a kind of childish thrill...and hot on its heels came a thousand questions. But then a strange kind of sixth sense buzzed through Meg.

Her heart drummed.

Shivering, she tried to shrug off the unsettling notion that she and the bottle shared a connection—a tenuous, but important link.

The feeling wouldn't go away.

Around her the tropical night was closing in. All that

was left of the sun was a blush of pink along the tops of the island's hills. The darkening waters of the bay threw themselves gently against the coral sand in a slow slap...slap...slap.

The rest of the world was going about its business, just as it did every evening, but Meg felt different...as if her life had been touched by an unseen hand.

Clutching the bottle to her chest, she hurried back up the beach and along the bush track to the car park. Carefully, she wrapped it in a towel and settled it safely under the passenger's seat of her Mini Moke. She would wait till she got back to her bungalow to open the bottle with great care and she would read its contents in complete privacy.

And then she would know...

CHAPTER ONE

THE last thing Sam Kirby needed was another pretty woman in his life.

His personal assistant, who spent her days juggling his crowded social calendar with his hectic business appointments, had told him so on many occasions.

So when he rushed into his downtown Seattle office straight from his latest corporate battle, he didn't expect to find a photo of a beautiful, bikini-clad girl smack on top of the paperwork needing his immediate attention.

'Ellen, what's this?' He spun around so abruptly he almost collided with his assistant, who'd been following faithfully at his heels.

Her eyes flicked anxiously to the photo. 'It came this morning in a courier express package from Australia.' She picked up several sheets from his desk. 'The operator of an island holiday resort sent it along with a news clipping and a letter.'

He frowned. 'If it's just an advertising gimmick, throw it in the bin. The way things are at present I won't be free to take a holiday any time in the next decade.'

'It's not advertising, Sam. I'm afraid there's more to it.'

With a grimace of exasperation, he took the clipping Ellen held out. The photo showed a lovely blonde standing on a postcard-perfect, tropical beach. Her name, the caption claimed, was Meg Bennet and she was holding an old bottle.

For a little longer than was strictly necessary, he let his gaze linger on her.

She wore a bikini top and a simple sarong in different shades of blue tied loosely around her slim hips. Her midriff glowed honey-gold and her hair was a pleasing tumble of sunshiny curls.

But she wasn't just another remarkably pretty girl.

What Sam found unexpectedly interesting, almost magnetic, was the disturbing directness of her smiling eyes as they looked straight out of the page at him.

It bugged him that he couldn't determine the exact colour of those eyes but, for a heady moment, he thought how interesting it would be to see them close up—just before he kissed her.

'Sam, your social diary is fully-booked well into next month,' his long suffering assistant remarked dryly, 'and that particular young woman lives on the other side of the Pacific.'

'Too bad,' he responded with a quick grin and a shrug before he refocused his concentration on the clipping from an Australian newspaper. 'Love letter found in bottle on tropical island,' he read aloud and, letting out an impatient sigh, he silently skimmed the rest of the story.

When he finished, he looked at Ellen with a puzzled frown. 'I don't understand why we've been sent this. Some American airman wrote a love letter to his bride back in 1942 and stuck it in a bottle and now it's turned up on the Great Barrier Reef almost sixty years later. So what?'

'Perhaps you were too side-tracked by the photo to notice,' Ellen prompted. 'But the story also mentions that they're trying to trace the American who wrote the letter, or his descendants.'

'But what has that to do with us at Kirby & Son?'

Ellen straightened her impeccably neat suit jacket.

And Sam felt a nasty jab of alarm. 'Ellen, what is it?'

She smiled gently. 'According to this letter from the manager of the island resort, the man who wrote the message in the bottle has been identified and his descendants have been traced.'

'And?'

'And his name was Thomas Jefferson Kirby—'

'My grandfather,' Sam completed in a choked, disbelieving whisper.

'Yes.'

'Whew!' He closed his eyes for a second or two. Slowly, he looked at Ellen again and shook his head. 'Tom Kirby died during the war. My father never even knew the poor guy.'

Again he stared at the photo and the bottle in the girl's hand. 'Who would have thought?' He held out his hand for the letter. 'What else does this Australian have to say?'

As he read, his stomach tightened an extra notch. 'What's he playing at? He reckons there was a new will in the bottle and he won't release the details until someone from my family goes over there.'

'There's no way your father could undertake that kind of journey.'

'Of course he can't, he's far too frail, but how the heck does this guy expect me to just drop everything and head off to some tropical island down under?' Groaning, he clapped a hand to his forehead. 'I don't have time to deal with this.'

Ellen looked at her young boss over her half glasses. 'There's a lot at stake. Kirby & Son has been in your family for four generations.'

'I know. I know.' Sam pushed aside thoughts of what

such stress might do to his ailing father. 'There's something suspicious about this Aussie. I don't like the way he's refusing to hand over the letter unless I show up in person.' With one hand rubbing his jaw, he added, 'I'll have to give this some thought.'

Ellen nodded and returned without comment to her desk in the adjoining office.

Tossing the photo and the papers onto his desk, Sam shoved his hands deep in his trouser pockets and strode towards the huge plate-glass window that overlooked the Seattle waterfront and the Bell Street Pier.

This sudden news about his grandfather had caught him way off-base.

It was the last thing he needed. Since his father's heart attack, Sam had sole responsibility for running the family's huge multimillion dollar construction company. He'd been working at a killing pace for the past three years and there was no sign of things slowing down.

Now, he'd been pitched a curve ball by an ancestor he'd rarely thought about and had never even mourned. He drew in an huge breath and let it out slowly, trying to diffuse the overwhelming sense of pressure.

Gloomily, he stared through the window at the world outside. From his vantage point, the whole of Seattle seemed stripped of any colour this afternoon. Although it was late spring, grey skies, and grey office blocks overlooked a grey waterfront. Even the offshore islands were dark charcoal smudges floating on dull slate-coloured water.

The idea of escape—especially of escaping to sunshine and warmth—had distinct appeal. He could collect this letter, steal a few days to dive on the coral reefs and smell the frangipani. Check out the colour of Meg Bennet's eyes…

Pacing the carpet back to his desk, his mind tussled with his dilemma. What he needed to know was whether this new will in Australia was genuine. If any of his competitors got wind of a will that could question the legal ownership of Kirby & Son, it would be like having an ace up their sleeves in a multimillion-dollar card game.

A discreet cough from the doorway interrupted his thoughts. 'Sam.' Ellen sounded hesitant, looked sympathetic. 'I just had a phone call from a reporter at the Seattle Times. He wants to talk to you. It seems the media already know about the bottle.'

Sam cursed under his breath.

'The press will make a field day out of it,' Ellen agreed. 'Especially after that society columnist dubbed you Seattle's favourite bachelor last week.'

He thrust an irate hand through his thick dark hair. 'I think I'm fast running out of options. I'll have to go to Australia and get this bottle business sorted out as quickly as possible.'

Ellen nodded. 'I can start making bookings.'

'Yeah, thanks. And I want my lawyers alerted to have someone on call round the clock—just in case this guy tries any tricks about my grandfather's will.' Sam paused and looked thoughtfully at the photo of the girl with the bottle.

Ellen followed his gaze and she sighed. 'Poor Meg Bennet.'

'Why do you say that?'

'She looks rather sweet. I can't help thinking that if you're planning to zip over to her quiet little island for a few days and zap straight back here again, you should be wearing hazard lights.'

Sam frowned and looked affronted. 'I'm not a danger to women. I'm just attracted to them.'

'Of course,' Ellen replied, but she walked away muttering something about charm having its own perils and wouldn't it be fitting if the tables were turned one of these days.

His glance flicked to the picture of the intriguing Meg Bennet. There was a spunky intelligence and honesty about her lovely face that suggested she wouldn't let any man get the better of her unless she wanted him to.

But he quickly dismissed such thoughts. It was the will, his grandfather's message in the bottle, that he was going to Australia to pick up. Not the beautiful girl who'd happened to find it.

Meg was pleased. The reef was looking its best this morning. As she snorkelled back towards the shallows of Florence Bay, no breath of wind stirred the surface of the pleasantly warm water, and the sun shone from a cloudless sky. The underwater visibility was perfect for her group of tourists to view the spectacular fantasy below.

Beneath them now, copper and gold butterfly-fish with elongated snouts were probing vibrant red coral clumps. Nearby, forests of branching staghorn coral, bright blue with deep pink tips, shimmered, pretty as Christmas trees.

A spotted ray, camouflaged on the sea bed, suddenly exploded in a cloud of white sand, the tips of its flat body rippling as it arched away.

All morning, she'd been guiding the resort's guests through a treasure trove of natural beauty. She always got a kick out of sharing the excitement of first timers when they discovered the incredible secrets of the tropical sea.

Reaching the shallows, she stood and balanced first on one foot and then the other, as she pulled off her flippers.

Then she removed her snorkel and mask and waited for the holiday makers she'd been escorting to join her.

The American, who was closest to her, ripped off his face mask and exclaimed, 'That was just fantastic. I never expected to see so many varieties of damselfish in the one spot.'

'So you know about damselfish? Sounds like you did some research before you came on holiday,' Meg suggested as they waded towards the crescent of sand that fringed the bay.

'I haven't had any time for research recently, but I've been interested in tropical fish since I was so high.' He gestured somewhere near his knee and grinned.

Oh, boy! Meg gulped as the full impact of that grin hit her. This man's smile outranked the big screen efforts of most movie stars.

And his eyes were an unexpected drowsy blue. She was perturbed by the way that just looking at him made her breathing quicken, dislodging the comfortable friendliness she usually shared with resort guests.

Dropping her snorkelling gear onto the sand, she reached for her towel and made a business of squeezing excess moisture from her hair. What was the matter with her? This American wasn't the first handsome tourist she'd taken skin-diving.

She promised herself that a reaction like that wouldn't happen again. This fellow could smile as much as he liked and she would remain immune. She'd seen one or two of her workmates get themselves into dreadful emotional pickles, breaking their hearts over resort guests. It just wasn't worth it.

Waving to the group of German tourists, who were making their way out of the water, she decided that it must be this blue-eyed boy's excitement about the reef that gave him an extra edge of attractiveness.

But she felt ridiculously self-conscious about unzipping the full-length Lycra bodysuit she'd worn as protection from marine stingers.

Her companion didn't hesitate to shed his suit and Meg found herself stealing a peek at the tall, wide-shouldered and tautly muscled body that emerged clad in simple bathers. She had no alternative but to step out of her suit, too. Nevertheless, she avoided his gaze.

It was very annoying that she should suddenly feel so bothered about something she did every day.

When they both hauled on T-shirts, she felt better, but there was still a self-conscious edge to her voice when she said, 'We'll head back to the resort now. You'll have time for a shower before lunch.'

The Germans, who had their own hired vehicles, were talking animatedly amongst themselves and so the American helped Meg to pile the snorkelling equipment into the back of the resort's Mini Moke and he sent her another breath-robbing grin. 'Thanks for a great morning.'

'My pleasure,' she murmured.

They both jumped into her Moke and, as she steered the little vehicle up the winding track leading out of the bay, her passenger leaned comfortably back in his seat, turned to her and asked, 'OK Miss Recreation Officer, what's planned for this afternoon?'

Surprised, she shot him a calculating glance, but smiled as she said, 'You Americans are so energetic when you come on holidays, aren't you? It's go, go, go the whole time.'

His eyebrows rose. 'That's so unusual?'

'I don't suppose so,' she admitted. 'But we don't have

a huge number of guests here at the moment and most of them seem to be fairly independent, so I didn't have anything organised for this afternoon.'

'I was hoping you might be able to take me on a guided tour of one of the island's walks.'

Meg pursed her lips. Was this fellow making a play for her already? When she'd come to work at the resort just three months ago, she'd discovered that far too many male visitors arrived on the island and assumed the female staff were part of the room service along with the free tea and coffee. She'd developed some pretty useful brush-off tactics.

'If you have a look in that glove box, you'll find a pamphlet that outlines all the walks. You're a big boy. You don't need a guide. Anyhow...' she added a white lie as an extra measure of protection '...I'm busy all afternoon. There's a VIP coming soon.'

'Big deal is it?'

'Oh, just some hotshot millionaire.' Meg rolled her eyes.

'You don't think much of millionaires?'

Her scowl was automatic. Five years ago, she'd watched her father's career and health suffer at the hands of a money-hungry tycoon and she'd developed a seriously jaundiced view of wealth. 'I'm sure those types are so busy counting their money, or protecting it, or making it grow, they don't have time for the important things in life.'

'I'm sure you're right,' he said in a strangely flat voice that made Meg look at him sharply.

They crested the hill and in front of them stretched a magnificent vista—a string of pretty blue bays sparkling in the midday sun like sapphires on a necklace.

As the American admired the view, he said casually,

'I heard something about a bottle being found on one of those beaches.'

'Yes.' A sudden sprinkling of goose bumps broke out on Meg's arms. 'I found it,' she told him.

Sam's guilty conscience gave him a bad time as he watched Meg's face grow wistful. He should come clean and confess to her that he was the very millionaire she had been talking about. He should tell her right now.

But an equally strong instinct urged him otherwise. She was already wary of him and a confession like that would make her clam up completely. Then he would miss this heaven-sent opportunity to pick up inside information about the bottle and its message before he tackled her boss.

They reached the resort, Magnetic Rendezvous. She steered the car into a parking bay and, after turning the engine off, leaned forward, linking her arms across the top of the steering wheel. Sam got the distinct impression she was pleased to talk to someone about this bottle.

She turned to look at him and he felt the full impact of her clear grey eyes. Yes, they were definitely grey, he decided—and sweetly framed by long dark lashes. And, he noticed uncomfortably, right now they were shimmering with a suspicious sheen.

'I don't know what made me pick the bottle up,' she said softly. 'I keep asking myself that and I know it sounds fanciful, but it was almost as if I was *meant* to find it.'

Her face softened into a sad, dreamy smile and Sam felt a surprising constriction in his throat. In the flesh, Meg was even lovelier than her photo had suggested. The photo hadn't shown the way she moved, light and graceful, with a sexy little sway of her hips. It couldn't record the delightful warmth of her voice or capture the way her smile could dissolve into a sweetly serious frown when she was lost in thought.

She was looking serious now when she said, 'That bottle spent sixty years bobbing around in the ocean. I'm only—well—it's more than twice my age.'

'So how old does that make you?'

'None of your business.'

Sam grinned. At a guess, he'd put her age at around twenty-four or twenty-five. He was thirty-two, so she was a bit young for him—not that he was thinking of her in that way, of course.

Then again…

She was offering him a view of her delicate profile and, as he watched the way she nibbled at her soft bottom lip, a guy couldn't help contemplating how nice it would be to try that himself sometime.

Meg's voice broke into his thoughts, dragging them away from highly unsuitable fantasies. 'I guess I'm looking at this whole bottle business in a hopelessly romantic way.' She flashed him a sudden smile.

He couldn't resist smiling back. 'What's wrong with romance?'

For a long moment their gazes held. An unspoken, highly charged exchange flashed between them. Sam only just resisted an urge to lean forward and taste her soft, startled mouth.

He couldn't be sure who looked away first but, eventually, they both stared back out through the windscreen at the stretch of lawn dotted with coconut palms.

He forced himself to remember that his family's business was at stake. Which was why he was relaxing on a tropical island and deliberately misleading this lovely young woman. He definitely shouldn't be planning to add seduction to his crime of deception.

He cleared his throat. 'So this message in the bottle, was it a love letter?'

She nodded. 'It's beautiful. That man sure loved the woman he was writing to.'

'He was writing to his wife, wasn't he?'

'Yes, but you can't read her name. There's some damage—from exposure to light we think.'

He repressed an angry sigh. If Tom Kirby's wife wasn't named, sorting out this will could be really messy. It was the worst possible news.

'You'd better not ask me any more about it,' Meg said with sudden briskness, 'I can't say anything else, not when the grandson of Thomas Kirby, the man who wrote the message, is coming here soon—tomorrow, I think.'

Sam's stomach tightened guiltily.

Meg added, 'He's the American VIP I was telling you about.'

'You don't say?' he murmured, and he switched his attention to a rainbow lorikeet as it settled in a nearby tree. After promising himself, *again,* to come clean very soon, he asked, 'So this guy is coming all the way out here just to pick up a sixty-year-old letter? Why couldn't you have posted it to him special delivery?'

Meg sighed loudly. 'That would be too easy. My boss wouldn't hear of it. He wants to get as much publicity mileage as he can out of this incident.'

He stopped studying the bird and turned to frown at her. 'What kind of publicity?'

'He sees this as a great opportunity to get media attention for the resort. Magnetic Rendezvous isn't doing all that well. The competition for the tourist dollar is very stiff.'

So that was what this guy was after! 'That's cheeky.'

'Oh, Fred's cheeky all right. He wants shots of me and

this bachelor millionaire with the bottle plastered in newspapers and on television screens all over the country. I'm not looking forward to it,' she said with another sigh.

'This man—this millionaire—'

'Yes?'

'He might—' Sam hesitated, uncomfortably aware that if he kept on talking about himself, he was taking this whole subterfuge thing way too far.

To his relief, Meg didn't wait for him to finish. She jumped out of the doorless Moke and grinned at him. 'I prefer not to think about him until I have to. Now, you're going to miss out on lunch if you don't get moving.'

He hopped out of the car too, and strode around to the back where she had begun to sort out the tangle of snorkels and flippers. 'There's something I should explain.'

'What's that?'

His eyes rested her. Her beauty was as fresh and natural, as untouched as the island itself. *Tell her,* an inner voice urged and he drew in a breath, ready to confess. 'There's something I should tell you...something I should get off my chest about why I'm here on the island.'

Meg stopped counting flippers and looked up abruptly to frown at him. 'Now you really have me intrigued.' She touched his wrist lightly. 'You'll have to explain...*Heavens!* I've been rattling on to you and I can't even remember your name. What did you say your name was again?'

'Sam.'

'OK, Sam.' Her grey eyes looked directly into his. 'Get it off your chest.'

Her gaze suddenly locked with his and, just as he had

earlier, Sam felt another startling sense of connection zap between them.

Her warm hand was still lying on his wrist.

Neither of them moved.

Chemistry could play sneaky tricks on a guy. Sam would have liked to feel more in control of this situation. Getting to know a woman was usually a pleasant game where he called all the shots. Many considered him to be an expert.

But right now, he had no idea where he was heading.

Especially when, out of absolutely nowhere, the unmistakable idea of kissing hovered between them in the dappled sunlight.

As if prompted by a magnetic force, he dipped his head towards Meg ever so slightly and, to his surprise, she didn't pull back. When he leaned lower, she raised her face a breathless fraction higher.

Their mouths met.

It was a hello kind of kiss. More than friendly, but not exactly the exchange of lovers. Apart from their mouths and her hand on his, they weren't touching. He smiled down at her and she smiled back and he felt the warmth and softness of her linger on his lips and the blood rush through his pulse points.

Meg was looking at him in dazed alarm as if she was as startled as he was. Then she jumped back, glaring at him and she said shakily, 'I make it a rule never to kiss guests.'

The flustered, breathless way she spoke sounded so sexy Sam stepped back too, in case he gave in to any more urges. 'I won't tell anyone.'

She grabbed a pile of flippers, as if she needed an armful of rubber to keep him at bay. 'You said you wanted to tell me something important about why you're here,' she reminded him sharply. 'What sort of work did you say you did?'

'Er—don't worry about my job. It's boring,' Sam replied hastily. 'But my hobby is marine science. I haven't studied it in depth, but I'd love to learn more about the life on the reef, underwater photography, salt-water aquariums—that sort of thing. We could make a great team. You could be my tutor.'

'Bad idea.' She scowled. And then, like a mother scolding a little boy, she added, 'I suggest you go take a shower and have some lunch.'

She looked so mad that any thought of confessing his identity seemed ridiculous now. But it also seemed important to set things straight with Meg. For some inexplicable reason, Sam really cared what she thought of him.

A flipper dropped from the pile she was clutching and landed at his feet. He picked it up and held it for a moment, his fingers flexing the rubber. 'Meg, what I meant to tell you was that this VIP you mentioned...'

He could sense her wariness, as if she'd pulled it on like protective armour. From beneath ash-blonde curls streaked with gold, her grey gaze darkened to a stormy charcoal. 'Don't tell me it's you,' she whispered.

'Yeah, 'fraid so.'

A red flush flared in her cheeks and he couldn't tell if she was embarrassed or just plain mad at him.

'I'm sorry. I meant to tell you earlier.'

'No one was stopping you,' she snapped.

'Maybe not, but I didn't see why I should give you a perfect reason to hate me.'

'Yes, but—' Meg gulped.

'And you handed me an excellent opportunity to check out the lie of the land. I don't intend to just waltz in to your boss ready to dance to his tune. After all, there's a lot at stake.'

'A lot of money.'

'More than just money. It's complicated.' He took a step closer and offered her what he hoped was a reassuring smile. 'But I have an even better excuse.'

Meg didn't smile back. She continued to stand stiffly to attention with her arms tightly wrapped around the flippers.

'I really appreciated being able to see the reef just the way I did this morning—just like an ordinary tourist. I had a great time. Thank you. From what you've said, the media will be hanging around tomorrow. Things will be different.' He smiled again.

But it seemed the effort was wasted.

Meg's chin lifted and she eyed him with a haughty glare. 'Things will be very different,' she said. 'For starters, you won't even *think* about trying to kiss me.'

He tucked the flipper into the bundle she was holding. 'In that case, I'm sure neither of us will look forward to tomorrow.'

Ignoring her startled gasp, he turned in the direction of his bungalow. And, as he walked away, Sam reflected that he'd been wise not to add a comment about just how slim Meg's chances were if she expected to control his thoughts.

Especially his thoughts about kissing her again.

CHAPTER TWO

AS SOON as she woke the next morning, Meg knew it was going to be a bad day. Her first clue was the way her mind flashed straight to Sam Kirby—exactly where she didn't want it to be. He'd taken up far too much space in her head all night.

Not even the rainbow lorrikeets that came to her kitchen window for their breakfast treat could lift her spirits. She watched the amazing birds peck daintily at tiny pieces of bread and honey. But this morning their bright purple heads, lime-green wings, and bright yellow chests, brush-stroked with scarlet, didn't fill her with admiration as they usually did. She was too busy feeling angry.

The cheek of the man—hiding his identity, encouraging her to talk about the bottle and then stealing that kiss—all in such a short space of time!

If ever a man spelled danger for Meg, Sam Kirby did. He was a super-rich big businessman and an international resort guest—he summed up everything she went out of her way to avoid. So how on earth had she stood there like a ninny and let him kiss her?

And the worst part was, it had been such a nice kiss.

Despite her anger, she'd found herself thinking about it over and over as she'd drifted off to sleep. Again and again, she'd remembered the warm, sensual pressure of his slightly open lips on hers. Then there was the impact of those deep blue eyes up close. They had been breathtaking. They'd made her think about...finding somewhere private…somewhere beneath whispering palm trees…or in the shallows on a secluded sandy beach…somewhere…anywhere he could go on kissing her…

But, for heaven's sake! These were things she most certainly shouldn't be thinking about on first meeting a man. Especially *this* man. She'd spent the rest of the night telling herself that.

Remember who he is. A corporate high roller.

A playboy millionaire. Forget him!

He'll be gone in a few days. Forget him, now!

The fact that he'd come to the island to collect the letter in the bottle was a snag. She'd already agreed to her boss's demands to pose with Sam for the publicity shots today, so she had little choice now, but to eat her breakfast, shower and get ready for the ordeal.

But, as she did so, Meg kept up a continuous pep talk in her head. By the time she left her bungalow, she was determined to be mentally prepared to face Sam again.

A swarm of journalists, television cameramen and photographers hovered around the reception area. When Meg arrived, some were pacing the slate tiles, while others settled back on the deep cane lounges to smoke and chat quietly.

Her boss, Fred Raynor, dragged her excitedly into his office. 'I was about to have you paged. All the media have turned up! They came over on the early boat. Isn't this great?'

He beamed and rubbed his pudgy hands together. 'And these are just the local press. When their stories get out, there'll be more.' He flung a hand to the view of the resort's tropical garden. 'It's going to be a beautiful day in paradise. We'll get excellent outdoor shots.'

'All we need is our millionaire,' Meg added dryly.

'He'll be here any minute.' Fred shook his head and ran a hand over his bulging stomach. 'Boy, did that guy upset my digestion last night.'

'Oh?' Meg couldn't help being curious.

'He wanted the letter out of the bottle straight away and was wild as a cut snake when I said he could only have it after he posed for a few photos.'

'Did he refuse to go ahead with the publicity?' she asked hopefully.

'I finally got him to agree. I told him flat I've got possession. He can carry on about his lawyers and rights, but down here it's finders keepers.' Fred's pale eyes gleamed as he looked at her meaningfully. 'Actually, I think what won him round was the fact that it gives him a good excuse to hang around—er, *here*—for a day or two.'

He looked over Meg's shoulder as someone entered the office and he lowered his voice. 'Here he is now.'

Standing stiffly to attention, Meg clenched her hands into tight little fists at her sides as she turned to face Sam.

'Morning,' he said with his usual smile.

'It's going to be good one.' Fred beamed.

'Hello, Meg,' Sam added when she didn't respond. His eyes held a twinkling warmth.

Meg nodded frostily. 'Hi.' She found herself needing to search for outward signs of wealth on Sam Kirby—things she might have overlooked yesterday—when she'd been taken up with his *other* attributes.

His watch was a sophisticated diving watch, but many men wore similar accessories. His dark blue, open-necked shirt, stone-coloured shorts and navy trainers were probably expensive, but spoke of taste rather than money. There was no hint of jewellery around his neck, at his wrist, or on his fingers.

So he wasn't flashy. That still didn't mean she could trust him.

Fred slapped them both on the shoulder and grinned broadly. 'Let's get this show on the road.'

Feeling annoyingly self-conscious again, Meg followed the men out of the office. As she expected, Fred wanted plenty of publicity shots set up in front of the huge Magnetic Rendezvous sign. She was required to pose with Sam.

'Smile into each other's eyes now,' a photographer called.

Meg tried to force a smile and focused on a point beyond Sam's shoulder. She knew he was looking straight at her, smiling with those baby-blue, super-cute eyes, but she was determined not to let them affect her again.

'Hey, miss, lighten up,' a photographer scolded.

She squeezed her smile muscles harder as Sam leaned closer.

'They're blue today.' His voice was a sexy rumble close to her ear.

Goose bumps prickled to unwilling life on her arms. Her gaze lifted to meet his. *Gulp.* No matter how she felt about him, Sam was still the best-looking guy she'd seen outside a cinema. 'What are blue? What are you talking about?'

'Your eyes,' he said softly. 'How do they do it?'

'Do what?' she muttered through her grimacing smile.

'Change colour. I've been trying to work out what colour they are and yesterday I decided they were definitely grey, but today I swear they're blue.'

Meg couldn't help it. She smiled.

Cameras flashed all around them. 'That's great!' someone shouted. 'Hold that smile! Gorgeous!' There were more flashes and clicks.

As a photographer rearranged them into a slightly different pose, Sam asked, 'How do they change like that?'

He was doing it again. Trying to win her over with charm. Most men usually focused their attention somewhere between her neck and her knees. No man, in her memory, had ever paid such flattering attention to her eyes.

'Does their colour depend on what you're wearing?' His approving gaze took in her aqua halter-necked top and shorts.

'I think so.'

'That's a really neat trick.'

But Meg was determined not to be won over by a few throw-away lines about her eyes.

Suddenly a female journalist in a trendy power suit stepped forward wielding a microphone. A cameraman and sound recorder crowded close behind.

'Mr Kirby,' the journalist asked silkily. 'I understand you've dated film stars and celebrities in America? So what do you think of Australian girls?'

Meg made a choking sound. Where on earth had this stupid question come from? What did it have to do with the letter in the bottle? Didn't the ditsy journalist know about sticking to the hard facts?

Sam looked a little startled by the question, too, but he quickly recovered. He favoured the journalist with a full-scale model of his sexiest smile. 'Aussie girls are enchanting.'

The journalist simpered and Meg might have scowled if the camera hadn't swung to focus on her. The interviewer spoke again, 'And, Meg, what's it like to have the attention of Seattle's favourite bachelor?'

'It's been an enlightening experience,' she replied coolly.

The journalist's eyebrow arched. 'Can you tell us exactly how you've been enlightened?'

Meg smiled slowly. 'No.'

Taken aback, the journalist stared at Meg for several long seconds before trying Sam again. 'We're told that this story isn't just about a romance that happened sixty years ago.' Her eyes slid meaningfully from Meg to Sam. 'I understand there's a little chemistry happening right now?'

Meg glared over her shoulder at her boss, who was slinking behind a clump of golden cane palms. She heard the angry hiss of Sam's breath. When she glanced his way, she saw that his smile had been replaced by a displeased, stony stare.

'You heard Miss Bennet,' he said. 'No comment.'

The journalist shrugged and rolled her eyes.

To Meg's relief, someone else called, 'OK, now we'll take some beach shots! Everyone down at the water's edge.'

On the beach, the morning sun hung above them, a dazzling white-gold blaze in the sky. Beneath it, the bay stretched like a shimmering sheet of liquid gold.

A cameraman hurried to set up his tripod.

And a bottle was thrust into Sam's hands. 'This is *it*? This is *the* bottle?' He turned to Meg.

She nodded.

The bottle was empty and Meg stood quietly as he examined the ancient, once clear, green glass carefully, turning it over and over, slowly. He seemed to be studying the surface, which was worn to an opaque haze by sand and salt and endless, endless water.

Her mouth quivered into a funny little trembling smile as she watched him and she wondered if he felt as choked up as she did. This was the bottle that had been held by Tom Kirby, his grandfather. All those years ago.

For days now, she'd been thinking about this moment when it was handed over to its rightful owner. She looked at Sam through moist eyes. 'It's good to know you have it at last,' she said in a voice choked with emotion.

Once more, cameras clicked and whirred as photographers crouched and hovered around them. 'That's lovely, sweetheart.' *Click!* 'Keep looking at him like that.' *Click! Click!* 'Beautiful.'

As soon as there was a break, Sam's face pulled into a wry grimace as he looked at her. 'I'll be happier when I get the letter as well as this bottle.'

Meg stiffened. All he cared about was the letter and the will and securing his family's business. She should have known a playboy bachelor from Seattle wouldn't have a sentimental bone in his body.

'Now, put your arm around her, mate,' another voice instructed.

Before she could prepare herself, Sam's strong arm settled around Meg's shoulders. She was gathered against him and of course her curves fitted perfectly against the hard planes of his muscular physique. This close, she could smell his skin, clean with a hint of expensive aftershave…and annoying, undeniable ripples of awareness heated her.

This was way too close for comfort.

'Put your hand on the bottle, too,' someone instructed. 'That's it—both of you holding it together.'

'Now, look deep into each other's eyes.'

Reluctantly, Meg dragged her eyes up to meet Sam's. This wasn't fair! Her resistance was wearing off. Suddenly, looking into those blue depths was like taking off from a high diving board. Her foolish heart leapt in her chest.

She tried for a joke—anything to take her mind off her body's embarrassing reactions. 'I guess we can regard this as practice for when we get married.' Then she cringed. *Idiot! Had she really said that?* 'I mean married to—whoever we marry,' she stammered, suddenly terribly flustered. '*If* we get ever married.' *How did she get into this mess?* 'Either of us, that is—' she added, floundering hopelessly. 'Either of us get married to anyone,' she finished lamely.

Looking into Sam's sexy eyes had emptied her mind of all cohesive thoughts.

'I get the picture, Meg.' He smiled.

'Have I gone bright red?' she asked him, as the cameras clicked away.

'Just a very becoming pink.' His amused eyes looked deep into hers as he tugged her a little closer.

His lips were so temptingly close. Meg had the distinct impression that he would have liked to kiss her again. She felt her own lips part and a little tremor of anticipation danced across them.

Thank goodness for Fred and the photographers! She was safe from Sam's kisses while they were around. How could any part of her feeble brain be contemplating kissing this man hot on the heels of yesterday's fiasco? Today she was supposed to be working doubly hard at keeping Sam at bay.

To her relief, the photo session was over at last. Someone mentioned that the next ferry would arrive soon, and the media dispersed, scrambling to leave for another assignment.

Meg squinted at the sky, taking deep breaths to regain her equilibrium. 'Time to get out of the sun.'

'You have a busy schedule today?' Sam asked as they passed under criss-crossing fronds of coconut palms on the way back to the resort.

She wasn't going to fall for any more of his come-on lines. 'I'm exceedingly busy,' she answered emphatically. 'I have meetings…'.

He nodded. 'But would you have dinner with me tonight?'

She pressed her lips tightly together. Not only did she have to ward off this man's charm, now she had to deal with his persistence as well.

Sam added softly, 'It can be my way of paying you back for the dirty hand I dealt you yesterday.'

Meg was proud of her crisp reply. 'You don't owe me anything.'

'I owe you a great deal.' He stopped walking and looked down at the bottle he was still holding. Then he tossed it lightly from one hand to the other. 'Whatever happens, my family will be grateful to you for my grandfather's letter.'

'Whatever happens?' Meg repeated. 'You sound like you're really worried about how this will turn out.'

His face tightened and he looked away at some spot down the beach. 'I'll feel a lot better when that will is safely in the hands of my lawyers.'

'You said there's a lot at stake.'

'Yeah.' His fingers toyed with the bottle's mouth. 'Meg—about my grandfather's letter—you've read it, haven't you?'

'Yes.'

'Can you tell me more about it? Are you sure there's no way of telling who it was addressed to?'

'No, I'm afraid not. As I told you, the top of the page was damaged.'

'And there was no other reference to his wife's name?'

'No. The rest of the time he referred to "my wife" or "darling" or "sweetheart"—that kind of thing.'

Sam sighed heavily. 'But there was definitely a will?'

'It definitely made mention of Tom leaving all his worldly goods to his wife.'

'Yeah, well, Fred had better hand it over soon.' He gripped the bottle tightly with both hands for a moment, then suddenly smiled at her.

If only he would stop doing that!

'Why don't you forgive me for yesterday? I hear there's a very good outdoor restaurant over in one of the other bays.'

Fighting back the wild urge to accept was like trying to put out a bushfire with a mere tumbler of water. For Pete's sake, Sam was by far the best-looking fellow who'd ever asked Meg out. But, she had to be sensible about this. He'd be gone in a day or two. She took in a deep breath and let it out slowly. 'Thanks for the invite, Sam, but I'll have to decline.'

Before she changed her mind, she turned and walked quickly away.

Sam watched her go, a wry, admiring smile tugging his lips. When she'd rejected his invitation, she hadn't added, *I can't trust you,* but that was what she'd meant.

Of course, he couldn't blame Meg for running. He'd given her every reason to be wary. Yesterday, she'd been totally upfront and honest with him and he hadn't returned the compliment.

Her disdain was exactly what he deserved.

But Meg Bennet was having a strange effect on him. Just thinking about her...about her eyes...her hair...her mouth made him...*restless.* Was it because she was different? Because she refused to be impressed by the thing that impressed most women—his money? Because she refused to be impressed by *anything* about him?

His gaze dropped again to the bottle in his hands and he reminded himself that he hadn't come to Australia looking for romance. He had a business to run and he had to get back to it as soon as possible.

By tomorrow, he'd be grateful Meg had turned him down.

Meg dropped a peach-coloured bath bomb into the warm water and watched it explode and fizz. The steam in her bathroom began to distil a sensuous mixture of citrus and flowers. Dipping her big toe into the fragrant liquid, she felt her body begin at once to relax. She visualised submerging beneath the heated, scented surface of the water.

Br-ring! Br-ring!

Heavens, no! Not the telephone! Hovering with one leg in the air, she glared at the slim, cordless machine lying on the counter next to her hand basin. She toyed with the notion of letting it ring. But, officially, she was still on duty. With an impatient sigh, she crossed the room and picked it up but, as she answered, she returned with it to the bath. There was no way she would waste that beautifully scented hot water.

'Meg! It's Fred Raynor,' the voice snapped.

'Yes, Fred?' She lowered herself into the bath and felt the warm liquid swirl softly, seductively around her body. Fragrance drifted upwards, teasing her nostrils, enticing her to relax.

'You're not busy tonight are you?'

'Oh? Not particularly.' Meg grimaced and rolled her eyes to the ceiling. What on earth could her boss want now? Since she'd refused Sam's invitation to dinner, she'd had an ongoing battle with her weaker self all afternoon.

That was the main reason she needed to relax now. To pamper herself after a nerve-racking, miserable day.

'I want you to take Sam Kirby out to dinner, over at Alma Bay.'

Meg gulped. 'I have to?'

'Damn right you do.' Fred snapped.

Frowning, she sat up higher out of the water. She held the phone closer to her ear. 'Fred, you know this is way beyond the limits of my job as recreation officer.'

'But we need to keep this guy on our side. There's a good chance we can get national coverage out of this. He's big time. We could even get an international story if we play our cards right.'

'I'm sorry, Fred. I posed for your photos, but this is definitely going too far. It's verging on sexual harassment.'

She was relieved when, after a noisy grumble, her boss rang off.

Surprised that he'd given in so easily, Meg was about to drop the phone onto the bath mat when it rang again.

'Give up, Fred!' she cried. 'I am not going to dinner with Sam Kirby. Got it?'

'I'm reading you loud and clear.'

'Sam?' she demanded. 'Is that you?'

'It is,' came a response from the other end of the line.

'For Pete's sake, what do you want?' She knew it was ridiculous, but Meg scrambled over the edge of the bath to grab at a fluffy white towel. Even talking on the phone to Sam felt dangerous when she was naked. 'Did you get Fred to order me out to dinner with you?'

'I won't ruin my reputation by answering that.' There

was a pause and then he asked in a lighter tone, 'Did I hear splashing?'

'Er, I doubt it,' she muttered, wrapping herself in the huge towel and perching on the side of the bath.

'I'm sorry if I interrupted something.'

Meg wanted to be angry. She wanted to depress the disconnect button and to slip back beneath the warm and welcoming water. But the weak side of her clung to the phone, liking too much the sound of his deep voice with that musical North American twang. Besides, she was desperately curious. 'What did you want?'

'Actually, it *was* to try one more time to ask you to dinner, but without Fred's assistance. Hey, if you were taking a bath, go right ahead. Don't waste the water.'

'I might just do that.'

'By the way,' he continued, 'I have a very interesting scientific question.'

'Oh?'

'Are you near a mirror?'

'What do you think? I'm in a bathroom.'

'Could you look in the mirror for me and tell me what colour your eyes are when you're not wearing clothes?'

Instinctively, Meg's glance flashed to the mirror. But then her cheeks warmed. 'I'll tell you no such thing.' She flung her towel aside and slipped back into the bath.

There was an exaggerated sigh on the other end of the line. 'Another mystery of science remains unanswered.'

'I guess your eyes stay blue all the time,' she heard herself say and she wondered how that sultry, flirtatious little hum had crept into her voice.

'Yeah. I'm afraid my eyes are boring, boring.'

Hardly boring, Sam, she thought, but didn't dare say so. She lifted her feet out of the suds and rested her toes on the end of the bath, wondering if she should apply some nail polish to make them more glamorous and, the very next second, wondered why they needed to look glamorous.

'OK,' he added, 'try this. While you're soaking in the tub, practise saying, "Yes, Sam, I'd love to join you for dinner."'

To her amazement, Meg heard herself purring a reply in her very best attempt at an American accent. 'Yes, Sam, I'd *lurve* to join you for dinner.'

'Wonderful. I'll meet you at your place at seven.'

She nearly dropped the phone. 'Hold on! I was only copying your accent! That wasn't a real acceptance.'

'Oh, but Meg,' he replied, his voice warm and hinting somehow that he was smiling his hottest smile, 'it was a very, very real invitation.'

When he didn't hang up but waited in silence for her response, Meg closed her eyes and willed herself to be strong. She was furious with this man. She should have hung up as soon as she'd heard his voice.

Letting out her breath on a gusty sigh, she told him, 'Nice try, Sam Kirby but, as I said at the start, give up.'

'Now, that,' he replied in a husky baritone, 'is a distinct challenge. I can warn you now, Meg Bennet, if I set myself a goal, I *never* give up.'

'And what goal are you aiming for?'

There was a long pause and Meg thought she heard a faint chuckle. 'I'd settle for your acceptance of my apology. For yesterday.'

Meg closed her eyes. 'OK. Apology accepted,' she whispered.

'Good,' he said simply. 'And dinner?'

After a beat, she answered, 'Dinner declined.'

She disconnected the phone and let it drop onto the bath mat and, sinking beneath the sudsy water, she wished she felt more pleased about turning Sam down.

CHAPTER THREE

AS SHE ate her simple supper of cheese on toast, Meg tried not to think about what it would have been like to be dining with Sam. She kept reminding herself that he and the bottle would soon be going home to the United States and she was wise to stay well out of the way. How silly she'd been to imagine that somehow her own destiny was linked to that bottle.

The only connection she had was stumbling across it on the beach and giving way to natural curiosity.

Finishing her meal, she carried her plate through to the kitchen and decided she'd seen too much significance in finding the bottle. Perhaps she'd been grasping at straws. There was a good chance she'd been looking for anything that would help her out of the depressing loneliness she felt these days. Ever since her father had died just three months ago.

It had been bad enough giving up her postgraduate studies in marine biology to nurse her dad through the last horrible months of his illness. But nothing had prepared her for the bereft emptiness of her life after he'd died. He was all the family she'd had. Her mother had died when she was only little and her father had meant everything to her. Since his death, Meg thought she had discovered the utter depths of loneliness.

But tonight she felt more desolate than ever.

The sand crunched beneath Sam's shoes as he walked towards the water. By the light of a glowing white moon,

Florence Bay looked beautiful. On either side of the bay, dark rocky headlands curved out to protect the deserted beach. Hoop pines, rising majestically from between granite boulders, were silhouetted in inky black strokes against the gun metal sky.

The dark water lapped gently.

Somewhere out there in the wider ocean beyond the reefs, Tom Kirby lay at rest. Thinking about his grandfather and the bottle, he hunkered down on the sand and stared ahead. These past few years, he'd been working so hard he hadn't stopped to contemplate anything deep or meaningful—like death and the hereafter. Or life for that matter.

Lately, he'd been sensing an uneasy awareness that his own life was hurtling forward like a runaway train and he wasn't at all sure he was heading in the right direction. He was doing the right thing by his family—carrying on the Kirby tradition—and working damn hard to keep it successful—and playing hard, too, when time permitted. But he knew deep down that neither his work nor his play was really making him happy.

Lost in thought, he didn't hear footsteps so, when a voice suddenly sounded close behind him, he jumped to his feet.

'Sam, what are you doing here?'

'Meg!'

She was standing a metre or so away from him, her face pale and her eyes wide with surprise. She was wearing a soft blue sweater and white jeans and, in the moonlight, her hair had a silvery sheen and she looked breathtakingly lovely.

He turned and extended an arm towards the sea. 'It may sound a little weird, but I'm paying my respects.'

'To your grandfather?'

'Yeah.' Sam shoved his hands in his pockets to prevent himself from reaching for her. 'I rang my lawyers this afternoon. They've been doing some research for me and I couldn't believe what they told me.' He kicked at a knob of bleached coral lying on the sand. 'Tom Kirby died on this day—this *very* day—in 1942. In the Battle of the Coral Sea.'

'Oh.' She sounded suitably shocked.

'Weird coincidence, isn't it?' He swallowed the constriction in his throat. Then he smiled at Meg. 'But maybe an even better coincidence is that I am seeing you this evening after all,' he murmured huskily. 'You never know, maybe we're destined for each other, Meg.'

Meg was sure Sam was teasing and she felt more than a little miffed that he might be making fun of her. Lifting her chin defiantly high, she shifted her concentration from his strong, handsome face to their surroundings— the little bay and the moon and the rocky headlands.

Time to leave, or to come up with a quick change of subject. Reluctant to hurry back to her lonely cottage, she changed the subject. 'For some reason, those rocks always remind me of shelled Brazil nuts.'

Sam's eyebrows rose. 'That's an interesting association of ideas. I wonder where it comes from?'

She smiled. 'I know exactly where it comes from. I'm crazy about Brazil nuts.' And for a moment she was absorbed by memory. She was sitting once more at a dining table, laden with Christmas fare, and she could see her father's strong hands wielding the silver nutcracker, breaking open the hard shell and handing her a pure smooth Brazil nut.

'My father always used to crack them for me and, when he gave me one, he would joke... ''Would you like a nut, Meg?" Of course, his nickname for me was Nutmeg.'

'Nutmeg,' Sam repeated. 'I like that.' He turned to look at her. 'Does your father live here on the island?'

'My father's dead,' she told him in a shaky whisper.

'I'm sorry.' His hand reached out and rubbed her shoulder gently.

'You know he used to warn me that there are no guarantees in life. He reckoned the only thing you can be sure of is that the angles of a triangle will always add up to one hundred and eighty degrees.'

'Sounds like he got one or two nasty shocks along the way.'

'Well, yes. He worked as a draftsman for the same company for thirty-five years and then suddenly they made him redundant.' She snapped her fingers. 'Just like that. Downsizing they called it. Profits were more important than loyal and talented employees.'

Sam's jaw clenched and he swung away so that he no longer looked at her. 'Sometimes the guys running big companies have to make difficult choices.'

'And their answers are always about money,' she responded bitterly.

'Money,' he repeated grimly. His hand was still resting on her and suddenly he smiled at her again and obviously decided to have his own stab at changing the subject. 'As you accepted my apology so nicely this afternoon, we can start afresh, can't we?'

Meg was sure she should have clarified exactly what Sam thought they were *starting*. But perhaps it was the setting, or her loneliness, or even moonlight madness, but she suddenly didn't want to be wary or cautious any more. 'Yes,' she said simply. 'I guess we can.'

'You know,' Sam told her. 'We actually have more in

common than you might be prepared to admit. I used to haunt the Seattle Aquarium when I was a boy. Tell me some more about the reef.'

Realising that he'd cleverly selected a topic she loved to talk about, she was happy to cooperate. 'Something I find very interesting is the coral-spawning that takes place every year. Have you heard about it?'

'I do remember reading something.'

'Marine scientists made the discovery here on this island. Every piece of coral on the Great Barrier Reef, even pieces in buckets and aquariums, becomes fertile and spawns in mass at a certain full moon in spring.' Her eyes danced. 'It's been described as the world's biggest sexual encounter.'

'World's biggest sexual encounter?' Sam repeated with a lazy smile and his gaze speared hers so intently she felt breathless and more than a little warm. 'That's exceptionally interesting.'

She couldn't help chuckling. 'Well, I don't know who actually judges these things.'

He turned towards her so that both his hands could grasp her shoulders. 'I warned you earlier, Meg, I can't resist a challenge.'

His face was in shadow but, as she heard the unmistakable rumble of desire in his voice, flames of unexpected heat darted through Meg. She wondered what she could do about her growing interest in getting close to this man. 'Surely you're not suggesting you want to compete with the entire Great Barrier Reef?' she asked in a strained, tight voice.

'I'm going to make a start.' His gaze centred on her mouth. 'I'm not planning to be upstaged by coral polyps.'

She knew then what was going to happen and she let it.

For the second time, Meg offered absolutely no resistance when he drew her closer. She had a desperate feeling that she had as much chance of resisting Sam Kirby as the tides had of resisting the pull of the moon. Fleetingly, she wondered if this was what destiny felt like.

In spite of her rules about guests, she had never felt so willing, so wanting to be enclosed in a man's arms.

Her heart jolted unsteadily as Sam's lips roamed her mouth and her own lips parted, as open and needy as a desert flower welcoming rain. His kiss deepened and, with a whimper of pleasure, she surrendered to his invasion. Sam tasted wonderful. His hard, strong body felt divine. Wanting more, she crushed herself shamelessly against him, as if she was afraid the world might end any minute and she would miss out on this vital experience.

Yesterday, Sam's kiss had been friendly and gentle. Tonight it quickly became wicked, wild and threatening. And Meg loved it! She loved the heat of his tongue as it plundered her mouth. Loved the hard, intimate force of his body driving and moulding against her.

She heard his desperately ragged breathing and suspected she was rushing headlong into danger. But it was a dark and alluring danger. A danger she suddenly longed for and welcomed.

Flash!

The blinding light startled them both, shattering their embrace.

Meg felt Sam swing angrily out of her arms. 'Get lost!' he cried and began to prowl towards someone in the darkness.

Shaking, Meg followed the direction of his gaze and saw what he'd seen—a man skulking behind a casuarina on the edge of the sand and clutching a camera.

'Let's just get out of here,' Meg called, running after him and grabbing his hand.

For a moment, Sam hesitated, but he shook her hand away and continued to stride towards the darkness in the direction the photographer had taken. There was the sound of a car taking off at speed. 'Who was he?' he demanded, turning back to her. 'I have enough trouble at home with the press.'

'Do you really think it was someone from a newspaper?'

'That's my guess.'

Meg cringed as she thought of all her workmates seeing evidence in tomorrow's paper of her lapse. So much for her personal code of ethics regarding tourists! 'I can't believe I let this happen again,' she whispered to herself.

She supposed she should be grateful to the photographer. He'd broken the spell that had been dragging her towards making a foolish mistake. Heaven knew what might have happened if they hadn't been rudely interrupted.

'Are you worried about your golden rule about kissing guests?' Sam's knuckle grazed her cheek. 'For my part, I'm very glad you broke it. I wouldn't object at all if you wanted to break a few more rules.'

Embarrassed, Meg drew back. 'You know I wasn't going to let you do anything but kiss me.'

'But you *did* let me kiss you,' he challenged. 'And I had the distinct impression that you were kissing me back.'

'I just got carried away with—with the atmosphere and the moonlight.'

'Is that what happened?' His voice suggested that he didn't believe her in the slightest.

'That's all,' she said as convincingly as she could manage. 'And I must go home now.' She had to get out of there before the moonlight or whatever it was started making her reckless again. Turning to head back to her car, she asked, 'Do you need a lift?'

'No. Don't worry about me.' Sam shoved his hands into his pockets and he turned to stare back out to sea.

When she reached her car, Meg looked back at him, but he hadn't moved. And that was good. Maybe it was sinking into Sam's thick skull that they must never take the risk of kissing a third time.

When Sam opened his door the next morning and found Meg standing there, he was mildly surprised. She was wearing a soft, floaty kind of dress that dipped in a low curve from shoulder to shoulder. In her hand was a folded newspaper.

'Good morning,' she greeted him primly, without smiling.

He returned her greeting carefully. 'Morning.'

There was no beating around the bush. Looking somewhere around the centre of his chest, she said, 'Have you seen this morning's paper?'

'Fred phoned and told me about it.'

With an impatient shake of her head, she thrust the paper at him. 'The publicity shot of us with the bottle on the front page is OK, I guess. But take a look at page three. The close-up shot of you and me—'

'On the beach?' Sam supplied as he took the paper and flicked to page three. He looked at the photo and felt his throat tighten. 'That's—er—some clinch, isn't it?'

Meg was blushing. 'What are we going to do about it? Fred wants to make more publicity mileage out of it. He wants us to go to a big function tonight for the handover of the letter—as a couple.'

'Yeah. He explained that when he rang.'

'Don't tell me you agreed?' she asked sharply.

'Sure. Why not?' Sam hoped Meg didn't quiz him too hard about why he'd agreed. He wasn't too sure himself that his motives would stand up to close scrutiny. 'But I take it you're not happy?'

'Of course not!' Meg exclaimed with a haughty lift of her chin that made her look especially stubborn. And gorgeous.

He looked again at the photo. Seeing that image of Meg's arms wrapped around him and her mouth meshed with his was interfering with his search for a rational argument. He tapped the page with a finger and replied in his most nonchalant manner, 'There's not much point in trying to pretend there's nothing between us. Why don't we attend this event together and brazen it out just for this one night?'

Meg stared at him. She looked ready to argue. Her arms were crossed belligerently across her chest and her eyes glistened as she tapped a tattoo with her foot.

Sam waited patiently in silence, unwilling to take the lid off this particular volcano.

Eventually she sighed. 'I'll go to this function on one condition.'

'Yes?'

'We only have the minimum contact necessary to keep the press happy.'

He had been leaning against the door frame, trying to look more casual than he felt. This situation was becoming more ridiculous by the minute, but sharing that opinion with Meg wasn't going to help matters.

Stepping back, he gestured towards the small sitting area in his resort bungalow. 'Why don't you come in? I find this a little difficult to discuss on a doorstep.'

She followed him in silence and assumed a stiff-backed, prudish pose at one end of his couch. Under other circumstances, he might have found it comic.

Selecting a single cane chair, Sam lounged back into the deep cushions. In a deliberately casual movement, he stretched his long legs in front of him, crossing them at the ankles. 'Now, tell me about these conditions of yours.'

She sat straight with her knees together, just as she might have been taught at deportment school, and made a little throat clearing sound. 'What I mean is, there'll be no flirting—no unnecessary touching. We'll just *pretend* we're—a couple who are—um—interested in romance.'

'And of course you're still insisting that you're not the slightest bit interested?'

'I'm certainly not.'

He watched a fascinating pink blush suffuse Meg's cheeks and he tried to ignore his body's inappropriate reaction.

'Just so I'm clear about this; that very romantic kiss on the beach last night—were you pretending, then?'

Her eyes shone with a threatening gleam. 'I told you last night, we can blame the moonlight and the mood for that. It was a slip.'

Remembering the sweet fire of her kiss and just how passionately Meg had *slipped* into his arms, Sam only just managed to keep his face solemn. 'So what do you think will keep the press happy? They already have a picture of us kissing.'

'We just have to be seen together. We can talk.'

'And can we look as if we're enjoying ourselves?'

Her eyes met his and she shrugged. The neckline of her dress slipped a little to reveal a tanned and shapely shoulder. 'I suppose we'll have to look reasonably happy.'

'We might have to dance.'

'Yes.'

'But you want me to hide the fact that I'm attracted to you, Meg?' He deliberately stared at her, trapping her gaze with his.

She stared straight back, her eyes the brilliant, clear grey of Cleveland Bay waters at dusk. 'That's right. You mustn't…' Her courage seemed to falter. Her neat white teeth worried her upper lip.

Sam suppressed a wild urge to leap out of his chair and crush those soft lips with his own, to force them apart, to taste again the sweetness of her mouth. Leaning forward, he dropped his linked hands between his knees. 'OK, fill me in. What mustn't I do?'

'Don't do anything that will make me—'

He waited.

'Don't you dare try to seduce me.'

Sam almost laughed. Here was Meg, looking like a goddess, driving him mad with her soft gold hair, her sea-grey eyes and her delicate air and she was trying to suggest that seduction was *his* agenda. Something he alone schemed and plotted. Something she had no part in.

He rose to his feet and said softly, 'If that's what you want, I'll do my level best not to seduce you, Meg.'

Meg jumped to her feet, too. 'If we have to kiss for any reason—and I can't imagine that there will be one—the lips stay shut.'

'Got you,' he agreed grimly, noting the continued heightening of colour in her cheeks.

'We can hold hands if necessary.'

'OK.'

'Do I need to continue this list of criteria, or do you get the picture?'

Was she serious? 'I think catch your drift.'

She glossed over his sarcasm. 'It's important that there's no misunderstanding.'

It occurred to Sam that this little conference could be more fun than he thought. 'Actually...' he glanced at his watch '...I've got an hour or two to kill. Why don't we make a really long list of all the things I mustn't do to you?'

Meg frowned. On the whole, she'd been relatively happy with this exchange, but had she missed something here? 'I beg your pardon?'

'Come on,' he urged with a slow smile, 'I'd quite like to discuss these rules in minute detail. It could take a while. For example, you've said we must kiss with our lips tight shut, so that means no—'

'I know jolly well what it means.'

'What about touching?' He stepped closer and uninvited little shivers prickled her skin. '*Where* mustn't I touch you? We really should talk about that.'

Meg felt shaky and weak. Obviously, Sam had no idea how much his kiss last night had affected her, or he wouldn't be teasing her like this. Kissing her had just been another bachelor game for him. Bimbo therapy for a bachelor on the loose.

But she hadn't been able to sleep for thinking about the taste of him. And the way he'd made her feel. If he touched her anywhere at this very moment, there was a good chance she would burst into a shower of sparks like an exploding sky-rocket.

'There's no need to discuss this,' she hissed.

'So it's no holds barred?'

'Very funny, Sam.' She walked away from him—out

of the danger zone. Up close, Sam was bad for her mental and emotional health. From the safer distance of the far side of the room, she explained, 'Fred wants us dressed up for tonight like something out of a soap opera.' She looked around the room—anywhere but at him. 'I guess that's appropriate. I feel like I'm caught up in some outlandish soap script.'

'I couldn't have described the situation better myself. That's *exactly* how I feel.'

'It would be easier if someone could hand us a script. Then our roles would be clear.'

He grinned. 'After I've organised to hire a suit, I'm free. We could spend today writing one.'

'Give it a miss, Sam.' She rolled her eyes. 'I'll see you tonight.'

CHAPTER FOUR

THE ONLY evening dress Meg had brought with her when she'd come to work on the island was a soft swirl of silvery grey chiffon over a silk slip with thin spaghetti straps that extended to lace across her bare back. 'I wish I had something with more back,' she told her reflection as she dressed.

If she had to dance with Sam in this dress, the whole business of touching would become a nightmare. His hands couldn't avoid her bare skin.

At exactly seven p.m., he arrived at her bungalow looking predictably scrumptious in a black dinner suit, white shirt and bow tie.

'Good timing,' she said lightly. 'I've just finished an extra coat of mascara—for the benefit of the photographers, of course.'

Her evening bag and a gauzy wrap lay ready on the dining table and she turned to gather them up. And heard his low whistle.

'That's some dress you're wearing.' His voice was rough as if he'd swallowed beach pebbles.

Half turning back in his direction, she found him looking at her with a puzzled smile. His eyes were paying fascinated attention to her exposed back. And she read admiration and interest in his gaze. This was going to be worse than she expected!

'You're planning to dance with me this evening wearing *this*?' He gestured to the criss-crossing of silvery ribbon that held her dress together. 'And—and you expect me to avoid all those no-go areas on that list of yours?'

'This is all I have that's suitable,' she muttered. 'You'll manage, Sam.'

They stood looking at each other, while the room seemed to vibrate with a thousand things they'd left unsaid.

Sam let out his breath. 'Of course I'll manage. As I've already warned you, I've never been known to knock back a challenge.' He offered his elbow so that she could link her arm through his. 'Allow me to escort you, Ms Bennet.'

Scooping up her bag and wrap, she stepped towards him and rested a cautious hand on the inside of his elbow. Her fingers met the luxurious silk and wool blend of his coat. He murmured close to her ear, 'You look much more beautiful than any soap star.'

Just in time, she remembered not to smile. 'No smooth talk, Prince Charming,' she warned.

'Spoilsport,' he muttered back, and they left her place and made their way through the tropical gardens to the restaurant.

A florid-faced Fred, dressed in an uncomfortably tight dinner suit and an outlandish rainbow-coloured bow tie, looked halfway between a clown and an Italian tenor as he rushed towards them. 'Our VIPs!' he gushed. He planted a noisy wet kiss on Meg's cheek and embraced Sam as if he were a long-lost brother. 'You two look great.' His eyes narrowed. 'Have you got your act together? No bickering?'

'Absolutely,' replied Sam. He draped a possessive arm across Meg's bare shoulders. 'We're totally smitten. Can't keep our hands off each other.'

Meg shot a scowl in his direction, but he wasn't looking. He was too busy smiling at her boss, while his thumb trailed devastating, lazy circles around the nub of her shoulder.

'Fantastic!' Fred beamed. He gestured to the gaily decorated dining room. From every table balloons floated above old bottles encrusted with glued-on sand. Fred was proud of his stroke of decorative genius. The assembled guests, mainly business associates of Fred's as well as the media, were all staring at Sam and Meg with undisguised curiosity.

Fred winked at Sam. 'Everyone's dying to meet you.'

As they progressed across the room, cameras flashed and Sam kept his arm firmly around Meg's shoulders. Through her teeth, she muttered, 'You're getting a bit carried away!'

'Don't panic,' he murmured, dropping his head so that his mouth was low against her ear. Her heart seemed to tremble in her chest when he whispered softly, as a lover might, 'Just remember it's only a game. And it will all be over in an hour or two.'

In an hour or two? Meg feared by then all that would be left of her would be a melted puddle. She reminded herself that Sam had a string of girlfriends at home on the other side of the world and that was exactly why she had to resist his charm. That was what she had to concentrate on.

'Don't pull away from me,' he ordered under his breath, as they reached a circle of guests. He dropped an unexpected kiss on her cheek. 'That's better. Just relax and enjoy.'

Relax and enjoy? No way. She had been relaxed when she'd first met Sam Kirby. Red Riding Hood had been relaxed when she'd met the wolf. She and Red Riding

Hood had both been very foolish young women. Tonight she planned to keep her alarm systems on high alert.

But it was intensely annoying that Sam could play his part so easily.

While dizzying, wild sensations danced along her skin, he remained cool and detached. He charmed Fred's guests by answering their questions and showing polite interest in their businesses and, at the same time, he kept her at constant fever pitch with casual touches and killer smiles.

When a photographer approached from behind, Sam had the audacity to run a daring finger down Meg's exposed spine. And when she reacted sharply, he smiled and whispered, 'Stay cool. This is just to keep Fred happy.'

Several cameras flashed.

A woman asked, 'When you return to the States, will you take Meg with you?'

'Oh, no!' Meg responded quickly.

Sam's hand squeezed her shoulder as he hauled her companionably against him. 'Meg and I have an understanding.'

With some difficulty, Meg muffled a gasp of dismay. Up close against him, his tantalising aftershave was distressingly arousing and she had the greatest difficulty speaking two sensible words in a row. She offered the woman a shaky smile.

'We're going to hate to be apart,' Sam added. His blue eyes twinkled as he smiled at Meg. 'Aren't we, sweetheart?'

'I'll—I'll be counting the days till he comes back,' she managed to reply.

To her relief, a meal was served and there was a chance to remove herself from Sam and sit down. Not that she was hungry. With him still at her side, her stomach was so tied in knots, she doubted her food would stay down.

'Having fun?' he asked and Meg noticed he wasn't having any difficulty wolfing down seafood and salad.

She crumbled a bread roll with nervous fingers. 'Not much.'

'What's the problem?'

'I think you're overdoing it.'

His eyes widened, pleading innocence, while his smile looked as guilty as sin. 'Overdoing what exactly?'

'As if you didn't know.'

'But I've stuck to your rules.'

'You have not,' she answered sharply. 'You're making up your own rules.'

He leaned closer and his thumb caressed her lower lip. 'You look gorgeous, Meg, but you're pouting when you should be smiling. Don't forget, as far as everyone here is concerned, we're at the beginning of a thrilling new romance. You're mad about me, baby.'

'As far as I'm concerned, I'm mad *at* you, not about you.'

'It's showing.' He touched her frowning forehead. 'The problem is,' he said, in a roughened whisper, 'I *want* to touch you and hold you and kiss you. It's not an effort for me at all.'

Meg dropped her gaze to her plate. Angrily she stabbed her fork into a pile of shredded lettuce. There could only be one reason why Sam found this ordeal so effortless.

He wasn't affected the way she was. She was burning up with every glance and touch, while he remained completely in control. This whole evening was just an amusing game for him. He was a love-'em-and-leave-'em millionaire, who was used to getting anything he wanted.

'If you've had enough to eat, I'd love to dance with you, Meg.'

She sighed. The band was playing a popular number and couples were leaving the tables for the dance floor. 'Do we have to?'

His gaze took in her dress. 'That's a dress designed for dancing.' Standing, he held out his hand. 'I promise this will be painless.'

I very much doubt that, Sam. Slowly, she rose to her feet.

His warm hand rested on her bare lower back as he steered her towards the dance floor. In a daze, she allowed him to take her hand in his, while she placed the other on his shoulder. She felt the hush of his breath against her hair. Slowly, without touching, their bodies swayed to the music. Then Sam began to move, leading her confidently. She sensed the strength and athletic grace of his body as he moved.

'Now, this isn't too difficult, is it?' he teased.

'No,' she whispered, feeling a surge of anger that gave her a new lease of strength.

It suddenly occurred to her that this man was far too self-assured and smug for his own good. And if he could dredge up this kind of will-power then, by Jove, so could she. It was time to listen to her head instead of her hormones.

It was payback time. Time to discover if Sam could handle the kind of treatment he'd been dishing out. Meg snuggled in a little closer.

Immediately she sensed his surprise.

'I'm going to play this your way,' she whispered huskily. 'After all, we only have this one night together, don't we?'

'Uh-huh.' He grunted his reply.

Resting her head against his shoulder, she did her best to ignore how good it felt to nestle against his strength. 'Is this what you want?' she asked.

Sam cleared his throat. 'Sure.'

'I admit I was being childish about all those rules,' she murmured. When he didn't reply, she slipped her hand out of his and wound both arms around his neck. By holding her breath, she was just able to keep the most sizzling zones of her body a hair's breadth from his. 'I must admit you have marvellous self-control.'

'Meg,' Sam asked, 'have you been drinking?'

'I've had half a glass of wine. Why?'

'You're acting—different.'

'Am I?' She raised innocent eyes to his.

She realised it was a mistake as soon as she saw the heat flaring in Sam's blue gaze.

'You know you're playing with fire.' He growled the words and his hands cradled her hips and he hauled her closer. '*This* is how much control I have.'

In a microsecond, her sensitive breasts were moulded against his hard chest...his thigh slid audaciously between hers...and dramatic evidence of his lack of control thrust against her.

Shocked, Meg quivered. Hot shafts of equally out of control feelings raced through her. Before she could protest or gather her wits, Sam held her even closer and his lips lowered over hers.

'Sam.' She spluttered his name.

'Keep your lips shut,' he murmured against her mouth, 'or you're in deep, deep trouble.'

But Meg knew she was already in all kinds of trouble. Leg-trembling, brain-melting trouble. The restaurant's lights had been lowered and, to the background crooning of a sultry saxophone, Sam held her close and danced slowly—very, very slowly.

Hardly conscious of her own movement, her senses were completely focused on the shocking yet wonderful way his body surged against hers and the way his mouth moved over her with admirable attention to detail.

And she was matching each wicked move of his with one of her own.

Vaguely, she realised that her plan to unsettle Sam was backfiring, but she was rapidly reaching a stage beyond caring. Her body was becoming fused with his in a slow meltdown that made common sense and the rest of the world fade away.

She didn't notice the music had stopped until a rude tap-tap-tapping on the microphone startled her out of her trance.

'Can I have your attention, ladies and gentlemen?'

As they looked up, Fred smirked in their direction.

Meg stepped away from Sam. Feeling suddenly cold and foolish, she stood stiffly self-conscious among the dancers still on the floor.

In the spotlight, Fred took a gulp from a wineglass and looked self-important. 'You all know why we're gathered here this evening. I've always been a sentimental sort of a bloke, and I wanted my friends to join me to celebrate this special occasion. Around sixty years ago, an American called Tom Kirby was facing the possibility of death in the middle of the Coral Sea and he sent a message—a love letter—to his wife. Two weeks ago, our very own Meg Bennet found that message.'

He paused for a polite burst of applause.

'And Tom's grandson, Sam, has come here to claim this letter. It contains some very important information for his family. Now...' Fred beamed, picking up the bottle and the letter from the table beside him '...if Sam could just come up here...' He looked around. 'Are the photographers ready?'

Meg watched as Sam, with shoulders squared and dark head arrogantly high, made his way to the microphone. She stood, three fingers pressed against the lips he'd so recently been kissing, as he shook Fred's hand, received the bottle and letter, and turned to the microphone. Fred adjusted it slightly to accommodate Sam's extra height.

When she'd first met him, she'd thought he looked like a film star. Tonight, he looked like a conquering hero as he waved the bottle triumphantly above his head and everyone cheered and clapped. 'This is a very special moment,' he began by saying. 'Wars do terrible things to families and this war robbed my father of the chance to know his dad, Tom Kirby.'

He paused and seemed to take a deep breath as he held the bottle out in front of him. 'Soon, I'll be able to place this bottle in my father's hands. Dad will be able to read for himself the letter Tom wrote to my grandmother.'

Meg's heart swelled with emotion and tears filled her eyes. It was happening again. Every time she thought about the bottle and the time it had spent at sea, she became totally caught up in the magic mystery of it.

'Of course none of this could have happened without one incredibly important person,' Sam continued. 'The woman who found the bottle—Meg Bennet.'

The spotlight from the stage suddenly caught her in its glare. Sam was standing with his arm outstretched towards her. Everyone was looking at her. People were clapping. Sam was smiling his sexiest, most heart-wrenching smile. Prince Charming.

She couldn't smile back, she was too busy holding back tears.

He looked down at the letter in his hand. The room was quiet, waiting for him to wrap up his speech.

The spotlight drew back and Meg had never been so grateful for shadows. Her heart was beating so loudly, its drumming filled her ears. Sam was saying something else, but she couldn't hear him. She was thinking of how she'd felt just now as she'd danced with him.

Tonight, it seemed so fitting that the bottle had brought this beautiful man from across the sea. To her. She had a very strong feeling that she was as helpless as a rock plunging off a precipice. Despite her best efforts to resist, she was falling in love.

Sam finished speaking. There was loud applause. He smiled some more, but, glad to get out of the limelight, he excused himself as soon as possible and made his way through the crowd towards Meg.

He grinned and shook the letter at her. 'Got it at last.' Then he looked at her more closely and frowned. 'You look upset. What's wrong?'

'Nothing.' She replied so faintly he probably couldn't hear her. After all the fuss she'd made this morning about rules, how could she tell him she'd changed her mind? She suddenly wanted him to go on kissing and holding her for the rest of the century.

He gave an embarrassed little shrug. 'I got a bit carried away before on the dance floor.'

Her gaze dropped to her hands, but she couldn't stop her lips from twitching into a smile. 'You were very badly behaved.'

'You want to get out of here?'

'Yes,' she muttered quickly. 'I'll just get my things.'

Together they made the necessary farewells and then walked back to Meg's bungalow along lamp-lit paths that wound through tropical shrubbery.

When they reached her door, she opened it and stepped inside. Sam followed quickly as if he expected her to try to lock him out.

She didn't have a clue what would happen now. And she wasn't sure what she wanted to happen. Her mind was at war with her heart and her wayward body. In her head, she knew she should be politely showing Sam straight back out the front door. But her body was urging him to stay close. Really close.

And her heart kept whispering to her about destiny.

'Do you want to read the letter?' she asked him.

'Yeah. I'll take a quick look at it.'

Meg kept her distance, allowing Sam to read in complete privacy.

She knew half of it off by heart anyhow. The part she loved was where Tom had written, *'Sweetheart, I want you to know that meeting you, knowing you, loving you is the most wonderful thing that ever happened to me. You've given my life shape and splendour.'*

'It's beautiful, isn't it?' she asked when Sam looked up.

He nodded his head slowly, his eyes returning to the piece of fragile paper.

'Do you want to ring your lawyers or your family?'

'Later.' He placed it and the bottle carefully on her dining table and stood stiffly in the middle of her small living room, looking distractingly handsome in his dark evening suit. 'Right now I want to figure out what's going on in your head.'

'About the letter?' she asked, confused.

'No. About us. About rules and conditions.'

'I'm giving myself a strict lecture,' she said quickly.

'So you should,' he replied with mock severity. 'All

those rules you've broken.' His face broke into a cheeky, boyish smile. 'But you know what they say about rules.'

Warning bells pealed in her head. But, she couldn't listen. Not any more. She couldn't bear it if Sam walked away now. She had to ignore them. 'I've heard that they are made to be broken.'

'Yeah,' he whispered. 'And that's what we're going to do now, Meg.' His smoky gaze roamed over her. 'We're going to break all your rules. One by one. Come here.'

Unable to resist, she walked towards him, her eyes fixed on his, until she was within arm's reach. Then she stopped.

'I think the first rule was about holding hands,' he murmured.

'We were allowed to hold hands.'

He held up his hands in front of him and, as her heart thumped, Meg placed her own against his, palm to palm. For heated seconds they stood, facing each other and her legs trembled. Slowly Sam slid his long fingers between each of hers till they were clasped, then he pulled her close till their lips touched and, against her mouth, he whispered, 'Next we need to break your kissing rule.'

His tongue traced a seductive line between her lips and they drifted open. And then his lips and tongue began to explore her mouth at a teasing, leisurely pace, and Meg wondered how such an easy, slow touch could ignite such a wild and violent longing. She was helpless to prevent herself from melting against him.

Dazed, with a drowsy, heated hunger, she threw her arms around Sam's neck and dragged him closer. She clung to him, craving more. 'Please, forget about rules.'

The shudder she felt in his strong frame and the responding clamour of her own body shocked her. An instant later, his kiss became urgent, deep and intensely intimate. The same shocking heat and wildness that she'd felt on the dance floor surged through Meg again.

She wasn't sure what excited her more—her own wild sensations or Sam's obvious delight in her. He began a lingering discovery of her bare back, playing with the lacing as he went.

Her breathing grew more and more ragged as his hands trailed slowly up to her shoulders. Tucking his thumbs under the tiny straps, he slipped them from her shoulders, before he settled his hands lower, cupping her breasts.

Meg shivered with delectable suspense and he whispered, 'You're so beautiful—just beautiful.'

Her body hummed with exquisite anticipation...while her fevered imagination raced ahead. And she could see the next few moments unfurling...herself and Sam shedding their clothes...until skin touched to skin.

She sizzled at the thought.

Except.

Except...*other* thoughts crept into her mind...*annoying, sensible thoughts.*

This man was famous in Seattle as a love-'em-and-leave-'em bachelor. Could she, *should* she trust him with her body?

Another fleeting misgiving flashed into Meg's mind. Her father had been too reserved to discuss romance, but she suspected that if her mother had lived to talk of such things she would have warned Meg about the folly of falling in love and making love all on the same evening.

Sam must have sensed her hesitation. He pulled back a little. 'You OK?' he whispered against her cheek.

Suddenly nervous, she whispered. 'I—I don't know.'

His hands stilled and, for a moment, he simply held her gently. 'I can't believe how I feel about you,' he murmured softly, close to her ear.

'What way would that be?' she had to ask, her heart thumping wildly.

Gently he settled her shoulder straps back in place and, cradling her face with his hands, he looked deep into her eyes. 'Like...like I've found something I didn't know I was searching for. But—'

Meg pressed her fingers to his lips. 'Don't say any more,' she breathed. 'That's scary.'

He leaned back a little, studying her face carefully. 'Scary nice or scary scary?'

'Scary amazing,' she whispered. 'It's exactly how I feel about you.'

He let out a rush of breath and gathered her close again. 'Oh, Nutmeg,' he said softly, a husky tremor in his voice. 'You don't mind if I call you Nutmeg?'

'No.'

'It's a name that sounds just right for a woman who has a touch of spice that makes her incredibly delicious.'

Her lips wavered into a shaky smile.

For a minute they stood close, their hearts pounding against each other's chest.

'This is going to happen, Meg. We both know that. But there's no need to rush. Am I rushing you?'

Meg couldn't answer. She was shaking and she had no idea what to say.

But a sudden vision of the distant future seized her! Maybe one day, when she was a little old lady, she would think about finding the bottle and she would remember Sam Kirby and she would wonder...

Sam's fingers were gently massaging the nape of her neck. She looked up into his face and saw his obvious desire warring with such a tender concern for her that her heart sang. He cared. Why had she ever doubted? She loved this man.

'Sam, you're not rushing me,' she told him.

'You're sure?' His voice sounded raspy.

The next moment, his strong arms began to enfold her once more and she knew with a beautiful certainty that this was the one place in the world she wanted to be. Sam made her feel vibrantly thrillingly alive.

She nodded against his chest. 'I'm sure,' she whispered.

Without a moment's hesitation, he lowered his head once more and again his lips began to work their heated magic, travelling on a sensual, mind-numbing journey, exploring her neck and then her ear and finally her mouth.

All doubts vaporised.

'I want you to stay,' she whispered.

CHAPTER FIVE

SAM woke first, just as the sun broke through the overhead trees and sent dappled light through the filmy curtains. Beside him, Meg lay with her hair tumbling over her face and one arm curled to hug her pillow. His heart swelled as he thought of the night they'd shared.

Carefully, he brushed her hair, soft as corn silk, away from her face so he could see the delicate outline of her profile against the snowy pillow. The urge to kiss her awake, to take her in his arms and make love to her again was overpowering.

But he resisted the impulse. Who knew where the media mafia were hanging out, or what sordid story they would concoct? To be fair to Meg, he should leave now—quickly and discreetly—before the resort workers were up and about.

He eased himself off the bed and dressed without making a sound. In bare feet, he padded out into her small living area. He looked around curiously, hungry for details that would tell him more about Meg.

Usually he was careful to retain a healthy ignorance about the domestic details of his women friends. As a confirmed bachelor, he'd found it safer that way. Women had an annoying habit of quickly jumping to the wrong conclusions if a guy showed interest in their day-to-day lives.

But Meg made him feel both incredibly curious and dangerously reckless. Right now, he didn't care what conclusions she came to. They were probably on the right track.

Not that this simple, tidy cabin, combining a neat little kitchen with a dining and sitting area, gave too many clues about Meg. The bowl of fruit on the kitchen counter held the usual healthy varieties. A cluster of spice bottles stood beside the stove.

Everything seemed very orderly, but the cottage had a temporary feel about it, as if Meg had brought few of her personal possessions with her. The only thing remotely out of place was a half-completed jigsaw puzzle on the coffee table.

He smiled. Meg probably collected a library of books, games and puzzles to keep less active guests entertained. This puzzle was of a painting by the ancient Italian master, Botticelli. It was called *La Primavera*. Spring.

Sam's smile lingered. The beautiful woman in the puzzle was dressed in a soft gauzy gown covered in flowers. She had a face like Meg's, sweet and slightly serious. Her hair was long and fair and her beautiful eyes were an indeterminate colour that might have been green, or grey or…blue? She reminded him so much of Meg that he almost headed back to the bedroom.

He spotted the piece of puzzle that depicted the spring maiden's bare pink foot and, picking it up, he fitted it into place.

Then he released his breath on a weary, drawn out sigh. If only his life could be as simple as that. Could it really be just a matter of finding the puzzle pieces and slotting them together? He'd tried to reassure himself that when this letter was handed over, everything would fall into place neatly. Kirby & Son's holdings would be safe and he could start planning a future.

He wanted to give a good deal of thought to his future.

Sitting on Meg's rattan sofa, he pulled on his socks and shoes, then quietly let himself out by the back door and made his way, as unobtrusively as possible, back to his own bungalow.

He'd showered and changed, and eaten breakfast from a tray delivered to his door when the phone rang. Draining the last of his coffee, he snatched up the receiver. 'Sam Kirby.'

'Good morning, Sam.'

The sound of Meg's voice unleashed a hot yearning, catching him unawares. He took a deep breath. 'How are you this morning, Nutmeg?'

'Fine—wonderful.' she purred the words. 'And you?'

'Missing you.'

'Yes,' she said softly. 'I miss you, too.'

'I didn't want to stir up trouble by hanging around at your place this morning.'

'I realised that. Thanks. Have you seen this morning's paper?'

Sam groaned and dragged stiff fingers through his hair as he thought of the possibilities. 'Not yet. I take it you have?'

'Yes. It's not as bad as I thought it might be, although now they're tagging this story as "Love in a bottle".'

'Sounds like an ad for alcohol or something.'

'There's another photo of us at the party in an embarrassing clinch.' After a pause she added, 'I hope you don't mind, Sam.'

Hearing the tension vibrating in her voice, Sam frowned. 'How do you feel about it?'

'I'm not too bothered.'

'You sound bothered.'

'That's—that's because of something else that's come

up. A couple of minutes ago I had a phone call from a little old lady.'

He felt instantly defensive. His hand gripped the phone more tightly. 'Don't tell me someone is giving you a lecture about your wicked ways?'

'No, Sam, it's probably worse than that.'

'How?' he snapped.

'She's claiming that she's Tom Kirby's wife and that the letter in the bottle is for her.'

Oh, God! Sam's heart thudded. He slumped against the wall beside him. 'Who the hell is this person?'

'Her name is Dolly Kirby. She lives on the mainland and she says she met and married Tom when he was based in this district during the war.'

Sweat was breaking out all over Sam. Dolly *Kirby?* Under his breath, he cursed and he rubbed the back of his hand over his damp forehead. 'I don't believe it.' He groaned. 'It can't be true. It can't be. Tom Kirby was already married to my grandmother before he left for the war. My grandmother was already pregnant with my father.'

'I agree this is really weird,' Meg admitted. 'Dolly doesn't want to talk to the papers,' she added gently, as if to calm him. 'She wanted to talk to me first. To us, actually.'

Sam closed his eyes and tried to think clearly, rationally. The fact that this woman didn't want to run to the press with her story had to be a good thing, didn't it? But hell! What on earth was going on here?

Meg spoke again. 'She sounds very sweet.'

'Does she, now?' he replied slowly as, out of nowhere, a pack of nasty suspicions raised their ugly, yapping heads. Just when he thought he had this business safely in hand, a new problem emerged. 'It sounds fishy to me.'

'*Sam?*' Meg's tone sharpened. He could hear the note of reproach in that one syllable. 'You should at least meet Dolly before you start jumping to conclusions.'

'Yeah.' He sighed. 'I'll meet her.'

'Fred's given me instructions to be at your—um—disposal today. We could go across to Townsville later this morning. There are quite a few ferry times to choose from.'

'OK.' Sam pinched the bridge of his nose between a finger and thumb. 'And, Meg...'

'Yes?'

'Let me handle this. We need to approach this whole exercise with extreme caution.'

'For heaven's sake, Sam. I think you're overreacting. We're going to check out a little old lady, not a hideaway for armed terrorists.'

He heard the iciness chilling her voice and, not for the first time, Sam wished he could forget the family business. Throw off his responsibilities to Kirby & Son. Surely, when a guy met a woman like Meg, he should be able to put the rest of his life on hold? He would give anything to forget about the will and to take Meg in his arms again.

And keep her there.

As they stood at Dolly Kirby's front gate, Meg and Sam exchanged wary smiles. During the ferry ride across from the island, Sam had been withdrawn and subdued and Meg had tried hard not to let her disappointment show.

She'd been following her instincts when she'd asked Sam to stay last night and those instincts had led her to the most sensational, magical evening of her entire life.

Today the bubble had burst.

It seemed that Sam was in danger of losing his millions

and it was clear where his priorities lay. The attentive lover, the fascinated, delighted companion of yesterday had been replaced by a cool, serious stranger.

Seeing him like this left a chilling, sad emptiness like a cold hollow around Meg's heart. Now she realised she'd been jumping the gun to imagine that last night's happiness had been based on a blossoming of reciprocal love—the kind of love that lasts.

She would give anything for just one of yesterday's smiles.

He reached forward and opened the latch on the rusty metal gate. It squeaked on its hinges as he shoved it open and he gestured for Meg to go before him. When they reached the low set of wooden steps leading to the front veranda of the cottage, his hand rested lightly at the small of her back. She noted with a grim smile that, even when he was dreadfully worried, his natural courtesy remained intact.

Dolly Kirby answered Sam's knock almost immediately.

'Oh, my goodness!' Her pale blue eyes riveted on Sam. They were rounded with shock. 'Oh, my dear Lord!'

Meg thought for a moment that the old lady was going to faint.

Sam dipped his head stiffly. 'Good morning, ma'am.'

Dolly continued to stare at him while her mouth trembled and her arthritic fingers clutched at the big brass doorknob as if for support.

'Mrs—er—Kirby?' Sam asked in clarification.

She nodded and at last she spoke. 'Yes. I'm sorry but you gave me such a shock. You—you look so much like him.'

'Him?'

Meg glanced at Sam and watched his face darken with discomfort.

'My Tom. His eyes were that beautiful sky blue just like yours—and with your dark hair. Oh, dear, you look so much like my Tom, and you sound just like him, too.'

Dolly's eyes glistened with sudden tears. Meg felt her own throat grow prickly with emotion. 'Dolly, I'm Meg Bennet. You spoke to me on the phone and, as you've guessed, this is Sam Kirby.'

Tentative handshakes were exchanged.

'Please, come inside.' Dolly led the way down the central hallway of her simple home and then turned into her lounge. She stood in the middle of the room and indicated they should sit on the old-fashioned, overstuffed sofa. When Meg and Sam were seated and leaning back against the frilly hand-embroidered cushions, she took her place on a carved wooden chair and continued to stare at Sam. 'I can't get over the likeness,' she whispered. 'It's like Tom walked back into my life.'

He cleared his throat. 'So—er—Dolly, you're claiming to have married my grandfather.'

'Yes, dear.' She nodded her head vehemently. 'Tom and I were married in April, 1942. Just before he headed off for the Battle of the Coral Sea.'

Meg wished Sam didn't look quite so stony, like a lawyer grilling a suspect in the witness box.

'There can't have been much time for a long courtship?'

'No, there wasn't. I think I shocked my family.' Dolly's face trembled into a wistful smile. 'It was a whirlwind romance.'

Meg felt a rush of understanding, of having shared the experience of falling in love with a Kirby at breakneck speed. She couldn't help smiling back at Dolly. If Tom

Kirby had looked even half as sexy as Sam—if he had smiled at Dolly with the same heart-stopping blue eyes as Sam's—she had no doubt at all that the other woman had fallen in love with the pace of a lightning strike.

She sensed Sam sitting even more stiffly beside her.

'You have evidence? A marriage licence?' he asked in the deceptively casual tone of a policeman making routine inquiries.

Meg bit her lip uneasily. She wished he could take the trouble to be more gentle with this elderly woman.

But, despite her fragile frame, Dolly was sprightly for her age. She was on her feet in a moment and crossing the carpeted room to an old-fashioned, beautifully carved sideboard. She picked up a framed photograph and a tattered manila folder and brought them across to him.

The black and white photograph in its delicate silver frame shook in her frail hand as she offered it. 'That's Tom and I. It was taken just before we were married.'

As Meg leaned closer to look at the picture he held, she bumped against Sam's shoulder and she tried not to think about how much she loved the feel of him against her. She focused on the details of the photograph and tiny, sensitive hairs rose on the back of her neck.

The laughing young man in the photo could have been Sam.

His height and build were very similar, but it was in their faces that the two men bore such a startling resemblance: the bright eyes, despite the lack of colour in the photo, the thick black hair; the strong line of the dark brows; the slightly crooked nose and squared, no-nonsense jaw. And the mouth; Meg could see that even Tom Kirby's lips were exactly like Sam's—surprisingly sensuous in such a strongly masculine face.

Her eyes caught Dolly's and they exchanged shy

smiles as a flash of sympathetic understanding sparked between them.

Behind the couple rose a familiar rocky headland.

'That looks like Florence Bay,' Meg cried out.

'Yes, dear.' Dolly smiled wistfully. 'Tom and I met on the island. Florence was a very special place for us.'

'You know, that's where I found the bottle?'

Dolly nodded and her face shone.

Sam made throat-clearing noises and shifted uneasily.

Meg looked at the young Dolly in the photo with her hand resting possessively on Tom Kirby's arm, demonstrating the same sense of connection and belonging that she felt for Sam.

The parallels were so strong, Meg couldn't help remembering the strange, mystical bond she'd felt when she'd found the bottle. It was as if she'd been caught up in some kind of time warp.

Dolly spoke. 'I had never been one to chase after boys. I didn't really know much about—er—passion. But with Tom, it was love at first sight and it was a love so big that neither of us could hold back.'

Meg was quite certain she understood. People *could* fall in love in a heartbeat. Look what had happened to her last night.

She thought with a sigh, poor Dolly. She'd met Tom, had loved him and had lost him in such a short space of time. She couldn't bear the thought of losing Sam when she'd only just begun to know him.

'Well, there…' Sam began to speak, but his voice cracked and he had to start again. 'There is certainly a strong family likeness.'

Dolly nodded. 'It's quite remarkable, isn't it?' She opened the manila folder. 'And here's the wedding certificate.'

In silence, Sam accepted the folder. Meg sat back and watched his face as he read the details carefully. She wished there was something she could do to make this easier for him. He looked so grim and worried. She would have loved to stroke that furrowed brow, or to kiss away the tension in those unsmiling lips.

Dolly spoke softly. 'I'm afraid we had to get married very quietly in a civil ceremony. The navy wouldn't have given Tom permission to marry in the middle of active duty, so it was all rather clandestine.'

Sam's expression grew darker than ever. He handed the photo and folder back to Dolly. 'Thank you for showing me these.'

After Dolly put them on a small side table, she sat down again opposite them.

Sam cleared his throat and nodded towards the folder on the table. 'I might have to let my lawyers take a look at that licence at some stage.'

Dolly nodded. 'I don't mind.' Her eyes gleamed as she smiled at him 'I would love to read Tom's letter.'

'Oh, Dolly, I hope you can see it soon.' Meg couldn't hold back her emotional outburst. 'It's just the most beautiful message.'

Sam swung around and glared at her. 'We still have to determine who it was written for,' he said coldly.

'Ease off, Sam,' Meg murmured reproachfully. *How could he be so hard? Couldn't he tell how disturbing all this must be for Dolly?*

His eyes met hers, read her dismay and flicked away again. He addressed the old lady. 'You know that my grandfather was already married before he left the States?'

For a long, awkward moment, Dolly stared at him,

open-mouthed. Slowly she began to shake her head. 'Oh, no, dear. I'm quite certain he wasn't.'

Sam's voice rose. 'Of course he was. My grandmother was already expecting a baby—my father.'

Dolly's gaze lowered and she fiddled nervously with the pleated skirt of her blue floral dress. Her lower lip trembled. 'I don't know anything about a baby. When I read in the paper that Tom had a grandson, I was quite shocked.'

'There was most definitely a baby. My father's name was Jefferson Thomas Kirby. He was born in 1942.'

'I'm sure Tom didn't know anything about a baby either.' After a pause, Dolly added, 'That's sad.' She raised her glistening eyes again and bit her lip. 'Tom told me about his fiancée. Her name was Judith, wasn't it?'

A strangling sound emitted from Sam's throat. Meg watched with alarm as a red tinge crept along his cheekbones and reached the tips of his ears. He drew in a sharp breath. 'Judith was my grandmother's name.'

Straightening her elderly shoulders as much as she could, Dolly spoke slowly, directing her gaze steadily at Sam. 'I am quite certain Tom and Judith were never married. He told me he would contact Judith and break off the engagement just as soon as he could. I know he tried, but I never heard if she received the message.'

Meg felt Sam's shock reverberate through his body. He slumped as if he'd been slugged with something heavy.

'You didn't try to contact her at all…after…afterwards?' he asked.

'Oh, yes.' Dolly sighed. 'I wrote several letters to Tom's family in Seattle during the war—and after the war. None of them was ever answered. If I'd had the money, I would have travelled over there to try to find someone.'

Slipping her hand into Sam's, Meg squeezed gently, but if he noticed he didn't acknowledge her attempt at sympathy. He seemed dazed.

'This is all very strange,' he said at last. Then, as if the fog cleared, he shook his head and snapped to alert attention again. 'I'm going to have to consult with my lawyers before we can—take this any further.'

He stood abruptly, letting Meg's hand slip out of his as if he hadn't even noticed it was there. She struggled to send Dolly a reassuring smile.

'Thanks for—for informing us. Good afternoon,' Sam said with a stiff little nod of his head. Then he frowned at Dolly. 'And I'd prefer if you kept this just between ourselves for the moment.'

'Of course.'

The three of them made their way back down the narrow hall to the front door. There was a hurried, unsatisfactory exchange of farewells, then Sam took off down the path with Meg following. She turned and offered one final little wave to Dolly before getting into the car.

They headed back into the city. Meg drove the car Fred had provided for use on the mainland, while Sam sank back in the passenger's seat and released his breath in a long, drawn-out sigh.

'That was tough,' she suggested as she turned into the main road.

He leaned an elbow on the windscreen ledge and rubbed his forehead slowly. 'This whole business about Dolly just doesn't make any kind of sense.'

'It must be a shock for both of you.'

'I can't believe my grandfather would...'

Sam shook his head as he left the obvious dangling.

He found it so hard to believe that his grandfather had been married to anyone else but Judith Kirby. When he was little, he'd been more than a touch afraid of his grandmother. She was a haughty, snobbish woman—who had always dressed impeccably and found small boys rather noisy and troublesome. She had been highly regarded in Seattle's best social circles.

Later, when he'd grown tall and had developed less noisy habits, she had favoured him more fondly. He wondered now, how she'd felt when he'd grown to look so much like Tom Kirby. He was mildly surprised that she'd never commented on the fact.

How would she have reacted to this news from Dolly? What would she have said to the possibility that her husband had committed bigamy? Of course, she would have dismissed the notion as rubbish.

It had to be rubbish.

The thought of his grandmother refuting such an idea with a toss of her silver hair and a sniff of her patrician nose reassured him for a moment. A very short moment.

But the evidence of that photo and the certificate was a little hard to ignore. If the documents were frauds, they'd been prepared by professionals.

He pressed tense fingers against his forehead. Of course, it wasn't beyond the realms of possibility that one of Kirby & Son's competitors had a hand in all this.

'A penny for your thoughts.' Meg's warm voice penetrated his speculations.

'You wouldn't like them.' He sighed. He had seen the way she'd been so caught up in Dolly's story. If the little old lady was a fraud, Meg would be devastated.

'Cheer up.' Her hand lifted from the gear stick to give his a friendly squeeze.

He sent her an attempt at a smile. Damn it, the last

thing he wanted to be doing with Meg was sifting through the sordid details of his grandfather's love life. They should be adding a few interesting details to their own.

'Sorry you had to get mixed up in this,' he told her.

'I started it,' she reminded him, flashing him a quick grin. 'I was the one who found the bottle. Maybe I should have just left it stuck in the sand.' She steered the car into the car park next to the ferry terminal. Once she had parked, she said. 'A necessary change of subject. Did you want to do anything else before you head back to the island?'

Reaching over, he touched her soft cheek. 'Changing the subject is an excellent idea.'

In the past, when the pressure of work had threatened to overwhelm him, he'd developed a habit of deliberately focusing on something else for an hour or two. He'd always come back to the problem with a clearer head. Often he'd drive off into the mountains of Seattle's hinterland. Sometimes he'd visit his favourite childhood haunt—the Aquarium.

He smiled at Meg. 'If we could shop for some exotic ingredients, would you let me into that neat little kitchen of yours, so I could cook dinner tonight?'

Her eyes widened and he noted that her irises reflected hints of the mint-green colour of her dress. 'You can cook?' she asked, her smile a cheeky challenge.

'Isn't cooking a part of every modern bachelor's repertoire?'

'Not that I've noticed.' She unsnapped her seat belt. 'The odd fellow might manage to barbecue sausages to a delicate shade of black, but that's about it. And you mentioned exotic ingredients. I'm impressed.' Leaning over, she kissed Sam. It was a playful, teasing kiss full on his lips.

And it was all that it took to *completely* change his focus.

Now wasn't the time to admit that he had only practised and perfected one recipe and that, after that, he was back to opening cans of beans. Instead, he trapped her lovely face between his hands and returned her kiss. The gear stick was a bit of a problem and they were both grinning, so their teeth collided a little, which meant it wasn't an award-winning kiss.

But it didn't matter. Hell, nothing seemed to matter when Meg was this close. This tempting.

She pulled away, giggling. 'If we hurry with our exotic shopping, we should still be able to catch the next boat.'

'OK. Now, where's a good seafood shop? I need crayfish, king prawns, scallops…'

As they made their way around the shopping centre unearthing Sam's ingredients, Meg tried to ignore the way her common sense kept pricking her. She didn't want to be reminded that this sudden flash rerun of yesterday's happy, charming Sam wouldn't last.

Any minute now, he could become reabsorbed in his problems. She decided the best she could do was make the most of this time out. Perhaps the story of Dolly and Tom's brief love had taught her a lesson? To seize the day? The hour? The moment?

The way she felt about Sam was so surprising. She had never expected to become so smitten by a man she'd only just met.

And she had certainly never expected to feel so ecstatically happy searching for udon noodles, baby bok choy or oyster mushrooms. The intensity of her feelings bubbled through her as if her veins had been filled with soda pop. There could only be one explanation. The same one she'd arrived at last night. She loved Sam. Loved him, loved him, loved him.

She hadn't been looking for love. It had just leaped into her life without knocking first. And, while Sam hadn't actually mentioned love, he'd told her that he'd never felt this way before either. Knowing that, felt good.

His smiling eyes met hers through a carefully stacked display of pumpkin-soup tins and a delicious, joyful shiver skittered over her. She felt like dancing a jig down the aisles. She sure hoped Sam didn't intend to spend too much time in the kitchen. She had other plans for this evening.

Last night's lovemaking had left her with an incredibly desperate need for more.

'All I need now is ginger and soy sauce,' he said.

'All I need is another kiss.'

A smile tugged at his lips. 'Come here, then.' He pulled her behind the tins of soup and, ducking his head, kissed her soundly on the mouth. 'How much time do we have?' He growled the words, nuzzling her neck just below her ear. 'I hadn't realised shopping was so seductive.'

She couldn't help grinning as she glanced at her wristwatch. 'We should just make the boat.'

There was a dreamlike quality to their happiness as they rushed through the checkout and sped back to the ferry terminal.

The only man who'd ever cooked for Meg had been her father. She loved the idea that Sam wanted to impress her with his skills in something as domestic as cooking.

She could visualise everything. She would tuck a tea towel around his waist, turn her stereo on and pour two glasses of wine.

Sitting on the end of the bench, she would admire the

way he chopped and sautéed. No doubt they would exchange quick, cheeky kisses whenever he came near her. They'd be laughing and joking...

And then, afterwards...

On the ferry, they sat outside on the upper deck, close together, while the wind and the sea rushed and slapped noisily about them. It was hard to talk. The ends of sentences were whipped away by the wind, so they smiled at each other instead. And they touched in deceptively casual little ways—a hand resting on a shoulder or a knee—a nose brushed against a cheek—lips against hair.

Each touch, each look set off flash points of longing so that it took all Meg's self-control not to throw her arms around Sam and make a public spectacle of herself.

On the island once more, Sam loaded the shopping into the back of the Moke, while Meg slipped into the driver's seat. All she could think about was being alone with him again. She was frustrated by the length of time it took to negotiate the narrow road to the resort. It followed a series of hills and valleys as it wound its way over headlands and skimmed along the flat edges of palm fringed bays. Finally, they chugged into the driveway of Magnetic Rendezvous.

'I'd like to pick up my laptop before I come to your place,' Sam said. 'At some stage, I need to send some e-mail messages back to Seattle.'

'OK,' Meg replied, trying to sound offhand about the fact that he could think about business right now when all she could think of was kissing him and touching him.

Sam captured her hand and swung her towards him. 'I'll see you in five,' he murmured. 'Don't go away. I'm going to need some help in the kitchen.' He rubbed his thumb gently over her lower lip and smiled slowly, his eyes trapping hers—making every pulse in her body throb. His mouth dipped to tease hers. 'Actually, any old room will do, but I'm going to need you there, Meg.'

She felt the flames leap into her cheeks and she couldn't reply. There was no way she could talk. She wasn't even sure she was still breathing. A feverish longing was eating her up. In a daze, she hurried to her cottage and shoved the seafood into the fridge. Her senses on high alert for the sound of Sam's footsteps, she hurried into the bathroom and cleaned her teeth.

She had never felt so fired up, so highly sensitised, so tingling with expectation. So hot! She was smouldering with such wild thoughts, there was every chance that, when Sam walked through her doorway, she would shock the socks off him.

When her phone rang, she ignored it. There was no way she could carry on a normal conversation with anyone right now. She checked her watch. Five minutes he'd said. Well, it was bordering on five minutes now.

Meg tried to calm down. She strode through to her kitchen and filled a glass with water. As she drank it, she closed her eyes and willed herself to relax.

Sam's phone rang just as he was heading for the door with his laptop under one arm. He grabbed the door frame for balance as he stopped abruptly and scowled at the squat little phone sitting on his coffee table. It continued its insistent ringing. Damn it! He knew a telephone could be annoying but, now, when he was on his way to Meg, it was an instrument of torture. Slamming his palm against the door frame, he hovered for another second, then stepped outside and shoved his door closed behind him.

Whoever was calling could wait.

*   *   *

Meg glimpsed Sam's profile as he strode past her kitchen window. Then she saw the back of his tanned neck and the neat line of his hair before he disappeared around the corner of the cottage. By the time he reached her front door, the slim laptop at his side, she was there too. He grinned, bent down and kissed her cheek.

'I missed you,' she whispered.

For a moment, he leaned away from her to deposit the laptop carefully on her dining table but, when he straightened, he reached to her, hauling her close. 'I'm here to stay.' His smiling gaze linked to hers. 'You know, those eyes of yours give you away every time.'

'What colour are they now?' she asked.

'Sweetheart, I'm not talking about their colour.' His kiss was hot and hard and Meg couldn't hold back her soft sighs of pleasure.

The telephone rang again.

'Damn phone,' Sam muttered against her mouth as he deepened the kiss. Her arms rose to entwine around his neck but, as the sound from the kitchen persisted, he groaned.

Reluctantly, Meg dragged her lips from his. 'There was someone ringing here earlier, but I'm afraid I ignored it,' she admitted.

'I had a call that I didn't answer, too.' Sam glared at the phone.

'Pity I don't have an answering machine.'

'I wonder if they'll keep trying all evening?'

'Best get rid of whoever it is.' With a heavy, regret-laden sigh, Meg released her hold on his neck.

'You want me to take it?' Sam asked.

'Thanks.'

She watched as Sam snatched up the receiver. After grunting his name, he listened in silence. A silence that went on way too long.

CHAPTER SIX

MEG watched as Sam stood with one hand propped against the kitchen wall and listened intently to the caller. He stared down at the white tiled floor and shook his head. 'There's got to be some mistake!'

Oh, no, she thought and her stomach clenched. What's gone wrong? She took a tentative step closer.

'There's got to be a record somewhere.' Sam yelled into the phone and she heard a note of rising frustration in his voice. His eyes closed as he concentrated hard on whatever his caller was saying. He nodded as he listened in agitated silence. 'OK. OK,' he said at last. 'Yeah. I met her. She has a certificate. Yes, yes, I'll get back just as soon as I can.' He pressed the disconnect button and dropped the phone before covering his face with his hands.

Meg's heart leaped wildly. 'What's happened?'

His head snapped up. His eyes were so fierce they'd darkened to navy. 'Our lawyers can't find a wedding certificate for my grandparents.'

'You mean, there's no record at all?'

'Sweet nothing.'

'So that means—'

'It means that almost certainly my grandparents were never married.' Sam shot a warning glance in her direction. 'Don't you start on about how happy you are for Dolly.'

Meg gasped. 'Well, I guess I am pleased for Dolly.' She took another step towards him. 'But I can understand your family's problems as well. This is awful for you. Are they going to keep looking, or are the lawyers certain there's nothing to be found?'

'They'll probably make a few more investigations. But there's virtually no hope,' he told her bluntly. With a despondent sigh, he shoved his hands deep in the pockets of his jeans.' They've already done an exhaustive search. It looks as if my grandmother's family did a cover-up job about the marriage. She and Tom Kirby were already engaged before he left—and she was pregnant. Somehow, I doubt Tom knew that.'

'But they never married?'

'No. My grandmother came from old blue-blood stock. Her family would have hated the stigma of illegitimacy.'

'I'm so sorry. This must be a terrible blow for you.'

'Yeah. It looks like Dolly was right all along. The letter was meant for her.' He pulled his hands back out of his pockets and banged one knuckled fist against the other. 'Which means Dolly is probably the legal inheritor of Kirby & Son.'

'Goodness.' Meg cried. 'Where does that put you and your family?'

His mouth stretched into a grimacing grin as he shook his head. 'Into a long, expensive, legal mess that could go on for years.'

'How terrible.' A feeling of dread swept through Meg. She hurried to Sam's side and gave him what she hoped was a reassuring hug. In return, he dropped a swift kiss on her cheek, but she could see his mind was distracted elsewhere.

'It looks like this whole business of coming over here to Australia for the bottle—has caused a huge problem for you and your family,' she said in a flat tone that matched the sinking feeling in her stomach.

He heaved a loud sigh. 'It sure has.'

The room seemed to sway abruptly. Meg reached for the back of a nearby chair to steady herself. What else had she expected Sam to say? That it didn't matter? That finding her had been the highlight of his life? That one night with her cancelled out the down side of losing millions of dollars, a family company and his father's legitimacy?

She willed the walls to stop closing in.

Sam spoke again. 'Of course, my lawyers will still want to take a good look at the letter. Nothing's certain until that's been sighted. That reminds me—' Abruptly, he picked up the phone again. 'Reception?' He barked the word. 'Sam Kirby here. I need to advance my return flight to Seattle. Can you organise that for me? That's right. I need the first available flight back. You've got my details, haven't you?'

As he replaced the phone, Meg stared at him openmouthed. She had known this news meant Sam would have to go home, but so soon? 'You're going back, just like that? Straight away?'

'I have to get back. You can see that, can't you?'

'Yes,' she said in a cold little voice. 'After all, there's a lot of money at stake.'

His jaw clenched. 'You really have got a huge chip on your shoulder when it comes to money, haven't you?' He glared at her and his shoulders stiffened.

Her stomach churned as she watched him pace the room, his face dark and grim.

'You don't realise what's *really* at stake here.' He hurled the words at her angrily. 'It's not just about money. Four generations of my family have worked hard to build up a fine, successful company. I've worked my butt off to keep it going since my father took sick. And now, it could all be lost. It's unbelievable that we could lose it just because—'

He plunged tense fingers into his hair. 'I'm still not sure this isn't some kind of incredible prank. If I take my lawyers' advice, everything should be under suspicion. Dolly's story is so hard to believe.'

Meg frowned at him. 'But Dolly has proof.'

He crossed his arms over his chest and she averted her eyes. The pose made his physique more impressive than ever. But her drooling days were over.

'We don't know yet if any of her papers are legitimate,' he said coldly. 'Anyone can mock up photos and certificates these days.'

Meg stared at Sam, aghast. 'Dolly wouldn't. How can you even suggest such a thing? You've got to be wrong about that.'

This was too much!

She thought of the smile she and Dolly had shared— the smile of one woman in love recognising the same blinding joy in the other. 'I'm sure you're wrong, Sam. You can't possibly believe it.'

'It wouldn't be the first time people have been hoodwinked by white hair and a sweet smile.'

Meg tried to suppress a growing suspicion that she'd been hoodwinked by blue eyes and a sexy smile. While she watched, Sam seemed to be transforming from a sensitive, exquisite lover into a hard-bitten, callous sceptic.

'Sam,' she said, deliberately keeping her tone sympathetic. 'I can understand how upset you must be by all this. But can't you believe Dolly's story? Can't you imagine how it was for Tom and her? Meeting here, just as we have, and falling helplessly in love?' Her voice broke on the word 'love.'

For a brief moment, his eyes linked to hers and their

flinty hardness softened. His Adam's apple moved up and down in his throat.

Please, Sam, she begged silently. *Please tell me you can picture what love was like for them.* Surely, if he felt only half the emotion she was feeling for him, he would know Dolly's story made sense.

But his next chilling words proved to her that he was on a completely different wavelength. 'Everything about this whole situation stinks. Look at the way Fred's used me to get his grubby publicity. Honestly, right now, I can't help thinking the whole business with the bottle and the letter has all been one huge hoax.'

Stunned, she backed away from him until she bumped into her sofa. She sank into it as his words echoed in her head. *One huge hoax? He didn't believe she'd found the bottle!* How could Sam doubt her? Last night he'd thanked her for finding it in front of a resort full of people.

And he'd given every impression that he was falling in love with her.

He had made perfect, beautiful love to her!

Tears slid down her face and she let them fall.

No wonder Sam hadn't trusted Dolly. He didn't trust anyone! For Pete's sake! When he'd first come to the island, he'd hidden his real identity. He'd been suspicious of her right from the start!

This was beyond terrible! Meg had never felt so wretched—as if she had fallen into a swirling black whirlpool and was drowning... She struggled to breathe.

Sam stopped pacing. His mind had been seething with shock and a hundred worries, but suddenly it penetrated that Meg had been silent for a long time. He blinked and looked around searching for her.

She was curled up on the sofa, her lovely, honey-tanned legs tucked primly to one side and her curls tumbling every which way around her face. He peered closer. Her face looked blotchy, streaked and strained. Concerned, he walked over to her and touched her cheek.

If she hadn't seemed so stiff and tense he would have stooped to kiss her, but something in the tight, held-in way she was sitting stopped him. 'Are you OK, Meg?'

Her answer was to haul herself off the sofa and to storm out to the kitchen. 'I'm getting extremely hungry.' She tossed the words over her shoulder. 'But I don't suppose you'll have time to cook dinner now.'

'Er—I guess that depends on what flights are available.' From the kitchen, he could hear the sounds of Meg opening the door of the refrigerator. 'Meg, I've been so agitated. I might have said something out of turn. I don't even know now what I said. I—'

Her hard voice interrupted him. 'Nice try, Sam, but don't expect me to buy it.'

He frowned. He still couldn't see Meg's face. She was hunting around in a cupboard for something, but she was sounding as edgy as a precipice.

Completely baffled, he offered an apologetic smile in her direction. 'I take it you're mad at me?'

Her head came out of a cupboard and she glared at him, her face flushed. 'I think you'd better take your seafood and your computer and get out of here,' she said slowly, her tone icily quiet.

Struggling to make sense of her anger, he held his hands out in a gesture of innocence. 'Don't I get any kind of explanation?'

Shaking her head, Meg folded her arms across her chest and looked away. He could have sworn her chin was trembling as if she were struggling to hold back tears. His heart lurched. 'Meg,' he shouted angrily. 'Speak to me.'

She almost—*almost*—weakened. Turning her tear-blurred eyes back to Sam, Meg saw his genuinely puzzled expression, as if he was honestly confused. It was tempting to simply throw herself into his arms, to have a sob that he could kiss better and to forget what he had just said about the bottle being a hoax.

But that was the weak option and she'd been weak around Sam Kirby just once too often. She'd given in to the ultimate weakness with a man she hardly knew.

Drawing in a deep, strengthening breath and then releasing it once more, she said softly, so softly she wondered if he could hear her, 'When we made love, I was offering you more than my body.'

She saw him stiffen. His face tightened, his shoulders straightened and he seemed to grow taller. 'Yes?'

'I told you I'm not in the habit of—of sleeping around.'

'Meg, I didn't think for one moment—What are you trying to tell me?'

'I have to feel emotionally involved with a man. I *did* feel very emotionally involved with you, Sam.'

His throat worked and he stared at her, his eyes puzzled. She wanted to tell him how she'd fallen head over heels for him—that already she loved him deeply, irrevocably. But it was way too late for that kind of admission.

'I *trusted* you.'

'Of course you can trust me, Meg.'

Tears threatened, but she willed herself not to cry. 'Trust has to be mutual.'

Sam's hands rose to his hips. He shook his head. 'Meg, I'm no good at guessing. This is driving me insane.' At that moment, the phone rang again and he snatched it up. 'Kirby.'

Meg's heart thumped and crashed harder than ever as she watched him listen carefully to his caller.

'That's good,' he answered with a grim nod of his head. 'Thanks. I'll be there soon.'

His eyes swung to Meg and she felt herself grow cold. 'They can get you a seat on a flight out *tonight*?' Couldn't he at least stay tonight? Just one more night?

'Yeah. I can get a flight out of Townsville to Sydney. That way I can catch the first connection to the US in the morning.'

'That's—that's what you want, isn't it?' Meg felt on the edge of panic. They were fighting. But that didn't stop her from wanting him. That didn't stop her from feeling desolate because Sam didn't need her the way she needed him.

He took a step towards her and reached out to touch her arm. 'What can I say to make amends?'

'Don't bother,' she cried and she made a dismissive gesture with her hand.

His eyes narrowed. 'What if I want to bother? What if I don't want to leave here with things in a mess like this?'

She shook her head, trying to convince herself that she wanted Sam out of her life. It was the only sensible way to handle this. She'd broken her own wise rule. She'd fallen in love with a resort guest.

And now she was paying the price.

She knew from the experience of her friends that once a man left the island he wanted to forget any romantic entanglements.

Looking straight at him, she said, 'You're—you're very—attractive, Sam Kirby, and it will probably take me twenty light years to forget about—last night.' She pressed her lips together tightly and took another breath before adding softly, 'But I can't trust my feelings right now.' Her eyes met his and she didn't look away as she added, 'And you're not thinking straight either. I'm afraid if I listen to anything else you try to say now I'll end up in a terrible mess.'

A wave of self-disgust clenched Sam's stomach. How could he have been such an A-grade ass? He had always prided himself on his diplomacy and now he struggled to place exactly where everything had started going wrong. How had he made such a royal mess of things?

Meg wasn't a girl who made love lightly. Intuitively, he had known that. In a way it had been part of why he'd found her so alluring.

Grimacing, he shoved his hands deep in his pockets. He had a fair idea he knew what was at the bottom of her hurt feelings. 'Meg, we aren't the same as Tom and Dolly.'

A weird little sob came from her direction. 'How do you mean?'

'They had a whirlwind romance and jumped straight into a hasty marriage.'

'Don't be silly. I don't expect you to marry me.'

He looked at her carefully, trying to guess if he was missing any subtleties of meaning here. 'It was different for them,' he suggested gently. 'They were in the middle of a war. Tom knew that any day he might die.'

'Of course, Sam, you don't have to—'

'Listen!' he ordered, his tension breaking through. 'I'm not saying that what I feel for you isn't just as strong. But our circumstances are completely different. We've had even less time to get to know each other than they had. I guess I should have known better than to—'

'I understand!' Meg cried. 'You don't have to spell out the fact that we both made a hasty mistake.'

He sighed. The way things stood, he really had no choice but to leave tonight. 'I'd really like to hang around and sort this out. But my company's in the middle of all kinds of hassles back home. Not just this latest crisis. My father's ill, so I have to get back to cushion the blow of this news for him. I'm not in a position to even think about the long term.'

She said through her teeth, 'I don't need a list of your explanations. I'm sorry things are so bad for you. I don't want to make it worse. Please, just go.'

'It'll take me quite a while to stop thinking about you, too, Meg.'

She gave him a look that said loudly and clearly that she didn't believe him.

'As soon as I've sorted everything out I'll come back.'

'Don't try to make me feel better, Sam. And, please, don't make promises you can't keep.'

'I want to come back and get to know you properly, Meg. I'll write to you.' He struggled to find a way to lighten the moment. 'But I do getting-to-know-you best face to face.'

She bit her lip, but he was rewarded by the tiniest chink of a wayward smile. 'Of course you do,' she said. 'You're even better at mouth-to-mouth.' She held up her hands as if to ward him off. 'That's the trouble with you, Sam Kirby.'

'I'll be back for sure next year for that coral-spawning you were telling me about. I can't miss out on the world's biggest sexual encounter.' He crossed the room and leaned down quickly to steal one final taste of her warm lips.

He felt her mouth tremble beneath his and heard the sharp intake of her breath.

'I'll be seeing you, Nutmeg,' he whispered. He wasn't feeling very cheerful, but he managed to wink at her.

Meg watched Sam disappear into the night and felt an enormous wave of hopeless misery wash cruelly over her. Her face crumpled as the tears began again. She tried to tell herself she had no right to feel so let down. She was being foolish.

All along she had known that Sam had only wanted a holiday romance. It was why she'd tried so hard to resist him. But last night, she'd honestly felt he cared for her in a way that went way beyond casual sex. She'd been quite certain she wasn't just another notch on a playboy bachelor's bedpost.

Now she was just as sure she'd been wrong. Sam might think he cared for her. But he couldn't have let fly with that hurtful remark about the bottle if he felt the way she did. It was clear that he didn't feel the same helplessness, the same sense of spinning out of control, the same all-consuming need that was eating her up.

Once he got home to Seattle—to his business, his family and his girlfriends—he would be like all the rest. He would soon forget this brief holiday affair.

Shivering, she wandered into the kitchen, dragged the bag of seafood out of her fridge, and, with an angry cry, tossed it into the freezer compartment.

So much for the romantic dinner!

How could she ever have imagined her destiny was linked to that stupid bottle?

And what in the world was she going to do about her feelings for Sam?

CHAPTER SEVEN

'SAM, darling, how lovely to see you.' Amanda Kirby beamed at her son as he strode into the familiar kitchen of his parents' waterfront home on the outskirts of Seattle. 'I was just going to make your father a cup of coffee. I'll bring a cup for you, too. Go find him. He's out on the deck. It's lovely this morning in the sunshine.'

Sam kissed his mother's cheek. 'I'll hang around in here while you make the coffee. Then we can go out together.'

Amanda sent Sam several thoughtful glances over her shoulder as she filled the coffee maker, selected cups and saucers and placed them on a tray. 'Are you keeping well, son?'

'Sure,' he replied quickly. 'Hey, don't rush straight into mother mode. I've only been here a minute.'

'I'm sorry. But you must be used to my fussing by now. It's just that, ever since you came back from Australia, you seem...strained. And you're looking thinner I'm sure.'

'I'm fine.' Sam watched in silence as his mother poured cream into a delicate porcelain jug and selected coffee spoons. 'I do have a few things weighing on my mind,' he admitted at last.

'I know that, dear.' Amanda crossed the room to where he stood leaning against the pantry cupboard and gave him a hearty, motherly hug. 'Would one of these things on your mind be a pretty blonde Australian girl?'

He eyed his mother shrewdly and released a half-sigh,

half-laugh. 'I heard that some photos found their way back here, but I didn't think you read those sorts of magazines.'

'I don't, but my cleaning lady does. She showed them to me. You seemed—er—quite taken with the young lady.'

Sam grimaced. His mother didn't usually comment about his appearances in the press. She was used to it. 'They caught me at an unguarded moment.'

'Several unguarded moments.'

His head jerked up. 'How many photos have you seen?' Then, shoving his hands in his pockets, he added quickly, 'Don't answer that. I'd rather not know.'

'She looks like a lovely young woman.'

'It's nothing serious,' he muttered, determined not to discuss Meg with his mother. 'You know how the press get carried away.'

'It's high time you did get serious about a girl. I don't know how your lady friends put up with your casual attitude.' Amanda stepped a pace away from her son and eyed him shrewdly. 'Julia Davenport seemed to miss you while you were away.'

Sam scowled. But his mind raced ahead. If he didn't make a quick response to this not-so-subtle hint, his mother would launch full steam ahead with another of her matchmaking ploys. 'I'm taking Julia to the theatre next week,' he said hastily. He'd have to remember to get Ellen to arrange that.

Amanda brightened. 'That will be lovely. What are you going to see?'

'Er...Julia's making the selection.'

She looked even more pleased. 'Julia has excellent taste. She's very knowledgeable about the arts.'

'I hope she chooses a comedy. I could do with some

lightening up. Look,' he said with a sigh, 'there's something completely different and much more important I want to talk to you about.' He paused for a beat or two. 'I have some bad news for Dad.'

Amanda frowned. 'How bad?'

'Bad enough that I think I should tell you first and you can see whether you think he can take it.'

'Oh, heavens, Sam.'

'It's about the will. The will in the bottle.'

'I must say, I've been very curious about that.'

'It wasn't meant for us.'

'Why ever not?'

Sam looked away from his mother's anxious eyes. 'It was written for Tom Kirby's wife.'

'Judith? But she was your father's mother—*your* grandmother.'

'No. Mother,' he said quietly. 'Not Judith.'

Amanda's face paled. 'But that's ridiculous.' She raised a shaking hand to her mouth. 'You don't mean…?' Grabbing her son's arm, she shook him. 'What on earth are you saying?'

He told her about Tom and Dolly and his grandmother's cover-up.

For several long, shocked minutes, Amanda Kirby stood perfectly still in the middle of her beautiful designer kitchen. Sam could see by her increasingly stricken expression that the full implication of his news was slowly sinking in—his father's illegitimacy and the threat to the Kirby family's holdings.

After some time, he said, 'One piece of good news is that Dolly Kirby isn't interested in any part of the family business, although legally she could lay claim to everything.'

Amanda nodded, her dark brown eyes wide in her still pale face.

'She says she hasn't contributed anything to Kirby & Son and she doesn't expect anything in return...except the acknowledged legitimacy of her marriage by this family.'

'This family? By that, you mean all of us? Including your father?'

Sam nodded.

Amanda walked unsteadily back to the stove. After a long moment of silence she said, 'There's no way I could keep a secret like that to myself...and your father's been much better lately. I think he can take this news.' She turned and shot Sam a warning glance. 'But we'll have to find a careful way to put it to him.'

'OK. I'll follow your lead.' Sam took the laden tray from his mother. 'And there's one other thing I'd like to discuss with Dad as soon as possible. It's to do with the business.'

Amanda frowned. 'Can we take this one step at a time?'

Meg watched the doctor's expression, trying to read her thoughts. Eventually, she said, 'Yes, my dear, you're pregnant. There's no doubt about it.'

Meg closed her eyes as alarm mingled with excitement. So it was true!

It was a shock, but not exactly unexpected. Over the past month, she'd experienced all the well-known symptoms of pregnancy and the kit she'd bought from the chemist had produced a positive result. But hearing the doctor's confirmation made it so definite.

Pregnant!

A tiny new life growing inside her.

The female doctor studied Meg over her half-glasses. 'Is this good news?'

Meg opened her mouth to answer and then hesitated. Was it good news? She couldn't tell. Couldn't think. The only thought that stayed steady in her head was that, now, she would never be able to forget Sam.

'Meg? Are you all right, dear?'

Startled, she looked at the doctor and realised she was expected to say something. 'I'm sorry,' she murmured. 'What did you ask me? We definitely used protection. It must have failed. I don't know how it failed.'

'Unfortunately, these things still happen.' The doctor sighed and reached out to give Meg's hand a reassuring pat. 'But don't worry. You're a strong, healthy young woman. You'll breeze through this pregnancy and, at the end of it, there'll be a beautiful baby.'

Meg nodded and attempted to smile, but her lips and smile muscles wouldn't respond. This was supposed to be a special moment. She should be rushing home to her husband to share the good news. That was how she'd always imagined news of such an event would happen.

Her handsome husband would be thrilled. He'd tell her to take it easy...and then he'd place his hand lovingly on her stomach...and he'd offer to bring her a cup of tea in bed in the mornings...

Now, she realised that a picture like that was only a silly, girlish dream. This was reality. She looked at the doctor. 'I was hoping to be able to pick up my postgrad studies next term.'

'That still might be possible,' the doctor said thoughtfully, but she sounded doubtful.

Meg dropped her head into her hands. No Sam...no marine science...just a baby... She felt so tired, so overwhelmed.

'Meg?' The doctor's voice sounded sterner and louder. 'You do plan to go ahead with the pregnancy, don't you?'

'Oh, yes.' She dragged her thoughts back to the present, to this room with its sensible carpet and the smell of medicine and the doctor sitting at her desk looking ultra neat and sensible. And concerned. 'I wouldn't consider— No, I definitely want to have this baby.'

'Good. That's settled, then.'

Now that she'd said the words out loud—*I definitely want to have this baby*—Meg felt a whole heap better. 'When is my baby due?' she asked. *My baby.* How strange those two words sounded.

The doctor consulted her chart. 'Going by your dates, I'd say somewhere around the middle of February.'

'February,' Meg repeated. Summer. The island was usually at its hottest and wettest in February. It was right in the middle of the wet season. Not the best time of the year to have a baby.

'We'll get a clearer idea of how far along you are when we see the ultrasound pictures in a few weeks' time.'

Meg nodded.

Glancing at Meg's ringless left hand, the doctor added, 'Do you have a partner to support you?'

'No.' Her mind flashed to what Sam had said about whirlwind romances and hasty commitments. *I'm not in a position to even think about the long term.* When she saw the other woman's faint frown, she added, 'But I'm OK. I'm fine.'

'What about your family?'

Again Meg shook her head. 'I'm afraid there's just me.' She tried to flash a bright, confident smile, but she knew the doctor wasn't fooled. 'I'll manage quite well,' she said more boldly. 'My father died earlier this year, but he left me enough to manage for the time being.'

A sudden vision of her father swam into her imagination and Meg was engulfed by a wave of sadness. Dad wouldn't see this little baby—his grandchild.

Just as Sam won't see his son or daughter, another thought whispered. She pressed the heels of her hands against her eyes.

'I'm sorry,' the doctor said gently. 'It's tough doing this on your own.'

'I'm just missing—' a sob escaped '—missing Dad.'

'Of course. And you'll find you're inclined to be a little weepy for a while. You can put it down to hormones.' After a sympathetic pause, she went on to outline some of the more routine aspects of monitoring a pregnancy and she gave Meg a pamphlet about pregnancy support groups. Eventually the visit was over.

Back out on the street, Meg was crossing the car park to her Mini Moke when the upside of her situation suddenly hit her. A baby meant that she would be part of a family again. A twosome. Mother and child. She and her baby would be close—just as she'd been with her father. She'd have someone to love her again. Someone for her to love back.

The thought of a baby's soft chubby arms clasping her made her smile as she turned the key in the ignition. She allowed herself to dream a little.

Maybe the baby would be a boy. A little boy with short black hair and sky-blue eyes. She could picture his cute, cheeky grin. Like Sam's.

That thought brought another painful block of tears damming her throat. *No, she didn't miss Sam Kirby!*

She wouldn't be able to tell him about the baby. Not after the way they'd parted. What could he do besides give her money? She didn't want his money and she certainly didn't want him directing her life, from the other side of the Pacific.

As if thinking about Sam today wasn't misery enough, there was a parcel from him when she got home. With fumbling fingers, Meg opened it and, nestling in a velvet-lined silver box was a beautiful Ceylon-blue sapphire pendant on a silver chain.

He had written a note on the accompanying card in funny, square handwriting: 'As soon as I can, I want to see how your eyes catch its blue sparkle.'

'Oh, Sam,' Meg whispered and began to sob at once.

Even from such a distance he could reach the most vulnerable corners of her heart. With very little effort, Sam could show up her weakness. Whatever he did made her want him. She was having his baby! What on earth was she going to do?

Sinking onto a chair, she clutched the pendant and raised her hands to cover her face. She could feel the cool stone pressing into her hot cheek and a miserable shudder shook her body.

Meg didn't know how long she huddled there weeping, but after a time the flow slowed to a trickle and a persistent thought kept nudging her attention. She *should* let Sam know about the baby. Part of her desperately wanted to tell him. Not that she thought for one moment that he would be pleased with the news. It would just be another complication in his already complicated life.

But it was *his* baby. She could reassure him that she was fine and she could insist that she didn't need anything. But she would feel better if he knew.

Frowning thoughtfully, she dug her diary out of her handbag and found the page that listed the various time zones.

* * *

And just before seven the next morning, she nervously punched in the numbers Sam had left her.

Her hand shook and her throat felt parched as she held the receiver to her ear. It took a few minutes for her to be put through from the main Kirby & Son office to Sam's personal assistant. Of course, it would have been expecting too much to think he had given her the number of his direct line.

'Sam Kirby's office. How can I help you?' asked a pleasant female voice.

'Oh.' Meg swallowed back a sudden surge of panic. 'Could I speak to Mr Kirby, please?'

'I'm afraid he's busy at a meeting right now. Who's speaking?'

'Ah—my name's Meg Bennet. Sam—um—has my number.'

'Meg Bennet!' the other woman cried and Meg was stunned by the rush of warmth and excitement in her voice. 'Oh, Meg, I'm so sorry. Sam is going to be tied up in meetings all afternoon. Perhaps you should try him at home this evening. Just let me check his diary and I'll see what he's doing tonight.'

Meg heard the sound of pages rustling. Then she heard what definitely sounded like a sigh on the other end of the line.

'Oh, dear,' Sam's assistant said. 'He does have something pencilled in for this evening. But if you ring around six, you should be able to catch him before he goes out.'

A wave of nausea almost prevented Meg from answering. Sam hadn't given her his home number, but this woman assumed she would know it.

'Is there any other way I can help you?' came the friendly voice again.

'Could you—I don't have—I seem to have lost Sam's

home number.' Feeling more embarrassed than ever, Meg asked, 'Could you give it to me, please?'

'Of course, dear. You *must* have Sam's home number.'

Slightly puzzled by the surprising friendliness of the woman's tone, Meg copied down the digits. But after the call disconnected, she sank into another depressed huddle on her sofa.

All night, she'd lain awake thinking about making this call. She'd practised a dozen different ways to tell Sam her news. *I'm pregnant. I'm going to have a baby. Your baby. You're going to have a baby. We're going to have a baby. When's Father's Day in America?*

She'd been so pent up with nerves, she'd almost chickened out of ringing him at all! And now she had to wait for several more hours!

Perhaps she wasn't strong enough for this.

Being distracted by work all morning helped, so she was feeling more relaxed at the beginning of her lunch hour, when she hurried back to her cottage to make an attempt at calling him at home.

But her relaxation evaporated when a young woman answered.

'Sam's place.' She purred the words. 'Julia speaking.'

'I—I—Could I please speak to Sam?' Oh, Lord! She panicked. A girlfriend! *Do I have to tell him he's about to become a father, when there's another woman standing right beside him?* She almost slammed the receiver down.

'Who's speaking?' the woman asked and the question sounded as if it had been dipped in ice.

Meg pressed her forehead with a damp palm. 'Meg. Meg Bennet. From North Queensland. Australia.' Her heart was thumping so loudly she wondered if it was echoing down the airwaves.

There was a distinct pause. 'I'm afraid Sam's busy

right now. He's taking a shower.' Another pause. 'But, as you're calling long distance, would you like me to take the phone through to him?'

'No!' Meg cried, and she cringed as she realised it was more like a scream. 'No,' she repeated in a whisper. 'I'll—I'll try again some other time. Goodbye.'

She crashed the receiver down and slumped against the wall, a hand pressed against her pounding chest. Sam had a girlfriend, who could casually talk about walking in on him in the shower without turning a hair!

She closed her eyes and tried to block out the images that thought conjured. She knew he was a handsome bachelor millionaire. Of course a cavalcade of *intimate* girlfriends went with the territory.

Why hadn't she expected something like this? Sam might have told Meg she was special. He might have thought he meant it at the time. But hearing that silky, sophisticated voice reinforced for Meg something she had known all along: Men put island holiday romances completely out of their minds as soon as they reached home.

She felt more miserable and alone than ever. If Sam wanted to forget about her, she'd give him every chance. And she would have to do her best to forget about him, too.

There was really only one way...

Still fastening his cufflinks, Sam walked into his lounge to fix himself a quick drink before Julia Davenport arrived. He needed a stiff one before he faced the evening ahead. Julia was pleasant enough company but, since he'd come home from Australia, his interest in women had lost its punch.

Perhaps it had been the intoxicating effects of the tropical sea air but, whenever he looked at another woman these days, visions of Meg seemed to haunt him.

Picking up a decanter, he glimpsed a slight movement in his peripheral vision. He double checked. Julia was sitting on his sofa, dressed in something black and skimpy. One long leg was elegantly crossed over the other and a long slender arm was draped along the back of the sofa.

Now she uncurled herself slowly, like a lazy cat.

'Julia. I didn't realise you were already here.'

'I let myself in,' she said in a sultry croon as she glided across the room towards him.

'How?' he asked, puzzled.

She smiled from beneath lowered lashes. 'Your mother gave me a key while you were away. So I could water your house plants.'

Sam's jaw clenched. 'I have a maid who attends to the house plants. My mother knows that.' He poured himself a doubly stiff Scotch.

'Sam.' Julia pouted. 'Don't be angry with me. I thought it would be good if I was more—*available*.'

He ignored her innuendo. 'There was a phone ringing earlier. Did you take it?'

A dark scowl clouded her face, undoing the effects of her carefully applied make-up. She flicked her head and said airily, 'It was just a wrong number.'

Had he imagined that slight shiftiness in her eyes as she'd answered? Sam downed his drink in an angry gulp. If Julia thought he wanted her to be available, she was in for a disappointing night.

The following week, Ellen brought Sam's mail through to his office and, instead of quietly placing it at one end of his desk and leaving again without disturbing him, she stood, holding a small square parcel and tapping it with a fingernail.

'This looks familiar,' she intoned darkly.

Sam jerked his attention away from the figures he was analysing. 'What's that?'

'This parcel looks remarkably like something you asked me to post a couple of weeks ago and it has Australian stamps.' She handed it to him.

A pulse in Sam's neck began to beat as he jumped to his feet. 'Thanks, Ellen.'

He waited till she'd gone before he opened it. With a sickening sense of foreboding, he ripped the paper off the package. Inside was a polite little note from Meg and the sapphire pendant he'd sent her, carefully boxed and re-wrapped!

He sank into a chair as he read and reread her note. Short and to the point, it covered the basic courtesies and managed to politely refuse his gift without any proper explanation. It was as impersonal as a bank statement.

It was a savage slap in the face!

With an angry cry, Sam tossed the note and its lilac-coloured envelope onto his desk and charged across the room. He hurt like hell! And the pain wasn't merely the smarting of a bruised ego.

Damn it! He really liked Meg. He liked her a lot. Maybe more than a lot. If he wasn't so tied up with this business, he'd be back there now finding out exactly *how* he felt about her.

Checking his watch, he calculated the differences between the time zones in Seattle and eastern Australia, reached for the phone on his desk and dialled.

When Fred Raynor grumbled into the phone, Sam asked to be put through to Meg.

'She's not here.' Fred barked the words out.

'Is she on leave?'

'No, mate. Resigned. She left last week. Just handed in her notice and took off.'

Sam felt as if he'd been hurled from a plane without a parachute. 'Why?' he managed to croak.

'Can't help you, mate. I wouldn't have a flaming clue.'

'Do you know where she went?'

'Haven't the foggiest idea. She didn't leave a forwarding address. You can't trust staff to hang around these days! No sense of loyalty.'

After hanging up, Sam snatched up the packaging and checked the postmark. It had been posted from the island just over a week ago. He scoured everything she'd sent, looking for a return address, but there was none.

Surely Meg hadn't taken off without telling him? She couldn't be hiding from *him*? He was shocked by the sudden slam of panic that clutched at his chest and stomach. Her terse note had piqued his ego, but now he was worried. Really worried.

He dialled Dolly Kirby's number. As soon as the opening pleasantries were over, he demanded, 'What's happened to Meg?'

'Oh, Sam.' There was an awkward pause. 'Meg's all right.' But Dolly's voice was decidedly cautious.

'You're sure about that?'

'Absolutely.'

'Quite certain, Dolly?'

'Yes,' she replied with an impatient huff. 'She telephoned me only yesterday.'

He let out a huge sigh of relief. He'd been so worried that something had happened to her. 'Where is she?'

'I'm afraid I can't tell you that.'

Something like a strangled gasp emerged from Sam's throat. 'You mean she asked you not to tell me?'

'For the time being.' Dolly's voice held none of its usual warmth and Sam's chest tightened painfully. What in the blazes was going on?

Meg couldn't do this.

'Do you know why she's—avoiding me?'

'I just know she doesn't want you in her life.'

'Dolly!' Sam was embarrassed by the angry hurt that sounded so clearly in his voice, but he couldn't help shouting, 'This is ridiculous!'

'Sam, from what I hear you have plenty of girlfriends. Give Meg a break.'

'Girlfriends? I—I—That's in the past, Dolly.'

This comment was met by a threatening silence.

'Dolly? Don't you believe me?'

'I suspect there's more chance pigs will start flying,' Dolly responded dryly. 'Look, I'm sure Meg will contact you in her own good time.'

Knowing that was all he would get out of Dolly, Sam ended the conversation.

Dropping the receiver, he crossed his office floor and leaned his heated forehead against the cool plate-glass window. He stared at the tiny figures on the street below as they scurried about their business. What a mess!

He should never have left Australia without resolving the tensions between himself and Meg. It was obvious they'd got their wires crossed, but if he'd stayed another few days, he might have cleared the air.

It hit him like the proverbial brick, that he'd never met a woman like Meg. It wasn't just her loveliness, it was everything about her. The sound of her laughter. Her love for the sea and its creatures. He'd never known another woman whose interests so aligned with his—or what his would be if he were free to explore them.

Then there was that very special light in her eyes...her

natural elegance, the way she moved like a dancer...and her way of listening to him...and the way she made love...with such tenderness and passion...unrestrained sweetness and fire.

He wasn't quite sure what he wanted from her, but he was damned sure it was a hell of a lot more than a polite little rejection note. He'd give her a little while to calm down and then he'd try again. And as soon as he could settle his business matters, he would be searching for her. He wouldn't stop until he found her.

When Meg rang Dolly towards the middle of September, she was surprised to hear that Sam had tried several times to trace her.

'What did you tell him?'

'I—I tried to convince him that I didn't know where you were.'

'Did he believe you?'

'I'm not sure, but I didn't give anything away. I just told him you were heading south.'

'I bet that didn't satisfy him.'

Dolly laughed. 'It did not.' She mimicked Sam's angry response. *'South? How far south? There's an awful lot of Australia south of Townsville.'*

Meg clutched the phone to her chest. Talking about Sam always made her edgy. 'Do you think he's going to come looking for me?'

'I'm sure he will eventually, but at the moment he seems to be very caught up with his business.'

Meg bit back a retort. Of course he would be. Business and money. They were always number one with Sam.

Dolly's voice brightened. 'I told him you're keeping very well.'

'Dolly!' Meg cried. 'Why on earth did you say that? You'll make him suspect something.'

'No, dear. Men are thick about things like that. He just scoffed, ''Of course she's well. Meg's a healthy young woman. Why shouldn't she be well?'' And then I had to mumble something about flu.'

'I'm fighting fit,' Meg agreed. 'Just about over the early-morning blues.'

'That's wonderful, dear. Did you know Sam arranged for a team of nice men to paint my house for me? It looks beautiful now.'

'It's the least he could do, Dolly.'

'And the man he hired to do my garden every week is wonderful. As for that beautiful pearl brooch on my birthday... Meg, Sam's a wonderful young man.'

'I'm sure half the women in Seattle would agree with you, but he can stay wonderful on the other side of the Pacific.'

'You don't mean that, dear.'

Meg didn't want to end up in another argument with Dolly about the wisdom of her actions. Dolly's reasoning was based on the assumption that Sam was as in love and as committed as her Tom had been and Meg didn't have the heart to set her straight.

'I'll warn you now that I'm sure he will come looking for you just as soon as he's settled his business matters,' Dolly assured Meg.

Just how much time it would take to settle business matters surprised even Sam. It wasn't just a case of organising a satisfactory settlement with Dolly. Sam had other plans for the company. He wanted to sell it.

Getting his father's support had been the surprisingly easy part.

'Look what Kirby & Son has done to me,' the older man had sighed. 'Years and years of hard work and stress. My heart's so clapped out, I have to sit around like an invalid…taking things quietly…'

What took an infuriatingly long time was working his way through the minefield of negotiations involved in finding the right buyer. But the waiting and the patience were worth it. By Christmas, the last negotiations had taken place and by New Year a deal was finalised. The new owners were ecstatic and Sam's parents were happy.

And he felt like a man who'd been let out of jail.

Not a day had passed that he hadn't thought of Meg.

The day after the sale had gone through, he rang Dolly again.

There was a longish pause. 'I can't, Sam. I can't tell you where she is. I promised.'

'Not even a hint?'

'Why do you want to find her so badly?'

'You know why, Dolly. It's nearly eight months since I've seen her. And—damn it—I think I might be—in love with her.'

'You want to marry her?'

Sam gulped. 'I don't know—' He gulped again. 'Maybe.'

'Oh, dear,' the old lady whispered.

'Dolly.' Sam persisted. 'Think of Tom. I'm in the same situation Tom was. I travelled over to Australia and found this wonderful woman…'

'Yes. I know, dear.'

'So you're going to at least tell me which state she's in, aren't you?'

'Yes,' Dolly repeated more definitely. 'I think I shall.' She paused again while Sam's heart pounded. 'She's somewhere on the Sunshine Coast. In the beach house her father left her. But that's all I'm going to tell you. That's all I can say.'

'Dolly, you're an angel.'

But finding Meg was not going to be easy. The Sunshine Coast, Sam discovered when he arrived two days later, was a beautiful but heavily populated string of beaches north of Brisbane. There was Sunshine Beach, Coloundra, Noosa, Mooloolaba, Alexandra Headlands…an endless list.

He began his search in the telephone directory, working his way wearily through the Bennets. He hadn't realised it was such a common name. Finally, he decided that Meg must have an unlisted number.

Over the next few days, he walked the esplanades of a dozen beaches, scanning the crowds. And at least a dozen times he thought he saw her. Once in a car when he was crossing the road; he was almost run over when he stopped to stare at a woman with Meg's colouring. Another time he actually went up to a blonde woman in a coffee shop and tapped her on the shoulder but, when she turned around, she wasn't Meg.

He caught a glimpse of a woman at the far end of a shopping mall and was convinced she was Meg. But she was too far away and kept walking quickly with her back to him. With so many busy shoppers getting in his way, he continually bumped into people and kept having to stop to apologise. He couldn't catch a proper look at her.

And then, finally, she turned slightly and, silhouetted at the mall exit, he caught sight of a heavily pregnant stomach.

Another mistake. He knew then that it couldn't be Meg and he gave up the chase.

He tried ringing a few of the resorts in the area to see

if they employed a Meg Bennet but, as he expected, they didn't give out that kind of information.

Now, as he stopped for a snack at an outdoor cafe, he had to admit that his options were dwindling to nil. Defeat stared him in the face. He could consider a private detective. But if Meg didn't want to be found, what the hell was he doing searching for her? Maybe he should just give up. Get on with his life.

Most men in their early thirties would give an arm and a leg to be in his shoes—masses of money in the bank and no responsibilities. There was a whole world out there, and it was filled to overflowing with pretty women.

Why had he become fixated with just one?

One stubborn, mule-headed, obstinate woman, who didn't want him.

One beautiful, loving, passionate woman who, once upon a time, had wanted him with burning, breathless abandon.

He reached for his mobile phone. 'This is not a good afternoon, Dolly.'

'Sam, is that you? Have you found her?'

He released a rueful chuckle. 'You know you sent me on a wild-goose chase.'

'Oh, so you've had no luck?'

'Dolly, you've heard the cliché about needles and haystacks?'

'It's that bad?'

'Worse.' Sam rested an elbow on the table and propped his forehead with a clenched fist. He spoke slowly and firmly into the phone. 'I need her address. I'm worried about her. I *have* to find her.'

'Oh, Sam.' Dolly sighed. 'I think maybe you do. I hope I'm doing the right thing. Do you have a pen handy?'

She gave him an address.

And half an hour later he found Meg's house.

She wasn't home when he arrived, but he snooped in her letterbox and found mail addressed to her, so he knew at last he'd found her.

Hungry for details, Sam wandered around the yard of the small, rather shabby, beach cottage. Despite its lack of paint and the fact that the garden was no more than a stretch of grass and a few shady trees, it had a dilapidated charm.

At the back, a low porch looked out across the Maroochy River. Sam stepped onto it and a floorboard creaked beneath his weight. There were a couple of old cane chairs lined with faded patchwork cushions. A collection of potted herbs caught the afternoon sun in one corner, and from the edge of the roof dangled a mobile made from pieces of beach debris—driftwood, shells, fishing line and pieces of coral. It danced in the breeze and the shells tinkled softly.

An empty glass and a women's magazine had been left on the floor beside one of the chairs. There was a fishing rod propped in one corner. A faint aroma of bait clung to it. Beyond the porch, the wide river looked slow, like an old man enjoying the sun.

Sam lowered himself into one of the chairs and settled to wait, suddenly nervous. He was more than nervous, he was terrified. He'd been so focused on finding Meg that he hadn't planned the next step. And he needed to plan. He needed to get this absolutely right. So much was at stake.

One thing he knew. She wouldn't be welcoming him with wide open arms. A woman didn't go into hiding just for the sake of it. He hadn't a clue what her problem was. No one would give him answers.

He stared at the sleepy river and tried to think straight.

Negotiating a complicated business deal was child's play compared with handling Meg Bennet. Meg, with eyes that changed from grey to blue, or green, just as the sea did. Meg, with as many moods as the sea.

He stretched out his long legs and tried to relax. Surely it was just a simple misunderstanding. Once he saw her again, he would find a way to sort out their problem.

CHAPTER EIGHT

MEG was smiling as she left the hospital. The midwife had told her that her baby was growing really well—exactly the right size for her dates. The heartbeat was strong and Meg was fit as a fiddle. Everything was as it should be. She was on top of the world.

She'd been astounded at the way her thinking had changed in the past months. Pregnancy involved so much more than a drastic expansion of her waistline. Her baby had become the centre of her world. While people all around her carried on as usual, discussing politics, the nation's economy or global warming, Meg found her vision growing more and more inward.

For her, the only significant event of the year was the birth of her child.

As the baby grew, she loved it more fiercely every day. Once in a while she got depressed when she thought about the responsibilities that faced her alone in the future.

But at least she was over Sam.

Moving away from the island had been the best thing she'd ever done. She'd been able to start afresh on her own. Her baby was the love of her life these days and, after the midwife's glowing report today, she knew she had absolutely nothing to worry about.

When she turned into her street and saw a sleek blue sports car parked outside her house, she felt a stab of dismay. She had no idea who it could be, so when she turned onto the dirt car track at the side of the house, she edged her car forward very cautiously.

There was a figure, waiting on the back porch.

Her heart began to thump so loudly she feared for her health.

It couldn't be. It couldn't possibly be…

Sam!

White-knuckled, her hands gripped the steering wheel. She stared back at him through the rear window and her heart drummed a desperate tattoo. Sam was lounging against the timber railing. Dressed in faded jeans and an even more faded black T-shirt, he looked completely at home. And as sexy as ever. Oh, sweet heaven, what was she going to do?

He couldn't come back into her life now.

Not now.

Breathless and panicky, she tried to think straight. How on earth had he found her? Thoughts of backing down the drive and taking off flashed through her mind.

But he was already coming down the steps.

Her shaking fingers fumbled with the ignition key.

He crossed the grass towards her and stopped a few feet from the car. She could see his smile through the passenger window.

'Hi there.'

How could she stay? She didn't have the courage to face him when he discovered about the baby. In sheer panic, Meg wrenched the key forward and the engine flared to life. Stepping on the accelerator, she began to back down the drive.

She heard Sam's shout and the car stalled.

She knew she was being irrational. Struggling to think calmly, she told herself that trying to run was ridiculous. Anyway, there was no place she could go. He would follow her, or he would wait until she came back. She couldn't stay away forever.

And, as if he had known that she couldn't escape, Sam stood waiting, his expression an unreadable mask, while she inched the car forward again.

'Hello,' she called and her heart continued its painful thump, thump, thumping.

He ducked his head to look at her through the passenger window. 'Good to see you at long last.'

She nodded.

'How are you?' His voice quaked a little, showing her he was probably as nervous as she was. He looked paler than she remembered, but his eyes were the same mesmerising, slumberous blue. One look into them and she felt a familiar tug of longing.

'I—I'm fine,' she managed to reply. 'And you?'

'Just great.' His attempt at a grin fell short of the mark. 'Hey, are you going to get out of this car?'

No! she wanted to scream. Not till next Christmas. He still hadn't noticed she was the size of a whale. There was still a chance to escape.

In her dreams!

Reaching over, she picked up her purse and two grocery bags from the passenger seat, shoved her squeaky door open, and stood with her packages hiding her stomach. From her side of the car, she looked at him over its bonnet.

He looked back at her and the intensity of his gaze showed her that this wasn't just a casual, passing visit. 'Anything else you need out of the boot?' he said volunteering.

She shook her head.

Get moving, she silently ordered her feet and at last she began a slow journey around the front of her car, avoiding meeting his eyes. She didn't want to see his face when he first recognised her condition.

But when she reached Sam and he didn't speak for the longest time, she was forced to look up.

And she knew as soon as she did that, to the end of her days, she would never forget the expression on his face.

'Meg!'

His agonised cry cut straight to her heart.

'There's been a little change in my life,' she whispered with a self-conscious dip of her head.

Pale-faced, he stared at her pregnant stomach, shaking his head slowly and obviously unable to speak.

So many times she'd pictured a scene like this because, somehow, she'd known Sam would find her. She'd envisioned his anger, his surprise, even his elation. But her imagination had never pictured him looking so frighteningly shocked—as if she'd dropped from the clouds and crashed to the ground right in front of him.

In the face of such raw, unprotected emotion, her plans to be cool and distant vanished. 'Come inside,' she said gently, feeling close to tears. 'I'll make you a cuppa. Or maybe you need something stronger?'

With another dazed shake of his head, he followed her.

Inside, Meg kept herself from thinking and feeling by fussing about making tea and pouring a Scotch for Sam. She felt light-headed—as if this whole scene was some kind of hallucination. When she took a mug from the cupboard, she rubbed it against the palm of one hand, as if needing the reassurance of its everyday smooth coolness.

'How far—when?'

His voice coming from behind, startled her. She spun around. 'The baby's due in three weeks.'

She could see him trying to calculate dates and she offered him the Scotch, which he tossed down in one angry gulp.

'Does that mean—?' He set the empty glass on a nearby book shelf and, shoving both hands deep in his pockets, squared his jaw and nodded his head in the direction of her middle. 'Am I the—?' He swallowed and tried again. 'Is it mine?'

Now it was Meg's turn to be shocked. 'How could you ask such a thing? Of course it's yours—I mean, of course you're the father.'

'But I don't see how. I used protection.'

'I know we did. They don't always work, but that's not your fault. I knew a baby was the last thing you'd want.'

She turned quickly back to the business of making tea. 'Find a seat.' She tossed the instruction quickly over her shoulder. 'I'll join you in a minute.'

It was a sign of how shocked he was, she decided, that, like an obedient child, he returned to the back porch and sat staring out at the river.

A baby!

Sam dropped his head into his hands while his stomach heaved. His emotions were rioting. In all the months he'd been worrying about Meg, knowing that she'd taken off, he'd never thought of this little bombshell. A baby! *His child!* He was damned if he knew how the pregnancy had happened. He'd been careful!

But what about Meg? Here he was feeling sorry for himself, but what a time she must have had. And what a blow to the old ego that she wanted to keep this to herself. She hadn't been able to trust him to be there for her.

Lifting his head, he stared out at the river. It was so

peaceful and languid in contrast to the turmoil raging inside him. *How could she read him so wrong?*

He felt hot prickles behind his eyelids and swiped at his eyes with a hasty action he hoped she didn't see.

Meg's hands shook as she brought the mugs outside. For an uncomfortable stretch of time, they sat side by side staring at the river without speaking.

'Now I know why Dolly made such a big deal about how well you're keeping,' Sam said at last.

'Dolly's been wonderful,' Meg admitted. 'I wanted her to know because, in a way, she's the baby's great grandmother.'

'Oh, yeah,' Sam snapped bitterly. 'Tell the step-great-grandmother, but not the father. That's really neat thinking.'

Meg felt her cheeks flame. 'I tried to ring you as soon as I found out. But I got one of your snooty girlfriends on your line.'

Sam frowned as he thought for a moment. 'I think that must have been Julia.' He let out a long, bitter sigh. 'She wasn't a girlfriend.'

'Whatever,' Meg responded. Who was he trying to kid? 'But even if I hadn't spoken to her, I still knew it was in my best interests to forget about you, Sam.'

'Why?' he yelled. An angry flush reddened his face.

'Please,' she whispered. 'Let's not fight about this.'

He sighed again. 'Just give me a little moment or two to—to adjust. I'm sure I'll behave myself when I get a little more used to the idea.'

She wriggled in her seat to get more comfortable. Her baby's foot was kicking hard against her ribs. Suddenly, she felt cold as if a rogue breeze had crept across the river. She sipped at her rose-hip tea. There was no way to make this easy.

Sam wasn't going to just wish her well and saunter off into the sunset like a vagabond cowboy. This was going to be the awful part, when he started to get possessive.

As if on cue, he took a deep swig from the mug and then turned to her hastily. 'I'm quite willing to marry you.'

Her eyes widened with shock.

'Sorry if that was too blunt,' he muttered. 'It didn't come out quite the way I meant it.'

'I certainly don't expect you to marry me, Sam. In fact, it's the *last* thing I expect—or want.'

'Last thing, eh? That's what I thought.' He looked away again.

'I've never believed in people marrying just because there's a baby on the way.'

'I can always help with finances, of course.'

'Sam,' she said, and her voice cracked on the single syllable, 'you don't have to worry about me. I'm managing just fine. I mean that.'

'What about after the baby's born? How will you manage then?'

'I have some money. And I'll study. Eventually, I'll go back into marine science.'

'What about the baby?'

'What about it?'

'Are you keeping it?'

'Of course. And don't you even think of lining up those lawyers of yours for some kind of paternal rights contract.'

He frowned. 'So you're quite settled on bringing up a little kid all on your own?'

'Yes.' She wished her answer sounded more definite. She meant it to sound totally convincing.

His face grew tight. 'Or do you have some other guy lined up for the job? A new daddy for little...'

'Of course there's no one else.' Jumping up, she stomped across the porch to stand near the railing with her back to him, hiding her quivering chin. When her anger had dropped from boiling to simmering, she turned back to him. 'For Pete's sake, Sam. That's twice already you've suggested I might have another man hidden away somewhere. Another lover. That's your department. It's not my style at all.'

'I just want to understand your situation,' he muttered defensively.

Meg took a huge breath. 'OK. Here's the situation It's quite simple really.' She held up one hand and, with the other, she ticked off her fingers as she made each point. 'We had a brief relationship. We made love once. You went home again, back to being Seattle's favourite bachelor. Now I'm pregnant. And I'm dealing with it. This baby's mine.'

'And mine. And normally—'

'Please,' she hissed through gritted teeth, clutching the mug tightly against her. 'I agree that, as the father, you have some rights, but don't start talking about *normally*. We don't have a normal situation. We both agreed when you left the island that marriage isn't part of our game plan.'

He rose and closed the gap between them. Meg shut her eyes. Whenever he came close, some traitorous part of her brain began to think about being closer. And that was insane.

'I can see where you're coming from,' he said with a

heavy sigh. 'When I left last year, there was too much still up in the air.'

She turned to the river and opened her eyes to stare out across the stretch of water.

'And, now, I guess it's too late,' Sam added.

'Yes!' Meg almost spat out the word. Then, ridiculously, she shot him a suspicious glance. 'Too late for what?'

He stood beside her, looking, as she was, at the river. 'Too late to start at the beginning and get things right.'

She nodded.

'If we had gone about this by the usual route,' he suggested slowly, 'we would have got to know each other over time—then we might have married—and *then* had kids. Things might have worked out. Might have even been perfect.'

'Please don't go on,' Meg implored him. 'There's no point in going over how things might have been.'

He persisted, in spite of her protest. 'But you're right. We met for a few days. There was a spark—'

'A spark?' she echoed, sounding surprisingly hurt even to her own ears. 'Is that what happened?'

His eyes held hers and, for the first time that afternoon, she saw a glimmer of the old humour she'd learned to expect from Sam. 'Actually,' he said with a slow grin that sent uncalled for waves of longing rippling through her, 'it was more like spontaneous combustion, wasn't it?'

She refused to answer, but suspected that her flaming cheeks did the job for her.

'And, hey presto!' He gestured towards her bulging middle. 'We skipped a whole bunch of vital steps in between.'

Meg's chin lifted. 'I don't think that means we should

automatically try to fill in the gaps now. You can't do relationships dot-to-dot.'

'No.' He sighed.

She crossed her arms over her chest, hugging herself. 'And that is exactly why I gave up trying to contact you.'

'But you can't keep me out of this, Meg,' he said softly.

She refused to answer.

'I'm already a part of it.'

Her chin lifted defiantly.

He went on. 'This little kid is half mine. As much as you might be trying to overlook the fact, you can't ignore the genetics. Your baby will be wearing my genes.'

She flashed a heated glance in his direction. 'But that doesn't give you the right to intrude into my life. I need you to respect my privacy.'

'You've had eight months of privacy.'

'Sam...' her voice held a note of warning '...I've spent that time adjusting. And I've done well. I've got it all together now. Leave me alone. You—you've done the wrong thing tracking me down.'

It was his turn to be silent. He stood staring into the distance and he tapped at her driftwood mobile with one lean finger, setting it swaying so that the shells clinked against each other.

Meg watched, feeling wretched.

Finally, he turned her way. 'We've probably said enough for the moment. We're both upset and we need a little space to—adjust.'

She nodded.

He crossed to the top of the porch steps and Meg wondered why she didn't feel relieved that he was leaving so soon.

'You're staying somewhere on the coast?' she asked.

He nodded, but she noticed he didn't seem to want to give her any details. 'I guess you should get some rest, Meg, and drink plenty of milk, or whatever it is that's good for pregnant women. I'll be in touch.'

Grabbing the rail, he swung himself down the low steps in one bound and jogged back down the car tracks as if he couldn't get away from her fast enough.

Sam resisted the urge to ring Meg or visit her the next day. And the next. Instead he visited the local library and unearthed a stack of books. She wanted her space and, for his part, he had a lot to learn.

Aside from how they started, he knew nothing about babies. He'd never given any considered thought to anything remotely linked to babies. Had never touched one—not even tentatively on the toe. The whole concept of fatherhood wasn't one he'd ever applied to himself.

Now, late in the afternoon, he was grappling with a staggering information overload.

He phoned her.

'Meg speaking,' she answered, sounding relaxed...and beautiful.

'It's me,' Sam announced. 'How are you?'

'Fine thanks.'

Had he imagined it, or was there a tinge of warmth in her answer? 'Doing anything exciting?'

'Oh, yes. My life is a thrill a minute. At the moment I'm ironing a maternity smock.'

A sudden picture of a domesticated, rosy-cheeked Meg, pregnant and standing at an ironing board, danced into his mind. Why the image should seem incredibly sexy was beyond him. It must be what happened to a guy after long periods of abstinence.

He banged a hand against his forehead in an effort to

clean up his thoughts. 'I was wondering if you've developed any of those food cravings that pregnant women get?'

'Curried spaghetti,' she responded impulsively.

He chuckled. 'That's an original one. Do you make it from your own recipe?'

'I like the tinned version best.'

'Uh-huh.' He paused for a moment. 'Anything else?'

'Hot chocolate with marshmallows. Sam, why do you want to know?'

'Just curious. I can see you've developed quite a sophisticated palate.'

'Most of the time I eat a well-balanced diet.'

'Glad to hear it.' He muttered as he scribbled a few notes. 'OK. I can do that.'

'Do what? What are you talking about?'

'I'm bringing dinner. My shout. I'll be there around six-thirty.'

'But, Sam, there's no need.'

He didn't bother to argue, deciding it was safer just to hang up.

As she set the table with simple red and white striped table mats and crisply ironed white serviettes, Meg tried to tell herself that she wasn't at all pleased that Sam was visiting again and bringing dinner after staying away for two whole days. Two tension-packed days when she'd wondered what on earth he was doing.

She ought to be dampening her unsuitable enthusiasm by focusing on the last time Sam offered to fix a meal for her. The exotic seafood dinner that had never happened. That had been the worst night of her life.

She also had to apply her thoughts to how to get rid of him quickly. He hadn't given her time to explain that she had a childbirth education class to attend this evening.

There was a knock at her front door and she hurried to open it.

Sam smiled down at her as he entered her hallway, carrying a shopping bag. His big frame was silhouetted against the setting sun and he looked like heaven in blue jeans. Her breath caught and her silly heart trembled with delight.

She'd been too distraught the other day, to dwell on his good looks but, tonight, she couldn't help registering every ruggedly masculine detail.

He dropped a kiss on her cheek so quickly, she didn't have time to duck. 'I didn't tell you the other day how lovely you look,' he said. 'Motherhood really suits you, Nutmeg.'

The unexpected compliment and the old nickname caught her unprepared. She couldn't hold back a pleased smile.

In her kitchen, he unloaded a bag of groceries and set them out on the bench. 'I could only find little tins of curried spaghetti.'

Smiling self-consciously, she nodded. 'I doubt it's the most popular item on the supermarket shelves.'

Besides the spaghetti tins, he'd brought a huge packet of fluffy pink marshmallows, a bag of green salad, some cherry tomatoes, a bottle of dressing and a litre of milk.

He grinned at her. 'A simple but tasty menu. How do you like your curried spaghetti?'

'Heated on toast.'

'Might I suggest a side salad?'

'That would be lovely, Sam.' Meg lifted a hasty hand to her mouth as she listened to herself. *That would be lovely, Sam.* What kind of limp-willed Lizzie was she? It was happening again. He was slapping on the charm. She was letting down her guard. The next thing she knew they'd be...

She shook her head. Next thing, if she had her way, he would be heading back to Seattle. After many ambivalent months, when she'd been uncertain about her future, the recent weeks had brought a reassuring feeling of focus and balance.

She knew what she wanted now: a simple, quiet life for her and her baby. She certainly didn't want a playboy millionaire pulling her strings as if she was a mindless puppet.

'How's your business?' she asked and was surprised when he didn't answer for quite some moments. She didn't think the long pause was justified by the difficulty of opening a tin of spaghetti.

'The business is fine,' he said at last. 'I've left it in good hands.'

'Your parents?'

'They're well. At least Dad's as well as can be expected. Where do you keep your microwave cooking gear?'

She showed him and, while he attended to the spaghetti, Meg made toast.

'I've been reading about ultrasound,' Sam said casually. 'Have you had that?'

'Yes.'

'And?'

'It showed that the baby's fine. Everything is as it should be.'

'That's great.' He adjusted the timer on the microwave and straightened to look down at her searchingly. 'So did they tell you the baby's sex?'

She nodded.

'Will you tell me?'

Meg drew in a sharp breath, remembering how real the baby had become for her once she'd known its gender. That kind of insider knowledge would bring Sam another step closer. Telling him probably wasn't wise.

'I'm just asking out of idle curiosity,' he added, almost too offhandedly.

She gave in. Keeping the news to herself had been hard. 'It's a boy.' She nibbled her upper lip.

His blue eyes—the eyes she so hoped her baby had inherited—widened. Then his face broke into an incredulous smile. 'A boy? That's kind of amazing isn't it?'

'You have a preference for boys?'

'Me? Not especially. I love girls.'

'Of course you do,' Meg muttered under her breath.

'I'm sure girl babies are especially cute. It's just…now I know it's a boy. Heck, it just brings home that your bump—' he indicated to her stomach with a nod of his head '—is aging to be a real, living, breathing person.'

'It hits you all of a sudden,' she agreed.

He returned to slicing tomatoes, but then he shot another cheeky grin in her direction. 'Hey, he'll need someone to teach him how to pitch a baseball.'

Startled, Meg cried, 'Hang on, Sam, don't get carried away. To start with, you won't be here. Secondly, this baby's going to be an Australian. He won't be playing baseball. He'll be learning to surf and playing cricket. He'll be—'

He held up his hands to slow her down. 'My apologies. I get the picture.' He surveyed the kitchen. 'Anyway, before we get too het up about our kid's future, I think this simple banquet is ready.'

With some misgivings about the way this evening was heading, Meg handed him two plates and he dished up their spaghetti on toast as carefully as he might a gourmet meal. And, as they carried their plates and glasses of milk through to her little dining room, he added, 'Do you have a video of the ultrasound?'

She only just restrained a sigh. 'I do.'

They sat down to eat before he said, 'I'd really like to take a look at it later.'

'I may not have time this evening. I have—an appointment.' She began to give her food her serious attention. For a few moments they ate in silence.

'What's it like?' he asked suddenly. 'Being pregnant?'

She couldn't help smiling. 'Fantastic.'

Both his eyebrows rose. 'So you don't feel trapped, betrayed by your biology...any of those feminist urges?'

'I did at first.'

He frowned.

'For about five minutes.'

'I wish I'd known. I would have been here earlier.'

'The first few months weren't worth watching. I hung over a bucket for ages. But the rest has been fine.'

'Do you know much about looking after babies?'

Was this a trap? Some kind of test? Meg considered pretending she was a baby-care expert, but her natural honesty prevailed. 'Not a lot,' she admitted. 'But I've bought heaps of books.' Looking down at her plate, she added, 'I don't seem to be able to think much past the birth at the moment.'

His eyes grew serious as he looked at her. 'I can never get my head around that whole delivery bit. Scares me witless just to think about it.' Then he looked embarrassed. 'I guess that doesn't make you feel any better.'

'I'm sure I'll be OK,' she said with forced cheerfulness. 'After all, look how many women have babies every day.'

She realised that she was starting to let down her guard. Here she was chatting away to Sam as if he was—a close friend. Continued loneliness could have that effect—of grasping at straws.

He frowned. 'But you're planning on doing all this on you own?'

'Yes,' she admitted unwillingly. 'Of course, there's a midwife…'

Sam shoved his plate aside, rested his elbows on the table and propped his chin in his hands. 'Meg, I think you're being selfish about this.'

'Selfish?' she cried. *'Selfish?'* How dared he make such a claim! Did he have any idea how much she'd given up?

Obviously he didn't. He continued his lecture. 'Look at your situation.'

'I *am* looking at it from the inside—day in, day out.' Her voice rose several decibels. 'This baby and I have been superglued to each other for some time now.'

'Sure,' he agreed with infuriating calm. 'But how about you listen to another point of view? '

She opened her mouth to protest. And shut it. 'OK, Mr Wise Guy,' she retorted shakily. 'You explain to me exactly what I'm doing that's so wrong.'

'Well, you've come down here, isolating yourself from your friends and your support base.' He paused. 'That's right, isn't it? You don't have family. Do you have friends here on the coast who know you well and are willing to be there for you?'

'I'm doing fine.'

'But you're going it *alone,* Meg.'

'That's the way I like it.'

He shook his head. 'Hell, it's not what being a human being is about. You wouldn't be clinging so stubbornly to this independence thing if you really thought about what's best for the baby.'

'How dare you!' she cried. Her knife and fork clattered to her plate as she glared at him.

Not the slightest bit intimidated by her anger, Sam reached across the table and touched his knuckles to her cheek—a gentle, feather-soft caress. Her heart jumped crazily.

'I dare because I—' his throat seemed to stick on whatever he'd planned to say '—I think someone should keep an eye on you.'

'I keep telling you, I'm fine.'

He shook his head. 'You might be fine but, whether you like it or not, I'm going to stick around till the baby's born.'

The cheek of him! Meg spluttered, overcome by the nerve of this man handing down his edict. She'd been managing on her own for so long... 'You want to swan around here and then as soon as the hard work's done you'll come bouncing into the hospital ward handing out cigars and announcing, "He's mine"?'

She knew she sounded catty, but she couldn't help it.

He surprised her by answering quietly, 'That's not what I'm on about at all. If you want me to, I'll leave as soon as I know you and the baby are fine. But, in the meantime, count me in.'

He looked so determined, like a fiercely beautiful guardian angel, she could feel all her arguments snapping, as if the strings that held them together had been cut with a single slash of a knife.

'You mean it? Once the baby's born, you won't start making demands? You won't be wanting to turn him into Samuel Kirby II or something? '

'Of course I mean it.'

'You promise you'll leave once the baby's born?'

He stared straight back at her, his eyes unflinching. 'I'll go, if that's what you want.'

'You're not going to try to—resume our relationship?'

He looked away and she saw the muscles in his neck grow tense but, when his eyes returned to lock with hers, he said, 'If you're not interested, what's the point?'

She sucked in her breath. 'No point at all. So, you're prepared to—'

'I want to support you through these last few weeks. My hotel is only twenty minutes away from here. I can drive you to the hospital in the middle of the night. The things prospective fathers usually do.' He took a small notebook out of his back pocket and scribbled on a page, tore it out and handed it to her. 'That's my mobile number and my address. Any time you're worried about anything, call me.'

It was a seductive idea. Meg hadn't admitted it to anyone but, as her time grew nearer, her courage had encountered one or two stumbling blocks.

She sent him a challenge. 'If you really want to help, prove it.'

'I'd be happy to, but how?'

'Come to my childbirth education class with me this evening.'

For a second or two she thought she'd caught him out. His eyes widened. His Adam's apple moved up and down. 'Fathers go to those things, do they?'

'Sure.'

'And it's just a class? We'll just sit around and take instruction, won't we?'

'There's a little more to it than that,' she mumbled. In fact, she was rapidly questioning her sanity. Why on earth had she thrown out that invitation? It was a crazy idea. All the other couples were married or in committed relationships.

Frantically, she juggled words in her heard, trying to figure the best way to retract her challenge.

But it was too late. Sam was already smiling and saying, 'I'd be happy to come.'

CHAPTER NINE

FOLLOWING Meg's directions, Sam drove her to the class. He pulled up the hood of his convertible and drove extra carefully, aware of his precious cargo. Tense and silent, Meg sat beside him, looking adorable in a black stretch-knit tunic and tights. Her hair was arranged into a cute little knot of wheat-coloured curls on top of her head.

He kept wanting to look at her. He'd never noticed before how attractive a pregnant woman could be. Until three days ago, he'd found them about as sexy as rolled oats.

The classes were held in a low building at the back of the hospital and, as they stepped into the room, he was unprepared for the enthusiastic greetings of the other couples.

A pale redhead with a stomach as round as two watermelons and with a square-jawed husband in tow, rushed forward screeching, 'Meg!' She dropped her voice to a stage whisper, 'Is this *him*? Your baby's father?'

Meg nodded shyly.

'Way to go!' The woman laughed. She grabbed Sam's hand. 'It's great to see you here—um—'

'Sam,' he supplied.

'This is Carol,' Meg explained quickly. 'And Todd.'

'Hey, where're you from, Sam?'

'Seattle.'

Carol beamed at him as if he were some kind of superstar. She winked at Meg. 'I can see why you've been hiding him, honey.'

Others gathered close and Carol took on the job of introducing Sam as if he were a special discovery. Everyone's excitement for Meg now that her baby's father had shown up was downright embarrassing. Sam was relieved when someone announced that a girl called Sara had given birth to a baby girl that morning and attention was suddenly directed away from him.

Excited cries and a hundred questions filled the next few minutes, but the arrival of a middle-aged woman with iron-grey hair brought the discussion to a halt. The couples took their places on yoga-style mats on the floor.

'Is everybody ready to talk about second-stage labour tonight?' the woman asked with a hearty chuckle. 'When we get to that point, we know the job's almost done.'

She paused and her eyes rounded as she saw Sam. He'd been trying to look unobtrusive as he sat on the floor beside Meg with his elbows resting nonchalantly on his bent knees.

She beamed at Meg and gave a little approving nod of her head. 'We have a newcomer in our class?'

Shyly, Meg made another introduction.

'Great to have you on board, Sam. Are you going to attend Meg's confinement?'

'Attend?' He gulped. *Attend the birth? Hell, no.* 'I—I don't know. I'm just her back-up support. I get to drive the car and carry the bags.'

One of the fathers behind him chuckled. 'You were there at the start, mate. They'll make sure you're there at the end.'

The instructor smiled serenely. 'That's for Meg and Sam to decide.' She looked around the room. 'Before we discuss your baby's delivery, let's go over some of our relaxation breathing. Nice, deep, slow breaths, now, mothers. We're having minute long contractions. Fathers, you can breathe along with them. Cleansing breath, and...'

Sam found his eyes riveted on Meg as she breathed. She sat cross-legged on the floor, with her eyes closed, and he could feel her drawing inward, focusing on something only she could find.

After a few, deep slow breaths, her right hand came up and slowly, slowly, she began to massage her rounded tummy—in big, soft circles. He could see her body relaxing. Her shoulders began to slump and her jaw to sag a little more as each breath was released.

She looked beautiful.

To his amazement, she lifted the black top she was wearing and exposed her bare abdomen. All of a sudden, he felt as if he'd swallowed a block of wood—perhaps an entire tree stump. He could see the true shape of her. Her skin looked so soft and creamy—and a faint line had appeared exactly down her middle. Now, she was trailing her fingertips over her skin, massaging once more. His eyes followed her fingers and he imagined how she must feel—so soft and warm.

He remembered a time when her hands had caressed his body and a film of sweat broke out all over him.

'Fathers,' the teacher was saying, 'remember, you can help during the first stage of labour, by reminding your wife to relax like this—or by rubbing her back if she has backache.'

Sam hadn't touched Meg for so long, the thought of rubbing her back—any part of her—brought an uncalled for thrust of desire. He took a deep breath. Time to try some relaxing of his own.

'Just remember not to over-breathe so that you hyperventilate. OK, that's great. This last contraction is coming to an end.'

He watched as Meg's eyes opened slowly. She looked at him, blushed prettily and pulled her tunic top back over her stomach.

He leaned close. 'You were fantastic. The best breather in the whole class.'

Looking pleased but also self-conscious, she gave him a playful push.

'What we're going to talk about for the rest of tonight is usually the most exciting stage of labour,' their teacher went on. 'When you feel the urge to push, you know it won't be long before you see your baby. For the first delivery, pushing may take a few minutes or up to three hours.'

Three hours! Sam hoped his shock didn't show.

He listened, fascinated, as the instructor went on to describe the various positions a woman might like to consider when pushing out her baby—squatting, lying on her side, on her back. He tried to switch off his imagination when she began to talk about stretching, burning, stinging sensations but, for the most part, he found himself listening carefully. If he couldn't be there with Meg, at least he could understand what was going to happen.

'OK,' she said at last, sweeping aside some charts she'd used to illustrate the progress of a baby down the birth canal, 'that's enough theory for tonight. Let's do some practice. I want each couple to choose a birthing position.'

Meg turned to Sam. 'I'll try lying on my side,' she said.

He tried to answer, but his throat wouldn't make a sound, so he nodded.

She stretched out on the strip of foam rubber, obviously unaware of the way her graceful movements affected him. It took all Sam's self-control not to get right down beside her.

'I'm—er—I'm going to have to support your leg,' he whispered.

She nodded and smiled, her silvery grey eyes glinting with a touch of amusement.

Damn her! She was enjoying his discomfort.

He crawled on his knees till he was positioned at the appropriate angle and then he touched her thigh. A quick glance around the room showed him the other guys were grabbing hold of different parts of their women without turning a hair.

It was all right for them, he thought. They curled up with their baby's mothers every night. They were kissing them night, noon and morning.

But he hadn't touched Meg in eight months—and even then it had never become a habit. Sweat beaded his brow. This was the first time he'd touched her in all this time and he was having to hold her legs apart. And on top of that he was supposed to keep breathing!

Fate, he decided, had a strange sense of humour.

'Are all our little fathers in place?' the teacher called.

There was a smattering of replies. Sam muttered something rude beneath his breath.

'Right. We're getting the urge to push. Here it comes. Tilt your pelvis, mothers. Round your shoulders, put your chin on your chest—and—push! That's it. Push, again! Keep pushing—a little more. That's it. Have a rest.' She beamed at her class. 'Well done.'

Sam lowered Meg's leg.

She smiled up at him and he only just resisted the urge to lean down and kiss her teasing lips. 'How are you doing?' she asked.

He wiped a shaky hand over his damp brow and tried

to crack a grin. 'Piece of cake,' he told her. 'By the time your baby comes, we won't need a midwife.'

Half an hour later, he emerged from the class, feeling a little shell-shocked, but rather pleased with himself. 'I'm an educated man,' he said to Meg as he walked with her towards the car.

She smiled back at him. 'You had your mouth hanging open for most of the night—especially during the film. I almost leaned over and shut it for you.'

He sent her what he hoped was a smile. They had reached the car and they both stood beside her door. Sam, about to open it, paused. 'You shouldn't talk about mouths and touching in the same breath, Meg Bennet.'

In the glow of a street light, her eyes shimmered as she looked cautiously up at him. Her slightly parted lips looked rounded, soft and sweet.

He lowered his head.

'Sam,' Meg whispered, 'there are people around!'

Of course there were.

With his lips millimetres from hers, he paused, then lifted his head again. What was he thinking of? There were car doors opening and shutting all around them. A dozen pairs of curious eyes had swivelled in their direction. He contented himself with sliding his thumb softly across her lower lip. She was petal soft...and she didn't pull away.

'Is it pregnancy that makes you softer and lovelier than ever?' he asked.

He heard her surprised gasp. She looked as if she wanted to cry.

Hastily he dropped his hand and opened the passenger door for her. And, as he hurried around to the driver's side, he cursed himself for a fool. His brains had dropped below his belt. If there was any way he was going to work out where he and Meg were heading, it wasn't by trying to get her back into bed.

Meg spent the next twenty minutes giving herself a long, silent lecture while Sam drove through the quiet back streets towards her home. Heavens, she was a lustful beast. And a foolish one. Sam had only to drop one little compliment—one *tiny* compliment—and she was ready to hurl herself into his arms.

Hadn't she learned anything since last May? Listening to his appealing sweet-talk had got her into this mess in the first place.

If only she didn't feel so physically attracted to him. She had expected that being pregnant would provide her with a measure of protection from his sex appeal. But she'd only had to compare him with every other man she'd seen in the past few days to know that he was one in a million. And that he still had the power to make her want him.

She'd felt a curious pride in him tonight. A feeling, she realised now, that she wasn't in any way entitled to enjoy. Sam might be the baby's father, but he didn't belong to her. Nor she to him. They had made a mistake, but they'd both agreed that, once the baby was born, they had to get on with their separate lives.

They were a contemporary couple. They weren't victims of the old rules that insisted that a couple expecting a baby should marry.

She tried to picture their future.

Ten years from now, Sam would pop over from the States for their son's birthday. He would bring his charming American wife and their handsome, intelligent children. Meg would probably be married to someone else and she and her husband might have a child of their own.

They would be the kind of patchwork family that existed quite happily all over the place these days. The various adults and children would all be thoroughly nice to each other.

Everyone would marvel at how well they all got on.

A new millennium family.

It was only when the lights of the houses they passed began to grow fuzzy that Meg realised she was crying. Surreptitiously, she blotted her tears with her sleeve. Why did such a practical and sensible, *realistic* picture of the future make her feel so sad?

She stole a sneak look at Sam. Illuminated by passing street lights, his profile wrenched her heart. Every little detail seemed utterly perfect—the jut of his nose, the sensual swell of his lips, the dark line of his jaw. Having him around—seeing him again—that was her problem. She'd never had an ounce of will-power where he was concerned.

Once this baby was born and he was gone, she would be able to get on with her life once more. She held on to that thought.

He brought the car to a stop outside her house and jumped out quickly, coming around to open her door. When he helped her out, she formed her lips to say the words good night. But she made the mistake of looking up.

And the look in his eyes stilled the words.

Meg's heart raced. He was standing close to her, their gazes locked. Under her ribs, her baby sent out a ferocious kick.

'What was that?' Sam stepped back a little.

'The baby.'

'Wow! The little guy kicks *that* hard?' He lifted his hand. 'Would you—would it be all right if I felt him?'

How could she refuse? Taking his hand in hers, she

placed it high on her stomach, exactly on the spot where the baby's foot always lay. Sensing the pressure, the little foot kicked again.

'Way to go, kid!' he exclaimed. 'That's a powerful kick. It's incredible.'

Meg's breath felt trapped in her throat. It felt ridiculously right to have his warm, strong hand there, under hers, cradling their baby.

His face was so close. Any minute, any *second* now, he might try to kiss her again. And if he didn't, she realised with a shock, she might go ahead and kiss him anyhow. Oh, how she wanted one or two of his kisses—his long and slow, sexy kisses right now. She'd been on her own for so long.

'Nutmeg,' he growled.

Strangely, it was the huskiness, the unmistakable shudder of desire in his voice that brought her to her senses, as sharply as a reprimand. The fact that he was wanting her as much as she longed for him, reminded her that this was a very dangerous game she was playing—getting close to Sam for just a little while.

She mustn't make the same mistake as last time.

Stepping quickly to one side, she drew away from him. Desperately, she struggled to think of something to say that had nothing to do with mouths or kissing. 'Would you like to see the ultrasound pictures of the baby?' she blurted out.

He stood, looking a little puzzled, his breathing a touch ragged. Sticking his thumbs into the loops of his jeans, he dropped his head to one side as he studied her carefully. 'Why not?' he asked at last. 'As long as it comes with a cup of hot chocolate and some marshmallows.'

Meg fumbled in her bag for her door key. 'Hot chocolate and a baby video,' she said with a shaky little laugh.

'What an exciting life Seattle's favourite bachelor leads these days.'

Seattle's favourite bachelor.

As he followed Meg into her house, the words echoed in Sam's head. If only she knew the half of it. The press's image of him as a playboy bachelor had died a quick and painless death in the past six months. Journalists had hovered around him for a few weeks after his return from Australia. When they discovered that he spent all his days and a hefty chunk of his nights closeted in his office, they pestered him for an explanation, but he sent them packing with a few cutting comments and they soon gave up.

He wondered how Meg would react if he told her the truth about his lack of social life since he'd seen her last. She probably wouldn't believe it.

It *was* rather unbelievable, he reflected now. If anyone asked him to explain why he'd given up dating other women since he returned to Seattle, he would be hard pressed to find a plausible answer. But the old appetite just wasn't there any more. A pretty woman was just that—a pretty woman. She wasn't—

'Here's the video,' Meg said, thrusting a slim rectangular box into his hand. 'You set it up, while I make the hot chocolate.' She hurried away into the kitchen, calling over her shoulder, 'But don't start without me. I'll need to explain it to you.'

He had everything ready when Meg reappeared carrying steaming mugs topped with fluffy pink marshmallows. They were almost overflowing. She set them down carefully on the coffee table beside some marine biology textbooks and then she fished two spoons out of her pocket.

'For scooping up the yummy bits,' she explained. She

took a seat on the sofa beside him. 'Can I have the remote? I'll need to stop and start so I can explain.'

'Sure.'

Sam dragged his gaze from the enticing vision of her flushed cheeks, dancing eyes and golden curls to the fuzzy black-and-white screen. At first, the video made no sense to him at all.

Meg pointed. 'Look, that little row of things like tiny rectangles shows the baby's spine. These are his fingers. Aren't they cute?' She gave a little giggle.

Fascinated, Sam hunched forward with his elbows resting on his knees. This was his son. A miraculous fusion of his and Meg's bodies.

'And there's his heart,' Meg was saying, her voice vibrating with hushed, happy warmth. 'You can see it beating.'

He located the tiny pulsating blob. 'It's so strong,' he whispered.

'It's beating at a hundred and thirty-six beats to the minute,' Meg elaborated, totally unaware of how radiant and utterly delicious she looked. 'Apparently that's a great speed for babies.'

'What about fathers?'

Her eyes shot to link with his. Her mouth rounded and stayed open as if she was going to ask a question, but changed her mind. She dampened her lower lip with her tongue.

Sam groaned.

'What about fathers, Sam?' she repeated his question.

'This one's heart has been galloping at a rate of knots all evening.'

'Oh.'

The urges that raged within him were frightening. He needed to pull Meg against him, to crush those soft pink lips against his and to plunder her beautiful, blossoming body. For most of the evening, he'd been envisaging a whole range of preposterous fantasies. All of them impossible.

And Meg wasn't helping things any. She was leaning towards him, looking flushed and making soft, breathy little sounds. Her eyes were grey pools with silver sparkles, like sunlight glinting off water.

If he didn't know better, he could swear she was inching closer, willing him to kiss her. But kissing Meg would be more temptation than he could handle right at this point in time. Like toppling dominoes, one thing would lead to another to…total disaster.

Meg was trusting him to keep his distance. He had promised her…

And he didn't know anything about making love to a pregnant woman. He was scared witless that he might actually hurt her if he stayed a minute longer. He jumped to his feet. 'That video was great…great to see the little guy. He looks in wonderful shape. But I'd better head off now. Let you get your beauty sleep.'

'What about your chocolate?'

'Oh, yeah. Thanks.' Scooping up the mug, he downed the drink in a long, scalding draught. Bits of marshmallow stuck to his lips and, chewing them off, he headed for the door.

'Thanks for coming to the class,' she called after him as he backed down her front steps.

'My pleasure,' he called back before vaulting her front gate and jogging to his car. Seconds later, he was accelerating down her street. In his rear-vision mirror he could see Meg standing in the yellow pool of light on her front porch, holding her front door open with one hand as she peered after him. The other hand was raised as if she'd been thinking about waving to him.

She looked so all alone.

He flicked his gaze back to the road and told himself that *alone* was exactly how Meg Bennet wanted to be.

With flaming cheeks, Meg watched the twin red tail lights disappear around the street corner. What on earth had come over her? She'd been cosying up to Sam on the sofa and had been seriously thinking about seducing him.

She'd wanted to get closer to the tantalising scent of him. She had visions of tracing her tongue over the dark shadow of his jaw, teasing him into kissing her. She had even imagined undoing the buttons of his denim shirt and sliding her hand over the hard planes of his chest.

Thank goodness her whale-like figure had put him off. The way he'd made a beeline for her front door had hardly been flattering, but at least it had saved her from making a foolish mistake.

If they had begun to kiss, or to do any of the dozen other things her febrile brain had been considering, all of her other carefully framed plans would have been ruined. She could hardly have her lustful way with Sam again and then insist on keeping him at arm's length for the rest of her life.

After standing, staring into the night for a long time, she wandered back into the house. Her cooled cup of chocolate was sitting on the coffee table. The pink marshmallows had melted and had begun to dissolve. They no longer looked tempting. The video had run through and her blank television screen cast a fuzzy light into the room.

Damn Sam! Up until now, she'd been managing so well on her own. She'd pushed him right to the back of her mind over the past months and she had become completely absorbed with her baby. She hadn't needed anyone else. All her emotions had been taken up by her growing son.

Almost every magazine she picked up these days carried a story about single mothers—fiercely independent women, loving their lives, free of the need to divide their loyalty between their baby and a man.

And now, here was Sam, back in her life, looking divine, charming her senseless, making her want him and totally messing her up again.

Switching off the television, she gathered up the mugs and carried them through to the kitchen where she washed them and left them on the sink to drain. Then she drifted through the darkened house towards the room she'd prepared for the baby.

She was proud of the mural of brightly coloured sea creatures she'd created along one wall and she'd continued the theme with a sea horse and starfish mobile. The remaining walls were sand-coloured, the carpet a soft blue like the sea on a summer's day and the furnishings were the crisp white of foam-tipped waves.

Running her hand along the glossy white rail of the cot, she tried to picture her baby curled up asleep.

Thinking about her baby boy, rather than his father, Meg felt calmer again. Through the window, she could see the river, where the moonlight spread its luminescent glow across the silken black water. This was a nice little home for him to grow up in. They would be happy here.

She and her little boy would be close, just as she'd been with her father. She blocked out other memories of her childhood: when she'd longed to be part of a larger family—with two parents and some brothers or sisters.

Lifting her arms to her hair, she removed the elastic

band and pins and shook her curls free. She turned to walk down the passage to her bedroom. But she had only taken three steps, when she felt a cramp, low in her belly.

And the next minute her tights were all wet.

Sam pushed open the heavy glass doors of his hotel and made his way across the foyer. In the time he'd taken to drive from Meg's he hadn't cooled down any, so he could look forward to another sleepless night.

'Mr Kirby?' A woman at the reception desk beckoned to him. 'Someone's on the line asking for you. Been trying to call you for the past ten minutes.'

Sam nodded. 'I'll take the call in my room.'

Frowning, the woman raised a frayed fingernail to her lips and gave it a hurried chew. 'Actually, maybe you should take it here. She sounds kind of desperate.'

'She?' In two strides he was at the counter almost grabbing the receiver out of the woman's hand. 'Hello.'

'Sam?' Meg's voice sounded tiny.

'Meg, what is it?'

'You turned off your mobile.'

He grabbed the machine from his hip pocket. 'I turned it off at the class. But anyway, why have you rung?'

'My water's broken.'

A jolt of adrenaline rushed through him so fast he had to grab the desk for support. Slapping his hand over the mouthpiece, he whispered to the receptionist, 'Her waters have broken.'

The woman's eyes bulged. 'She's needs to get to a hospital straight away.'

'You need to get to a hospital straight away,' he told Meg.

'I know that, Sam.'

'Can you hold on till I get back to your place?'

'I—I guess so. Yes. I'm sure I can.'

'OK. I'm coming, sweetheart. Listen, the mobile's back on now. We can keep in contact while I'm on my way. Hang up and I'll ring you back.'

He almost threw the receiver at the receptionist and dashed back out through the hotel doors to the car park. Once he had his car heading back down the highway towards Meg's place, he phoned her. 'How you doing?'

'OK. I'm getting contractions.'

'Are they strong?'

'Fairly. About three minutes apart.'

'Three minutes!' Sweat broke out all over Sam. 'Maybe we should get an ambulance.'

'I'd rather wait for you.'

He accelerated. 'Are you remembering to relax?' he managed to ask. 'Are you doing your deep breathing?'

There was a silence at the other end.

'Meg?'

'No, I haven't been very relaxed,' she said and he thought she sounded weepy. 'I guess I panicked.'

'That's OK, honey,' he murmured, as he manoeuvred a sudden curve. 'You can do it, now. Do it just like you did at the class tonight. You're terrific at it.'

'Yes,' she whispered. 'Thanks. I forgot. Oh, there's another one coming.'

He heard a little gasp and then the sound of deep, slow breathing. 'That sounds real good, Nutmeg.' He pulled up at traffic lights, his stomach a bunch of knots. This baby was coming a few weeks early. He hoped like crazy everything was all right. Pounding his fist against the steering wheel, he cursed the red light. 'Change, damn you! I can't hang around all night.'

'Sam?' Meg's voice came through again.

'I'm right here. How are you?'

'A lot better. Thanks for reminding me to breathe. I forgot all about it, I was so scared.'

The lights changed and he took off once more, taking full advantage of his sports car's ability to duck and weave through the traffic, while cursing the fact that they drove on the wrong side of the road down under. 'That's what I'm here for,' he replied, trying to sound a whole heap calmer than he felt. 'Now, do you have your hospital bag packed and ready?'

'Yes.'

'Good girl.'

'Are you comfortable?'

'Hardly. I feel like I've got a coconut pressing down inside me.'

'That'll be the baby's head. That's good, Meg. It means everything is at it should be.' Where he'd got that information from, Sam wasn't sure, but it seemed to reassure Meg.

'Where are you, Sam? How long do you think you'll be?'

'I'm about ten minutes away.'

'OK. Oh—oh!'

The breathing started again and Sam took a deep breath in sympathy. He could feel his own gut squeezing tight. He hadn't prayed in a while, but he suddenly sent a silent plea for Meg and a quick request for strength for himself. No wonder Meg was frightened. He was absolutely terrified.

Again, he wondered if he should be dialing for an ambulance, but decided for the time being to take his cue from Meg. From what he'd read, first babies usually took their time coming. And besides, she wanted *him*! His heart swelled with an uplift of emotion.

Meg's voice came through again. 'Oh, boy, that was a stronger one.'

'You still OK?'

'Yes, but I can't wait to see you.'

Despite his anxiety, he smiled.

'Oh, no. There's another one already. Oh, Sa-a-am!'

The anguish in her cry sent panic surging like a tidal wave through Sam. He was hot and cold at once. 'Stay calm, darling. Just breathe. Come on, now—calming breaths. You can do it.'

Suddenly, he didn't care about safety. He slammed his foot down on the accelerator and charged towards Meg's place with his heart in his mouth. In the background, all he could hear were her desperate whimpers and sobs coming over the phone. She sounded so distressed, he wanted to kill someone.

It occurred to him in a blinding flash that, if anything happened to Meg now, he might do something really reckless. *He loved her!*

Tom had told Dolly she'd given his life shape and splendour. Now he understood what the old guy had meant. Without Meg, Sam knew his life would be empty and worthless.

After what seemed like an endless, frustrating maze of right and left turns, his tyres screeched as he roared to a halt outside her house. Luckily, she'd left the front door unlocked and Sam sprinted inside, shouting as he ran, 'Meg! Where are you?'

There was no answer.

CHAPTER TEN

'MEG!' Sam shouted, dashing and skidding through the house, checking rooms as he ran. Every nightmare, every fear he'd ever dealt with paled to nothing beside the overwhelming terror that seized him now.

Her bedroom was at the back of the house, but at last he found her. Curled on her side, she was in the middle of the bed, her golden hair in disarray and her face bleached white with fear. She was clutching at a bed sheet.

'Meg,' he whispered. 'What's happening?'

She couldn't answer. Suddenly her face screwed up in pain and her body stiffened.

'Hey, sweetheart,' he whispered. 'It's OK. I'll get you to the hospital. Try to relax. Breathe for me. You can do it.'

She shook her head and tears rolled down her cheeks.

Sam felt a painful sob rising in his throat. Somehow he held it back.

On one reckless night last May, he'd made passionate love to this beautiful woman and now she was in agony. All because of him.

At last the contraction seemed to be over.

'I think I'm in transition,' Meg whispered. 'I feel awful. Oh, Sam. I'm so scared.'

Transition! From what he'd read, that meant the baby would be arriving soon.

'Let me carry you to the car.'

'No!' she wailed. 'Don't move me. *Please!* I can't move.'

'I'm going to call an ambulance,' he told her.

This time she didn't object.

Snatching the phone out of his pocket, he began to punch in numbers, but he was hit by sudden confusion. 'What's the number for emergencies in Australia?'

'Triple zero,' Meg whispered urgently through gritted teeth.

Once again he punched the numbers.

'Oh, no! Oh, no! Sam, I think the baby's com-i-i-ing!'

Coming? It couldn't be! His heart slammed against his ribs. Babies weren't supposed to come this fast! 'Hold on, Meg!' he cried, shocked to the core by the signs of strain in her face.

'I ca-a-n't,' she cried back. 'I've got to push!'

'Hello,' said a voice in Sam's ear. 'Which department did you want, ambulance, fire or police?'

'Ambulance!' he shouted.

'Sa-a-am! Help me-e!'

Meg looked terrified.

'Ambulance service. How can I help you?'

Panic stricken, Sam yelled, 'We're at thirty-seven Casurina Drive. There's a baby coming! Get here fast!'

He threw down the phone and crouched close to Meg. She had rolled onto her back and her eyes were dilated with fear. He was frightened too. He had no idea how long it would take for the ambulance to arrive.

'It's coming, Sam.' She sobbed. 'We don't have time to go anywhere. I think I'm going to have it any minute now. I'm so scared! Don't leave me.'

'I'm not going anywhere, Nutmeg. I'm staying right here to help you. Are you comfortable like that?'

'I guess I need to—o-oh!'

Once more her face crumpled. He could see the strain in her neck as she began to bear down again.

'Don't fight it,' Sam murmured, hoping his advice was correct. 'Go with the pain. I guess you may as well push. You can do it.'

In a little while, she relaxed back against the pillows, looking flushed, but calmer.

'Let me get you more comfortable.' There was a glass of water on her night table. 'Would you like a sip of water?'

She nodded and he lifted her head to take a little drink.

When she began to grunt with another contraction, he sat beside her, supporting her back, helping her to lean into the urge to push, just as they'd practised a few hours before.

'You're fantastic, Meg!'

'How am I doing down the business end?' She nodded to her lower regions.

He moved down the bed, more than a little scared about what he would find. 'It's just great! It looks just like in the movie at the class.' He managed a crooked grin. 'Only better.'

Her mouth quirked into the tiniest of smiles and Sam stepped forward and kissed her cheek. Somewhere, amid the panic that rioted inside him, he managed to think that she'd never looked more beautiful.

'I didn't mean to have the baby at home,' she said with another sob. 'Oh!' She let forth a swear word Sam hadn't realised she used and, once again, she began to bear down. A loud, grunting groan burst from her lips.

'I can see the baby's head, Meg!' Sam called suddenly and he felt tears of panic, excitement and joy clogging his throat and welling in his eyes. 'He's got black hair.'

Meg smiled through her pain. After a moment's respite, she panted. 'Black—that's good!'

Sam shot a frantic glance through the bedroom window to the street outside. His heart raced as if he'd swum clear across the Pacific.

Slow down, baby!

Where's that ambulance? he wanted to scream but, for Meg's sake, he kept quiet, hiding his fright. What on earth would he do if the baby kept coming and he was here on his own? Facing a tiger shark on the bottom of the ocean would be a piece of cake compared to this.

But he didn't have any choice. The contractions were forcing Meg to push again and the baby's head was moving slowly forward. Sam gulped. 'You go, girl!' he whispered. 'He's looking great.'

'Oh—oh!' Meg cried. She dragged in another deep breath and began to push once more.

'His head is on the way out!' Sam told her. 'I can see his forehead. Here come his eyes...his nose!' His heart clattered in his chest as he stared at the tiny head. It was wrinkled and wet and dark. 'I'd say he's kinda cute-looking.'

Red-faced, Meg managed another quick smile before she began another push. She was looking tired and he raced to prop her back with more pillows. Then he darted to check on the baby's progress. The shoulders were emerging. The baby seemed to be turning slightly. He rubbed his hands nervously together, took a deep breath and grasped his son's tiny shoulders.

To his amazement, the little guy continued to progress forward without any assistance. Smart kid! All Sam needed to do was be there. Soon the rest of the shiny body was slipping away from Meg and into his hands.

Awestruck, he held his son, as his little arms and legs

flung wide. Through a throat choked with emotion, Sam managed to cry, 'He's here, Meg! You have your little boy.'

At the sound of her cry of triumph, a new fear clutched at Sam. What in heaven's name was he supposed to do now? The tiny body in his hands was slippery and wet. The kid looked incredibly like a startled frog. Meg had done her part. Was this where he was supposed to spank the poor little guy? In the movie, they did medical-type things like suctioning out the baby's nose and throat.

Sam felt a primal male urge to get the hell out of there.

Suddenly, the little arms flew wide open again and a lusty, 'Waa' erupted from the baby's mouth. His tiny face grew red as his cries gained volume. 'Thank God!' Sam breathed.

A relief such as he'd never known before, flooded through him. Relief! Elation! Overwhelming love. An urge to shout from rooftops! A dozen emotions shook him.

'My baby!' cried Meg. 'Let me see him.'

With intense concentration, he gently lifted the little fellow onto her stomach. 'Here you are, you clever girl.'

'Oh, Sam, he's beautiful.'

'He's perfect,' Sam agreed, blinking his eyes, but not really caring about tears any more. This little creature with a scrunched-up face was the most perfect kid in the whole world.

He sat beside Meg and helped to support her so she could see the little miracle she'd produced.

'He's a funny colour,' she whispered. 'But I think brand new babies look like that.'

'He's fine, honey. He's getting pinker by the minute.'

'Look at his little hands. His tiny fingers. Oh, his eyes are open.' Little black eyes blinked at them. 'Sam.' She sobbed. 'He's gorgeous.' Through her tears, Meg looked up at him. 'Thank you,' she whispered.

Now it was over, he was shaking. 'Hey, you did it all by yourself. You were fantastic.' He kissed her forehead and tenderly brushed damp curls from her face. 'You were so brave.' Clearing his throat, he added, 'Am I—are we supposed to do anything about the cord?'

'The ambulance should be here soon. They'll look after it,' Meg responded. Now that she had her baby, she didn't seem to be worried about anything else.

Their son began to cry again and Meg stroked his back gently. 'He feels so soft,' she whispered.

'Maybe we should keep him warm.'

'There's a baby blanket in my bag.' She pointed to a suitcase standing near the doorway.

'I'll get it and then I'll check again where the ambulance has got to.' Sam flipped open the locks on the case and sorted through the neatly folded items. He found a soft white blanket dotted with tiny blue sea horses. Smiling, he covered the baby and Meg.

There was a knock at the door.

'That'll be the ambulance.' He dropped another kiss on her warm cheek and stood up, calling loudly, 'We're in here!'

Meg smiled at him and she looked as if she would be smiling from now until Christmas.

Meg lay in her hospital bed and stared at the tiny form in the crib beside her. A tiny pink and perfect face topped by thick black hair peeped out of a neatly bundled bunny rug.

It's all over! her mind kept repeating. *I have a baby and he's fine! He's beautiful!* She had never known such exhilaration. Such a sense of achievement.

She had never known such love. She was bursting with goodwill towards the entire universe. Love for the baby. Love for Sam. Especially for Sam.

Where was he?

Once the ambulance had arrived, there had been so much action. And when they'd got to the hospital, people had kept buzzing continuously around her, doing things to her and the baby. There had been a constant flow of people checking one medical detail or another and Sam had disappeared into the background. Even when she'd been settled into this private room, which he'd insisted she must have, the nurses had sent him away so she could rest.

But she'd rested all night and now she wanted him. She needed him.

Sam had delivered her baby! The very thought filled her with awe. He'd been magnificent. Without him, she would have been a screaming, sobbing mess!

And afterwards! The three of them—Sam, herself and their little boy—it had been a moment of such closeness. An experience of bonding beyond her wildest dreams.

There was a telephone on her bedside table and, impulsively, she decided to dial his mobile.

'Sam Kirby.'

'Hi there, Daddy.'

'Meg! Are you OK?'

'Wonderful,' she whispered back. 'Where are you?'

'In the hospital foyer, wondering whether I should visit you so early.'

Meg found she was grinning. 'Get right up here at once,' she ordered.

'I'm on my way.'

She slipped the telephone receiver gently into its cradle and sank back onto the pillows, satisfied.

Within minutes, Sam's tall dark frame appeared in the doorway. He carried a huge bunch of roses.

'How did you know I love pink roses?' Meg asked, delighted. Everything seemed delightful on this wonderful day.

'Oh, I can be quite intuitive at times.' He smiled down at her. 'You look really well, Meg.' He reached down to lightly brush her cheek. 'I guess radiant would be the right word.'

'I'm on top of the world.' She sighed happily.

He settled on the side of the bed nearest the baby and peered into the crib. 'Doesn't he look different now he's all scrubbed up and wearing clothes?'

'I have to keep telling myself he's real. Isn't he the best looking baby you've ever seen?'

'My experience doesn't count for much. The only brand-new creatures I've met at close quarters have been puppies and guppies.' Sam studied his son and then grinned at Meg. 'But, yeah, he's a great looking guy.'

'He looks just like you.'

Sam shook his head and laughed.

After a moment of silence, while they both gazed at the sleeping baby, Meg reached out with one finger and touched the back of Sam's hand where it rested on the counterpane. 'I'm so grateful for the way you helped me.'

Rolling his hand over, he captured hers and squeezed. 'All part of the service, ma'am.'

His eyes held a soft glow that snaffled Meg's breath. She dropped her gaze and gently removed her hand from his grasp.

'What are you planning to call him?' Sam asked.

Meg took a deep breath. 'Tom.'

'Tom?' he repeated, sounding shaken. 'After my grandfather?'

'He would never have been born if it wasn't for your grandfather's letter in the bottle,' she said softly. 'I was thinking I'd like to call him Thomas Samuel.'

An emotion Meg couldn't identify tightened Sam's face. He got to his feet quickly and, staring down, shoved his hands in his pockets.

'You have any objection?' she asked cautiously.

'No.' He shook his head. 'No, they're fine names. They go well with—with your name—Bennet. Thomas Samuel Bennet. It sounds—solid.'

Meg's eyes misted. She didn't know where her ridiculous brain had been trailing but, somewhere in the past hours, between the baby's birth and this moment, she'd stopped thinking about a future without Sam.

She pressed four fingers to her lips. Soon, he would be heading back to Seattle.

'Can I hold him for a moment?' Sam asked.

'Sure,' she said and bit her lip as he bent over the cot and gently picked up his sleeping son. Tom looked so tiny in his father's big strong arms. You mustn't get weepy, she lectured herself. But the tears came anyway. She couldn't help it.

And Sam looked so cute standing there, holding the tiny bundle in his big hands and looking down into the baby's sleeping face. He stared intently, as if he were imprinting every detail to store up memories.

'Well, Tom,' he said softly, 'I dare say you won't always be as angelic as you look right at this moment, but I want you to be a good kid for your mom. Do you hear me, bud?' His glance stole swiftly in Meg's direction and, when he saw her tears, he frowned. 'Are you OK?'

Snatching up a tissue, she blotted her face and blew her nose. 'Just feeling a bit emotional.'

'You must still be tired. I should head off soon.'

'Will you come and visit us later?'

Sam's face darkened and, bending over the crib, he placed the baby down once more. 'I don't think so.'

'Oh?' Meg tried not to sound disappointed, but failed miserably.

He straightened and folding his arms over his chest, eyed her steadily. 'We have a deal, remember. You made me promise not to hang around once the little guy arrived safely.'

'But I—I didn't think you'd want to get away this quickly.'

His jaw jutted forward as he stood considering her words. He spoke to the opposite wall. 'Hanging around now isn't going to help anybody.' Slowly he swung his gaze to look her in the eye.

Meg's mind twisted and turned, trying to make sense of her sudden misery. Sam was right. She'd made him promise not to make a nuisance of himself once the baby was born. Yesterday, this arrangement had seemed the perfect solution. A wonderful idea. Of course, she hadn't expected Tom to arrive so soon.

What a difference a day could make.

She was tempted to blurt out that she'd changed her mind—that she wanted him to stay. Surely everything was different now? They'd been through so much together. But somewhere in the back of her head a little niggle of common sense warned against making a rash decision.

He sighed. 'If I'm going to head off, I'd prefer to do it sooner rather than later.'

It was hard to sort out her feelings right at this moment, but she knew she might regret saying or doing anything on an impulsive whim. Over the past eight months she'd planned exactly how she wanted her life to be. She'd be foolish to change her mind in just eight hours.

Her lips trembled as she whispered, 'Are you going straight back to Seattle?'

He didn't answer at first. He stood looking at her, his eyes searching her face as if trying to read the turmoil of thoughts she kept hidden. Finally, he said, 'I thought I'd like to spend some more time up north. Probably on Magnetic Island. I want to take a really good look at the reef.'

Somehow, Meg felt better knowing that Sam would still be in Australia. But not much better.

'Meg, you made me promise I would go after the birth. You still want me to go, don't you?'

No! No she didn't want him to go anywhere. She wanted Sam right here, looking at Tom with her, agreeing with her that he was the most wonderful baby in the universe.

He thrust his hands deep in his pockets and let out a ragged sigh. 'Don't make this hard for me.'

She suspected she was being selfish again. Feeling vulnerable and emotional wasn't a good reason to cling to Sam. In a few days she'd feel stronger.

'You should go, Sam,' she said softly.

He quickly looked away. 'OK,' he said, sounding efficient.

'I'll keep in touch.'

'Good. That'll be—great.'

'I'll write and tell you what Tommy's doing.'

'Thanks. Yeah, I'd like to keep track of him.' He was looking at the highly waxed hospital floor as if something down there was fascinating him.

'I can send you photos.'

His head jerked up. 'Photos? Yeah. Good idea. I forgot

to bring a camera.' And then, without another word, he held his hand up in a funny little saluting sort of gesture and headed for the door.

Not even a kiss goodbye!

'Sam!' she called.

In the doorway, he swung back.

She knew he would stay if she asked him to. Just lately, he'd given the impression that he would do anything she asked...

Right this minute she didn't know what she wanted. Perhaps it would help if she asked him what *he* really wanted?

She sat up straighter, the question poised on her lips. But he looked so ready for flight, her courage faded. 'Take care,' she called.

He gave a curt nod and, the next minute, he was gone.

CHAPTER ELEVEN

Sam swam to the far end of Florence Bay to where the jumble of smooth basalt boulders met the sand. The afternoon sun was already slipping towards the western hills, taking the heat out of the day as it went. In a lazy overarm crawl, he turned, planning to head back for one more lap across the bay, when a seagull took off from a nearby rock with a sudden noisy shriek.

Sensing that something or someone must have startled the bird, he blinked salt water from his eyes as he looked towards the shore. But the beach was empty.

It was a weird thought, but he could have sworn that someone had been there. Shrugging, he set off again, churning across the bay once more, just as he had every afternoon for the past six weeks.

These days, he was free to do exactly what he wanted whenever he wanted. It was the kind of freedom he'd craved when he'd been chained to a desk at Kirby & Son, but now he found his freedom had a bitter edge. It wasn't quite the blissful life he'd imagined. Of course, in time, he'd feel better.

When he'd stopped thinking about Meg and Tom.

After another lap, he could feel the familiar ache in his muscles that told him he'd pushed himself far enough for this session. He liked to stretch his body to the point of exhaustion. It made sleep come more easily. Turning for the shore, he let a small wave carry him into the shallows and then he stood and walked towards his towel.

A strand of seaweed clung to his chest and he flicked it off.

Out of the corner of his eye, he saw it land on a bottle sticking half in, half out of the sand.

The humid March air closed in and dark clouds along the horizon hinted at a hovering storm. Peeling his stinger suit down, Sam towelled himself dry then hauled on an old pair of track-suit bottoms.

The bottle, draped in seaweed, caught his eye once more as he bent over to recover his towel. For a ridiculous moment, he had a fanciful notion that there was something inside the bottle.

Like a piece of paper.

But that kind of coincidence didn't happen in real life. Without giving it another thought, he snatched up the towel and began to jog along the beach towards the car park.

One more time he looked back at the bottle, but the shadows were lengthening across the sand and all he could see now was a dark blob. With a shrug, he headed for his car.

Meg felt so much better now she'd finally come back and had booked into a holiday cottage at Magnetic Rendezvous. Her little house on the Sunshine Coast had been fine but, ever since Sam had decided to stay on in Australia, she'd felt a force drawing her inevitably to the north.

She tucked little Tom into his basket and covered him with a light cotton blanket. Considering the state of her nerves, she was amazed he'd fallen asleep so quickly and easily this evening.

Leaving a night light burning, she tiptoed out of the room and headed for the mirror in the bathroom to check her hair and make-up. She was pleased with what she saw. Apart from the fact that her breasts were fuller, there weren't any obvious signs that she'd recently had a baby. The white trousers and silky knit top she wore tonight were ones she'd been able to wear in pre-pregnancy days.

Leaning closer to her reflection, she touched up her lipstick and dabbed a little extra scent to her wrists.

In the tiny kitchen, a chicken casserole was simmering in the oven. A chilled bottle of white wine, a bowl of green salad and a cheese platter waited in the fridge. Everything was ready. She looked at her watch. If her plan had worked, she calculated that Sam should be knocking on her door any minute now.

Once again, she checked the table setting. The little bowl of brown and yellow bush orchids looked just right as a centre-piece. The lamps in the lounge were casting a welcoming glow across the small room.

Perhaps she should turn the oven down just a fraction, to prevent the chicken from getting too brown on top? Again she checked her watch.

She decided to turn the television on and to try to act as if she wasn't desperately waiting for him. She flipped through the channels. News...more news...sport...a games show. She couldn't pay attention to any of them this evening. All she could think about was Sam...and what she would say to him when he came...

Fifteen minutes later, she began to wonder if he had seen the bottle! She had placed it close to his towel and she was sure that he would find it there but, perhaps, by some quirk of fate, he'd walked straight past.

Now, she wished she'd stayed on the beach, but it had been threatening to rain and she'd been worried that Tom would get caught in a storm, or that Sam might have seen her. That would have spoiled the surprise and ruined her plan.

Another possibility seized her. Sam could have seen the bottle, read her message and disregarded it. That thought was unbearable.

Surely her beautiful plan wasn't about to fall flat on its face?

Meg's optimism faltered. If he still hadn't come after another five minutes, she would ring through to the helpful woman in reception—the new woman called Ellen, with the American accent.

In the shower, Sam flexed his shoulders and let the hot water stream over his back, releasing the tension in his muscles. It felt good.

Idly, he picked up the soap and began to lather his chest. He let his mind drift as he relaxed some more and, unexpectedly, the weirdest thought struck him. It came so suddenly that the soap slipped from his hand and slithered to the floor. His head shot up and he stared at the water pinging off the tiles.

He'd seen an image of that bottle in the sand again.

And it hit him, out of the blue, that the bottle hadn't been there when he'd first arrived at the beach. He had a perfectly clear picture of walking onto the beach and tossing his towel down on the sand. It had been a bare stretch of sand. A perfectly bare patch.

And yet when he'd come out of the water, there had been a bottle right next to his towel.

He tried for calm as he turned off the taps, but wild thoughts persisted.

When he'd been swimming, he'd sensed someone was there on the beach. He remembered the seagull's startled reaction. Now, he was sure someone *had* been there.

And that someone had left a bottle near his towel.

Trying to tone down his sense of agitation, he quickly dried himself and hauled on a T-shirt, jeans and trainers. In the kitchen drawer, he found a torch. Maybe he was going crazy, but it was suddenly incredibly important to get back to the bay straight away and find that bottle.

'I'm sorry,' the woman from reception told Meg. 'Mr. Kirby doesn't seem to be in. I've rung his unit several times, but there's no answer.'

'Thank you. Maybe I'll try again later.' Meg let the receiver drop.

What a prime idiot she was.

She'd been totally carried away by a romantic fantasy! Over the past six weeks, her feelings for Sam had become so powerful, so overflowing, that she hadn't been able to hold back any longer. She'd reached the point where she had to find a way to win him back.

When she came up with the wonderful, superbly romantic idea of sending Sam a message in a bottle, she'd been so pleased with herself.

Now, as she wandered listlessly into the kitchen and turned off the oven, she realised it was an impractical, pathetic idea. *A drippy, desperate, downright dumb idea.* Maternal hormones must have withered her brain.

Snatching up oven gloves, she lifted the casserole dish out of the oven and set it on a tiled mat to cool. Two huge, fat tears plopped onto its lid and sizzled.

She'd been so foolish. Like a dizzy balloon that had lost its air, she felt totally deflated and empty. All day she'd floated on excitement. Her energy had been fuelled by such high hopes. She'd flown up from Brisbane, had travelled across to the island on the ferry, had dashed around frantically preparing dinner, had raced down to the beach with the stupid bottle...

And now...

Disappointment was such an exhausting emotion!

She didn't feel like eating, or removing her make-up. Suddenly, all she wanted was to curl up in bed and howl herself to sleep.

'Ellen, has anyone been trying to contact me?' Sam panted as he dashed into reception, frantic with frustration. By the time he'd reached the bay, the tide had come in and had completely covered the sand. He hadn't been able to find the bottle anywhere.

And now he was desperate.

His receptionist looked up, surprised. 'There you are, Sam. Yes, a young woman has been very anxious about your whereabouts.'

'Young woman?' he repeated, seriously short of breath and not because he'd been running.

'Meg Bennet,' Ellen elaborated, her wide eyes speaking volumes. 'Didn't you know she's booked into unit sixteen?'

'Oh?' Sam responded, suddenly trying to sound casual, while shock waves jolted and ricocheted through him. *Meg was here on the island?* His heart pounded as he glanced at his watch and lifted one shoulder in an attempt at a careless shrug. 'I guess she'd be asleep by now. No doubt she'll contact me in the morning if she really wants me.'

He managed to make his way back out of reception at a normal walking pace, but once he hit the pathway leading to the bungalows, Sam sprinted.

Unit sixteen was in total darkness.

He stared at the black cabin and the curtained windows

and groaned. Meg was inside! She'd been trying to reach him. Knowing that, how could he wait all night? He walked up to the door and thought about knocking. She wouldn't appreciate it if he woke the baby. Heaving a heavy sigh, he turned away again.

But damn it. How could he give up? It was *Meg* inside. Seconds later, he knocked on the door, not worried if he woke the entire resort. 'Meg,' he called, 'are you there?'

From inside the cottage, he could hear little bumps and thuds as if someone was stumbling in the dark. Then footsteps. A light came on. He tried to calm his breathing as the door opened.

Dressed in an oversized button-through T-shirt, Meg peered out at him through red and swollen eyes, ringed with smudged make-up.

'Sam?' she whispered. 'Is it you?'

'Yes. I—er—believe you've been trying to contact me.'

'I have.' Her voice sounded squeaky with surprise.

'I thought maybe there was something wrong with the baby. Is he OK?'

'Yes, yes, he's fine. I—I wasn't expecting you to come now. It's late.' One hand darted to her dishevelled curls while the other clutched at her nightdress.

It occurred to Sam that any other girl would look terrible, but Meg still managed to look graceful and sexy.

'I'm sorry if I've woken you up.'

'No, you didn't.' She hesitated. 'Do you want to come in?'

'Sure.'

Meg looked a little confused but, after another slight hesitation, stepped back to allow him through the door.

'Crumbs,' she muttered half to herself, 'I must look a fright.' She turned and cast him an embarrassed smile over her shoulder. 'Can you give me a minute to wash my face?'

'Of course,' Sam agreed.

She disappeared and he was left to pace the room, feeling jittery and nervous, as if he was about to sit for an important test without any preparation. He didn't have a clue why Meg was here on the island. It was obvious she'd been crying but, if he let his brain try to come up with reasons, he feared he would go crazy.

She looked like a racoon with hay fever! Meg scrubbed furiously at her face. What a disaster! She'd so wanted to look nice for Sam. Everything was supposed to be perfect—the meal, the flowers, the clothes. She patted her skin dry and brushed her hair quickly. The black rings were gone from around her eyes, but she still looked pale and strained.

She sent her reflection a hopeful smile. It would have to do. Sam wouldn't appreciate being kept waiting.

In the lounge, he was looking grim and frowning. She'd been hoping for a relaxed and pleasant evening, not more worry and tension! Taking a seat, she gestured for him to sit down, too.

As he did so, her eyes honed in hungrily on all the things she loved about Sam—his dreamy blue eyes, the sheen of his hair in the lamp light, the shape of his hands—well, all of him really. He was looking tanned and very fit and his hair had grown longer. Living on the island suited him.

'I guess you're surprised to see me here,' she said shyly.

He nodded.

She felt awkward, not sure where to begin her explanation.

'How's Tom?' he asked.

'He's fine.'

'Has he grown much?'

'Heaps. Would you like to see him?'

'Ah—yeah. That'd be great.'

Jumping back out of her chair, she led him down the short passage to the bedroom. In the glow of the night light, little Tom lay snuggled on his side with a chubby pink hand curled close to his mouth. His head was covered by a downy cap of dark hair. A little bubble of milk rested on his lower lip and he pouted gently in his sleep. Meg smiled, enjoying the warm glow of motherly love that was so much a part of her life these days.

She looked up at Sam.

'He's so much fatter,' he murmured.

'He certainly has his priorities figured out,' Meg agreed. 'Food's the most important thing in his life at the moment.'

'That's the trick, bud,' he murmured. 'Don't let your life get too complicated.'

They exchanged self-conscious smiles and tiptoed back outside.

Once more they sat in separate chairs, facing each other a little awkwardly.

Glancing to the darkened kitchen, Meg said quickly, 'I cooked dinner, but it'll probably be cold now.'

'You cooked dinner? You were expecting me for dinner?'

She sighed. 'It was a really silly idea. I put a message in a bottle and left it on the beach near your towel. I guess you didn't notice it.'

'So there *was* a message in that bottle,' he said softly, almost to himself.

'As I said, it was a stupid idea. One of those things that seem brilliant when you first think of them...'

'By the time it occurred to me that there might be a message, I'm afraid the tide was in. I couldn't find the bottle.'

Meg rubbed one bare foot against the other. 'You went back tonight looking for it? Oh, boy! I've really botched things up.'

He leaned forward in his chair, linking his hands loosely between his knees and her heart turned over when he sent her one of his slow, lazy smiles. 'Maybe things aren't all that botched. I'm here now. Tell me now whatever you wanted to say.'

She gulped. 'I spent ages trying to write that note—getting the wording right. There are so many things I wanted to explain.'

Sam cocked his head to one side. 'I'm a good listener.'

It was probably now or never, but Meg wished her stomach wasn't jumping around like a grasshopper trapped in a jar. 'Well, I wanted to explain that maybe I was sorry I sent you away so quickly.'

He didn't say anything, just sat there watching her, waiting for her to finish her explanation.

Anxiously, Meg wetted her lips with her tongue. She felt sick with nerves and her hands clenched into tight fists. She wanted so badly for Sam to hold her. 'I should have given you a chance to tell me how *you* felt—about—everything,' she cried. 'I was so busy worrying about myself. But, Sam, what you did for Tommy and me—the night he was born. It—it was just so special.'

She was grateful that she managed to keep tears out of her voice, but he was staring at her with such fierce concentration Meg's courage almost faltered. Feeling flustered, she pushed herself out of her chair and began to pace the room. 'I've been thinking over what you said—about how we didn't get to know each other by the usual route. Everything happened so quickly and we didn't give ourselves the chance to understand each other. We need to fill in the gaps in our relationship.'

His eyebrows rose.

'And so I thought that while you're still hanging around on the island—' She paused for a minute and frowned at him. 'Why *are* you still here, Sam? Aren't you'd supposed to be back in Seattle by now?'

'We'll get to that later. Tell me more about your plans for our relationship.'

'So you're interested?'

'Mildly.'

'I see.' Meg's cheeks flamed and her throat felt very parched.

Sam rose too and stood looking at her with a disturbing glimmer in his eyes. 'Meg, I was teasing. I'm sorry. The truth is I'm exceedingly interested in anything you have to say about us.'

She swallowed.

'What did you have in mind?' he asked in a husky voice.

'I think it really would be an excellent idea if I tried to get to know my baby's father better.'

A smile spread slowly to reach his eyes. Meg's stomach grew even more jittery as he began to walk towards her. Just out of reach, he stopped and their eyes locked.

Her voice was a breathy whisper. 'You told me you do getting-to-know-you best face to face. That's why I came.'

Reaching out, he took her hand. 'And you told me I was even better at mouth-to-mouth.'

He drew her closer and, with one hand lifting her chin,

his face lowered towards hers. 'Just a taste test,' he whispered, as he lightly nibbled her lower lip.

'Taste as much as you like,' she whispered back.

'Don't worry, I plan to.' He took her hand in his and he rubbed his thumb slowly back and forth over her knuckles. 'But tell me a little more about why you're here.'

Meg swallowed again. 'This is how it's been with us, isn't it? We've been through some amazing times together.' She felt her cheeks warm. 'Making babies—delivering babies. We seem to be quite good at the big moments.'

'We're *great* at the big moments, Meg.'

'I got around to thinking maybe we could be good at the little things, too.'

'Like becoming friends?'

'Yes. We could keep it low-key if you like—just one step at a time.'

'Low-key,' he repeated, his voice rumbling with an unreadable emotion. His thumb stopped moving. He frowned as he looked down at her. 'Please don't tell me you want to go through all those rules again?'

'Rules?'

'You can't have forgotten. If we kiss the lips have to stay tight shut. No touching certain…'

'Actually, no.' Meg felt frumpy talking about such details in her old nightdress, but it couldn't be helped. Sam had seen her looking worse. 'If I'm honest, I don't want that kind of low-key at all.'

'That's a relief.'

She drew in a deep breath. 'The absolute truth is, I—' she took another breath '—I've had all these arguments going on in my head about why I should stay away from you. But they're losing out. My heart's winning hands down. I love you, Sam.'

'You're sure about that?' he whispered.

'I thought I was sure about it last year, but I *know* I've been sure about it for the past six weeks.' Her throat was so choked with tears she could hardly get the words out. An embarrassing sob broke through and, when she spoke again, the tears flowed. 'I've reached the point where I want you so badly I can't think about anything else.'

'Oh, sweetheart.'

His arms closed tightly around her and she sobbed against the soft ribbed cotton of his T-shirt. Beneath it she could feel the rock-hard strength of his shoulders and chest.

'So, now you know.' She squeaked the words out. 'I expressed it a lot better in the letter.'

'Nutmeg, you couldn't have said it any better,' he murmured against her cheek. 'There are no better words the world over.' His warm lips kissed her forehead, her tear-stained cheek and her damp eyelids.

With an embarrassed little smile, Meg raised her eyes to meet his. 'I sent you away, and now here I am throwing myself at you.'

'Keep at it,' Sam murmured. 'You're doing a great job.'

Feeling braver, she scattered greedy kisses over his stubble-roughened jaw. 'Before I throw myself too far, perhaps I should do a bit more about getting to know you.'

'What would you like to know?'

'How long do you plan to stay here on the island?'

'I'm going to be here for ages. You see—' he smiled down at her and with one finger brushed a wisp of hair from her cheek '—I've bought the place.'

'You've bought Magnetic Rendezvous?'

'Yeah.'

'You've got to be joking.' She shook her head in bewilderment. 'Why?'

'Two reasons.' He kissed the tip of her nose. 'You're one.' He kissed her chin. 'And Tom's the other.'

Meg's heart fluttered wildly in her chest. 'But, Sam, I thought you were a hotshot businessman. I don't know if this place is a viable proposition. Fred never seemed to make much money. Did you check it out properly?'

'I've run a complete survey. It will be a runaway success by the time I've finished with it. I've big plans for an eco-friendly resort—a marine studies centre. It's the kind of challenge I've always dreamed of taking on.'

'Wow! That sounds brilliant. But what about Kirby & Son?'

'We've sold it.'

'My goodness.' Meg was flabbergasted.

'I'll explain more later,' he murmured, gathering her close again. 'Right now, there are more important things to consider.'

'Did you want—?'

He spoke into her hair. 'I only want to think about us. You and me and Tom. Look at me, Meg.'

When she looked into his sexy blue gaze, his eyes were so filled with emotion, her legs threatened to give way.

'Right now, I want to concentrate on you.' With parted lips, he drew a sweet, slow caress over her mouth. 'I want to tell you over and over how much I love you.'

'Oh, Sam,' Meg whispered.

'It hit me the night Tom came along, that I've been in love with you for months and months. I think it probably happened when I first met you, but I was slow to catch on. It nearly killed me to drag myself away from you when you were in hospital.'

She frowned. 'But you did it—'

'I did it because I loved you and it was what *you* wanted. When I realised I could put your needs before mine, that's when I knew for sure I was a goner.' He rubbed his chin in her hair as he held her closer. 'But I mustn't lose you again. I need you in my life, Meg.' His eyes smiled into hers. 'Every day.'

Meg's heart swelled. She couldn't speak.

But it didn't matter. Sam's strong arms were lifting her, carrying her across the room and then settling her onto his lap as he lowered himself onto the sofa.

Unable to restrain herself any longer, her hands began to explore the beautiful strength of his shoulders as her body arched against him. She buried her lips against the dark warmth of his neck, relishing the familiar smell and taste of his skin.

'Will you marry me, Nutmeg?' Sam's words feathered her cheek.

Yes! she wanted to cry, but her throat was so filled with happiness, her voice made no sound. But it didn't matter. She nodded and lifted her face so Sam could read her answer in her shining eyes.

And everything else that needed to be said was accomplished mouth to mouth.

EPILOGUE

EVERYTHING was so quiet as Sam Kirby walked through the open-plan living area of his home, that he wondered where his family was. Then he smiled when he saw Meg sitting with Dolly, out on the deck. They were enjoying the late afternoon breeze as it drifted up to them from the bay below.

When he pushed aside the sliding glass doors and stepped outside to join them, he realised the breeze wasn't the only thing drifting from below. The sounds of excited, girlish voices reached him.

'Our shell seekers are returning,' Dolly commented as he stooped to kiss her papery cheek.

'Hi there.' Meg reached up and squeezed his hand and she sent him a happy, welcoming smile. As always, when he kissed her, his heart responded with a little leap of joy.

The girls' cries became clearer. 'Granny Dolly, look at the pretty shell I found!'

'I got one, too!'

Sam looked in the direction of the voices. All that could be seen at this stage were two straw sun hats atop the two little girls, as they clambered up the cliff path towards the house. He chuckled. Beneath those look-alike shady hats, were his six-year-old twin daughters, Bella and Claire—as different as chalk and cheese.

Bella would be the one in front, bursting with impatience to show off her find, her round face flushed beneath a tumble of glossy, dark curls. Claire would be following at a calmer pace, clutching her prize carefully, her thoughtful grey eyes peering from beneath a straight blonde fringe.

Taking a seat beside Meg, he draped an arm around her shoulders as they watched the girls reach the top of the cliff path and bound eagerly up the steps and onto the deck.

'Mine's a spotty shell.' Bella puffed, dropping a speckled cowrie into Dolly's lap.

'It's beautiful, darling.' Dolly beamed.

Dolly's sprightliness continued to amaze Sam. Although she was ninety now, she didn't seem any older than when he'd first met her ten years ago.

'And what have you found, Claire?' the old lady was asking.

The other little girl placed a perfect, pink and white volute into Dolly's outstretched hand. He might have predicted that Claire's shell would be less showy but just as beautiful as her sister's.

'This is lovely, too. It's so delicate. Aren't you both clever shell collectors?'

'They're for you,' Bella explained.

'Why, thank you so much. I'll find somewhere very special for them when I go home.' Dolly smiled at them both. 'I thought you might want to give these to Tom for his birthday.'

'He says shells are for girls,' Claire explained. 'He only collects sea-urchin skeletons.'

'Oh, I see.' Dolly sent Meg and Sam a knowing wink.

'He got a proper full wetsuit for his birthday, a weight belt and an underwater torch,' Bella elaborated. 'So he can go skin diving with Daddy.'

'Ten years' old! Tom really is growing up, isn't he?' Dolly sighed.

'That's what Mummy was saying this morning. She and Daddy were talking about when Tom was born,' Claire announced, and Meg and Sam exchanged smiles.

Bella, not to be beaten, added, 'But then Daddy started kissing Mummy—right in the middle of breakfast. Not just an ordinary kiss. A real long one.'

'Hey! Who's telling tales?' Sam laughed. He threaded his little finger into one of the wheat-coloured curls lying loose against Meg's neck. She turned and shot him a secret, sizzling smile. Luckily, his daughters didn't know the half of what he and their mother had been up to earlier this morning.

'They're not telling me anything I didn't already know,' remarked Dolly and her eyes misted.

Meg jumped to her feet. 'How about you girls go and look for your brother? It'll be time for his birthday tea soon. Just remind him we're having his favourites—lasagne and chocolate-layer cake.'

'I saw him down at the sea-horse tank,' Sam called after the girls as they eagerly headed off once more. To Meg, he commented, 'The staff have started calling Tom the apprentice, he spends so much time after school each day hanging about the research area.'

'He certainly loves the sea horses and he was so excited when they started breeding,' Meg agreed.

Dolly turned to them both. 'I meant what I said before. I'm so happy that you two have a very special marriage.' She smiled and her eyes glistened a little tearily. 'I know it might sound silly, but I've told my Tom about it and I know he's happy, too.'

'Oh, Dolly.' Meg stepped closer and took Dolly's hand in hers. 'We are just so grateful to your Tom. Sam and I would never have found each other without him. I'm sure he knew when he threw that bottle overboard that, whatever happened, it would bring happiness, somewhere, some time.'

'Yes, I think that, too, dear.'

Sam switched his gaze to the horizon—to the Coral Sea—where Tom had sailed and had not come back. It always choked him up to think that his grandfather had missed out on a happily married life, when his own was so full and satisfactory in every way. Even his job was fulfilling. Now he had the fun of making good money while doing something he really loved.

Dolly's voice broke into his thoughts. 'I just feel so blessed that I've been able to enjoy your little ones.'

'And you'll be able to enjoy them for another ten years. You'll be here for your hundredth birthday, Dolly,' Sam assured her. He jumped to his feet. 'Now, I'm going to break open a bottle of champagne. You ladies will join me in a celebration, won't you?'

'Of course!' they chorused.

Minutes later, he'd popped the cork and was filling their glasses.

Meg helped Dolly to her feet and the three of them stood together and looked out to sea.

Then Sam raised his glass. 'To Tom Kirby senior,' he said. 'Dolly's husband and my grandfather—and a brilliant letter writer.'

They clinked glasses and drank.

Smiling down into Meg's eyes, he kissed her and she tasted of champagne and laughter and love. Then he added, 'And to Tom Kirby junior, our son and great-grandson.'

Just then there was a clatter of feet on the stairs and Tom, his black hair windswept and his blue eyes sparkling, raced ahead of his sisters. 'Are we really having lasagne and chocolate-layer cake?' he shouted breathlessly.

The adults laughed. And Sam reached over and wrapped an arm around his son's shoulders. Once more he raised his glass. 'As I was saying, to Tom junior—a kid who, right from when he was born, has always had a great sense of timing.'

Once more they laughed, clinked their glasses, toasted and drank their champagne.

Meg's and Sam's eyes met.

'Oh, oh,' he heard Bella warn Claire. 'They look like they're thinking about kissing again.'

His daughter was a mind-reader.

Cathy Williams is originally from Trinidad but has lived in England for a number of years. She currently has a house in Warwickshire which she shares with her husband Richard, her three daughters Charlotte, Olivia and Emma and their pet cat, Salem. She adores writing romantic fiction and would love one of her girls to become a writer although at the moment she is happy enough if they do their homework and agree not to bicker with one another.

**Don't miss Cathy Williams's latest seductive story: AT THE ITALIAN'S COMMAND
On sale in November 2005,
in Modern Romance™!**

THE BABY SCANDAL

by

Cathy Williams

CHAPTER ONE

RUTH heard the sound of footsteps striding up the staircase towards the offices and froze with a bundle of files in one hand. The wooden flooring, which was the final word in glamour, unfortunately had an annoying tendency to carry sound, and now, with the place completely deserted except for her, the amplified noise travelled with nerve-shattering precision straight to her wildly beating heart.

This was London.

She had laughed off all her parents' anxious concerns about the need to be careful in *The Big Bad City*, but now every word came flooding back to her with nightmarish clarity.

Muggers. Perverts. *Rapists.*

She cleared her throat and wondered whether she should gather up some courage and confront whoever had sneaked into the empty two-storey Victorian house, which had been tastefully converted one year ago to accommodate a staff of fifteen.

Courage, however, was not her forte, so she timidly stood her ground and prayed that the bloodthirsty, drug-driven maniac would see that there was nothing to steal and leave the way he had come.

The footsteps, which seemed to know precisely where they wanted to go, materialised into a dark shadow visible behind the closed glass door of the office. The corridor light had been switched off and, although it was summer, autumn was just around the corner, and at a little after seven-thirty night was already drawing in.

Now, she thought frantically, would be a very appropriate time to faint.

She didn't. Just the opposite. The soles of her feet appeared to have become glued to the floor, so that not only could she not collapse into a convenient heap to the ground, she couldn't even move.

The shadow pushed open the glass door and strode in with the typical aggressive confidence of someone with foul intent on his mind.

Some of her paralysed facial muscles came to life and she stuck her chin out bravely and said, in a high-pitched voice, 'May I help you?'

The man approaching her, now that she could see him clearly in the fluorescent light, was tall and powerfully built. He had his jacket slung over one shoulder and his free hand was rammed into the pocket of his trousers.

He didn't *look* like a crazed junkie, she thought desperately. On the other hand, he didn't look like a hapless tourist who had wandered accidentally into the wrong building, thinking it was a shop, perched as it was in one of the most exclusive shopping areas in London, between an expensive hat shop and an even more over-priced jeweller's.

In fact, there was nothing remotely hapless-looking about this man at all. His short hair was black, the eyes staring at her were piercingly blue and every angle of his face and body suggested a sort of hard aggression that she found overwhelming.

'Where is everyone?' he demanded, affording her a

brief glance and then proceeding to stroll around the office with proprietorial insolence.

Ruth followed his movements helplessly with her eyes.

'Perhaps you could tell me who you are?'

'Perhaps you could tell me who *you* are?' he said, pausing in his inspection of the assortment of desks and computer terminals to glance over his shoulder.

'I work here,' she answered, gathering up her failing courage and deciding that, since this man obviously didn't, then she had every right to be as curt with him as she wanted.

Unfortunately curt, like courage, was not in her repertoire. She was gentle to the point of blushingly gauche, and that was one of the reasons why she had moved to London. So that some of its brash self-confidence might somehow rub off on her by a mysterious process of osmosis.

'Name?'

'R-Ruth Jacobs,' Ruth stammered, forgetting that he had no business asking her anything at all, since he was a trespasser on the premises.

'Mmm. Doesn't ring any bells.' He had stopped inspecting the office now and was inspecting her instead, perched on the edge of one of the desks. 'You're not one of my editors. I have a list of them and your name isn't on it.'

Ruth was no longer terrified now. She was downright confused, and it showed in the transparent play of emotions on her smooth, pale face.

'Who *are* you?' she finally asked, lowering her eyes, because something about his blatant masculinity was a little too overpowering for her liking. 'I don't believe I caught your name.'

'Probably because I didn't give it,' he answered drily. 'Ruth Jacobs, Ruth Jacobs...' He tilted his head to one side and proceeded to stare at her with leisurely thoroughness. 'Yes, you could do...very well indeed...'

'Look...I'm in the process of locking up for the day...perhaps you could make an appointment to see Miss Hawes in the morning...?' It finally occurred to her that she must look very odd in this immobile position, with her hand semi-raised and holding a stack of files in a death-like grip. She unglued her feet from the ten-inch square they had occupied since the man entered the room, and darted across to Alison's desk for her appointment book.

'What's your job here?'

Ruth stopped what she was doing and took a deep breath. 'I refuse to answer any more questions until you tell me who you are,' she said in a bold rush. She could feel the colour redden her cheeks and, not for the first time, cursed her inability to dredge up even the remotest appearance of *savoir faire*. At the age of twenty-two, she should surely have left behind all this ridiculous blushing.

'I'm Franco Leoni.' He allowed a few seconds for his name to be absorbed, and when she continued to stare at him in bewilderment, he added, with a hint of impatience, 'I *own* this place, Miss Jacobs.'

''Oh,' Ruth said dubiously.

'Doesn't Alison tell you *anything*? Bloody awful man-management. How long have you been here? Are you a temp? Why the hell is she allowing a temp the responsibility of locking up? This is damned ridiculous.'

The rising irritation in his voice snapped her out of her zombie-like incomprehension.

'I'm not a temp, Mr Leoni,' she said shortly. 'I've been here virtually since it was taken over, eleven months ago.'

'Then you should know who I am. Where's Alison?'

'She left about an hour ago,' Ruth admitted reluctantly. She was frantically trying to recognise his name, and failing. She knew that the magazine, which had been a small, money-losing venture, had been taken over by some conglomerate or other, but the precise names of the people involved eluded her.

'Left for where? Get her on the line for me.'

'It's Friday, Mr Leoni. Miss Hawes won't be at home. I believe she was going out with...with...with her mother to the theatre.'

The small white lie was enough to bring another telling wash of colour to her face, and she stared resolutely at the bank of windows behind him. By nature she was scrupulously honest, but the convoluted workings of her brain had jumped ahead to some obscure idea that this man, whether he owned the place or not, might not be too impressed if he knew that her boss was on a dinner date with another man.

Alison, tall, vivacious, red-haired and thoroughly irreverent, was the sort of woman who spent her life rotating men and enjoying every minute of it. The last thing Ruth felt equipped to handle at seven-thirty on a Friday evening was a rotated boyfriend. And this man looked just the sort to appeal to her boss. Tall, striking, oozing sexuality. The sort of man who would appeal to most women, she conceded grudgingly, if you liked that sort of obvious look.

And if you were the type who didn't view basic good manners as an essential part of someone's personality.

'Then I suppose you'll just have to believe me when I tell you that I'm her boss, won't you?' He smiled slowly, watching her face as though amused by everything he could read there. 'And, believe it or not, I'm very glad that I bumped into you.' A speculative look had entered his eyes which she didn't much care for.

'I really need to be getting home...'

'Parents might be worried?'

'I don't live with my parents, *actually*,' Ruth informed him coldly. After nearly a year and a quarter, the novelty of having her own place, small and nondescript though it might be, was still a source of pleasure for her. She had been the last of her friends to fly the family nest and she had only done so because part of herself knew that she needed to.

She adored her parents, and loved the vicarage where she had lived since she was a child, but some obscure part of her had realised over the years that she had to spread her wings and sample what else the big world had to offer, or else buckle down to the realisation that her life would remain neatly parcelled up in the small village where she had grown up, surrounded by her cosy circle of friends all of whose ambitions had been to get married and have big families and never mind what else there was out there.

'No?' He didn't sound as though he believed that, and she glared at him.

'No. I'm twenty-two years old and I live in a flat in Hampstead. Now, do you want to make an appointment to see Miss Hawes in the morning or not?'

'You keep forgetting that I own this company. I'll see her in the morning, all right, but there's no need for me to make an appointment.'

Arrogant. That had been the word she'd been searching for to describe this man. She folded her arms and stared at him.

'Fine. Now perhaps you could see yourself to the door...?'

'Have you eaten?'

'What?'

'I said...'

'I heard what you said, Mr Leoni. I just wondered what you meant by it.'

'It means that I'm asking you to have dinner with me, Miss Jacobs.'

'I beg your pardon? I'm afraid...I couldn't possibly...I don't usually...'

'Accept dinner invitations from strangers?'

Yes, of course he had known what she had been thinking. She didn't have the knack of dissembling.

'That's right,' Ruth informed him, bristling. 'I know that must seem a little unusual to you, but I...' Where was she going with this one? A long monologue on her sheltered life? An explanation on being a vicar's daughter? Hadn't she come to London in the hope of gaining a bit of sophistication?

'I don't bite, Miss Jacobs.' He pushed himself away from the edge of the desk and she looked at him guardedly. If he was trying to make her believe that he was as harmless as the day was long, then he was living on another planet. Innocent and naïve she might be, but born yesterday she was not.

'You're my employee. Call it maintaining good relations with someone who works for me. Besides...' The assessing look was back on his face, sending little tingles of apprehension racing down her spine. 'I'd like to find out a bit more about you. Find out what you do in the company... And in case you still don't believe who I am...' He sighed and withdrew his wallet from his pocket, flicked it open and produced a letter to Alison, with his name flamboyantly emblazoned in black at the bottom, and his impressive title typed underneath.

Ruth scanned the letter briefly, noting in passing that it implied, with no attempts to beat around the bush, that the magazine had not accumulated enough sales and that it was time to get to the drawing board and sort it out. Presumably the very reason he had made an appearance at the ridiculous hour of seven-thirty on a Friday evening.

'There now,' he said, without the slightest trace of remorse that he had allowed her to wallow in nightmarish possibilities when he could have eliminated all that by simply identifying himself from the beginning. 'Believe me?'

'Thank you. Yes.'

'What do you do here?'

'Nothing very important,' Ruth said hastily, just in case he got it into his head that he could quiz her on the details of running a magazine. 'I'm an odd-job man...woman...person...I do a bit of typing, take calls, fetch and carry...that's all...'

'Tell me all about it over dinner.' His hand brushed

hers as he retrieved his letter and rammed it back into his pocket, and she could feel something inside her shrinking away from him. She had never met anyone quite like him before. Her boyfriends, all three of them, had been from her town, and they had been nice boys, the sort who were quite happy to trundle through life with modest aspirations and no great appetite for taking life by its head and felling it.

Franco Leoni looked the sort who relished challenges of that sort, thrived on them.

'Now, why don't we lock up here and find ourselves something to eat?' He was now so close to her that the hairs on the back of her neck were standing on end. Up close, he was even more disconcerting than he was with a bit of distance between them. Underneath the well-tailored clothes, every inch of his body spoke of well-toned, highly muscled power, and the impression was completed by his swarthy olive colouring, at odds with the strikingly light eyes.

She cautiously edged away and snatched her jacket from the hook on the wall and slipped it on.

'Good girl.' He opened the door for her and then watched as she nervously locked it behind her and shoved the jangling keyring into her bag.

'My car's just outside,' he said, as they walked down the staircase, 'and please, try not to wear that fraught expression on your face. It makes me feel like a sick old man who takes advantage of innocent young girls.' There was lazy amusement in his voice when he said this, and she didn't have to cast her eyes in his direction to know that he was laughing at her.

His car was a silver Jaguar. He opened the door for her, waited till she had shuffled inside, then strode to the driver's seat. As soon as the door was shut, he turned to her and said, 'Now, what do you fancy eating?'

'Anything!' Ruth said quickly. The darkness of the car made his presence even more stifling, and she cursed herself for having been railroaded into accepting his invitation. Yes, so he might well be the owner of the company she worked for, but that didn't mean that he was trustworthy where the opposite sex was concerned.

She wryly recognised the outdated prudery of her logic and smiled weakly to herself. As an only child, and a girl on top of it, she had been cherished and protected by her parents from day one.

'A girl without pretensions,' he murmured to himself, starting the engine, 'very refreshing. Don't care what you eat. Do you like Italian?'

'Fine. Yes.'

She could feel her heart pounding like a steam engine inside her as the car pulled smoothly away from the curb.

'So, where do you fit into the scheme of things at *Issues*?'

'If you own the magazine, how is it that you've never made an appearance there?' Ruth blurted out curiously. She was pressed against the car door and was looking at him warily with her wide grey eyes.

'The magazine is a very, very minor company of mine.' He glanced in her direction. 'Have I mentioned to you that I don't bite? I'm not infectious either, so there's no need to fall out of the car in your desperation to put a few more inches between us.' He looked back to the road and Ruth shuffled herself into a more normal position. 'I bought it because I thought it could be turned around and because I viewed it as a sort of hobby.'

'A sort of hobby?' Ruth asked incredulously. 'You bought a *magazine* as a *hobby*?' The thought of such extravagance was almost beyond comprehension. '*What sort of life do you lead?* I always thought that hobbies involved doing things like playing tennis, or squash or bird-watching...or collecting model railways...*Your hobby is buying small companies just for the fun of it?*'

'There's no need to sound quite so shocked,' he said irritably, frowning as he stared ahead and manoeuvred the honeycomb of narrow streets.

'Well, I *am* shocked,' Ruth informed him, forgetting to be intimidated.

'Why?'

'Because, Mr Leoni...'

'You can call me Franco. I've never been a great believer in surnames.'

'Because,' she continued, skipping over his interruption, 'it seems obscene to have so much money that you can buy a company just for the heck of it!'

'My little gesture,' he pointed out evenly, although a dark flush had spread across his neck, 'happens to have created jobs, and in accordance with the package I've agreed with all my employees, *including yourself*, you all stand to gain if the company succeeds.'

Ruth didn't say anything, and eventually, he said abruptly, 'Well? What have you got to say to that?'

'I...nothing...'

He clicked his tongue in annoyance. '*I...nothing...*' he mimicked. 'What does that mean? Does it mean that you have an opinion on the subject? You had one a minute ago...'

'It means that you're my employer, Mr Leoni...'

'Franco!'

'Yes, well...'

'Say it!' he said grimly.

'Say what?'

'My name!'

'It means that you're my employer, Franco...' She went hot as she said that, and hurriedly moved on. 'And discretion is the better part of valour.' That was one of her father's favourite sayings. He spent so much time listening to his parishioners that he had always lectured to her on the importance of hearing without judging, and taking the wise course rather than the impulsive, thoughtless one.

'Hang discretion!'

Ruth looked at him curiously. Was he getting hot under the collar? He hadn't struck her as the sort of man who ever got hot under the collar.

'Okay,' she said soothingly, 'I take your point that you've created jobs, and if it succeeds then we all succeed. It just seems to me that *buying a company as a bit of fun* is the sort of thing...' She took a deep breath here and then said in a rush, 'That someone does because they have too much money and might be...bored...'

'*Bored?*' he spluttered furiously, swerving the car into a space by the pavement as though only suddenly remembering the purpose of the trip in the first place had been to get them to a restaurant, which he appeared to have overshot. He killed the engine and turned his full attention on her.

Ruth reverted to her original position against the car door. Her shoulder-length vanilla-blonde hair brushed the sides of her face and her mouth was parted in anticipation of some horrendous verbal attack, full frontal, no holds barred. He certainly looked in the mood for it.

He inhaled deeply, raked his fingers through his hair and then shook his head in wonderment. 'How long is it since I met you?' He glanced at his watch while Ruth helplessly wondered where this was going. 'Forty-five minutes? Forty-five minutes and you've managed to prod me in more wrong places than most people can accomplish in a lifetime.'

'I'm—I'm sorry...' Ruth stammered.

'Quite an achievement,' he carried on, ignoring her mumbled apology.

'I don't consider it much of an achievement to antagonise someone,' she said, aghast at his logic.

'Which is probably why you're so good at it.' He had regained his temporarily misplaced composure and clicked open his door. 'I'm looking forward to dinner,' he said, before he slid out of the driver's seat. 'This is the first time I've walked down a road and not known where it was leading.'

What road? Ruth thought, *as she stepped out of the car onto the pavement. What was he talking about?* She hoped that he didn't expect her to be some kind of cabaret for him, because she had no intentions of fulfilling his expectations, employer or not.

The Italian restaurant was small and crowded and smelled richly of garlic and herbs and good food. It was also familiar to the man at her side, because he was greeted warmly by the door and launched into fluent Italian, leaving her a chance to look around her while her mind churned with questions about him.

'You speak fluent Italian,' she said politely, as they were shown to their table. 'Have you lived in England long?'

They sat down and he stared at her thoughtfully. 'You look much younger than twenty-two. Where are you from?'

Ruth had spent her life being told that she looked much younger than she was. She supposed that by the time she hit fifty she would be glad for the compliment, but right now, sitting opposite a man who bristled with worldly-wise sophistication, it didn't strike her as much of a compliment.

'A very small town in Shropshire,' she said, staring at the menu which had been handed to her. 'You wouldn't have heard of it.'

'Try me.'

So she did, and when he admitted that he had never heard of the place she gave her shy, soft laugh and said, 'Told you so.'

'So you came here to London...for excitement?'

She shrugged. 'I fancied a change of scenery,' she said vaguely, not wanting to admit that the search for a bit of excitement had contributed more than a little to her reasons for leaving.

'And what were you doing before you moved here?' He hadn't bothered to look at the menu, and when the waiter came to take their orders, she realised that he already knew what he wanted. Halibut, grilled. Her choice of chicken in a wine and cream sauce seemed immoderate in comparison, but a lack of appetite was not something she had ever suffered from, despite her slight build. She had eaten her way through twenty-two years of her mother's wonderful home cooking, including puddings that ignored advice on cholesterol levels, and had never put on any excess weight.

'Secretarial work,' she answered. 'Plus I helped Mum and Dad a lot at home. Doing typing for Dad, going to see his parishioners...'

'Your father's a...priest?' He couldn't have sounded more shocked if she had said that her father manufactured opium for a living.

'A vicar,' she said defensively. 'And a brilliant one at that.'

He smiled, a long, warm smile that transformed his face, removed all the aggression, and sent little shivers scurrying up and down her spine like spiders.

'You're a vicar's daughter.'

'That's right.'

'Your parents must have had a fit when you told them that you wanted to move to London.'

He was watching her as though she was the most fascinating human being on the face of the earth, and the undiluted attention addled her brain and brought more waves of pink colour to her cheeks.

'They were very supportive, as a matter of fact.'

'But worried sick.'

'A little worried,' Ruth admitted, nervously playing with the cutlery next to her plate and then sticking her hands resolutely on her lap when she realised that fiddling was not classed as great restaurant etiquette.

'So...' The speculative look was back in his eyes as he relaxed in the chair and looked at her. 'Let me get this straight... You worked as a secretary after you left school, lived at home with your parents and then moved to London where you...did what until you started working at the magazine?'

'I found somewhere to live... Actually, Mum and Dad came with me a month before I left home and made sure that I had somewhere to go...I think they imagined me walking the streets of London and sleeping rough on park benches...' She smiled again, the same slow smile that transformed the features of her pretty but not extraordinary face into a quite striking glimpse of ethereal beauty.

'I got work temping at an office in Marble Arch and after a few months, when I was hunting around for something more permanent...' she shrugged and reflected on her stroke of luck '...I happened to be in the agency when Alison, Miss Hawes, arrived to register a job for a dogsbody, and I was given the job on the spot.'

'So you run errands,' he murmured to himself. 'And you're satisfied with that line of work?'

'Well, I do enjoy working for the magazine,' Ruth said thoughtfully, 'and hopefully I might be given some more responsibility when my appraisal comes up...the pay's very good, though...'

'I know. I've handled enough businesses to know that motivation and loyalty are heavily tied in to working conditions, and good pay makes for a good employee, generally speaking.'

Their food arrived and they both sat back to allow the large circular plates to be put in front of them.

'How many businesses do you own?' Ruth asked faintly.

'Sufficient to allow me very little free time, hence my non-appearance at the magazine. I spend most of my time out of the country, overseeing my divisions in North America and the Far East, although I *have* been to see how Alison was getting on a couple of times. You weren't there. I would have remembered you.'

Ruth, more relaxed now that she had something aside from him to concentrate on—namely the brimming plate of divine food in front of her—lowered her eyes and said to her forkful of chicken and vegetables, 'No, you wouldn't. I'm not one of life's memorable women.' Her parents had always told her that she was beautiful, but then all parents said stuff like that. She only had to look in the mirror to know that she simply wasn't flamboyant enough ever to cross the line between being reasonably pretty and downright sexy. She couldn't be sexy if she tried.

He didn't say anything.

Unusually for him, he was finding it hard to keep his eyes away from the woman sitting opposite him, her soft face downturned as she tucked into her food without inhibition.

He couldn't remember the last time he had been in the company of a woman who still had the capacity to blush. They could laugh, they could flirt, and they were adept at revealing enough of their bodies to incite interest, but when it came to the hesitant air of innocence that this woman in front of him possessed, they none of them could have captured it if they tried.

And it was this dreamy, uncertain shyness that had aroused him almost from the minute he had clapped eyes on her. He broke off to eat a mouthful of food, but his eyes slid back to her face of their own volition.

He had a ridiculous urge to impress her. To say

something or do something that would make her look at him with the hot interest he had become accustomed to in members of the opposite sex. He watched the way her blonde straight hair slipped across her face as she ate and the way she tucked it casually behind her ears. She looked about bloody sixteen! He must be going mad!

'You never told me,' she said, interrupting his thoughts, which were veering off wildly into the arena of sexual foreplay. 'Are you from Italy?' She blushed and smiled. 'Silly question. Of course you are with a name like yours. How long have you lived in London?'

'Most of my life. My mother was Irish, my father was Italian.' What, he wondered, would it feel like to reach out and touch that peach-smooth face? The thought fascinated him. He realised that he wasn't eating and shovelled some mouthfuls in while his mind wandered away again. What would her body look like? It was difficult to tell underneath her demure calf-length skirt and neat white blouse. He toyed with the fantasy of divesting her of both, very, very, very slowly, and he could feel himself stiffening at the thought of it.

This was ludicrous! He was responding like a teenager who had never touched a woman in his life before!

'How exotic!' she responded, and it occurred to him that, however damned exotic she might find his ancestry, it wasn't quite enough to distract her from the business of eating. In fact, he thought with a twitch of resentment, she seemed a lot more interested in the food than she did in him.

'There's no need to show polite interest,' he said abruptly, and her grey eyes registered dismay at his reaction.

'I *am* interested,' she protested, unnerved by the sudden brusqueness in his voice. She was boring him. Of course she was. How could a gauche woman like herself ever hope to capture the interest of a man like him, all glamour and fast-lane living. 'The food's wonderful, isn't it?' she volunteered tentatively, feeling her way towards a topic that might smooth the undercurrent that seemed to have inexplicably developed.

'I can see that you've enjoyed it,' he said wryly.

Ruth gave a sheepish smile. 'I have a very unladylike appetite, I'm afraid.' She had managed to eat every mouthful, and if she had been in the company of anyone else would have happily bolted down some dessert as well. Instead, she closed her knife and fork, declined pudding and accepted coffee.

'I guess you read what was in that letter I sent to your boss,' he said casually, eyeing her over the rim of his cup. He had pushed himself away from the table so that he could sit at an angle, crossing his long legs.

'Not really,' Ruth answered. 'I mean I scanned it…'

'But still managed to get a pretty good idea of what I was trying to say.'

'I don't think that Alison would approve of my discussing something that was meant for her eyes only,' Ruth eventually told him.

'I shouldn't trouble your head with such concerns,' he dismissed. 'I intend to have a little talk to the entire staff. Sales have picked up since we took over, but not enough. I've read what the three journalists have written over the months...have you?'

'Oh, yes,' Ruth said enthusiastically.

'And...? What's your verdict?'

She couldn't quite understand why her opinion should be of any concern, considering her lowly status in the company, but there was an interested glint in his eyes, so she sighed and said slowly, 'I think it's all been good. But I suppose there's a little element of having lost the way. I mean,' she said hurriedly, 'their articles are so varied that there's a bit of doubt as to what sector of the market the magazine is supposed to appeal to. Not,' she felt compelled to add, 'that I'm in any position to criticise.'

'Why not?' he asked bluntly, leaning forward so that his elbow was resting on the table and his eyes bored into her like skewers.

'Because I'm not an editor.'

'But you care about the company enough to want to see it improve?'

'Of course I do!' When she had joined it had been a fledgling firm, and was even now, and consequently, loyalty was abundantly given by everyone who worked in it.

'Enough to do your little bit?' he asked, leaning forward yet further.

'Naturally I do my best... I can't write, if that's what you mean...but I help out...' She looked at him, bewildered.

'Good! Just what I wanted to hear.' He signalled for the bill but kept his eyes on her face. 'Because I have a proposition to put to you...'

'What?' There was enough of a predatory expression on his face to give her a clue that whatever he had in mind was not going to be to her liking.

'I'll discuss it with Alison first, but, yes...it's time for a few changes, and you could be right where it matters...'

CHAPTER TWO

WHEN she arrived at work the following Monday morning, it was to find Alison in her office, door shut, which was a rare phenomenon, and, even rarer still, an atmosphere of hushed efficiency amongst the staff who had managed to pole up for work at a quarter to eight—an hour before their due starting time on a Monday, this was always limited to a handful, which increased as the week progressed.

She walked across to Janet Peters, one of the editors, opened her mouth to ask what was going on and, before she could get the question out, was greeted with a series of facial movements and twitches that left her a little confused.

'Are you feeling all right, Jan?' Ruth asked, concerned, and in reply Janet crooked her finger for Ruth to lean forward,

'Guess who's in with Alison...' she hissed. 'Hence the unnatural deathly quiet in this place...'

'Franco Leoni, owner of *Issues*?' Ruth hazarded, and then grinned when Janet fell backwards in her chair and stared at her with profound consternation.

'How did you know?'

'I knew...because...I am possessed of strange mystic forces that leave me with the uncanny ability to *see into the other realm.*' She giggled and played with the blunt edge of one of her plaits, a sensible hairstyle that kept her hair away from her face though unfortunately made her look no older than twelve.

'Be serious!' Janet said sternly, by which time they had been joined by three others and the atmosphere was drifting inexorably back into cheerful, noisy confusion.

'How *did* you know?' Jack Brady asked, sitting on the desk and giving her a frank and open stare. Jack Brady, who looked only slightly older than twelve himself, with his freckles and thick fair hair, specialised in frank and open stares which fooled no one but the uninitiated.

'He came here on Friday night, just as I was about to leave. Scared me to death as a matter of fact.'

'Was that,' Jack asked, frowning and tilting his head to one side, 'before or after he asked you to lie prone on the desk so that he could have his wicked way with you?'

'Before,' Ruth said with a serious face. 'I felt fine afterwards.'

'Ruth Jacobs!' Jack said, shocked. 'You're not *supposed to say naughty things like that*! Especially looking the way you do, all fetching, sexy innocence with those two blonde pigtails and big, tempting eyes...' He playfully pulled the ends of both the plaits with his hands, so that she was more or less compelled to incline her body towards his, and it was while they were in this awkward stance, both of them laughing, that Alison's door opened and there was a general flurry of scattered bodies as Franco stood and watched what was going on.

Ruth and Jack were the last to detach themselves from the situation.

'An office hard at work,' Franco said, pushing himself away from the doorframe and strolling towards them with the friendly expression of a barracuda on the prowl for food. 'Such a reassuring thing to see—especially when I have just finished having a meeting with your boss to work out why the magazine isn't doing as well as it should.'

He was dressed in a silver-grey suit, which he managed to transform into something elegant rather than functional, and a pale blue and white shirt with a dark blue tie. Very conservative, very traditional yet, on him, shockingly attractive.

Jack, who had been reduced to a state of tongue-tied embarrassment, launched himself into a comprehensive stream of apologies, which Franco, not bothering to look at him at all, waved aside.

He somehow managed to turn his broad back on the assembled eight members of staff now busily working at their desks, heads down, eyes focused, so that he could devote every scrap of uninvited attention to Ruth, who was the last one left still standing and with nowhere to conceal herself.

'So,' he said softly, which just succeeded in making his exclusion of the rest of the office from their conversation all the more complete, 'does flirting list among your dogsbody jobs?'

'I wasn't...flirting!' Ruth protested in a low, heated voice. 'Jack was just...'

'Playing with your hair...'

She tried to slide her eyes around him to see whether their tête-à-tête was being observed, but decided that she would rather not know.

'That's r-right...' she stammered absent-mindedly,

as her eyes flitted over the downturned heads and rapt faces staring at computer screens.

He clicked his tongue impatiently, 'Would you mind looking at me when I'm talking to you?' he snapped, sharply enough for her to literally jump to attention.

'Of course!' She nearly saluted, and then had to stifle a giggle at the thought of what his expression would be like if she dared do any such thing.

'Do you recall our little conversation on Friday?'

'Which bit?' Ruth asked cautiously. Her smoky grey eyes wandered away as she tried to recall what they had spoken about. She knew that if she put her mind to it she would have no trouble at all, although the overwhelming impression that remained with her of that night, like a thorn driven deep into her side, was the unwelcome feeling of being bludgeoned into the ground by something much like a steamroller.

'Could I have your attention?' he asked in a grim, irritable voice, and she shot him a nervous smile in response.

Did he realise that he had just raised his voice one or two decibels, and that in the small office all those downcast eyes were quietly boring a hole in the back of his neck, and that all those subdued voices would be eagerly anticipating his departure so that they could lay into her with a thousand and one questions?

Having never been the focus of gossip, the thought of it now was enough to bring Ruth out in a cold sweat.

She could hardly tell him to lower his tone, though, so she compensated by reducing the level of hers so much that he had to bend down to hear what she was saying.

'I *am* paying attention, to every word you're saying,' she whispered furtively, feeling like a dodgy character in a third-rate movie.

'I've spoken to Alison about my little proposition...'

'What little proposition?'

'Do you have *any* concentration span *at all*?' he snapped.

He glared down at her. Most of the women he knew—had ever known, for that matter—achieved a near perfect complexion through generous, skilful application of make-up. This girl, staring up at him, her teeth anxiously worrying her lip, had the most perfect complexion he had ever clapped eyes on, without the aid of any make-up at all. God, he could feel his mind beginning to drift, *again*, and he glared even more ferociously at her, further maddened by the glaringly obvious fact that although she was hearing every belligerent word he was saying she wasn't seeing *him* at all.

Who was that boy who had been playing with her hair? Was there something going on there?

He fought to impose a bit of self-control and managed a stiff, artificial smile which appeared to alarm the object of his attentions even more than his aggression had done a minute before.

'Maybe we could continue this conversation in Alison's office. A bit more private.'

'Oh, yes!' Ruth breathed a sigh of relief. She had just managed to accidentally catch Jack's eye and had quickly looked away when he had grinned and winked at her.

'After you,' he said, stepping aside so that she could precede him.

Ruth, in her usual uninspiring attire of neat powder-blue skirt and long-sleeves blouse, was acutely conscious of his eyes behind her, following her movements. She was also conscious of Jack shooting her telling, questioning looks from where he was seated at an angle away from his desk, and with a sidelong glance she smiled at him and flashed him the smallest of waves. A conspiratorial wave that combined bewilderment at Franco Leoni's inexplicable shepherding of her into Alison's office and dread at what it indicated.

'Mind if I have a word with Ruth alone?' Franco asked, as soon as they were in the office, and Alison obligingly exited at speed, either relieved to be out of his presence or else frantic to obey his every command.

'Take a seat.' He indicated the black chair in front of the desk and Ruth sat down, only to find that he had remained standing, so that to look at him she had to crane her neck.

He strolled across to the bay window which opened onto the busy view of a London street in full swing, and, after idly staring out for a few seconds, he turned to face her, relaxing against the windowsill, arms folded.

'I won't be telling you anything that the rest of your colleagues will not hear for themselves very shortly, but the gist of my chat with Alison concerns what we briefly discussed last Friday evening. The magazine seems to have found itself in something of a rut. As you rightly pointed out, neither one thing nor another.'

Ruth felt a sudden warm glow at the unexpected compliment.

'We have three talented reporters with good, solid styles of writing, but their subject matter is too disparate. Sport, fashion, natural disasters. Are you following me?'

'Of course I'm following you. I'm not a complete idiot, you know!' She felt a sudden flash of anger at his patronising attitude. Why had he called her in on her own to give this little speech? He hadn't made it clear, unless it was to sack her, but she couldn't really see why he would do that. Her contribution had nothing to do with the actual running of the magazine. She was a gofer, and a pretty good one at that, with lots of enthusiasm.

No, the only reason she could see for this one-to-one chat was to given him a chance of shooting down everything she said in flames. Maybe her soft nature was just too much of a temptation for a man like him. He simply couldn't resist walking over her.

However soft she was, Ruth had no intention of being walked over. When pushed, there was a stubborn streak in her that made her dig her heels in and refuse to budge.

'Sorry,' he said, with a shadow of a smile. The apology, so unexpected, was enough to pull her down a peg or two, and she responded helplessly to the sincerity in his voice.

'That's okay,' she said with a half-smile, lowering her eyes and then belatedly realising that all this timidity was no way to deal with this man. She looked at him fully and he stared back at her in silence for a few seconds.

'I don't suppose you were familiar with the magazine before we took it over?'

Ruth shook her head.

He went to the desk, but instead of sedately sitting on the chair he perched on the surface of the desk, so that he was still staring down at her—though from a lesser height, and infinitely closer.

'It failed because there simply wasn't enough money to pay any half-respectable reporter, and as a result, the articles were shallow and superficial. But, as far as I am concerned, the essence of the magazine was good. It dealt solely with topical problems. Drugs in the schoolyard, corruption in local politics, that sort of thing.'

'Oh. Yes,' Ruth said faintly, wondering what this had to do with her.

'I think we need to drag it back to that formula, but handle it better than our predecessors.'

'What does Alison think of your idea?' Ruth asked, leaning forward to rest the palms of her hands on her knees and staring up at him.

The pigtails were a mistake. She had not expected to be confronted with Franco Leoni first thing in the morning or else she would have tried for a more sophisticated look. She could tell from the way that he looked at her that he was finding it difficult not to click his tongue impatiently at the image she presented.

'Oh, she agrees entirely,' he said. 'In fact, she's probably out there explaining all of this to your colleagues…' he looked at her for a fraction longer than necessary '...and friends,' he ended on a soft note, which made Ruth frown.

'Well, I hope you don't mind my asking, but why have you taken me to one side to explain all this when I could have been out there hearing it along with everyone else?'

'Because...' He inclined his head to one side and, worryingly, appeared to give the question quite a bit of thought. 'Because there's a further little matter I wanted to discuss with you...'

'What?' She inadvertently stiffened at the tone in his voice.

'I think you could be a great deal of help in getting this magazine back on the straight and narrow.'

'Me...?' Ruth squeaked. She almost burst out laughing at that, and managed to contain the urge in the nick of time.

If he thought that she was, mysteriously, a wonderful and gifted reporter labouring under the disguise of a dogsbody, then he was way off target. The most she had ever written were essays at school, and she'd occasionally helped her dad to write the odd sermon for Sunday's congregation.

Hard-hitting articles on topical issues were quite outside her realm of capability.

'Yes, you. And there's no need to sound so shocked. Don't you have any faith in your abilities?'

'I couldn't write to save my life!'

'Why not? Have you ever tried?' There was curiosity etched on his dark, handsome face as he leant a little closer towards her while she continued to stare at him with frank disbelief.

'Of course I have,' Ruth said firmly, 'at school. I

managed to get my A level in English, but I certainly wouldn't want to put it to the test by writing an article. And I fancy,' she said with a slow smile, 'that not very many readers would thank me for the effort either.'

'So you never considered university?'

Ruth eyed him warily, wondering what this had to do with anything.

Franco, leaning towards her, felt his eyes stray to the blunt edges of her plaits, and he wondered what she would do if he took them and tugged at them, the way the boy in the office had. She certainly wouldn't respond with laughter. Apprehension, more like it. The thought generated another surge of hot antagonism towards the young lad who was clearly on familiar enough terms with her to touch her hair, play with it.

Were they sleeping together?

He would find out. He would make it his business to find out. In fact, he would make it his business to find out everything he possibly could about this girl sitting in front of him, if only to sate his gnawing curiosity.

He felt another urge to *make her notice him*, and scowled at such an adolescent response.

'No,' she laughed. 'I'm no brainbox. My only virtues are that I'm enthusiastic and I'm prepared to work hard.'

'Really?' he drawled. 'Admirable virtues, I must say.' His blue eyes lingered on her face, which turned crimson in response as the ambiguity of his observation sank in. 'You blush easily. Is that because I make you feel uncomfortable?' He was staring at her so fixedly that Ruth disengaged her eyes from his face. A fatal mistake, because as they travelled the length of his body, they came to his hands, resting casually over his thighs. Just a couple of inches higher and she could discern, beneath the fine silk of his trousers, the faint but unmistakable bulge of his manhood. The sight of it made her feel a little faint.

'No,' she denied quickly, staring back into his blue eyes. 'I blush with everyone...no discrimination there, I'm afraid...I'm just hopeless when it comes to that kind of thing. Anyway, you never said what you wanted to talk to me about...'

'Oh, didn't I?'

'No,' she said drily, 'you didn't.'

He flashed her a smile. 'Perhaps that's because I've been beating about the bush trying to think of how best I can put my suggestion to you. And, before you ask, it has nothing to do with writing articles for the magazine.'

'Then what?'

'Like I said to you, I think we need to get back to hard-hitting articles, the sort of stories that people are interested in and can identify with.' He rubbed his chin thoughtfully with his finger, then stood up and began pacing through the room, as though his brain needed the physical movement to work clearly. 'And I intend to lead by example.'

'Oh?' Ruth felt like someone who had accidentally strayed into a maze and was in the process of getting more and more lost.

'I intend to tackle the first article myself—get a feel for what's out there and what our best vantage point is when it comes to reporting it...'

'I thought you were a businessman,' Ruth said,

aware that she must have missed something vital but not too sure what it could be.

'I have lots of strings to my bow,' he murmured, waiting for her to ask for clarification and then disproportionately irked when she simply nodded and informed him that diving in the deep end and doing some reporting himself sounded a very good idea to her.

'Was that your intention when you bought the magazine?' she asked, and he frowned his incomprehension at her question. 'I mean,' she elaborated slowly, 'to get involved in the reporting side of things. Must make quite a change from working in an office...'

'I don't *work in an office*!' he growled. 'I *run companies*.'

'I know. But from the inside of an office.'

'Yes, admittedly, I *have a desk*, and all the usual accoutrements of my trade, but...'

'I'm sorry, I didn't mean to be rude.'

He muttered something inaudible under his breath and wondered how on earth he could have such chokingly erotic fantasies about someone whose eyes barely rested on him long enough to establish that he was a man. Never mind an immensely rich and powerful one.

'I just wondered,' she ploughed on, 'whether your decision to get involved has to do with your boredom at the office...'

This time the indecipherable noise was somewhat louder and more alarming.

'I'm sorry,' Ruth said a little desperately, wondering how she had managed to put both feet in it with such apparent ease. 'I forgot. You don't work at an office.

Well, you more or less own the office, and you're not bored. I'm sorry. I don't know why I said what I did. I must be tired. It's been an awfully tiring weekend.'

'Has it? Doing what, Ruth?' he asked slyly. 'Are you and that boy out there involved? Because I tell you from now that I don't encourage office romances. The first thing to suffer is usually the work.'

'What?' Ruth asked, appalled at his sweeping assumptions. How had they swerved off onto this topic anyway? She thought that they had been discussing his idea to do a spot of reporting. Now here they were on the subject of her personal life, and her non-existent love-life at that.

'I asked you whether—'

'I heard you! No! Of *course* not! Jack and I are friends! I wouldn't dream of... *No...*'

Franco tried not to smile with satisfaction. He couldn't have explained why, but from the minute he had come upon the two of them in the office, clearly at ease with one another, he had been determined to find out what was going on. The surprise on her face at the thought of being romantically involved with the boy was enough to persuade him of the honesty of her reply.

In some part of him he could feel that this was getting out of hand. Mild interest was fine, but she was getting under his skin, making him want more of her... He shifted his position and abruptly sat down, because his body was responding to her with its now familiar obstinate refusal to obey the commands of his head.

'Good, because for what I have in mind romantic involvement is not such a good idea.' He glanced up at her and asked casually, 'You're not involved with anyone, are you? I mean, no lovers on the scene?' He knew that he was shamelessly exploiting his situation, taking advantage of his position to prise answers out of her that he wanted to know and she, quite possibly, did not want to reveal, but he blithely squashed any guilt.

'No!' Her face was flushed and she fought down her instinctive embarrassment at his forthrightness to say, somewhat belatedly, 'And you have no right to ask me questions like that. What I do in my private life is...'

'I know, I know...' he said, ready to apologise now that he had heard what he needed to know. 'And I'm deeply sorry at having to intrude into your privacy, but my proposition... I want you to work alongside me on a certain project I have in mind.'

Ruth thought that she must have misheard what he had said, but, when no further clarification was forthcoming, she said, with a regretful smile, 'I thought I'd made it perfectly clear. I'm hopeless at writing. I don't think I'd be any good at all.'

'You won't be asked to *write* anything. I intend to commence a new series of insights into twenty-first-century life in this so called civilised country of ours by running a selection of interviews with young girls who find themselves lured into teenage prostitution.'

At what point, Ruth wondered, was she supposed to roar with laughter at this outrageous idea of his? Or at least outrageous if he intended to include her in it.

Hadn't she told him that she was a vicar's daughter? She could no more work on such a project than she could strip off all her clothes and streak through a football ground.

'No, I'm very sorry, but I can't...'

'Why not?'

'I'm afraid I'm totally unsuitable for any such assignment,' she amended, smiling. 'Not the right kind of girl at all...'

'Why don't you let me be the judge of that?'

Wasn't he listening to a word she was saying?

'What do you think the *right kind of girl* is?' he asked, walking towards her and then stopping directly in front of her, so that now she had to virtually bend her neck backwards to see his face.

'B-Bold, brassy,' Ruth stammered. 'Self-confident. Perhaps you should ask Jan to do it...'

'That's not the sort of girl I have in mind for this at all,' he said, brutally bulldozing her input without qualm. Then he leaned forward and propped himself up against her chair, gripping either side so that she found herself suffocatingly trapped by him. 'In fact,' he continued softly, his face close enough now so that she could feel his warm breath against her cheek and see the dark flecks streaking the blue irises of his eyes, 'the minute I laid eyes on you I knew that you were the woman I wanted...' He paused, relishing her discomfort. 'For the job.'

At last he stood back, massaging the back of his neck with one hand before taking a more orthodox position on the chair behind the desk.

'My parents...' she protested weakly.

'Would, I'm sure, like to see you spread your wings. It *is* why you came to London, isn't it? Wasn't that what you told me?'

Ruth glared at him, resenting the fact that he had homed in on a passing remark and was now capitalising on it to justify what he wanted her to do.

'You're a big girl now, Ruth,' he pressed on mercilessly. 'Time for you to stop running to Mummy and Daddy whenever you need to make a decision. Time for you to face the big, bad world out there and stop trying to hide away from it.'

'I am *not* trying to hide from anything.' Ruth dug her heels in stubbornly. 'I am just being realistic. My background hasn't prepared me for dealing with a job of that nature...'

'So what do you intend to do with your life? Has it ever occurred to you that the most interesting challenges in life are also often the most threatening?'

He was conscious that what he was trying to do was toe a very delicate line. On the one hand he wanted to coerce her into accepting his offer, into working with him. Partly because he genuinely thought that she would be well suited to what he had in mind; partly because the temptation of being close to her was virtually irresistible. On the other hand he was aware that if he pushed too hard she would set her soft mouth in that mute, obstinate line, avert her eyes and simply not budge an inch.

'I'm not going to ask you to do anything dangerous, Ruth,' he said in a gentler voice, resisting the urge to steamroller her into doing what he wanted, even though he knew full well that, underneath the shy exterior, this woman was probably immune to being steamrollered. 'I just know that we'll be dealing with young girls, asking them questions of a personal nature. They would respond to you far more quickly than they ever would to someone brash and self-assertive. You're gentle and calm enough to draw confidences out of the kind of girls we'll be dealing with, and—who knows?—you might even sway one or two of them to reconsider the road they've chosen.'

Ruth went pink. She couldn't help it. She could feel her soft nature being played on by a master musician, but then he was right. She couldn't run away from everything that had a ring of adventure or risk about it.

He could see the indecision in her eyes and pressed on smoothly, effortlessly, tasting victory. 'Most of our work will be done at night, which is why it's important that you don't have a partner. I wouldn't want to be accused of taking you away from your loved one. You'll be able to work here normally a couple of days a week, but you might find that as your body adjusts to working by night you just want to sleep during the days. And it won't be an assignment that lasts for ever. Two weeks at the most, probably less. Just enough time for us to gain an accurate picture of what's happening to our young people out there and what's being done by the government to put an end to it.'

'Why are *you* so keen to get involved?' she asked, buying time while she mulled over the possibilities in her head. 'Any one of your reporters out there would be more than capable of handling the job.'

'I like to lead from the front.' He shot her a wry smile. 'And maybe you're right about that remark you made to me about being bored.' He shrugged expressively and tried to look humble. 'I have all that I could ever need—or want, for that matter. I started out as a reporter myself, you know.'

He linked his fingers behind his head and leaned back into his hands, staring broodingly up at the ceiling. 'First on a provincial newspaper, ferreting out dirt and scandal, then on a city newspaper as a financial reporter. Good fun and, as it turned out, a useful passport when I decided to branch out and play around with the money markets myself. Since then I've made my money and now—who knows?—maybe I fancy getting back to my roots. Or maybe what I'm looking for is a little...' he leveled his eyes to hers '...excitement.'

Ruth, inexperienced, marvelled at how he could invest a single word with so many hidden, tantalising possibilities.

'Have you told Alison about your idea...for me? I wouldn't want to rub anyone's back up the wrong way...'

'Absolutely,' he said expansively, bringing the palms of his hands to rest on the desk and adopting a businesslike expression. 'Alison thinks it's a fabulous idea, and she's going to rally the other reporters to start working on similar contentious issues so that we can pull something together for the issue due at the end of next month. When you've finished your stint with me, you'll be pulled into a more responsible position—maybe occasionally working alongside one of the reporters as back-up.'

'Oh!' Ruth said breathlessly, a little awed by the suggestion of such a tremendous promotion.

'Naturally, this unexpected change of job will be reflected in your pay.' He whipped a sheet of paper from underneath a paperweight on the desk and waved it in the air, talking at the same time. 'An immediate increase in your salary, to be followed by another increase in three months' time if you prove yourself up to your additional responsibilities—if, indeed, you *want* additional responsibility.

'All you have to do...' he leant across the desk and rapped his finger imperiously at the bottom of the sheet of paper '...is sign here...' He produced a fountain pen, seemingly from thin air, and handed it to her before she could open her mouth to protest at the sudden speed of things.

Ruth's eyes scurried over the closely typed page, briefly taking in the description of her new role, containing an undignified gasp at the enormity of her salary increase.

'At the bottom,' he said. 'Your signature. And then everything's formalised.'

'I'm still not sure...' she said on a deep breath, shifting her eyes away from the piece of paper in front of her with its frightening promises of adventure and money and excitement.

'Of course you are,' he said gently. 'Apprehensive, but sure.'

Ruth frowned, uncertain whether she cared for his ten-second summary of her reaction and then irritated because he was right.

He looked at his watch. 'You're not putting your life on the line with this assignment,' he urged her, raking his long fingers through his hair. 'A week—and if you hate it, believe me, I won't force you to carry on. But give yourself the chance to see whether this kind of thing appeals to you.'

A few more seconds of hesitation and then she put her name at the bottom of the piece of paper. Okay, so she wasn't signing her life away, but the minute she pushed the piece of paper across the desk back to him she felt as though she was signing *something* away, though what she wasn't too sure.

Or maybe it was just that trace of smugness tugging the corners of his mouth that made her feel just a tad nervous about what she had agreed to. She was very nearly tempted to snatch the piece of paper out of his hands, rip it into a thousand pieces and then hustle back to her desk. But, with a speed that left her wondering whether the man was a mind-reader, he folded the paper in half, stuck it into his open briefcase, which was perched on the side of the desk, and decisively slammed it shut.

'Now that's all settled,' he said, standing up and shrugging on his jacket, 'just one or two suggestions before we start work on Wednesday.'

'On Wednesday?' she squeaked.

'Why waste valuable time? No point meeting here. Meet me at The Breakfast Bar in Soho. Here's the address.' He scribbled it down for her and she took the paper from him. 'Eight p.m. sharp. I gather it's where a lot of young girls hang out when they hit London for the first time. It's cheap, in the centre of things, and has a reputation for being a useful place to meet people.'

'How on earth did you find all that out?'

'I'm clever and talented. Hadn't you noticed?' he said in a silky voice, addressing, as it turned out, her downturned head. 'Anyway,' he continued crisply, 'just a couple of suggestions.'

That got her attention. She looked up at him with

her peach-smooth skin and wide grey eyes, now holding a hint of a question in them.

'Dress casually. Jeans, trainers, nothing too...formal. If anything, you'll want to blend in with some of the girls we'll be meeting...that way they'll be more relaxed and more expansive about revealing themselves to a couple of reporters...'

'How do you know they won't laugh in our faces and walk away?'

'I think, actually, they'll either be flattered or relieved that someone's taking an interest in them.' He was by the door now, hand on the doorknob. 'The way we'll play this is: questions in the night, and the following evening we'll debrief over dinner before we start again.' He smiled at her. 'And don't be scared. I'll look after you.'

CHAPTER THREE

'I DON'T know if I'll be able to handle this.'

She had rehearsed a long speech about this, had even stood in front of the bathroom mirror and practised, making sure to keep her eyes focused, to try and control the temptation to eat her words, and to appear confident and firm.

Now, sliding into the seat opposite Franco for the first of their so called debriefing meetings, she found that all of her painstakingly contrived self-assurance had vanished through the window. Her words came out in a rush, and from the expression on his face she could see that he thought she was deranged.

To be greeted by someone whose opening remark was, *I don't know if I can handle this*, must, she conceded, be a little disconcerting.

'Would you like a drink?' was his response, and she looked at him, exasperated.

'No, I would *not* like a drink. I would like to say what I have to say.'

'Go ahead, then.' He sat back in the chair, left ankle resting on right knee, and proceeded to look at her with an interested, patient expression that made her even more nervous.

They had arranged, the night before, to have their debriefing dinner at a pub in Hampstead, which, at six-thirty, was still virtually empty. A few lost souls were perched on bar stools, drinking in a desultory way, and a few more couples occupied tables, but the crowds would not start piling in until later.

Ruth sat very straight on the chair and pressed her hands into her lap. 'I've thought long and hard about this,' she began. 'In fact, I've spent most of the day thinking about it...'

'Are you *sure* you don't want a drink? Dutch courage and all that?'

Ruth hesitated and then nodded briefly. Perhaps a glass of wine. Making her speech had been considerably easier with only her reflection as audience. She watched as he strode off to the counter, leaning against it with his back to her.

He was wearing jeans again. As she had discovered the night before, the attire of jeans, on him, was even more unsettling than a suit, which, rightly or wrongly, exuded more soothing connotations of good behaviour and civilised self-restraint. Seeing him in a pair of jeans for the first time had made her realise that he was younger than she had first thought. He had appeared more overtly sexy in them as he had sat astride his chair, so that the denim tautened and tightened alarmingly over his powerful legs and thighs, chatting easily with two girls who couldn't have been older than seventeen or eighteen.

'So. You were saying?' He handed her the glass, sat back down and proceeded to look at her questioningly over the rim of his glass of lager.

Ruth gulped down some of the wine and then licked her lips thoughtfully. 'I don't think that I handled last night very well,' she began. 'I don't know what I expected when I agreed to this assignment, but the reality of it was just a little too much for me.'

'I thought you were rather good, actually,' he said, massaging the back of his neck with the flat of his hand. 'Concerned, gentle, unthreatening. Kate and Angie seemed to be opening up to you quite a bit.'

'Yes, well, that's the problem. I don't think I want to...' She hesitated, tripping over what was going through her head. 'I'm not gritty enough...'

'Stop right there.' He pressed, palms down, on the circular table and looked at her grimly. 'Now you listen to me, because I'll only say this once. If you don't want to do this, then that's all well and fine, but don't think that you can hide behind a lot of hogwash about *not being gritty enough* and *not being prepared for this kind of thing because you're a vicar's daughter* and *not being the right sort of person*. Just come right out with the truth, which is that this particular assignment doesn't appeal to you. Perhaps you don't like the thought of working nights. Perhaps you just find the girls we'll be interviewing distasteful. Is that it? Have I put my finger on the button? Do you fancy that you're better than they are?'

Ruth's face had turned as white as a sheet, and when she picked up her glass of wine her hand was trembling.

How could he say those things? He had got it all wrong! She had spent hours thinking about what she was going to say, working out her explanations in her head, and when it had come to the crunch her own tongue-tied, gauche, immature stupidity had let her down again! Had left him with all the wrong impressions.

'No!' she protested defensively. 'I have no objection to working nights at all...I don't have any family commitments...and I don't... How can you say that I find those girls...distasteful?' Her voice was shocked and mortified at the assumption, and she watched his expression change from brutal, punishing grimness to something gentler.

'Then what is it?' he asked quietly.

'I...I feel inadequate for the job,' she said finally, which hadn't been part of the rehearsed speech at all. 'I was appalled by those stories last night. Girls who leave home for no better reasons than lack of space and arguments with step-parents—leave home and at the age of seventeen drop the lid on their futures for ever. I wanted to take them home with me and, I don't know...save them, I suppose. Instead I had to jot down every word they said, ask questions and then say goodbye, because tonight we'll move on to a couple of different faces, with different stories and different little tragedies.'

'But you can't make everything better, and hiding away from certain unpleasant realities doesn't mean that they no longer exist. It just means that you remove yourself from the inconvenience of having to confront them.'

Ruth hadn't tied her hair back. Nor had she tied it back the night before. It fell like silk to her shoulders. With her hair loose and wearing a skirt that was a little shorter than normal and a blouse that was a little less buttoned up than customary, she felt strangely vulnerable. She felt like a woman instead of a girl. Particularly here, now, sitting opposite someone so potently masculine and in a situation where the dress code of formality was not in existence.

The night before she had maintained a healthy distance, physically, from him. She had taken up her position on the chair furthest from his, allowing the two young girls to sit between them, facing one another, but, even so, her eyes had slipped towards him with unerring regularity. It was almost as though she had needed to feed off him, feast her eyes on his image, allow his overpowering masculinity to seep into her like a liquid.

She suspected that all this was a little bit puerile, a little bit unhealthy.

Her reaction to him frightened and confused her, and, because she had no slide rule against which to measure it, she ingenuously justified it as perfectly natural, absolutely normal to be fascinated by a member of the species who was so utterly different from any of his kind she had ever met before. She equated it with a lack of logic that she failed to recognise, with the same sort of fascination that might grip her were she to find herself in the company of a two-headed monster.

'I don't have a problem confronting reality,' she said awkwardly.

'Correct me if I'm wrong, but I think that you've led a very sheltered life, very protected, very cocooned. You worked hard at school, did ballet, maybe a bit of horse riding, had every angle of your life mapped out…'

'There's nothing wrong with that!' Ruth burst out vehemently. 'I'm glad I had a sheltered life! I would hate to have been like those girls!'

'Is that why you find it so hard to be in their company? Because you can't identify with them? Because they seem like aliens to you when in fact they're just less fortunate?'

'No,' Ruth said wearily. 'I told you, I just feel too much compassion... I also feel around a hundred next to them, when in fact I'm only a few years older. I feel like their mums and I respond as thought I were...'

'You feel older because of the way you project yourself.'

'What do you mean?'

'I mean...' Here he drew in a long breath and looked at her steadily. 'Look at the way you dress.'

Ruth automatically glanced over herself and blushed.

'You spent the whole of last night huddled in your denim jacket as though you were terrified you might catch something if you took it off.'

'I felt cold.'

'The place was packed with people and it was boiling hot.'

'I...I...' She searched around for a logical reason for her sartorial reticence of the night before and found none.

The truth of the matter was she hadn't dared expose the tiny skin-fitting top she had daringly slung on before she'd left the house. It clung lovingly to every inch of her body. It was the sort of top which was comfortable enough for her to wear at home, when there was no one around, but was absolutely the last thing she would be seen wearing in public. She had no idea why she had worn it. Perhaps she had been imbued with a feeling of recklessness, but, in all events, she had lacked the courage to remove the jacket, even though she had felt stiflingly warm in the café. She was amazed that he had noticed.

'You have the face of a girl, an angelic child, and you dress like someone's matronly aunt, as though you're ashamed of the way you look.' His eyes skirted over her blouse and she nervously responded by fiddling with the top button.

'I'm not a child,' was all she could find to say, hurt by the description.

'You don't have to become these girls' social worker. You simply have to understand what makes them tick—the emotion will transfer itself into what we write, and what we write might change the lives of some of them. There are very good places of sanctuary where they can seek refuge, just until they get their heads together and their lives a bit more sorted out, but, like everything else, these places need government backing. The printed word can work wonders sometimes.'

He could see the awkward embarrassment gradually ebbing away and her eyes lighting up with interest. Woman she might well be, but she responded with the transparently telling emotions of a girl. He could sit and watch the changing expressions on her face for ever. It was as fascinating as watching the rise and fall of the sea on a moonlit night. Her grey eyes reflected the smallest shifts in her moods, from blue-grey, when she felt serene and dreamy, to a stormy dark grey when she was defensive and bristling. Observing all these minute alterations was more fun than reading a good book.

He was also feeling wonderfully fired up. He had watched her covertly the night before, had seen the way her eyes had rested on him before hurriedly flitting away, as though she'd been terrified of being caught out doing something unmentionable. It had been a most amazing turn-on.

She had sat there, her legs discreetly but somehow sinfully clad in what had looked like the thickest possible black tights, her jacket kept severely buttoned so that his mind had been obliged to wander and speculate on what lay beneath it. And when she'd taken notes, which she'd done with remarkable efficiency—he really must see about getting her status at the office changed—her hair had brushed against her cheeks and her fringe, which was short and straight, had become permanently tousled from the way she'd expelled her breath upwards whenever she felt hot or bothered or both.

She was saying something to him, and he shot her a penetrating, earnest look to cover up the fact that his mind had been on a walkabout involving her and her intriguing personality, which seemed to grow more beguilingly addictive with every passing minute.

'Yes,' he said automatically to whatever it was she had said—obviously a question, judging from the way she was looking at him, head tilted to one side, mouth semi-parted so that the smallest sliver of her pearl-white teeth was showing.

'Sorry?' she asked, puzzled.

'What did you say?'

'I asked you what you thought the chances are that those two girls will straighten their lives out.'

'Oh, yes! Right. To be honest, my impression was that they'd done a bunk from Manchester, found themselves in London and were realising that they'd bitten off a bit more than they could chew. I wouldn't be surprised if they started asking themselves whether going back to face irate mums and aggravating siblings mightn't be preferable to the unknown down here.'

'Mmm. I thought that too, actually. In fact...' She rummaged in her bag and extracted her notebook, which she then proceeded to peruse, frowning in concentration. 'Kate pretty much admitted that she was already thinking along those lines. I think it helps that they travelled down together. They prop each other up, whereas they might be more vulnerable if they were on their own, more of an easy target for...undesirable types...you know what I mean....'

'I do,' Franco said gravely. 'Now, what do you want to eat?' He watched her as she glanced around the pub, absent-mindedly pushing her hair behind her ears.

'Anything with chips. I'm starving.'

He fought to conceal a smile. 'Haven't had anything for the day?'

'Not much. Cereal, toast.' She leaned a little forward so that she could decipher what was written on the blackboard on the wall towards the back of the room. 'Fruit and sandwiches for lunch. Nothing since midday, though, which is probably why I'm so hungry.'

He felt a wave of laughter surge through him and he covered his mouth with one hand to stifle the sound. He knew, with unerring instinct, that laughing at her appetite was something she would not find very appealing. He suspected that she might mistakenly assume that he was sneering at her, treating her like a country bumpkin lacking in social graces.

'Are you all right?' she asked, when he was forced

to camouflage his laughter as a choking cough, which made him sound like an old man whose fifty-a-day habit was finally catching up. 'Have you got something in your throat?' She stood up and administered a resounding firm slap to his back, which propelled him forward, mostly through sheer shock.

'What are you doing?' he gasped.

'I thought you might have had something stuck in your throat.'

'What?'

'*I* don't know,' Ruth said, sitting back down and giving him a ladylike glare.

'Must have swallowed the wrong way,' he mumbled. 'Anyway, chips you say?'

'Thank you. With some fish. I see that they do haddock and chips with bread and a salad.'

'Anything else?' He stood up and turned away with an exaggeratedly grim expression, because his lips were beginning to twitch again and another of those slaps administered to his back might cause untold damage to his spine.

Ruth consulted the blackboard again while Franco watched, dumbstruck at the thought that she might actually be considering adding to what she had already ordered, but eventually shook her head in polite denial.

The pub was slowly but surely filling up. Most of the tables were now taken and the only room at the circular bar in the centre was elbow room. Ruth watched as Franco smoothly found a gap and caught the bartender's eye with the practised ease of someone for whom attracting attention was as effortless as drawing breath.

In fact, as she looked at him now, she could see that

the attention he had managed to attract was not limited to the bartender. Women had angled their bodies so that they could surreptitiously snatch a glance or two at the striking man with the pint in one hand, the glass of wine in the other, weaving his way back to the table and... Ruth thought of the image she presented and glumly acknowledged that *the stunningly sexy woman* didn't fit the bill. More likely *fetchingly homely lass*.

'Now,' he said, resuming his seat and pushing the glass of wine over to her. 'What's it to be? Your decision? In or out?'

Ruth gently twirled the glass in a circle on the table, lightly holding it by the thin stem. 'In. But...'

'But...what...?' he asked softly.

'But you put up with me if I occasionally get weepy and sentimental over some of the girls.'

'I'd be surprised if you didn't.'

She wondered whether he would have qualified that as *pleasantly* surprised. 'I'm a weepy, sentimental person at the best of times,' she said, sticking her chin out and daring him to argue the merits of that, which he didn't.

'Don't tell me that you cry at movies?'

'Loudly.'

'And lose sleep over sad stories in the press?'

'To the point of insomnia.'

'And fret if you think you've offended someone?'

'*Ad nauseam.*'

'Then we have a lot in common. I do all those things as well.'

The thought of Franco Leoni sobbing during a movie made her burst out laughing, and she threw her head back and arched into the back of the chair, wiping her eyes. He smiled at her, a long, slow smile, and the laughter dwindled from her lips. The moment of hilarity was gone, replaced by a split second's worth of devastating awareness that seemed to continue into eternity.

Eventually she dragged her eyes away from his face as a harassed waitress appeared with their food, and then the moment was gone, replaced with suitably appropriate chit-chat about their interview the evening before, and how it could be formatted into the report they were building.

Another couple of interviews with youngish girls, he said, perhaps ranging in experience from the newly arrived to the well and truly ensconced. Though those might be less tempted to pour out their hearts and souls because bitterness could be a very effective plug when it came to free speech.

Then they would interview older women, women who had started out down the road years before and ended up at its most logical destination.

'Think you can stand it?' he asked casually, as she tucked into her food, and she nodded without speaking as her mouth was full.

'I shouldn't have any more wine,' she said, when she had swallowed both food and wine.

'Goes to your head?'

'Horribly.'

'And what do you do when that happens?' He leaned forward and his eyes raked over her in a manner that was both casual and searingly intimate. 'Anything that could feed my night-time fantasies?' he murmured in a teasing, playful voice.

'Very funny,' Ruth said severely. She wondered if

he thought she was so thick that she wouldn't recognise that he was making fun of her and her outmoded approach to life, so inconsistent, she knew, with someone her age. 'Now that I've decided...' Was that quite the right phrase? Or would *been persuaded* have been more appropriate? '...to carry on, what shall we do tonight? It's nearly eight-thirty and, well, do we see whether we can do some more interviews? Or not?'

'We do.' He fished in his pocket and withdrew a crumpled-up piece of paper which he proceeded to flatten out. 'I have a couple more contact names and places that we could check out. Nothing quite as salubrious as last night's rendezvous, but then we're looking at girls who are a bit more hardened by life in the big city.'

'Where on earth do you *get* these names and places from?' Ruth asked, peering at the piece of paper.

'Having friends who work in the press can be of great help sometimes.'

He grinned and she said slowly, 'You're really enjoying all this, aren't you?'

'So far.'

'Because it makes a change?'

'Possibly,' he said, with a shrug. He drained the contents of his glass in one long gulp, deposited the glass on the table and said, 'You'll have to change. You're going to stand out in clothes like that where we're going this evening.'

'Where exactly is that?'

'It's the sort of place where good girls don't go. Which is why tonight you're going to have to look like a bad girl so that you can blend in.'

'*Look like a bad girl?*' she asked faintly, her face

registering the impossibility of achieving any such look. 'How does a person *look like a bad girl*? I haven't got that sort of face,' Ruth continued, anxiously contemplating the task and wondering whether this was another well-disguised leg-pulling exercise. 'Would I have to snarl a lot? Bare my teeth? Chew gum? I don't smoke, so that's out.'

'A simple change of outfit should do it. The sort of girls we'll be seeing will be older than the two last night, older, more experienced, and if we want to try and engage their conversation then I suggest you get rid of the buttoned-up shirt and the knee-length skirt.'

'What difference will it make?' Ruth persisted stubbornly. Her skirt, she wanted to point out, was actually a couple of inches above the knee, but he clearly hadn't noticed that.

'It'll be the difference between a possible interview and the possible giving of confidences. A fine but important line if we're to humanise this article we'll be working on.' He stood up and she hurriedly followed suit. 'So. To your place.'

'There's no need for you to come with me,' she said dubiously, eyeing the tall, masculine figure slinging on his battered tan airforce-style bomber jacket and experiencing just the smallest twinge of unease at the prospect of this man being under her roof. 'I can always meet you there...if you give me the address...'

'Absolutely no way. We'll take a taxi to your place. Where do you live?'

It's ridiculous to feel nervous, she lectured herself sternly on the drive over to the flat. It's hardly as though you haven't worked alongside the man now. And anyway, there won't be anything of the social visit about him being in the flat. He'll just be there, waiting while you change. If you change quickly enough you can leave him standing by the front door, even. Maybe. Certainly there won't be any cups of coffee being offered or *Please have a seat; I won't be a minute*.

Why had she thought that he might obligingly remain rooted to the front door while she dashed into the bedroom to change? No sooner had she unlocked the front door and pushed it open than the man was inside the flat, strolling around it with undisguised curiosity, inspecting the books on the single bookshelf over the television set, peering at the family pictures on the mantelpiece by the blocked-up fireplace.

Ruth watched from the open doorway, then she stepped inside and said sarcastically, 'Make yourself at home.'

'This isn't too bad at all, is it?' He made that sound as though his expectations of her place had run along the lines of rat-infested basement studio flat with mould-encrusted lino flooring and peeling paint on the walls.

'What had you expected?' Ruth asked, clicking shut the door and looking at him with her arms folded.

'Nothing as big as this, for a start. Flats in London aren't cheap to rent and I wouldn't have expected that you could afford a decent-sized one-bedroom place.' He looked around him in the manner of an estate agent summing up a potential property. 'With a pretty big kitchen in a respectable area.'

'Actually, Mum and Dad do help me out with the rent,' Ruth admitted.

'Ah.'

Their eyes met and she looked away, nettled by what she felt was going through his head. 'I'll just go and change,' she informed him, scuttling past him towards her bedroom.

She would show him that she wasn't the ineffectual child he seemed to think she was. She glared at her wardrobe, daring it to let her down in her moment of need, desperate to do *something*, project *some* kind of image that would blast a great big gaping hole in his preconceived ideas of her as little Miss Goody-Two-Shoes who thought that a good game of Scrabble was as exciting as sex and who couldn't even make it on her own in the Big Bad World without her parents propping her up on either side.

Useless to explain to him that her parents' financial help was something she accepted because it afforded them peace of mind rather than because she was scared of living somewhere dingier.

Her assortment of clothing was, she was forced to admit, sensible and practical rather than sexy. In the end she made do with a pair of jeans, which she omitted to cinch at the waist with a belt so that they hung low against her slender hips, exposing her belly button. She teamed these with a black and white cropped bra that revealed most of her stomach, over which she flung a cream-coloured cheesecloth shirt which looked the essence of respectability when buttoned up and twinned with one of her pleated skirts, but which reeked of wildness when left hanging open to reveal bare stomach underneath.

She gazed, wonderingly, at her reflection in the mirror and felt a surge of heady abandon.

The girl staring back at her, with the make-up and

the mascara and the figure-hugging, body-exposing clothes, was not Ruth Jacobs. Oh, no. The girl staring back at her was someone wild and sexy and utterly daring.

Well, just for the night anyway.

Ruth grinned at her reflection and stuck her tongue out, then she took a deep breath and went outside.

Franco, staring out of the bay window to the pool of illuminated pavement outside, into which came and went the hurrying figures of people on their way to homes, families, lovers, turned around at the sound of the bedroom door opening.

He'd been thinking how right she was. He *was* having a good time, chasing behind this story with the sort of fervour that reminded him of himself ten years ago, before the acquisition of money had jaded his palate and turned his enthusiasm into dry-tongued cynicism.

And he had to admit that having her along for the ride made things infinitely spicier. Looking at her, enjoying the way she aroused his imagination, succumbing to the novelty of having to take cold showers every night because the slightest passing thought of her turned effortlessly into a network of complex fantasies that would not have gone amiss on the pages of a men's magazine. Yes, he had to admit that his tired soul had been re-ignited in more ways than one.

Even so, it had still surprised him how disproportionately thrown he had been by her suggestion of leaving. He didn't care to question the insanity of his response.

'Well?'

He realised that he had been staring at her. For how

long? He couldn't have said. He knew that his mouth was hanging open, though, and he shut it.

Bad girl. In the low-slung jeans and the small top with enough bare skin peeping through the crack in the unbuttoned blouse to make any red-blooded man need several cold showers on the trot. And, worse than that, there was still enough of the blushingly shy Ruth Jacobs evident to make the picture she presented more hauntingly erotic.

He felt a steady flush creep into his face and he hurriedly cleared his throat.

'Definitely more of a...suitable...suitably appropriate...look. Yes.'

'I haven't overdone it, have I?' Ruth enquired anxiously, peering down at herself, twisting so that she could try and achieve an overall view of herself.

Her fair hair swung over her face and Franco savoured the image she presented of slender, unconscious beauty, moving with the natural grace of youth. Her breasts, he saw, were much bigger than they appeared beneath her normal garb of buttoned-up blouse. The close-cropped top barely provided restraint, and they bounced gently as she inspected herself. He could feel himself begin to perspire and he cleared his throat nosily in an attempt to take control of the situation before he found himself hunting down the nearest shower.

'Not at all. Now, shall we head off?'

Ruth straightened immediately.

His voice was curt, and when she glanced at his face she could see that his expression matched his tone of voice.

Of course she had overdone it. She had been stupidly trying to prove something and now resembled a clown of sorts, right down to the ridiculous clothing and the painted face. As some token gesture to modesty she slung on her denim jacket, so that at least the top half of her body was covered, and then trailed behind him, hovering self-consciously in the background while he summoned a taxi.

She noticed that he barely looked at her for the duration of the drive, which covered a honeycomb of unrecognisable streets and alleys to emerge finally in a long, narrow road which was erratically lit and sported a selection of women lurking in the shadows. Against the walls, in doorways. Singly or else in twos and threes.

Ruth's heart dropped. This was very different from what she had encountered the night before. There was something gritty and depressing and scary about this scene. She drew the jacket a bit tighter around her.

'This'll do,' Franco said, staring impassively out of the window. 'Okay?' he asked in a low voice, when they were out of the taxi, and she gulped and nodded. 'Don't look so terrified.' He walked up to a twosome, who smiled invitingly and told him they were available for some action, whatever he wanted, to which he replied that they were looking for a woman by the name of Mattie.

The process was repeated over and over, until they finally hit jackpot. They were pointed to a building which resembled a warehouse primed for demolition and were told to wait a few minutes because she was with a client.

'How do you know she'll see us?' Ruth whispered, squinting at the black doorway. Ever so often a car would cruise by very slowly. Sometimes there was the sound of doors being opened and closed, then the swish of tyres as the car slipped away. Ruth heard it all like background noise but she couldn't bring herself to look around.

'We don't. In which case we'll just have to try our luck with some of the others. But I think she'll see us. I was given her name by a guy called Robbie, well-known veteran reporter who mostly sits behind the desk now, but years ago he helped her with some police aggro and she's always been grateful to him for that. Now and then they even meet up for a drink. He takes her out for the occasional meal at Christmas time, says that it makes her feel like a worthwhile human being.'

They waited in silence. Ruth had become so accustomed to the slow purr of cars breaking the ominous hush of the dark street that she barely noticed when a car stopped and a man rolled down his window and asked. 'How much, love? When you're through with the next one?'

CHAPTER FOUR

'ARE you *sure* you're all right? Perhaps we ought to go to the doctor…' It was the fourth time in the space of half an hour that Ruth had asked the question, but as she gazed anxiously at the bruised fist resting on his thigh she felt the same mixture of shocked dismay and guilt. 'This is all my fault, isn't it?' she said miserably, thinking aloud rather than posing a question. 'If I hadn't donned this…' she glanced down at herself with scathing disgust '…ridiculous garb, none of this would have happened.' She ran a finger gently along the scraped knuckle and winced on his behalf. 'Is it very awful?'

'Nothing that I can't handle,' Franco informed her stoically. It had taken ten minutes of solid walking and frantic searching before they had managed to find a taxi, during which time he had been pleasantly warmed by her charming show of concern for his welfare.

Whom did it hurt if he had exaggerated a minor scrape into something worryingly more painful?

'I should never have worn this stupid outfit,' Ruth repeated, hunkering down into her jacket as though endeavouring to bury her way through it and vanish completely.

'Will you stop saying that!'

'How can I? I shudder to think what kind of sight I made if that man…that *foul, disgusting, revolting* man thought that I was...available for sale.' She made a choking, disgusted sound under her breath and gazed at her co-passenger in the car with stormy grey eyes. 'I have *never* attracted that *sort of attention* in my life before!' She sounded as horrified as she felt. Her pale blonde hair caught the passing lights and, when it did, shimmered like spun gold. She flicked the spun gold carelessly behind her shoulders and then irritably stuffed it into the back of her jacket.

'You can't be *that* unfamiliar with attention from the opposite sex,' Franco said heavily.

'How much further is it to your house? I did a first aid course when I was at school. I should be able to patch you up in no time at all.'

'Forget the hand,' he answered irritably, not caring for the fact that his usually captivating personality was in competition with a mildly swollen bone on his right hand. 'You haven't answered my question.'

'What question?' She looked up from her frowning inspection of his hand and favoured him with a long, beautifully guileless grey stare.

'I *said*,' Franco repeated, hanging onto his patience, 'you must be quite accustomed to attracting male attention.' He moved his fist from his left thigh to his right, just in case she avoided taking the conversational path he wanted by becoming sidetracked by his now virtually pain-free knuckle. That way, if she was so damned interested in inspecting the offending part of his body, she would have to lean over him which, regretfully, he doubted she would do.

'Well, I haven't got a boyfriend at the moment...' In the darkness of the taxi he could glimpse the faint blush that swept into her cheeks. 'I believe you asked me that question already,' she said, making him feel uncomfortably like a bore.

'Actually, I *wasn't asking you about whether or not you're involved*,' he said, with the bewildering feeling that he had been walking down a straightforward street that had suddenly revealed itself to be a honeycomb of back alleys and side paths. 'I was merely remarking that a girl like you must be accustomed to men staring at her.'

'A girl like me? What kind of girl would *that* be?' Her voice had become frosty with disapproval.

'I'm not implying that you're *any kind of girl* or at least not the kind of girl that you're implying...*I'm* implying...God.' He raked his good hand through his hair. 'You're making me tongue-tied!' He automatically grinned a sexy, rueful grin, but its impact was lost as she was staring fixedly through the car window.

'*Where* did you say you lived? I don't recognise this area at all.' She felt a slight tremor of nerves and wondered whether it had been such a clever idea to offer to help him. He could just have easily have cleaned himself up, but why would he do that when she had rushed in with her exclamations of horror and sympathy and her saint-like insistence that he take her immediately to the nearest first aid kit? Which, he had returned with alacrity, was in the bathroom cabinet of his house.

If she had been thinking with her head and on her feet, instead of with her soft, emotional heart, she would have briskly sent him on his way and headed home to recover from her ordeal.

But guilt had stopped her. She had unwittingly provoked an inappropriate response from a kerb-crawler and Franco had been swift in dealing with the situation. No attempt at an explanation had been made. No sooner had the words left the driver's mouth than he had been yanked unceremoniously from his car, punched even more unceremoniously in his jaw and then flung back into the offending vehicle with a string of abuse, the memory of which was enough to make her go red.

Was it any wonder, she thought now, fighting down her ridiculous surge of nervous tension, that she had felt guilty about the whole thing?

'Chelsea. Just off the King's Road, as a matter of fact. You must have been there since you arrived in London...'

'Oh, yes,' Ruth said vaguely. 'I *did* go shopping there a couple of times, but it was a bit pricey for my liking. The last time my mum came down for a couple of days I took her there, but she spent most of the time telling me that she couldn't imagine *what section of the human population some of those garments in those strange little shops catered for.*

A look of mischievous amusement crossed Ruth's face. 'She can be a *little* old-fashioned. Poor dear.' She looked with mock gravity at Franco's rapt face. 'She *has* led a rather sheltered life, you know, what with being married to a vicar... Thank goodness she has me to snap her out of it!'

In the silvery light of the car he caught the wicked self-ironic expression on her face and they grinned at one another, momentarily delighted to have found themselves so perfectly attuned on the same wavelength.

Ruth was the first to look away. For some reason

her heart had begun to beat wildly, and maintaining his even, teasingly amused gaze had proved impossible. 'What are *your* parents like?' she asked, licking her lips and struggling not to wilt under eyes that were suddenly strangely disconcerting.

'*Were,*' Franco corrected. 'My father died eight years ago and my mother died three years ago this December.'

'I'm so sorry,' Ruth said impulsively. 'Still, how proud they must have been of you! You've done so much! Built businesses and companies and empires! The lot!'

'Actually,' he said drily, 'my father had done very well for himself on similar lines, so my accumulation of money was not as impressive a feat as it might have been. Not,' he added swiftly, 'that they *weren't* proud of me. Of course they were.

'They were mildly disappointed, though, that I never did the expected thing and married and produced a horde of children. My mother had always longed for a big family, but there were problems and, as it turned out, she was lucky to have had me. But you can imagine the combination of Italian and Irish.' He sighed with heartfelt regret. 'Yes, they would have liked to have seen their only son settled.'

Ruth had a sudden, intriguing image of a settled Franco Leoni, married with lots of miniature Franco Leonis running about. Franco Leoni and babies. Babies and Franco Leoni. Her mouth became dry and her erratic heartbeat did a few flips and carried on at a slightly more accelerated rate.

'Shall I tell you something?' he said, in a faintly

surprised voice. 'I've never come close to telling anyone what I've just told you.'

'Why? Are you ashamed of the fact that your parents would have wanted you to settle down and raise a family?' Personally, she couldn't think of anything more pleasurable than settling down with the man you loved and having a family. A nice, large family in a rambling, cosy house where there was always the sound of laughter and music and chatting, where problems were aired and where everyone lent a helping hand to everyone else. She gave a little sigh and half smiled.

'Where are you?' he asked curiously, and she snapped back to the present with a small start.

'I beg your pardon?' she asked, blinking away the pleasant daydream.

'For a minute there I lost you. You just suddenly vanished into a world of your own.'

What he didn't voice was the depth of his frustration as her expression had grown wistful and she had dreamily succumbed to some magical picture in her mind. What he could barely admit to himself was the sharp stab of jealousy as he had sourly surmised that the one thing most likely to put that goofy, happy expression on her face was the thought of some man. Was there someone hovering in the background? Someone perhaps, whom she was not technically *dating* but who still had the power to render her doe-eyed merely at the thought of him?

'Oh, just thinking.' She gave him one of those bland, vague smiles and he frowned at her.

'What about?'

'Nothing in particular.' Her shrug was the physical equivalent to the vague smile and his frown deepened.

'How is it that you never settled down?' Ruth asked, in her soft, direct voice.

With a jolt of awareness he realised that, for all her blushing and ultra-feminine appeal, she was not in the slightest intimidated by him. He was one of the most eligible bachelors in London, if not *the* most eligible, and was respected in every corner of the business community and feared in quite a few. Women flocked around him without encouragement and he had become accustomed to dismissing them with little more than a glance if he so desired. People, he knew, tiptoed around him because of the power and status he wielded. No one, but *no one*, had *ever* asked him why he was still unmarried.

'I mean,' she continued slowly, 'there must be women who find you appealing.'

'Yes, I suppose out there, somewhere, there lurks one or two who don't run screaming from my presence,' he said in an amused, wondering voice.

'I'm sorry. I didn't mean... I just meant that... well, you're... successful, self-employed... and... and...'

'And...?' he encouraged silkily, enjoying this delicious moment, praying that the taxi would linger so as not to spoil it by arriving at their destination with unwanted haste.

'And not ugly,' she said in a rush. 'But really it's absolutely none of my business.'

'Does the classification of *not ugly* count as a compliment?' he asked, with a crooked smile, and Ruth could have groaned aloud in sheer despair.

She had never been the most verbal, gregarious person on the face of the earth, but neither had she ever been quite so stultifyingly gauche as she was in the presence of this man. He had the mysterious power of rendering her almost completely speechless.

'I'm s-sorry...' she stammered. Again. But was thankfully spared a lengthy examination of her clumsy vocabulary by the arrival of the taxi at their destination.

She had expected a house. Out in the country it was a general rule of thumb that the bigger and grander the house and the larger and more impressive the plot of land, the wealthier the inhabitants.

Instead, she found herself peering out at a dubiously large Victorian building which had clearly been sectioned off into apartments. The street itself was divinely quiet, and carried the unmistakable smell of the privacy only vast money could purchase in the heart of London, but she was still surprised at Franco Leoni living in a flat.

'I own a rather grand collection of bricks and mortar out in the wilds of Dorset,' he said into her ear, reading her mind. She heard the smile in his voice and realised that yet again her every passing thought had been displayed on her face.

'How does your hand feel?' she asked, slipping out of the taxi and ignoring the taxi driver's curious examination of her attire in the light of where he was depositing them.

Franco very nearly confessed that he had forgotten all about his so-called injury; then he remembered that the only reason she was here with him now was *because* of his hand. The prospect of her vanishing blithely away in the taxi if he informed her that it felt as right as rain was a possibility he refused to consider.

'Still a bit tender,' he murmured, without a twinge of guilt. He bent over, paid the taxi driver, who was voluble in his gratitude for what had clearly been an over-the-top tip, and then nodded at the block of flats. 'Home sweet home.'

'You mean, *home sweet home, mark one.*'

'Mark three, actually,' he said, extracting a key from his pocket and slotting it neatly into the door. 'I also own another place in Italy.'

'Of course,' Ruth said with gentle sarcasm, turning to look at him fully, 'I'm now beginning to understand how it is that you could buy a company for fun...' She smiled and then turned away to inspect her surroundings.

If, Franco thought wryly, his enthralling personality had taken a back seat to a minuscule bruise on his hand, then it was clear that he had been completely forgotten, lock, stock and barrel, in her absorption with her surroundings.

She audibly gasped as they entered the spacious, heavily modernised hall, which was really presided over by a uniformed porter.

While George, the porter, handed over mail, and pleasantries were exchanged with the comfortable familiarity of two people who see one another daily and go back some way, Ruth stared around her with open-mouthed fascination.

Far from being dark, poky and irremediably Victorian, which had been her expectation, the interior of the grand, renovated house was light and spacious. The cream carpet was thick piled and the paintings on the walls were tasteful and modern. On one wall, stretching all the way up the winding stairwell and breathtaking in its sheer size, was a complex mural that appeared to depict a series of interconnecting mythical creatures. Chandeliers shed a mellow glow and plants were decorously placed here and there so that the overall impression was of space and grandeur.

'Shall we take the lift?' he asked, and she dragged her gaze away from the mural.

'There are *lifts*?'

'Three. One for each of the residents.'

'But surely it won't take long to walk to your flat...?'

'In which case, we follow the winding road until we can't go any further.'

On the way, he explained the mural to her, pointing out some of the well-known mythological figures and most of the more obscure ones. Her child-like enthusiasm invigorated him in a way he would not have dreamt imaginable. He had the empowering feeling that with this chit of a girl at his side he could accomplish anything. How foolish could one grown man get? he wondered.

As they neared the top floor, Ruth felt a sense of apprehension begin to creep over the light-hearted frivolity that had taken them over.

The same plush cream carpet had followed them up the elegant curved staircase, but as soon as he opened the door to his apartment she was confronted with a dose of unbridled masculinity.

Gleaming wooden flooring replaced the thick-piled carpet. As she followed him inside she noticed, in passing, that most of the furniture was solid and exquisitely made but unabashedly modern. Sleek lines, unfettered designs and an absence of anything that was fussy.

'The country house is so full of antiques,' he said, reading her mind again, 'that I decided to go for a totally twentieth-century look. What do you think?'

Ruth paused to glance into the sitting room, where the colours were pale off-whites, creams, with hints of deeper hues in the lush carpets strewn liberally across the floor.

'It's fabulous.' She looked around her and blurted out, a little sheepishly, 'I never knew a Victorian house could look this...this *modern*. The vicarage is Victorian, but...' she smiled fondly at the thought '...absolutely cluttered. Dad's hopeless when it comes to sticking things in drawers, and Mum's almost as bad. This apartment looks as though no one lives in it from one day to the next.'

She gave him a brief, questioning look, and he mildly acknowledged that, once again, his privacy had somehow been infringed.

'I travel a lot,' he found himself saying. 'In fact, as I've mentioned to you previously, I'm out of the country more than I'm in it. And, when I *am* here, I tend to socialise out of the house...'

'Why is that?' She took a few curious steps into the sitting room and looked around her.

'What? Why is what?'

'Why is it that you don't socialise here, when it's obviously huge enough to entertain any number of people? I mean...' She opened her mouth to say something, then promptly shut it again.

'Carry on, carry on,' he told her irritably.

'Nothing. Where have you got your first aid box?' She glanced at her watch, which instantly made him scowl.

'What were you going to say?' he demanded, barring her exit from the room.

'I just wondered whether you never brought anyone back here. There seem to be no feminine touches at all...no flowers in vases or soft cushions...' She looked up at him with interest.

'*Flowers in vases? Soft cushions?* I don't think I've ever dated a woman who was interested in flower-arranging or cushion colour co-ordination.'

'Of course not,' Ruth said quickly, regretting the directness of her question. She could tell from the expression on his face that he was rapidly becoming fed up with her.

'Anyway, I don't care for the thought of some woman spending too much time in my apartment. Naturally I...entertain them here...but I always make it perfectly clear that traipsing in with little jars of female unguents won't do. That's only one short step away from them attempting to make their mark on what they see, which is one even shorter step away from them attempting to do the same to *me*.'

It occurred to Ruth that he had had no problem letting *her* in, listening to *her* remarks about the decor, and was suddenly deflated to realise why. Because he was so uninterested in her as a woman that whether she nosed around his place and proffered her opinion or not was of no concern to him.

'If we could sort your hand out?' she said a little coolly. 'It's late, and I really must be on my way home. I'm whacked.' She yawned in a convincing attempt to provide further evidence of her exhaustion, and in fact, when she had consulted her watch, it was a great deal later than she had imagined.

'In the bathroom,' he said, watching her. He turned away abruptly and headed past a couple more rooms, all equally clinically beautiful as the first, and flung open the door to his bedroom, upon which Ruth halted in her tracks.

'This is your bedroom,' she stated flatly. There could be no mistaking it.

It was dominated by a commanding king-sized bed with an imperious wrought-iron bedhead. The wardrobes were sleekly wooden, and obviously designed and made by the same person who had been responsible for much of the furniture, but there were black iron details picked out in their detail that rendered the final appearance harshly masculine. A tapestry depicting a hunting scene hung over the bed, its rich colours bringing life to the aggressive monochrome scheme. The throw on the bed was black, with ivory lines in abstract patterns, and the pillowcases on the pillows were quite clearly silk, or satin—one black, one ivory-coloured.

It was a room that breathed heavy sensuality. A room that instantly brought on an attack of nerves as Ruth peered around her with alarm.

'Come in, come in,' he commanded, walking towards a door that was old wood halfway up and intricate stained glass for the remainder. 'Don't just stand hovering by the door!'

Ruth cautiously entered the den of iniquity, treading with the delicate hesitancy of someone crossing a minefield. She would get this hand-fixing business over in rapid time and clear out before her nerves got the better of her and induced some horrendously embarrassing Victorian swooning fit.

'Sit on the bed,' he called out, halting her in mid-step. 'More comfortable there. I'll bring all the stuff out.'

'It's just a bruise!' Ruth joked weakly to the stained glass. 'No need for that handy vial of anaesthetic!'

He poked his head around the door and shot her a wicked grin. 'I'll just put it back, then, shall I?' He disappeared once more for a few seconds, then emerged with an assortment of things in both hands.

'This is the first aid kit?' Ruth enquired dubiously, shifting back to accommodate the sudden depression in the mattress as he sat down next to her.

She removed her jacket and then examined the sum total of his bathroom cabinet. Some cotton wool, some antiseptic liquid that appeared to have turned a strange, off-putting colour, several assorted plasters, none of which were much good for anything but a minute nick, and, mysteriously, some talcum powder.

'I never said it was comprehensive.'

'Well, it'll have to do.' She took his hand and felt a flutter of awareness as she rested it on her leg, splayed out so that she could examine the bruises, three in all. 'It's really not bad at all, is it?' she mused, head downturned.

For a few seconds Franco was caught between boasting about the fact that the man's face would be looking a damn sight worse than his hand was and assuming the air of a wounded martyr, appealing to the fair maiden for sympathy. He opted for the macho image and said smugly, 'Not bad, considering I probably put the bastard out of action for a few days.'

'You men always think you're so clever, sorting things out with a fight.' She raised her eyes to his and smiled. 'I'm teasing. Actually, you were very gallant. Thank you.' She returned to what she was doing and he felt a wash of unparalleled warmth rush through his body like a tidal wave.

With a mixture of amusement and horror he realised that his body was reacting in its own inimitable fashion, pushing against his trousers, and he shifted his body, crossing his legs awkwardly.

While she worked away on his hand he watched, and gave free rein to a tingling array of erotic fantasies because, with his erection hard and throbbing, thinking chaste thoughts seemed fairly pointless.

'Am I hurting you?' she asked, dabbing the grazed knuckles with the antiseptic ointment.

'No, but you probably could.'

'Sorry?' She looked up and he flushed darkly, quite startled at what had emerged from his mouth.

'What I meant was that you probably *could* hurt me if this ointment wasn't completely ineffective because it's probably been in the cupboard for ten years,' he improvised.

'It *does* look a bit dodgy, doesn't it? Why have you brought talcum powder?'

'Just in case.'

'In case of what?'

'Just in case you wanted to mop things up.'

'Oh. Well, I don't think it'll be necessary.'

'You've missed a bit...there.' He pointed to a scratch that was almost invisible to the naked eye, and as she bent to squint at it, braiding her hair in a makeshift plait to keep it away from her face, he was afforded the sweetest sight he could have imagined possible. The tempting indentation of cleavage, separating the full swell of breasts.

She held his hand between hers, her fingers soft and gentle, and stroked the spot he had pointed out.

'I don't see anything.'

'Are you sure?' His voice was rough and unsteady. Rough and unsteady enough for her to look at him, her hand stilling as she read the flaring attraction in his eyes.

'I think it's time I left,' she said. A similar flush was spreading over her, and her voice sounded wobbly and high pitched.

'Of course,' he said gruffly. 'You need to get to bed.' Neither of them moved a muscle. The silence in the room was now resounding. In her own ears, she seemed to hear the booming of her heart. She had never felt anything as powerful as this. The heat in his eyes scorched her. She felt, literally, as though she was burning up.

'I...I...' she began, unable to rip her gaze away from his.

'You have the most exquisite skin.' He lifted one hand and stroked it. It felt like satin beneath the sensitive pads of his fingers. He watched her pupils dilate, saw the very slight flaring of her nostrils, the fleeting drop of her eyelashes as his finger touched her face, and the impact those physical responses had on him was the equivalent of a powerful electric charge. She tilted her head back a millimetre and her breathing became more ragged.

Looking at her, Franco felt as though he had never before experienced the pull of true passion. It was like being hit, full-on, by a freight train.

Her lips parted, and he leant forward and gently touched her mouth with his, tracing the contours of her pink lips with his tongue, and Ruth gave a moan of desire.

The force of wanting him was so tremendous that she abandoned herself to it. She pulled his head towards her, melting exquisitely as his gentle mouth became hard and hungry and the kiss deepened into a wild, mutual exploration with tongues. She was gasping as his hands found her shoulders and tugged down the lightweight shirt.

Pure sensation seemed to have taken her over, like an alien force, rendering her power to reason completely useless. It was as though her brain had been temporarily switched off at the mains.

She closed her eyes and arched back, supporting herself on her hands. Her legs couldn't be still. They fidgeted of their own accord, lubricated with the feminine moisture oozing like honey from between her thighs.

He leaned to kiss the slim column of her neck and her head fell backwards, her braid coming undone. With his hand, he roughly unravelled what remained tied back and pushed her up the bed, moving with her so that their bodies remained no more than an inch or two apart.

As the palm of his hand pressed between her legs, a firm, moving, rousing pressure through the thick fabric of her denim jeans, she released a long, shaky moan. He undid the button, tugged down the zip and then slid his hand down beneath the tiny underwear, pushing his finger against the pulsating bud of desire and inducing a sharp, sweet feeling of satisfaction.

His finger moved and rotated and she fumbled, eyes still closed, with her tight, cropped top, finally pushing it up and over her breasts in sheer frustration. Her nipples were large and swollen with excitement, and as his finger kept moving against that magical place and his mouth covered the throbbing tips of her breasts, she could no longer contain her mounting need for fulfilment. The thrill of orgasm ripped through her body and she felt herself tense as the waves of pleasure rolled over her.

As she turned to him, appalled at the wanton abandon of her response, wanting only to touch him as he had touched her, the telephone rang.

One loud, shrill summons, followed by another, and another.

'Answer it,' she said, her face stamped with mounting horror as she contemplated what had just taken place between them.

'No way.' He pulled her towards him, but she pushed herself away.

'No!' she cried wildly. She scuttled away from him, rapidly trying to put herself in order and avoid his eyes. 'I shouldn't have... Oh, dear Lord...what have I done?'

'Ruth!'

'Please!' She was almost weeping with shame. 'I'm sorry. Please!'

The phone had stopped and she ran, as fast as she could, past a bewildered George as if the devil was after her.

CHAPTER FIVE

FRANCO had been utterly sure that Ruth would stop working alongside him. The certainty, as he had lain on the bed, cursing himself volubly and aloud for his inept, stupid, thoughtless and downright juvenile handling of this shy woman-child, had twisted in his gut like a blunt knife.

Eight days later and here she was. She hadn't jacked in the assignment, as he had feared, and he could only assume that some little voice in her head had preached to her the values of maturity which would be exemplified if she refused to allow their all too brief moment of exquisite carnal pleasure to come between her and her job.

Now, with their last evening together drawing to a close at a little after midnight, he could feel a disturbing sense of panic that when they parted company now, it would be for good.

He stared at her broodingly, watching how she handled the woman sitting next to her, asking questions without stammering, nodding, murmuring sympathetically now and again, leaning forward to say something so that her hair brushed the sides of her face. She had grown in confidence with every passing day, but far from diminishing her appeal it had added to it.

When the woman finally stood up and took one last long drag on her cigarette, he went through the motions of shaking her hand and thanking her for her time, but he could barely keep the agitation out of his body.

'Do you think we've managed to get enough for the article?' Ruth asked, slipping on her denim jacket.

'I should think so.'

She yawned, and he tried to suppress a childish desire to insist that she give him her full attention. She wasn't even looking at him when she spoke. In fact, she hadn't *looked* at him since the little incident in his apartment. Not once had she mentioned it, but he knew that she hadn't put it to the back of her mind.

The awareness was there all too powerfully in those carefully averted eyes, the surreptitious sidelong glances when she thought he was looking elsewhere, the way she shifted her body away from him whenever he got too close to her, as though she thought that proximity might lead to combustion.

He was experienced enough to recognise all those little give-away signals that told him just how much he still excited her. Unfortunately, he was powerless to do anything about it. His attempts to tease her into relaxing were met with a blank politeness that had driven him crazy.

Now, she was getting ready to go, sticking her little notepad into her bag, checking her jacket pockets, the way she did every night, to make sure that her house keys were tucked away safely in the inner pocket on the inside. In a minute she would get irritated with her hair and shove it into the back of the jacket.

He felt as though he knew her intimately and, worse, still wanted to find out more. Everything, in fact.

Panic was burgeoning into desperation. It was an

emotion so alien to him that he could hardly cope with it.

When had he *ever* been desperate about any woman? His repertoire of emotions when it came to the opposite sex ranged widely from desire to mild curiosity, but certainly never *desperation*.

'Fancy a nightcap?' he asked lightly, slinging on his battered jacket. 'Little celebration to mark the completion of what we set out to do?'

'No, thanks.' She yawned and shoved her hair into the back of the jacket. 'I'm very tired.'

The response, expected though it had been, was still unbelievably maddening.

Begging, he told himself grimly, was an avenue he had no intention of exploring. He could no more beg for a woman than he could swim twice round the world. In fact, swimming twice round the world was probably the easier option.

'What shall I do with all the information we've compiled?' she asked, half turning to him, though still, he noticed, not actually looking at him. 'I could transcribe it onto disk over the weekend. My handwriting is hardly legible!' She pushed open the door of the café and then paused outside for a few seconds, looking around her, getting her bearings.

'Hmm. The information. Good point.' The wind whipped up a bit and he zipped up his jacket, pulling the collar up to warm his face. 'You look as though you're freezing,' he said. 'Have my jacket.'

'No! Don't be silly! I'll be fine once I get into a cab.' She turned and stretched out her hand, which was trembling. 'So it's goodbye, then.'

Ruth smiled at him. The stiff wind had flicked

strands of hair out from the jacket, whipping them across her face so she was forced to gather them up with one hand and then hold them in place.

Thank goodness it was dark. Could he see the tears gathering in the corners of her eyes? Could he see the trembling of her outstretched hand? If he did, she hoped that he would put that down to the cold and not to the dreadful sinking feeling that was pouring through her system like poison.

Of course it was a tremendous relief that they would be parting company. She had tried her very hardest to shove the memory of that humiliating night to the back of her mind, to tell herself that *these things happened*, but it hadn't worked. She had not been able to look him in the face, and it had taken every last ounce of courage to survive the past week and a half.

Once she hopped into the cab and sped away she doubted that she would ever see him again. He hadn't made much of an appearance at the company in the past and he was unlikely to in the future. If anything, her presence there would be enough to ensure his absence.

It hadn't been lost on her that for the past week he had done his best to be kind to her, cracking jokes, teasing her, gamely going along with the pretence that nothing had happened, but she wasn't a fool. He felt sorry for the poor little vicar's daughter who was obviously as well versed in the games adults play as she was in nuclear physics. Which was not at all.

'About all that information...' he said thoughtfully, as they briskly began to cover ground out into the more populated streets, where finding a taxi might pose less of a problem. 'No point transcribing the lot onto disk. For starters, it'll take you for ever.'

'No, it won't. Honestly. I'm quite a good typist.'

'How much have you actually got?'

'Quite a bit, as a matter of fact,' she admitted, panting as she tried to keep up with his much longer strides. 'I had no idea how much note-taking I'd done until a couple of days ago when I gathered it all together.'

'As I thought,' he said, trying to keep a note of crowing triumph out of his voice. 'Reams of information. Far easier if I sift through it first and highlight the important areas. *Then* you can transcribe it to take in to work.'

'Okay,' she said easily. 'Shall I get a courier to take it to your office on Monday?'

He appeared to give this a bit of thought. ''No,' he finally said, drawing out the single syllable so that it reverberated with sincere regret that he couldn't be more accommodating. 'Don't forget, time is of the essence if we're to get this out for the next issue, or at the very least the issue after. I'll come over to your place tomorrow evening, let's say around seven? Seven-thirty?' He had spotted a taxi and was flagging it down.

'My place?' Ruth gulped, and with the best will in the world couldn't keep the tremor of trepidation out of her voice.

'Don't put yourself out by cooking anything elaborate. Just something simple, or I could bring a takeaway…' He had pulled open the door to the taxi and was shovelling her inside. 'I'll get another taxi,' he informed her, leaning into the cab. 'So, that's settled, then, is it? Your place tomorrow. Takeaway? Or will you rustle something up?'

'Well...' she began desperately. Visions of any such scenario transpiring had not occurred to her. Consequently, she had no weapons at hand with which to deal with it.

'Honestly, Ruth, pasta will be great.' Before she could frame an answer to that self-imposed invitation, he had turned away and was rattling her address to the taxi driver, then he gave her a brief salute, nodded, and said, 'See you tomorrow, then.'

'Yes, but...' Her words were lost in the heavy slam of the door and then the taxi was pulling away from the kerb and Franco, as she looked back, was a rapidly diminishing figure, before disappearing altogether as the car rounded a corner.

She was dimly aware of having been railroaded into something, but then decided that she was being fanciful. What incentive did Franco Leoni have to railroad her into anything? His primary concern was for the magazine, and he was right. They couldn't afford to sit around, and if he sifted through all her transcripts tomorrow then she would have all of Sunday to type up the relevant information.

So why, she wondered, did she spend the whole of Saturday feverishly buying food and tidying her little flat and generally acting as though his casual visit, arranged out of necessity rather than choice, was *a date*?

His suggestion of a simple pasta meal had been the starting point for one of her specialities, a prawn and tomato dish, lathered in a rich, creamy sauce, which was excellent with penne pasta and asparagus. Going strictly in accordance with her own appetite, she made sufficient to feed a small army.

It was only when the cooking had been accomplished, and she stood back to survey her handiwork, that a sudden, unappealing thought occurred to her.

Franco had mentioned, in passing—she couldn't remember exactly *when*—that he disliked women fussing around him. She wondered, with a groan of despair, whether he might read all the wrong things into what for her had been doing something she basically enjoyed. Would he imagine that she was trying to impress him with her culinary skills? Ingratiate herself under his skin?

Once the notion had taken root, it grew with remarkable speed. By the time six-thirty had rolled around, Ruth's imagination had leapt ahead to a scenario that involved Franco inspecting her lavish offerings with contempt and then leaving as quickly as his feet could take him, forgetting all about her transcripts in the process, and having to bellow up to her to fling them down.

To compensate for the meal, she opted for the least attractive clothing in her wardrobe. A pair of green chinos that were a size too big for her and consequently made her look ridiculously thin and unfeminine and an off-white shirt that had belonged to her father before she had decided to appropriate it for her own use years previously.

The shirt hid everything and the trousers made her look like a boy. In fact, the whole get-up was eminently satisfactory, given that she wanted to imply to her uninvited guest that his presence was something she could take or leave, that she had certainly gone to no trouble on his behalf, and that the abundance of food was more to do with her own hearty appetite than it was to do with impressing him.

By the time the doorbell rang at precisely seven-fifteen, Ruth had collated every single piece of paperwork and had stacked it with mathematical precision in the middle of the coffee table in her tiny sitting room. Even someone with appalling vision would not have missed the telling bundle.

'For you,' were his opening words.

He was dressed as casually as she was, though his uniform of jeans, which he had adopted for their nightly meetings, had been replaced by dark grey cotton trousers and a grey and black striped polo shirt, just visible beneath his jacket.

'You shouldn't have,' Ruth said automatically, taking the bottle of wine from him and thinking, dubiously, that she was less than grateful for the gesture, though she knew that it stemmed from nothing more than politeness.

''Course I should. I've disturbed your weekend. Made you rearrange your plans, most probably.' He paused, and then added casually, 'Have I? I hope not.'

'Oh, nothing that I can't arrange for another evening,' she answered vaguely, stepping aside to let him enter and then shutting the door behind him.

Her cagey reply, Franco thought with a twinge of irritation, was not exactly an auspicious start to the evening, but he would overlook it, skirt round the temptation to pry further, until he elicited a response that was more to his satisfaction. It was just ridiculously good to see her again.

'Smells good in here.' He sniffed the air appreciatively while divesting himself of his jacket. 'You haven't put yourself to any trouble, have you?'

'No more than I would have for anyone coming over for a meal, even if it *is* a working meal.' She took his jacket, placed it on the hook on the wall by the front door and headed towards the bundle of paperwork.

'Aren't you going to offer me a drink?' He reached for the bottle of wine. 'Point me in the direction of a corkscrew and I'll pour us both a glass.' He didn't wait for an answer. Instead, he spun round on his heels, and she hurried in front of him before he could get to the kitchen and start making himself at home, rooting through her drawers in search of a corkscrew, peering into her cupboards in his hunt for two wine glasses.

'Give it to me,' she said breathlessly. 'You can wait in the sitting room. In fact, you could start having a look at my notes.' If she lingered in the kitchen long enough he should have ample time to flick through what she had written, which would speed the evening up no end.

He seemed to have taken over her small flat with his presence and her hands were shaking as she tried to manipulate the wretched corkscrew. Eventually she managed to pop the cork out and she tipped a generous glassful into two water goblets, which were all that she possessed that remotely resembled wine glasses. Similar shape, loosely speaking, although, she noted wryly, they held considerably more. She would have to take her time with hers or her brain would be further addled.

She returned to the sitting room to find him poring

over sheets of paper. Very businesslike, very promising, very *not* a social visit.

'Ah, glad you came.' He patted a space next to him on the sofa just as she was about to hand him his glass and retreat to the furthest corner of the room. 'You were right about your handwriting. Very difficult to read. I'm afraid you're going to have to decipher some of these squiggles for me.'

Caught on the hop, Ruth hovered uncertainly for a few seconds, then she handed him the wine glass. He beamed encouragingly at her and patted the vacant space a little more firmly.

'What, for instance, does *this* say? It looks as though something small and eight-legged decided to go for a walk across the page.'

Ruth scuttled around the table and perched next to him, peering at the paper.

'Oh, that's a word-for-word account of the conversation we had with Amanda? Do you remember Amanda?'

'Short spiky hair? Bad complexion? Fidgeted a lot?'

'Yes, that one.' She rattled off what was on the page, bending slightly across him.

'And what about this?' He jabbed another page, just as she was about to pull away.

'Here, hand me the paper,' Ruth told him, suddenly aware of his clean, crisp masculine smell and the fact that her arm had been only an inch or so away from his thigh. She pulled it out of his hand towards her and he edged closer until their bodies were touching very lightly, then he bent a bit, his left hand sliding over the back of the chair behind her head.

He had a hot vision of her nakedness, the way her fiery body responded to his touch, every inch the passionate woman underneath the gauche, sweetly shy, dreamy girl.

He tried to focus his eyes on the piece of paper in front of him, knowing that he had to keep her talking just to be near her like this. He crossed his legs and attempted to shove the insidiously erotic images out of his head. The sight of his erection pushing against his trousers would be enough to send her running out into the street in a state of terror, most probably.

'Sorry?'

'I said that I'll write the indecipherable bits a bit more legibly in the space above.' She tilted her face to his and narrowed her eyes. 'Are you listening to me?' She became aware of his arm extended behind her and abruptly stood up. 'I'll go and see about the food. If you could just highlight the bits you don't understand in one colour and highlight the bits you want transcribed in another, then we should be able to go from there.'

'What about the bits I can't understand but *might want transcribed*? Use both colours? Or do we bring in colour number three?'

Ruth gave him a stern, reproachful stare. 'Now you're just being silly.'

'Sorry,' he said meekly. 'Saturday night levity.'

'I'll be in the kitchen.' She spun round on her heels and was busily setting the small pine table and heating the food when she became aware that he was in the kitchen with her.

'Have you finished already?' she asked, turning

round to face him, her face flushed from the heat, and drying her hands on the striped apron she had slung over her clothes. She had scraped her hair away from her face into a high ponytail. It swung gently behind her every time she moved her head.

'You *have* put yourself out,' he said, beelining to the saucepan and the pots simmering gently on the stove.

'No, I haven't!'

'There's enough food here to…'

'Go away. You're…you're disturbing my concentration!'

'Oh, really?'

She felt his attention on her as she turned away and realised that her words could easily be misconstrued.

'I mean,' she said, very quickly, 'I hate people being in the kitchen when I'm cooking, peering at the food and…' she looked at his hand '…sticking fingers in to taste.'

The hand was immediately withdrawn and he threw her a sheepish little-boy look which just made him look even more alarmingly sexy.

'I'll just sit at the table,' he told her. 'You won't notice that I'm here. You just carry on. I'll be as quiet as a mouse.'

'What about the work?' she asked, watching in dismay as he settled comfortably into one of the four small pine chairs.

'Work can wait a while. I have a feeling it won't take as long as I thought.' He gave her a charming grin. 'I take it you enjoy cooking?'

Ruth stirred the pasta and then fetched the salad out of the fridge and stuck it on the table in front of him.

'Yes, I do.' Her voice softened. 'Mum and I used to spend every Sunday in the kitchen when I was a girl. She'd let me roll pastry for pies and knead dough for bread, and when I got a little older I'd chop and mix and stir. I've always associated cooking with fun.' He had brought her glass of wine into the kitchen and she absent-mindedly picked it up from the kitchen table and swallowed a mouthful.

Then she drained the pasta and stirred in some black pepper and parmesan cheese. She brought it to the table with the pasta scoop stuck in, then the prawns, thick and creamy and a rich tomato-red.

'Just help yourself,' she instructed. She divested herself of the apron, slung it back over the hook, and didn't demur when he topped up her glass with some more of the crisp white wine.

'Now sit down,' he commanded, when she continued to hover as he helped himself to food.

Ruth sat down, politely waited until he had finished, and then helped herself to her usual giant-sized portion of food. When she looked up, Franco was staring at her plate with wonderment.

'I enjoy eating,' she said defensively, and his mouth curved into a slow, long smile.

A man could grow ridiculously accustomed to her honesty, he thought. All of a sudden, memories of drawn-out games he had played with the sophisticated women he had always tended to date seemed trite and pointless. Why didn't *all* women say what was in their heads, instead of batting their eyelashes and flirting and never calling a spade a spade?

Meals for the rake-thin glamour models of his experience were lettuce leaves and carrot shavings and fat-free vinaigrette. Anything more substantial was tentatively nibbled and then fashionably left. Conversation never expressed real thoughts or opinions or feelings. Conversation, he realised, was always merely a prelude to sex.

'Do you know,' he murmured, following her lead and devouring his food with the zeal of someone unexpectedly rescued from starvation, 'that the enjoyment of food is often linked to a sensual nature?'

'Sorry?' She paused in mid-mouthful to look at him.

There was a dab of sauce in the corner of her mouth and she licked it away with a gentle flick of her pink tongue, like a kitten. Franco wondered how it was that there wasn't a barrage of men beating down her door. Was it only him who found her the most erotic woman on the face of the earth? He shovelled a mouthful of pasta and prawn into his mouth.

'I *said* that appreciation of food is often linked to an appreciation of all things...physical.'

The gist of what he was saying crawled into her head, delightfully fuddled by the single glass of wine she had consumed, and a slow spark of excitement began to burn.

He stuck his fork into his salad and looked at her. 'You are a very sensual woman, Ruth.'

Ruth stared at him, shocked at the unexpected directness of his remark. She carefully returned her wine glass to the table and took a deep, steadying breath.

'I don't think this conversation is...is... appropriate,' she said in a whisper, clearing her throat.

'I'm paying you a compliment, not launching into a debate.'

'Yes, well, that's as may be...'

'But...? Are you so unused to being complimented by men that you're incapable of accepting one? In the manner in which it was intended? Or maybe you find it uncomfortable to think of yourself as a woman who might enjoy sex...'

The fork, which she had been holding, clattered to her plate, and she hastily retrieved it and licked it clean. Her eyes skittered from plate to glass and back to plate, frantically trying to avoid resting on his face.

'Were your parents inhibited when it came to the question of sex?' he pressed on, watching as her face went from pink to white and back to pink. 'Was it something that was never mentioned at home? Are you ashamed of your body? Of how it feels when you're turned on?'

'No! No, no, no!' She stood up, her hands pressed over her ears, her eyes shut.

Why was he doing this? Why was he pushing her to the limit? What did he want her to say? That, yes, she liked being touched? That he turned her on? That she couldn't lay eyes on him without every pore in her body going into hypersensitive overdrive?

She felt his hands on hers and he gently pulled them away from her ears.

'I can't go on pretending that nothing happened between us, Ruth,' he said softly. 'Even though I know that's what you want more than anything else...isn't it?'

'I don't see the point of discussing it,' she whispered miserably.

'But it won't go away, will it?' He tilted her face up to his and smiled crookedly at her. 'The last week has been agony. Looking at you, wanting you, knowing that you want me as well. Because you do, don't you…?'

'No!' Ruth cried wildly, struggling against hands that were gripping her like bands of steel. He waited until her futile struggles had petered out.

'So if I kiss you,' he murmured, his voice deepening, 'you won't respond…?'

She looked at him then, her eyes wide with dismay.

'I…I…' The balance of what she had intended to say was lost as his lips found hers, then it was as if a dam that had been feebly contained had suddenly and irrevocably broken its barriers.

She was clutching him, gripping his arms and returning his kiss with fierce, hungry craving. She could taste sauce and wine on his tongue and she sucked it compulsively, enjoying his fast, uncontrolled breathing and the way his hands, behind her head, curled into her hair, dragging it free of its ponytail.

He scooped her off her feet and into the bedroom and she watched, feverishly, as he stripped off his clothes. Oh, his body! Lean, hard, every muscle toned and rippling as he yanked off the shirt and then his trousers, flinging them to the ground impatiently.

His erection was hard and big and he smiled as her eyes fastened on it.

'This is what you do for me,' he said thickly, touching himself, and she moaned softly under her breath. Instinctively she began undoing the buttons of the shirt, frantically tugging at them while he watched, enjoying every deliciously sweet moment of what was happening between them, of what was to come.

Anticipation had never before been filled with such agonising, piercing ecstasy.

She heaved a sigh of relief as he unclasped her bra and tossed it to the ground, where it joined the discarded shirt. His sharp intake of breath as he looked at her naked breasts hitched her levels of excitement yet higher. Considering her build was slight, her breasts, she knew, were full, with large nipples now pointing upwards, as though beckoning his mouth. She touched one with the tip of a moistened finger and his throbbing member stirred in heady arousal.

Her trousers felt heavy and cumbersome against her legs and she ripped them off with shaking hands, watching him all the time. Watching him, watching her.

Restraining himself was excruciating, but Franco had learnt from his one experience with her. He wanted everything to go slowly now. No fast foreplay and urgent, solitary orgasm. He wanted to touch everywhere, with every part of his body.

He waited until all her clothes were off and she was lying in naked splendour on the bed, her hair falling against the pillow in a pale sheet, her slender body hovering on the boyish were it not for the full, ripe swell of her breasts. Then he moved slowly towards the bed and over her, his body skimming hers but not resting on it.

Very delicately he explored her mouth and lips with his tongue, and when she tried to press him harder against her he laughed softly and stroked her hair.

'Oh, no, you don't. This time I want us to enjoy one another.'

So she steadied herself, and gradually her body

melted under the slow, erotic, lingering caresses. One touch and her whole body tingled. Her breasts she offered to his mouth like ripe fruit and watched his dark head as he suckled on them, slowly taking his time, moving down her stomach and finally finding the honey sweetness he craved.

He nuzzled and burrowed into the shell-like pink lobes that hid her quivering womanhood, enjoying the thrusting of her hips which she couldn't control as the waves of pleasure rippling through her grew more intense.

Her body, under his touch, was like a magical instrument, and he felt both privileged and humbled by her granting him permission to play.

And he seemed tuned in to her in a way he had never felt with a woman before. When he knew that the urgency of her movements would soon spill over into unstoppable pleasure he moved over her, kissing her neck, her lips, her eyes, wanting to kiss every bit of her, missing nothing out.

'Oh, my darling.' His voice didn't sound as though it belonged to him. It was husky and unsteady and unrecognisable.

Her eyes flickered open.

'What is it?' he asked, stilling.

'I've never...you know, I...I'm a virgin.'

'I'll be gentle.' Was he in heaven? He closed his eyes and breathed her in deeply.

Oh, his love, and for his eyes only.

CHAPTER SIX

Quick learner had never been a description applied to Ruth. At school, she had got there in the end, but she had never been one of those bright young things whose hands had always been raised to tell the answer, who had achieved B grades without benefit of revision, who had been able to spend their time giggling with the boys at the back and yet, mysteriously, had still known the answers to the maths questions when asked.

Ruth had plodded. *Tries hard* had always been somewhere in her end of term report cards.

Now, in the space of four weeks, she had proved a very quick learner indeed. She had returned to her normal duties at the office and had known, without having to be told, that what was going on between her and Franco was not for public consumption.

She had caught on in double-quick time that, although she had lost her footing and was falling inexorably in love with him, the feeling was not mutual. *Love* was a word that had not once crossed his lips, and she took great pains to hide the way she felt because she knew that if he discovered the truth he would politely turn away, and she preferred the agony of her pointless love to the certainty of his absence.

So at work she smiled, and was as obligingly in the background as usual, happy to run her errands and pleased that she was being given more responsibility.

There was some mention of her going on a short writing course, so that she could help out on some of the more straightforward feature articles, which would be exciting, and when that happened she would be released from some of her more mundane duties.

She had never been one for talking about her private life, which she had always considered deeply boring anyway. People had become accustomed to her shy reticence on the subject. No one suspected that now, beneath that quiet, smiling reserve, was a new and thrilling love-life. No one would have guessed in a million years that three or four times a week now, when she left the office, it was to rendezvous with Franco, whose company, against her better judgement, became more addictive by the day.

He never failed to delight her. She could listen to him chat for hours, although that never happened because he always insisted on hearing what *she* had to say. He always seemed to find her anecdotes amusing. He could be so tender and yet so hungry, taking her with a passion that left her breathless.

The only thorn in her paradise was the fact that their relationship had been doomed from its inception. One day, sooner rather than later, the hot desire that simmered in his eyes every time he looked at her would fade away into bored uninterest. His amusement at her gauche little ways, which she could no more help than she could prevent the sun from rising in the sky, would turn to indifference. He would cease to complain at the times they could not spend together and instead begin to find ways of lengthening the absences between them.

She found herself swaying on the underground train one morning, lost in her reverie of doom and gloom.

It couldn't get any worse, could it?

The thought, which had been creeping under her skin, burrowed deep in her subconscious like a malignant germ waiting for the right moment to emerge, began to gently flower amongst the rich soil of her depressing thoughts.

A wash of hot blood flowed upwards to her face and she could feel a fine perspiration break out over her body.

By the time she arrived at her stop, five minutes later, her limbs were numb. Of course she was worrying needlessly. Hadn't that always been one of her traits? Hadn't her parents always fondly told her that she was a little worry-wart?

But where *was* her period? She didn't keep a rigid check on them, although she usually more or less knew when they were due, but she was uneasily aware that she was late. *How* late she couldn't say for sure, and she clung to this thought as her feet swerved away from her normal route to work to detour into the chemist's on the corner.

I can't be pregnant, she thought, sick with panic. *We've been so careful.*

But there had been that one time, hadn't there? The first time they had slept together had been unprotected, hadn't it?

Her mind continued to conduct a two-way debate on the subject even while her hands reached for the pregnancy testing kit and her eyes read the brief directions on the outside. She weakly struggled to convince the treacherous inner voice in her head that she was being silly while she paid for the kit, and her feet somehow found their way out and began walking to work.

One minute. It took one minute for her world to fall to pieces. In the small confines of the office toilet, ears attuned to the slightest sound of anyone coming in, the give-away box and its wrappings scrunched up into a small bundle and shoved into the disposal unit next to the toilet, Ruth watched in horror as one thin blue line was joined by another above it.

'Oh, no!' She realised that she had groaned aloud, and she clasped her hand to her mouth, biting back the cry that wanted to come out. 'I can't be.' She picked up the plastic gadget and stared at the message it was flamboyantly telling her. Her hands were shaking violently and she sat down on the lid of the toilet and tried to order her thoughts.

Eventually she shoved the tube into the disposal unit, washed her face with ice-cold water and looked at her reflection.

A baby. You're going to have a baby. You're pregnant!

Who would ever have convinced her that the one event which she had spent her life looking forward to would induce feelings of horror, shock and sick despair?

She was hanging onto either side of the sink, fighting down the nausea clambering up her gullet like acid, when the door was flung open and Alison strode in, bursting with vitality and in the middle of some particularly pleasing thought that had brought a smile to her lips. She stopped dead in her tracks when she saw Ruth, now hurriedly trying to look normal, inclined over the sink.

'What the heck...? What's the matter, Ruthie?'

Ruth gave her a watery smile and desperately racked her brains for something to say. 'Nothing. I just...it's not a good morning for me,' she finished lamely, and truthfully.

'What's wrong? What's the matter?'

The door was pushed open and Alison flew to it and snapped at the hapless intruder to leave, then she turned to Ruth.

'Has something happened? What? You'd better sit down. You look as though you'll fall down otherwise.' She guided Ruth to the chair in the corner and sat her down, invalid-style, then she squatted next to her and held her hands. 'Has something happened to one of your parents?' she asked anxiously. 'Is someone ill?'

An idea stirred in Ruth's head and she took a deep breath. 'It's my mum. She's not very well at the moment.' It wasn't, technically speaking, a lie. When she had last spoken to her mother two days previously her mother had been complaining of a cold, some nasty little virus that was flying round the village and taking its toll.

'Oh, Ruth.' Alison's eyes brimmed over with sympathy and Ruth felt a twinge of unpleasant guilt, but what else could she do?

In the space of three seconds, as soon as she had discovered that she was pregnant, she had known two things very clearly. The first was that she was not going to get rid of the baby and the second was that she would have to leave her job, leave London, and leave

Franco for good. The baby would be *her* responsibility and hers alone.

Now Alison, unwittingly, had provided her with a way out. At least a way out of the job, and, much as it sickened her to play on her boss's softer nature, she could see no way around it.

'Shall we go into my office and discuss it?'

Coffees were brought in, and the force of curiosity pressing against the closed office door was almost enough to break it down.

Ruth hatched her plan, through necessity and desperation. She would take a few weeks off, at her insistence unpaid, keeping in contact with the office by phone.

'We've got your address on file, so we can contact you if needs be, can't we?'

The only address on her work file, Ruth knew, was her London address, and she planned on being out of the city before the week was finished. No one knew the whereabouts of her parents. She tried to remember if she had mentioned it to Franco at any point, but she was sure that she hadn't.

He knew that she had grown up in a village and that her father was a vicar, but that could apply to millions of villages in the country, so if he tried to look for her he would bump into dead ends, and she doubted that she was an important enough fixture in his life for him to pursue it too assiduously.

'Are you sure there's nothing more we can do to help? I'm sure Franco would—'

'No! Please,' Ruth interrupted quickly. 'Honestly, Alison, he's done enough for me already, what with this promotion and stuff. I'm only sorry that I won't be able to take advantage of it.'

'You will when you return.'

'Yes, that's true.' She looked down briefly at her hands and her eyes fell onto her flat stomach. In a few months' time she would be feeling the movements of this baby inside her. Her job at the office was over, thanks to one night of stupidity. 'It's been brilliant working with you. With all of you.' Her voice trembled and the worry returned to Alison's face.

'Why are you talking as though we're losing you for good, Ruth?'

'Well, you can never tell...'

'Don't be so pessimistic. Your mum'll be fine. My mum fell and broke her hip a year ago, and we all thought that she would be out of action for good. But two months later she was back on the golf course, hale and hearty as a horse and chivvying the lot of us around, as per usual.'

'Yes, well...' If only it were as simple as that. She hadn't even gone down the road of contemplating how her parents would react to her news. She would have to brace herself for that, but she knew that it would break their hearts. She felt her eyes begin to sting and she blinked rapidly, and shoved the thought to the back of her head.

By the time the day was done Ruth had returned to her flat, drained. At least there would be no Franco to face. He was out of the country for the next week and, although he would call, she could easily cope with his voice down the end of a line. Alternatively, she could always fail to pick up the telephone and let the answer-machine take a message. Cowardly, but so much easier than dealing with him verbally.

Everything moved so quickly after that, that Ruth barely had time to pause for breath.

Two phone calls to the office, to inform them that she would keep in touch, and Franco's calls she steadfastly ignored. Though she listened to them as they were recorded on the answer-machine, her stomach clenching into knots as, over the week, his tone of voice became progressively angrier at her absence. If she hadn't known him for the man that he was, allergic to all forms of commitment, she might well have imagined that there was a possessiveness to his voice that she had never noticed before.

A gullible fool might well have read all sorts of things into that, but time had hardened her. Before, she had been able to put up with him because she loved him, and because she had been prepared to face the inevitable hurt when he grew weary of her. The baby changed everything. Several options presented themselves if she stayed to tell him the glad tidings.

The first was that he would be furious. He might even see it as some kind of elaborate trap to force him to settle down, and she would have to watch any fondness he might have had for her curdle into contempt and dislike.

The second possibility was that he might actually force her to marry him, and thereafter she would have to endure a life chained to his side, helplessly in love, while he did his duty as a father and fulfilled his needs as a man elsewhere. Because there could be nothing more conducive to rotting a relationship than a shotgun wedding.

The worst scenario involved him fighting her for custody of the baby, and, naïve though she was, she was not so naïve that she didn't know that money spoke volumes. He had lots and she had none.

Whichever way she looked at it, running back home was the only solution she could see to her dilemma.

On the Friday morning she stood at the door of the flat which had once brimmed over with all her hopes and dreams and excitement, and looked at the impersonal space staring at her. She had packed all her clothes into two large suitcases. The rest she had crammed into the small van which she had rented for the trip back home.

It had taken under three hours, but in that time she had felt as though she was packing away her youth. When she arrived at the vicarage it would be gone and she would begin a new life altogether. One where love was only a memory and the past was something to be unlocked at night and treasured.

At least, she thought, as she cautiously began the long drive back home, she had concocted something to tell her parents. It was a lie, and a fairly horrendous one at that, but Ruth steadfastly told herself that it would be a lie in a good cause. There was no way that she would be responsible for breaking her parents' hearts.

It would be bad enough when they discovered that she was pregnant, but they would be devastated if she told them the circumstances behind the pregnancy. Out of wedlock, deeply in love with a man who did not return her love. The unspoken postscript to that would be the tacit admission that he didn't love their daughter but he was willing to use her for sex and, worse, she had allowed him.

Sex, the most beautiful demonstration of love between a man and a woman, degenerated into an animal act to satiate lust. They would never dream of castigating her, but it would be in their eyes for the rest of their days and Ruth just couldn't face a lifetime of silent reproach.

So as the van neared the vicarage she plastered a joyful smile on her face as her mother ran out to greet her. They were expecting her. There would be an enormous welcoming lunch, probably her favourite of fried fish and homemade chips with lots of bread and butter and mushy peas. They would sit down with anticipation glowing on their faces to hear this incredible news she had promised them.

Please let me look excited and thrilled, Ruth prayed, as she sat down at the table and looked at her parents across the weathered tabletop. They could barely contain themselves, but they had insisted that she eat first before she told them what she had to say.

With all her possessions in tow, Ruth knew that they expected to hear something about work—probably that she had landed some wonderful job close to home and would be moving back. They had helped her every step of the way in her decision to go to London, but they would be overjoyed were she to tell them that she was returning home.

'I'm not sure where to begin,' Ruth said, when she could no longer postpone the dreaded moment.

She looked at her parents, as wildly dissimilar as two people could be. Her mother was slender and fine-boned, with short fair hair that lent her the same gamine appearance as her daughter. Her father was plump, bordering, as he often said, on beach-ball-shaped. His dark hair was receding faster than he cared to believe and his dark brown eyes were gentle and ironic.

'So I'll just say it in one rush and please don't interrupt till I'm finished.' She drew in a deep breath. 'I met someone a few weeks ago.' She didn't dare look at her parents as she spoke. 'And I fell in love. Problem is, he has a nomadic kind of job. Well, actually, he's a reporter, and he goes away for long periods of time at a stretch.' Uri Geller couldn't bend his spoons more convincingly than she had just bent the truth. 'We hadn't planned on rushing into anything, but...' Here was where the waters got a little choppy. 'But I'm afraid...I was a little bit careless...'

'Darling, you're not...!'

'Which is why we...well, jumped the gun a bit...and got married!' Her voice was thick with a certain unnatural gaiety which fortunately her parents appeared not to notice.

'You're married!' The exclamation, uttered in identical tones of shock, was shrieked in unison, and Ruth raised miserable grey eyes to them.

'I know it's an awful shock...' she said, wringing her hands. 'I wanted to say something...but...'

'But, darling, where *is* he?' Her mother had reached out her hand to Ruth's and was now patting it comfortingly across the remainder of their lunch.

'That's the thing...' Ruth took a deep breath and pleaded with God that she really was doing all this to spare her parents, whom she loved more than anything. So could He please not strike her down just yet with a bolt of lightning? 'He was called away on an urgent matter and he could be gone for weeks... months, even...that's why we rushed into things...'

'Oh, darling, *where*?'

'Where what?' Ruth looked blankly at her parents.

'*Where* has he gone to do his reporting? Is it one of those war-torn countries?'

Ruth, not wanting to get too technical over the details, sought refuge in a forlorn expression and expressed a heartfelt desire not to talk about it.

It was to become her refrain as the days lengthened into one week, then two. Twice she called the office, and the second time she called after hours, leaving a brief message that they should perhaps start thinking about her replacement. Her conscience was unquiet as it was, and lying into an answer-machine somehow seemed less unforgivable than lying to her boss.

Her parents, having ridden the shock of their daughter's pregnancy, had taken to proudly announcing it to all and sundry in the parish, wistfully explaining that the father of the baby was out of the country, risking life and limb for the freedom of others.

Wherever she went she could not escape the well wishes of one and all and constant questions as to her husband's whereabouts.

After a week and a half Ruth had resorted to briefly explaining that her beloved husband was out of telephone contact due to the precariousness of his situation. In time, she knew, the fracas would fade, and she personally couldn't wait. Telling the lie had been monumental enough. Maintaining it threatened to drive her to an early grave.

She was quietly skulking at home, putting the finishing touches to the roast leg of lamb she had prepared for their supper, when she glanced through the kitchen window at the sound of a car crunching up the gravel drive to the house.

A childhood spent in various vicarages had inured her to this—unexpected visits from parishioners at the least appropriate times. Many was the time when grace would have been said and knives and forks raised, and the doorbell would ring.

Her brain half registered the fact that she would now have to stop her preparations and make social small talk for half an hour or so until her parents returned from doing their rounds. She had a fleeting impression of a big car in a dark colour, then the doorbell went. Several short, sharp rings that had her clicking her tongue in annoyance and hurriedly drying her hands so that she could rush to get the door.

She pulled it open, wondering which of her father's elderly fan club members had become so demanding, and the welcoming smile on her face froze.

Her facial muscles, now in a state of paralysis, were quickly joined by the remainder of her body.

'Surprised?' The smoky, sexy voice that had not too long ago been capable of turning her legs to jelly, was cold with contempt. 'Did you think that I wouldn't come looking for you? Did you think that you could run away without explanation and I'd just accept it?'

Ruth gave an involuntary squeak of horror. What was he *doing here*?

He should be...he should be...*he should be in some war-torn country, incommunicado, possibly for ever.*

The possible ramifications of her elaborate lies came

home to roost with terrifying force and she held onto the doorframe to stop herself from collapsing.

She had to get rid of him before her parents returned.

'Inside!' she hissed, pulling him in and then peering outside to see whether there was anyone about. The vicarage, thankfully, was well out of range of passers-by, by virtue of its location, set in three acres of sprawling gardens, but there still always seemed to be someone, somewhere, hovering.

'*What* are you doing here?' she demanded, shutting the door and hitting him with the full force of her desperation. She placed her hands squarely on her hips and did her best not to be destabilised by the cold blue eyes looking at her with avenging rage.

Having spent the past three hours in a car, battling with traffic and an eminently unhelpful map, Franco was in no mood for reasonable discussion, even though reasonable discussion was precisely what he had told himself he wanted when he had set out earlier that afternoon.

Naturally, as soon as she opened the door and he saw the face that had driven him crazy for the past few weeks, any possibility of reason had flown through the window. He had been engulfed in a black, smouldering anger that he could feel physically wafting from his body in waves.

It was infuriating enough that he had found himself here, running behind some damned chit of a girl, when every bone in his body had told him that he should just leave the wretch to get on with her life, wherever she chose to live it and with whom. He had never had to wage war with his better judgement and it still galled him to admit that he had lost. He had just not been able to let the things go.

Even more infuriating was the fact that a less remorseful visage he had yet to encounter. If she had been wrapped up in self-pity and regret, ruing the day she walked out on him, ready to plead for entry back into his life, then leniency might have crept in somewhere, but she looked every bit as angry as he felt. And allied to that anger was something else, something he couldn't put his finger on but which could only mean one thing: another man. It was a possibility he didn't dare even contemplate.

'What do you want?' she repeated, casting anxious glances behind him to the closed door.

'Expecting someone, Ruth? My replacement, perhaps?' He gave her a twisted smile.

It occurred to Ruth that arguing was not going to win the war, nor was it going to get rid of him, and get rid of him she must, so she smiled sweetly and forced her posture to relax into something a bit less uptight.

'Look, this isn't a good time. Perhaps if we arranged to meet up later. Maybe tomorrow.'

'I'm not going anywhere until you answer one or two questions.' He pushed himself away from the door and strolled into the hall, looking around him with frank curiosity. 'So this is where you live.'

'How did you find me?' Ruth glanced at her watch and followed a few paces behind him.

'You must have forgotten. You mentioned where you lived the very first time we met. It didn't take long to trace your full address.' He turned around and looked at her. 'Why did you up sticks and leave? I won't begin to tell you how disappointed everyone at the office is with your behaviour. They became worried about you, you know, when they kept telephoning your London number and got nowhere. They had no idea where you lived, because, happily for you, your parents' address had never been recorded on your application form. They all assumed the worst about your mother.'

Ruth blanched. 'I'm sorry...I didn't mean to...'

'To what, Ruth?' His voice was like a whiplash. 'Lie? Deceive people who trusted you? Run away because you couldn't handle what was happening between us? Because that's why you ran away, isn't it?' His blue eyes bored into her until she felt giddy. So far she had experienced no morning sickness during the pregnancy, but right now she felt very nauseous indeed.

'No. You don't understand.' She was almost weeping now. 'You *must* go. Please!'

'Or else what?'

Ruth looked at him helplessly.

'And don't give me that innocent stare!' he exploded. 'Why didn't you wait for me and tell me to my face that you wanted out? Why run away?' He bore down on her and she flinched, faltering back against the wall, pressing herself against it, thankful for the scant support it provided.

'Because I'm a coward!' Ruth babbled. 'I was scared so I did the first craven, cowardly thing I could think of. I ran home to my mum and dad!' Whose absence she fervently hoped would continue just long enough for her to get rid of him.

'You're well rid of me! I'm too gauche for you, too

inexperienced. Do you think that any woman with her wits about her would *run back to her parents the minute she got cold feet?*' She gave a laugh that sounded like a deranged shriek. 'I know this means that you now have no respect for me, but I deserve it! I've behaved abominably. Okay? Is that good enough?' She chewed her bottom lip and frantically willed him to disappear.

This was not what Franco wanted to hear. It reeked of insincerity, although when he thought about it he wasn't too sure *what* he wanted to hear. Something less self-abnegating. But the bottom line was that she was telling him to get lost. She wasn't back in her home town dealing with a broken heart. She had wanted him out of her life and so she had used the quickest method and walked out. Without a backward glance.

He had opened his mouth to give her a piece of his mind, which she richly deserved as far as he was concerned, when there was the sound of fumbling at the front door and two things happened at once.

Ruth gave a groan and sank elegantly to the ground, and a middle-aged couple walked through the door, their chatter drying up on their lips as they absorbed the scene that confronted them.

CHAPTER SEVEN

RUTH opened her eyes to the sight of her mother's worried face inches away from her own, and within seconds the nightmarish memory of *why* she was lying on the ground came flooding back. She gave a short cry of shock and tried to angle her head upwards to see whether Franco really *was* there, or whether it had all been some dreadful figment of her imagination. Some obscure pregnancy symptom, perhaps.

'Darling, now don't try and stand up. Not in your condition...'

'Shh!' Ruth hissed dramatically. She didn't have to look up after all to know that Franco had not been a convenient mirage brought on by a sudden attack of morning sickness. Just behind her mother, two pairs of shoes indicated four feet. Her father's and Franco's. She would have recognised those classy handmade Italian brogues anywhere.

She groaned softly and felt like finding temporary refuge in another attack of the vapours.

'Whatever happened, darling?' Her father's rotund face, now wreathed in lines of concern, joined her mother's, and Ruth smiled weakly at them both.

'I'm afraid that I'm to blame, sir.'

In the fuss after she had passed out, she realised, introductions had not been made. Knowing her parents, they would barely have afforded the stranger a second look after they had seen their daughter swooning on the floor like a Victorian maiden in a melodrama. Now, they both looked up, and there were a few seconds of silence while they digested the man who had managed to shift into her line of vision and was looking down at her with what she loosely interpreted as a nasty smile.

She struggled up onto her elbows, frantically trying to work out what damage limitation exercise she could adopt, and his hands swiftly pulled her to her feet, fingers gripping hers hard enough for her to massage her hand as soon as he had released her.

'Mrs Jacobs, I do apologise for barging into your house like this.' Franco, all dark, persuasive charm, extended his hand to the fair-haired woman staring at him with a perplexed frown. 'How are you feeling?'

'I beg your pardon?'

'Fine!' Ruth inserted, blushing wildly and clasping her hands behind her back. 'Mum's fine!'

'Ruthie, what *are* you talking about?' her mother asked, turning to her. 'Have I missed something here? And shouldn't you be sitting down? We can't have you falling all over the place, can we?'

'No!' Ruth responded in a high voice. 'Mum, this is Franco! Now, why don't I take him into the sitting room and you and Dad can...' her eyes flitted desperately from face to expectant face and settled on her father's '...can...check the progress of supper! The lamb's probably burnt to a crisp...!'

Her mother's expression was beginning to look depressingly alert, Ruth noticed, and she slid her arm around her parents in an attempt to cajole them into the right direction.

'Ruth...' her mother began to whisper, catching her

eye and smiling delightedly. 'Oh, darling, I'm *so* pleased for you...'

'I'll be back in a moment!' Ruth trilled, pushing her parents towards the kitchen and looking over her shoulder to Franco. 'Just wait in the sitting room, why don't you? It's just through there on the right.'

'Is he who I *think* he is, darling?'

'Who's that? Who's that?' Having safely arrived at the kitchen with both parents in tow, Ruth leaned against the kitchen door and breathed deeply. Surely this had to be a nightmare? In a minute she would open her eyes, discover that it was eight in the morning and everything was as it should be. Real life, after all, didn't have this surreal quality of farce about it.

She sighed and looked at her parents.

'Yes,' she admitted, 'but he won't be staying. He...he...he's in the middle of doing something *terribly* dangerous, very espionage, and he *literally had to sneak out under cover of darkness* to get here. In fact, he was just on his way out when you came home!' The palms of her hands were sweating so profusely that she had to surreptitiously wipe them on her jeans.

'Oh, no!' her mother said with dismay, edging towards the kitchen door—which Ruth resolutely barred.

'Darling, your mother and I really would like to meet your husband, and I'm sure he partly came here to meet us. He seems a fair enough kind of chap...'

'I absolutely refuse to let the man leave until we've at least had a word with him. And why are you behaving so *oddly*? You're as red as a beetroot, Ruthie!'

'I...it's a bit *hot* in the house, Mum,' she stammered, pressing herself against the door.

'Away! Away, away, away!' Her father shooed her, giving her gentle little pushes to dislodge her and then stepping aside so that both females could walk past him.

For the first time ever Ruth speculated on the virtues of running away from home. Twenty-two might seem a bit old to be doing that kind of thing, but then, she thought giddily, how many twenty-two-year-olds had to deal with the horrendous situation staring her in the face?

She would be exposed as a liar in front of her parents and their hearts would be doubly broken. She would never be able to explain why she had lied in the first place and her deepest desire to keep her pregnancy under wraps would be smashed to smithereens. Her only slim hope was to somehow get rid of Franco before either of her parents could blurt out her condition. Perhaps they might imagine that he wasn't aware of it, in which case they would leave it to her to break the news in private.

Franco was lounging in the sitting room by the bay window, staring moodily outside at the impeccably maintained gardens, now shrouded in darkness. He turned around when they entered, his eyes seeking and finding Ruth's with the accuracy of laser-guided missiles.

'Well, old chap,' her father said, beaming. 'Thought we'd never get to meet you!' He strode across and shook Franco's hand vigorously, then he stood back, rocking on his heels, and inspected Franco with paternal thoroughness. 'I gather it's been quite an exercise getting here in the first place!' He patted his shoulder heartily.

''Course, as the father of the most beautiful daughter on the face of the earth, I can happily appreciate why you did your utmost! Now, we *know* you can't stay for long, but surely you can stay long enough to have a quick glass with us...? Some wine, perhaps, or sherry? Might even have a couple of cans of lager—have we got a couple of cans of lager anywhere, darling? So what's it to be...?'

'He'll have the one glass of wine!' Ruth interceded, fairly running across the sitting room and positioning herself next to Franco, with one hand resting warningly on his arm. 'But then he *really must be on his way*. Mustn't you, darling?' She smiled up at him and he shot her a ferociously questioning look.

'Wine would be terrific.'

'Oh, we haven't even introduced ourselves!' Ruth's mother came forward, looking lovingly at her daughter and then transferring her affectionate gaze to Franco. She had a naturally expressive face, quick to smile, and her readiness to see the best in everyone lent her a quality of endearing appeal that few could resist.

'I'm Claire, and that portly chap over there, who absolutely *refuses* to go on a diet, is my husband Michael.'

'I would happily go on a diet, my dear, but I know you would be offended.' He winked at Franco. 'Loves to cook—couldn't bear it if she had no one to experiment on.'

'And Ruth has taken after her in the culinary aspect,' Franco said smoothly, patting the hand that was still resting on his arm and then giving it a squeeze that was unnecessarily firm. 'Hasn't she?'

'The way to a man's heart!' Claire said, laughing. 'Now, cheers to the both of you!'

Ruth, on orange juice only, knocked back her glass with determined speed and then offered a bright smile to no one in particular.

'Now, darlings, I expect you want to spend the last few minutes together, so Dad and I will leave. I *know* we've only exchanged pleasantries,' Claire said seriously, proffering her cheek to be kissed by Franco, 'but I just have a gut feeling that you're going to make an absolutely wonderful son-in-law. Isn't he, Michael?'

'He'd better! Or he'll have me to answer to!'

If Franco was flabbergasted by the revelation of his status, Ruth thought with reluctant admiration, he hid it well. He smiled, murmured one or two polite things, shook hands and then, as soon as her parents were out of the room, turned on Ruth, dropping all semblance of civility.

'Like to tell me what the hell is going on? I feel as though I've walked into a madhouse.'

Her hand dropped from his arm and she nervously took a few steps backwards.

On the plus side, her parents had not breathed a word about her pregnancy. Uncertain as to whether the expectant father knew or not, they had, luckily for Ruth, opted for discretion and silence.

On the minus side, she now faced the uphill task of explaining the inexplicable and, on top of that, persuading Franco to leave with only a fuzzy explanation as to why her parents thought that he was their son-in-law.

'Well?' he growled in a menacing voice, taking

three steps forward to match her two. Ruth backed into the sofa and half fell into a sitting position, watching warily as Franco took up position next to her, uncomfortably close.

It seemed like only yesterday that they had not been able to keep away from each other, touching, feeling, exploring. In another sense all that seemed like an eternity away, part of some youthful game which she had now abandoned for good.

It hurt just to look at him, to breathe him in, to remember.

'Don't even *think* of fainting on me,' he warned silkily, 'or I'll have your parents running in here, and by God I'll drag an explanation out of them as to what the heck's going on around here. So, if you've got any sense at all, you'll keep your wits about you. Got it?'

He stretched his arm out along the back of the sofa and edged threateningly close to her.

'Must you?' she breathed unsteadily.

'Must I *what*?'

'Come so *close*.'

'Why, is this the same Ruth talking? The Ruth who couldn't get close enough to me? The Ruth who once begged to be touched when we were in a restaurant so that we ended up having to leave before the meal was finished?'

'P-Please,' Ruth stammered.

'Please what?' He looked at her grimly, loathing himself for the way those limpid grey eyes could make his stomach clench into knots, even though he knew that he had been taken for a ride.

'Explanation time, darling,' he said softly, shifting into the sofa and flashing her a humourless smile.

'And, contrary to what your parents seem to think, I have all the time in the world to listen to what you have to say.' He crossed his legs and folded his arms behind his head. 'So many questions,' he murmured, 'I hardly know where to begin. Care to help me out there?'

Ruth, frozen into petrified silence, did not respond.

'As I guessed. Well, having come here on a quest to find out why the hell you ran out on me for no apparent reason, I now find that a veritable *nest* of more interesting questions have sprung to life. For instance, *why do your parents think that I'm their son-in-law?*'

'Because...because...' Ruth stared down at her entwined fingers. She could hear her heart thudding madly in her chest, the desperate boom, boom, boom of someone whose options were fast running out.

It was worse than rotten luck that Franco had remembered the one time she had uttered, foolishly, the town where her parents lived. And that he had travelled all the way from London on an explanation-seeking mission to soothe his ego. If he had telephoned she knew that she would have fobbed him off, or at least arranged to meet him somewhere very neutral, where there was no chance of her sweet and blissfully ignorant parents putting in an appearance.

'Because...?' Franco prompted silkily. 'I'm all ears.' There was a thread of sheer menace in his voice that sent a shiver down her spine.

'Because they...it's all a mix-up,' she finally said, clutching at the faint hope that he might believe her. She looked at him evenly and he sighed and shook his head.

'It's no good, you know.'

'What's no good?'

'You trying to lie to me. You just can't do it. Your face gives you away. So why don't you just stop beating about the bush and tell me the truth? Or else your parents are going to find it very perplexing indeed that their daughter has led them to believe that I'm in some frantic rush when in fact I'm still sitting right here when supper's served.'

He rubbed his chin thoughtfully and Ruth realised that he was enjoying all this, enjoying having her at his mercy. She supposed she had done the unforgivable—walked away from a man who had probably never suffered the indignity of being dumped in his life before.

'I suppose...' he drawled with shark-like relish, 'that I could always *ask* your good parents to tell me what this is all about...'

'No! Okay, I'll tell you.' She took a deep breath and then said in a rush, 'They think you're their son-in-law because I told them that we were married.'

'Well, *obviously* that's why they think I'm their son-in-law. The question is *why have you lied to them*?'

He looked at her narrowly, at the slender hands twining miserably on her lap, at the impossibly fair hair framing her delicate face, at the varying shades of colour tingeing her cheeks, giving away her discomfort.

Well, quite frankly, she couldn't be too uncomfortable for his liking. Something was afoot. All would be revealed in due course, but, for the while, he was remarkably content to watch her squirm under his questions and beady-eyed gimlet stare.

It was all the more satisfying since—against all reason, considering the way she had walked out on him without a backward glance—he still had a compelling desire to touch her, to stroke her, to make love to her.

Thank God her parents were in the house. He had a sickening suspicion that if they hadn't been he would have been sorely tempted to let his hands and mouth do some of the arguing on his behalf. Which would have inevitably met with rejection. It was a thought he found impossible to contemplate.

'Please go,' Ruth whispered, without bothering to try and think of a reasonable explanation. There *was* no reasonable explanation. All she could do now was to appeal to his better nature, and she knew that he *had* a better nature. Despite his air of formidable self-confidence, and despite the fact that he had an uncanny talent for appearing utterly and calmly in control of every possible situation, she knew that he was kind and humorous and thoughtful in ways that could be incredibly unexpected.

And really, for the sake of the good times they had shared, surely he would leave her alone if she asked, if he could see how much it meant to her?

It wasn't as though she was the beginning, the middle and the end of his universe. However intense their relationship had been, it had been brief, and if *she* had emerged scarred from the experience, then he was intact.

If she could somehow persuade him not to let his curiosity get the better of him, then perhaps he would go away quietly and she could keep her secret safely hidden.

'Now, why would I do that?' he asked, pouring

himself the remainder of the wine from the wine bottle which her father had left on the coffee table in front of the sofa, 'when things here are so riveting?'

'Because,' Ruth said, meeting his relentless blue eyes without flinching, 'it would please me. I'm sorry I lied to them, it was a mistake, but if you would just leave and not look back, then it's a mistake that can be remedied.'

A dark flush spread through his face and he swallowed the contents of his glass savagely, then banged the glass on the table and looked at her.

'No,' he returned coldly. 'My name's been played with and I am owed an explanation. And if *you* won't provide it, then I'm sure your parents would be more than happy to oblige.' He began standing up and Ruth feverishly pulled him back down.

'Okay. I'll tell you.' She looked at him tremulously. 'I'm pregnant.'

The word dropped between them like a hand grenade. Ruth, eyes squeezed tightly shut, waited for the fall-out.

When there was no loud explosion of rage, she tentatively opened her eyes and immediately realised that an explosion would have been preferable to the shocked stillness of the man sitting next to her. Her revelation had rendered him speechless in the worst possible way.

A tear drizzled to the corner of her eye and she wiped it with the back of her hand. There was to be none of that. It mattered not that any number of horrendous complications could ensue from his awareness of the situation—the first involving her parents, who were currently innocently chatting in the kitchen, unaware of what was to come.

'You're pregnant,' he said flatly, standing up and walking across to the bay window. Putting, she thought bleakly, as much distance now between them.

'I wasn't going to tell you...' Ruth began in a shaky voice. 'It was a mistake...'

'But we were using contraception,' he said harshly.

'But not the first time.' She got up and quietly shut the door to the sitting room. The last thing she needed was for her parents to witness unnecessarily a slanging match between their daughter and so-called son-in-law.

'I know that maybe I should have told you...'

'No.' His voice dripped with glacial sarcasm. 'Why should you? The fact that you're carrying *my* baby is only a minor detail that really hasn't got much to do with me at all, isn't it.'

'Can you blame me?' Ruth's eyes flashed with sudden anger.

'Yes, I damn well can, as a matter of fact!' His eyes smouldered with rage. She could feel it emanating from him across the length of the room, suffocating her.

'Why? Why?' she cried, leaning forward. 'What's so difficult for you to understand?'

'Are you a *fool*?'

'No, I'm not!' She could barely speak because her voice was so unsteady. 'As far as I was concerned, I was doing you a favour!' She glared at him, and all of a sudden the strange calm that had carried her along for the past few weeks shattered into oblivion. The starkly grim reality of what was happening to her was like a blow to the stomach.

This was no ordinary situation. With the best possible intentions in the world, she had lied to her parents and had stupidly involved Franco in the lie. Now he could blow the whole thing apart. They lived in a small village where the parishioners would not be backward in passing judgement on the vicar and his unwed, pregnant daughter. Not only would *she* suffer, but so might her parents, two people who had done nothing but believe the story their daughter had fabricated.

'*When first we practise to deceive...*' Why, oh, why hadn't she remembered that at the time? She should have told him everything. Now, in trying to conceal it all, she risked the worst possible outcome.

'You and I...we had a fling. A baby was not part of the agenda, and when I found out that I was pregnant, I suppose I just...panicked. I couldn't imagine that you would want a baby in your life and I had no intention of...getting rid of it. I just thought that the easiest thing to do would be to leave, let you get on with your life.

'I lied to my parents because I was a coward. I *am* a coward. It would have broken their hearts if they had known...the truth, that I was pregnant and unmarried. I know it happens all the time, and they wouldn't have flung me out the house and told me never to darken their door again, but they're old-fashioned, and it would have been tough on them what with Dad being the vicar.'

'And what did you intend to tell your parents when your husband failed to make an appearance? Misplaced your address, perhaps! Had second thoughts about the whole thing? Or maybe you painted him as some kind of inveterate bum whom you'd idiotically married on a whim?'

'I hadn't thought that far ahead,' Ruth whispered. 'I suppose I might have killed you off.'

'Killed me off?'

'Well, you *were* involved in a dangerous line of business.'

'What? What line of business?' He came back to the sofa and sat down heavily.

'Reporting from war zones.'

'What?' He resisted the urge to burst out laughing. There was nothing funny about the situation, but her ingenuity amused him. 'Any in particular?' he asked pleasantly. 'Or just the most life-threatening?'

'I hadn't specified. What are you going to do?' She raised her eyes to his and looked at him steadily.

'Well, here's what I'm *not* going to do,' he informed her bluntly. 'I won't be walking away from my responsibilities; that's the first thing. So, whether you like it or not, you'll be seeing me on a regular basis from now on. You lied to your parents about my fictional hair-raising occupation so you can un-lie your way out of that one. As for our status as husband and wife—well, I'll have to think about how I decide to deal with that...'

'But...' She frowned as the innumerable complicated permutations of that particular lie sprang to mind. 'You can't hang around...people will wonder why we don't live under the same roof if we're married.'

He shrugged. 'Well, you can work on that, can't

you? You're so gifted in the art of fabrication, you should be able to come up with something...' He stood up and flexed his muscles, rubbing the back of his neck. 'So why don't we go and see your parents? They'll be thrilled when they realise that I won't have to go rushing off after all, won't they?'

He politely allowed her to lead the way, maintaining a telling silence, while his brain whirred with the connotations of what she had just told him.

He was going to be a father. *He was going to be a father!* He didn't know whether he felt deliriously happy or abjectly terrified, or whether he just felt bloody confused, but the one thing he *did* know was that the ground had very neatly been pulled out from under his feet.

When he thought of the fact that none of this would have been revealed had he not made the journey to find her, he felt the blood rush to his head. He was consumed by a rage that was so pure and undistilled that it seemed to have enough force to blow him off his feet.

His baby! So what if he had never indicated an interest in fatherhood? So what if he had always implied that his life was just too full for the responsibilities that came with a family? Was that any reason for her to keep the fact of her pregnancy hidden?

She turned to give him a brief, hesitant look as the sound of her parents' voices reached their ears, and he frowned coolly at her.

They would have beautiful children.

A beautiful child. He instantly corrected the errant thought.

'Franco. Have you come to say goodbye? Such a

shame that you have to disappear just when we were getting to know one another.' Claire walked over to where he was standing by the doorway and reached out her hands to him in a gesture of warmth and acceptance.

At that, he gave Ruth, who was busy contemplating this scene, a meaningful look, and she cleared her throat and said, in a high-pitched voice, 'Actually, Mum, Franco might be able to stay for supper with us.'

As expected, her mother's face broke into a radiantly pleased smile, and, without ado, she drew him into the kitchen and sat him at the table. From behind him she made lots of mouthing motions to Ruth which were clearly visible as *Have you told him about the baby?* and Ruth, unsure where things were going now, wore the baffled expression of someone conversing with a mad person and pretended to misunderstand.

What if he revealed everything? The marriage that never was, the love that didn't exist, the fling that had more to do with sex than anything else? Would her mother believe *her* if she then proceeded to talk about love and how meaningful it had been for *her*? Or would she emerge as a cheap tart who had fallen prey to stupidity?

For the millionth time her mind drifted away as she contemplated a future of parental disappointment and social ostracism.

She snapped back to the present to hear Franco charmingly informing her parents that he would be staying for longer than merely supper, and she shut her half-opened mouth with a snap.

'W-what did you say?' she stammered, looking at

him and trying to work out what that self-satisfied expression on his face was all about.

'I *said*—' he smiled, catching her eye and beckoning her over with his finger '—that my brief visit might well extend to something a bit...more substantial.' He patted his lap and Ruth blushed furiously, confused as to what that gesture was supposed to mean.

Out of the corner of her eye she saw her parents exchange knowing winks and was further mortified.

'More substantial?'

The patting of the lap now bordered on a silent command, and Ruth reluctantly went across to where he was sitting and primly perched on his lap.

'Isn't it wonderful? Darling?' His lips nuzzled the nape of her neck and she brushed the tingling sensation away with one hand.

'Wonderful. Hang on, Mum, let me give you a hand with those things.' Her heart was slamming against her ribcage. She couldn't figure out what he was playing at and her uncertainty was nerve-racking.

'So, how did you manage to wangle that?' her father asked, beaming. Both her parents were beaming. It was enough to make you sick.

'One or two phone calls,' Franco said mysteriously. 'After all, now that *fatherhood* is on the way, I can hardly leave my blushing bride to cope on her own, can I?'

'I wouldn't want you to abandon your duties,' Ruth returned quickly, slamming the dishes on the table until she caught her father's eye and adopted a less aggressive approach to the table-setting. 'After all, you know how *stimulating* you find what you do.'

'Well, yes. Working as a top reporter in some of the most dangerous hotspots in the world *is* stimulating, but...' He reached out and stilled her frantic hand, stroking it and then giving it a gentle squeeze. 'What could be more stimulating than being by your wife's side so that you can witness the creation of new life?'

'How long are you planning on staying?' Ruth asked, appalled by the way events appeared to be unfolding. She took the platter of lamb from her mother and deposited it on the table.

'Oh, I think I can stay for at least a few weeks...'

'*A few weeks?*'

'That's wonderful!' Claire said brightly, giving her daughter a brief hug in passing. 'Isn't that tremendous news, Ruthie?'

'But what about your...*job?*' She turned to her parents and said, a little wildly, 'Franco just does the odd bit of troubleshooting. In fact, he also works in an off...sorry, has a company.'

'What company would that be?' her father asked, and Franco gave a self-deprecating shrug of his broad shoulders.

'Just a few small concerns...one of them is practically a hobby, isn't it, my darling?'

'Won't those *small concerns* miss you if you stagnate here in the middle of nowhere for weeks on end?' Ruth hissed, infuriated by the smile tugging the corners of his mouth.

'Oh, I can pop up now and again to check on things! And I can bring my laptop here.' He turned to her father. 'Computers have shrunk the world, wouldn't you say? If I wanted to, I could probably do most of my business from one room in a house, provided I had the right equipment around me! Have computers reached religion as yet?' He settled comfortably in the chair with every appearance of someone getting used to surroundings they had no plans on leaving in a hurry.

'Dear boy—' her father leant forward, warming to his pet subject '—you'd be surprised. Bit of a computer boffin myself, actually.' He winked at his daughter. 'Good to have a man around to discuss it with…'

CHAPTER EIGHT

IT HAD been the longest dinner Ruth had ever endured. The lavish meal of roast lamb with all the trimmings appeared to be incidental to the main business of Franco winning her parents over.

Every mouthful of food had been punctuated with some fascinating evidence of wit and charm, and by the time she and her mother had begun clearing the table her parents had been hooked and reeled in like two helpless flounders.

She had tried her utmost not to catch his eye, but whenever she had she'd been rewarded with a look that promised a *very long chat* on the subject of her pregnancy.

At least, though, her parents, misinformed as they were, had not seen their illusions shattered, and for that she owed him a debt of gratitude. The question still remained: *what happens next?*—she had no doubt that he would fill her in on that without sparing her feelings. Making life easy for her was not, she suspected, at the top of his list of *must dos*.

And really, in a way, it was almost a relief to have everything in the open with him. Her decision to run away, necessary though it had seemed at the time, had encrusted her soul with a layer of ice and turned her into someone she didn't much like. Deception had never been a trait she admired, and to have succumbed so completely to it herself, whatever the circumstances, had made her feel sick inside herself.

She sighed and thought that the only passably good thing to have emerged from the evening was the fact that Franco would not be sharing her room with her. It had given her a surge of pleasure to say, with regret in her voice, that her bed, like the bed in the two free bedrooms, was of a single size. She didn't know if she had the strength to lie next to Franco's blatantly masculine body without reaching out to touch him, and that would be a disaster. She had forfeited any passing claim she had ever made on his affections.

Right now he should be safely ensconced in the small bedroom down the corridor from her, with the sloping roof and the patchwork quilt. He was so tall that his feet would stick out at the bottom of the bed and he would probably spend the night tossing and turning and trying to get into a comfortable position. He was not accustomed to small dimensions. His bed in his apartment in London was of the king sized variety. Enough room to hold a party.

Unfortunately, or fortunately, in this instance, the myriad rooms in the vicarage had mostly been turned into other things. One of the unused bedrooms had been turned into her father's office, one had been converted into a sewing room for her mother, and another two housed various *projects* which the parishioners seemed to have on the go on a fairly regular basis.

It wasn't unusual for Ruth to stroll into one of these rooms and be confronted by a barrage of hand-knitted stuffed dolls, waiting patiently for some charity fair or other and staring at the door with blank, woolly eyes, or else a vast assortment of brightly coloured cushions which seemed to be crying out for the addition of nubile girls in harem outfits.

The sheer eccentric chaos would get to him after a while. After, she suspected, a very short while. That, and the boredom of small village life, where eating out at a decent restaurant involved a forty-five minute trek into the nearest large town and the main topics of conversation were not stocks and shares but roses, manure and the weather.

In the darkness of her bedroom, she smirked to herself.

She was revolving in her head what other aspects of village life would get up his nose when there was a brief knock on the door, then it was pushed open, and, outlined against the light from the corridor, was Franco. A dark, well-built silhouette wearing a pair of boxer shorts and a tee shirt which he had borrowed from her father.

She realised that she wasn't surprised to see him. She had more than half expected it. Was that why she had abandoned her favoured night gear of skimpy vest and little shorts and opted for the one flannelette nightie she possessed?

He had retreated to his bedroom at a little after ten-thirty with the docility of a lamb, having trapped her into walking up the stairs with him but unable to prevent her from scampering back downstairs before they could make it to the isolated confines of his bedroom. His last words had been *Later, my darling*, which had barely made her steps falter.

The threatening little syllables had obviously been lodged somewhere in the forefront of her brain, though, because her eyes barely flickered now when she saw him.

Without saying a word, she switched on her bedside lamp and watched in silence as he pushed himself away from the doorframe and sauntered into the bedroom, carefully closing the door behind him. He had obviously waited until he assumed her parents to be asleep. Their bedroom was well within earshot of raised voices.

A little shiver of awareness slithered through her as he sat on the side of her bed, depressing the mattress with his weight. That, she thought gloomily, was the snake in the grass. It didn't matter how much she reasoned things out on a logical basis, how much she told herself that it would be a huge relief when he abandoned her as an object of revenge for walking out on him and, even worse, walking out on him when she was carrying his baby, she still felt an electric thrill whenever he was around. In fact, the past few weeks seemed to have been lived in cotton wool, and now that he was in the house and threatening to get under her skin she felt truly alive again.

Of course, that didn't mean that she *really wanted him around*, she reasoned to herself, screwing up her life for all the wrong reasons.

'I know you're going to shout at me,' she began defensively, 'and there's no point. It might make you feel better but it won't change anything.' Despite the fact that she had semi-rehearsed these lines, she still failed to sound firm and convincing. In fact, she was only a hair's breadth away from subsiding into a nervous stutter.

'Shout at you? Wake your parents up after they've

been so welcoming and hospitable? Perish the thought.' He smiled at her and she shivered.

'Thank you,' she said, looking away, 'for not...'

'Exposing their shy, unassuming daughter for the inveterate liar that she is?'

'I'm not an inveterate liar,' Ruth said mutinously.

'No? Well, it doesn't matter now. What matters is how we intend to deal with all of this.'

'We could have talked about it in the morning. There was no need for you to come here tonight.' As a form of protest, it sounded pretty unconvincing to her ears, considering he'd now been sitting on her bed for a good ten minutes.

'Oh, but you're my *wife*. I can do whatever I please with you!'

Ruth reddened and drew her knees up to her chest under the quilt, dragging it up, then she hugged her legs and rested her chin on her knees. 'You know that's not true,' she said in a faltering voice.

His eyes caught hers and her pulse began to beat with a quickened, steady pace.

'Well, we'll leave that for the moment, shall we?' Another one of those smiles that made her nervous system go into overdrive. 'Let's talk about the immediate future.'

'You can't possibly stay here for weeks on end,' Ruth said, with a question in her voice.

'Why not?'

'Because you've got things to do in London.'

'Yes, well, as it transpires, I've got things to do here as well.'

Her grey eyes glinted in the mellow light and, involuntarily, his eyes dropped to the slender column of her neck and the slight body bulked out by the quilt. She was wearing a thick nightgown. Nothing like she used to wear in bed with him.

To his lasting amusement, she had always refused to sleep naked, blaming it on her upbringing, but her nightclothes had never been of the granny variety. Baggy boxer shorts and loose white vests that always showed the twin peaks of her breasts, pushing against the cotton like pointed buds, begging to be touched. His eyes shot back to her face and he frowned.

'Would you ever have told me?' he asked quietly. 'Or would you happily have allowed my child to be born into this world without ever knowing the identify of its father?'

Ruth felt her mouth go dry. 'I hadn't really thought about it,' she whispered truthfully.

'You hadn't really thought about *anything*, had you?' He knew that he was beating this to death, but he couldn't help himself. She had been quite happy to go it alone! In fact, he thought darkly, she had probably been enjoying her independence before he showed up on the scene, while *he*, on the other hand, man of the world, eligible bachelor infamous Houdini when it came to the opposite sex, had spent *weeks* torn apart by her absence from his life.

'I thought I was doing the right thing.'

'The *right* thing? Surely, as a vicar's daughter, you *must* know that the last thing you were doing was the *right thing*!' He could feel himself on the verge of exploding and was obliged to surreptitiously take a few deep breaths to regain some self-control.

Think of the nightgown, he told himself with grim satisfaction. She was wearing what could only be called the ultimate man deterrent. Because, he decided, *because* just in case he showed up, which she had half expected him to, judging from her lack of outrage, she didn't want to be clad in anything remotely sexy. Because the thought of sex and him still did something for her. Still, he decided, *turned her on*.

'All right, then, the *best* thing.'

'For whom? The best thing *for whom*?' He watched as her fingers plucked nervously at the quilt cover and she licked her lips. Then she straightened her legs, revealing the true depth of her sexless nightwear in all its splendid *spinster aunt* glory.

It had all the hallmarks of sexlessness. A ruffled neckline, a few little pearl buttons down the front, long sleeves. Probably reached to her ankles as well, he thought, staring at her face yet, mysteriously, still managing to see the swell of her breasts under the unrevealing cloth. He felt himself harden and adjusted his sitting position accordingly.

'For...everyone...'

'Tomorrow...' he said, getting up and strolling across to the window, out of which he proceeded to stare before turning to face her tense figure on the bed. Her hands, demurely linked on her lap, fidgeted continually. 'Tomorrow I intend to go to London to sort out one or two things. I'll probably be there a couple of days, then I'll be back. With clothes. And while I'm gone you'll have to do a little bit of furniture replacement.' He moved across to the bed, where he proceeded to tower over her prone form, his fingers fractionally tucked into the elasticised waistband of the boxer shorts.

'What do you mean?'

'You know what I mean,' Franco said on a long-suffering sigh. 'This sleeping arrangement isn't going to work. For starters, what are your parents going to think? That your besotted husband, fresh back from those war zones, is content to sleep in a separate room from his coy, young wife?' He looked at her with hooded eyes. 'No.' He shook his head, 'As your husband, I have one or two rights...'

Ruth felt her heart begin to flutter madly. Wasn't this taking the game too far? But how on earth could she complain without giving everything away?

'I can't redecorate my parents' house,' she attempted feebly, and he sprang onto her reply with alacrity.

'In which case we could always move out. Get a cosy little flat somewhere. Or a house. Yet, flats are for the city; houses are much more what we'd want here, in the middle of this beautiful countryside. Something small and ivy-clad, perhaps a thatched roof.'

'You've been looking at too many chocolate box covers,' Ruth declared, with a sniff. 'Houses like that don't exist in this part of the world.' She found herself drifting into a very pleasant world of Franco, the baby and cosy evenings spent in front of a roaring log fire in some wonderful, fictitious thatched cottage, and metaphorically pinched herself back to the present.

'Why are you doing this?' she asked, looking at him. How could a man look so obscenely spectacular in an oversized tee shirt with a cartoon logo on the front? It wasn't fair. Little wonder she had stupidly fallen in love with him. He was the type of man who was positively lethal when it came to virginal country girls with marginal experience of men and a head full of romantic dreams.

'What's the alternative?' he asked smoothly. He had known that she would ask him that question sooner or later, and the truth was that his answer had been a little too long in coming for his liking.

He might well rage and rant and hurl accusations at her, but the facts were straightforward enough. She was pregnant and had involved him in a lie to spare her parents a small part of the truth. Well, even if it hadn't occurred to her, it had certainly occurred to him that everyone could emerge a winner from the situation.

All he had to do was go along with the lie for a while, perhaps disappear on some fictitious mission, reappearing when the baby was born and thereafter vanishing again until it became clear that his presence was not a constant and a divorce was inevitable.

Seeing the child would be no problem because he could simply persuade her to move back to London, perhaps even hand her back her job with a few more perks thrown in so that she had ample money, and visits could happily occur during the week or on weekends. End of complicated story.

However, this version of possible events was not what he discovered he wanted.

He didn't want to be a part-time father and a pretend husband. He wanted more than that, although whenever he got to that point in his head he firmly switched off rather than meander down the twisty road to its shady, unwelcome destination.

He watched her face closely in the semi-darkness

and had to resist the urge to hurry the conversation along until it got to the point he wanted.

'You could always go away,' she suggested timidly. 'I mean, I wouldn't try and stop you from seeing the baby whenever you wanted...'

'No can do. You involved me in this and I don't intend to emerge from it looking like a cad and a bounder.'

'Who would know?' Ruth asked, trying to follow his train of thought.

'Every single friend I possess, for a start. I mean, Ruth, *think about it*. I'm a single man one minute, and the next minute I'm visiting a baby, having abandoned the mother to her own devices. And what about your parents? Eh? *Their* opinion of me is hardly going to be sky-high when I vanish off the face of the earth leaving you to get on with things on your own.' *Why* that mattered, *exactly*, was hard to say, but matter it did.

'You could always pay child maintenance if that makes you feel better.'

'*No!*'

'Shh! You'll wake my parents. They're very light sleepers!'

'No.' He lowered his voice but didn't alter its tone. 'Doesn't it make more sense for me to go along with this and for things to taper off if needs be?'

If needs be? he thought. What does *that* mean? Why did his vocal cords insist on forming ridiculous sentences that had nothing to do with his thought processes?

'If needs be? What does that mean?'

'It means,' he said heavily, 'that I intend to be

around for a while and there's nothing you can do about it.' He stood up and looked down at her, challenging her to question his decision further, ready for any verbal fight she might care to indulge in, but she seemed bemused by the course of events.

'Just make sure,' he said, turning to her, his hand on the doorknob, 'that you get the bed.'

Which was a request that she found nigh on impossible to obey.

Like the devoted husband he wasn't he called her every evening for the five nights he was away, making sure, she suspected, that he called at dinner time, when he knew that her parents would be around. Why, she had no idea. If his sojourn in her life was to be temporary, why go to any lengths to impress her parents, two people he would never see again?

It made no sense, and she quickly decided that she was reading meaning into something basically meaningless. He called at the same time every evening because it was the most convenient time for him *to* call.

Which left quite a bit of free time, she thought. What did he get up to after eight in the evening? Back home to his apartment to sit in front of the telly with a pre-packaged meal for one on his lap? Hardly. But, if not, then where *was* he?

On the night before he was due to return, Ruth finally gave in to impulse and dialled his home number. She was so utterly convinced that he would be out, living down to her worst suspicions, that she was flabbergasted when the telephone was answered and she heard his dark, velvety voice down the end of the line.

'It's me,' she blurted out, and then added hastily, in case he didn't recognise her voice, 'Ruth.'

'I *know* who it is. What's the matter? Is everything all right?' His voice was laced with sudden, urgent anxiety and Ruth allowed herself a moment of sheer pleasure during which she indulged in the brief but sweetly tempting fantasy that Franco actually *cared* about her.

'Yes! Nothing's wrong with the baby. I'm fine.'

There was a small, telling pause.

'Then why are you calling?'

'I'm sorry,' Ruth said stiffly. 'Am I interrupting anything?'

'Depends...'

'Oh, I see.' She saw a tall, leggy glamorous woman sitting at the rough, incredibly expensive hand-made dining table, swirling a glass of champagne in one hand, long raven-black hair falling in a mass of curls over one shoulder, smouldering Latin eyes thickly fringed, promising him who knew what antics in the bedroom later that night.

'I've just this minute got back from work, actually.'

'At this hour?' Ruth heard her voice rise in suspicious disbelief, and she cleared her throat and continued with ghastly formality, 'You must be exhausted. I'm sorry I disturbed you.'

'Forget it.'

In the background she heard the clink of ice being tossed into a glass. He was on the mobile, probably in the exquisitely and rarely used high-tech kitchen. She strained her ears to see whether she could discern another lot of clinking ice which would be a telltale sign that he had company, but there was nothing, and she found herself momentarily breathing a sigh of relief.

'You never said what you wanted.' He spoke into

her ear, and for a wild moment she imagined that she could almost feel his breath against her cheek.

'Nothing!'

The one telling word was out before she could take it back, and she heard a dry chuckle down the end of the line. 'You mean you were just missing me?'

'I was doing no such thing!'

'Then perhaps you wanted to check my whereabouts. Could you have become seized with a sudden attack of jealousy because I wasn't around?'

His wild but accurate stab at the truth made her give a forced cackle of laughter.

'Don't be ridiculous. You have an ego the size of...the size of...'

'C'mon, Ruth, can't you think of anything else I have that's as big as my so-called ego?'

She felt her face begin to burn as her mind swerved off obligingly in the direction he had pointed to, only skidding to an abrupt halt when he said, with amusement, 'You're blushing, aren't you? I can feel it down the line.'

'Oh!' She made a few strangled sounds under her breath. 'I just *called* as a *matter of fact*—' at last, inspiration! '—to tell you that I've wasted hundreds of valuable man hours tramping through the nearest towns in search of a wretched bed that can be delivered by tomorrow and...' She allowed a few seconds to elapse, thoroughly, and childishly enjoying the anticipation of satisfaction about to come. 'The earliest any double bed can be delivered is in four weeks' time.'

'No problem. Leave it with me.'

'Leave it with you? And what can *you* do that I

can't?' Her moment of triumph had lasted the length of time it took for her to blink.

'You'd be pleasantly surprised. I'll make sure it's delivered by tomorrow afternoon.' His voice dropped a couple of notches. 'Aren't you excited, darling? We'll be able to sleep together! The way we should...seeing that we're married now...' He gave a throaty chuckle, and she slammed the receiver down.

She'd worked it out. At long last, she'd worked it out, and it amazed her that she hadn't slotted the pieces of the jigsaw together before now.

Yes, he wanted to take responsibility in the matter of the baby, but Franco Leoni was a charming, sexy, self-confident predator when it came to the opposite sex, and he intended to stick around and take full advantage of the situation in which he found himself, to continue sleeping with her. He still wanted her and he intended to have her, until he grew tired and bored with his conquest, at which point, and not a minute before, he would do his convenient vanishing act, only reappearing at intervals to do his fatherly duties.

There was nothing she could do about it. In public, he had licence to do whatever he pleased. He could touch her, stand as close to her as he liked, allow his hands to wander wherever they wanted, within reason, and she had unwittingly handed him this freedom.

And in private...

Ruth shivered and began heading up the stairs to the bedroom and the short-lived comfort of her single bed.

He knew that she was still attracted to him. Her body and face revealed as much even if her mouth insisted on paying lip service to politeness.

What if a bed *did* arrive tomorrow?

She pushed open the door to her bedroom and stared forlornly at her conveniently sized bed for one. She had visions of the two of them, back to sharing a bed, their bodies touching even if she tried to edge to the furthest part of the bed as possible. He knew how to touch her; he could break her in a matter of seconds....

'How wonderful!'

Those were her mother's words as the lorry backed up the drive to deliver the bed.

'I can think of plenty more wonderful things,' Ruth muttered under her breath.

'What's that, dear? How did he *manage* to get this all sorted out in a matter of a few hours?' Her mother had taken charge of the situation and was crisply giving instructions and leading the way up the stairs to the bedroom. 'And such a marvellous bed, as well! I've always longed for a wrought-iron bed.' She sighed dreamily and Ruth was sorely tempted to tell her mother that she could have the thing, no charge. 'There's something terribly *romantic* about a wrought-iron bed, wouldn't you agree, darling?'

'No. I prefer wood myself.'

Her mother peered back over her shoulder to give her a chiding look. 'I hope you won't be indiscreet enough to tell that to your husband!' she scolded. 'He must have spent *hours* choosing this and arranging the whole thing.'

'Mum, he probably spent five minutes on the phone!'

'He must be awfully persuasive in that case.' They watched in silence for a few minutes as the delivery men wrestled with the base of the bed through the door of the bedroom. The single bed had been ignominiously put in one of the outbuildings a couple of hours before by her father and three of the parishioners, who had needed quite some cups of tea to recover from the exertion.

'It's called rich, I think.'

'Now, Ruth, it's not like you to be cynical. Franco is a delightful man and he clearly adores you. Super! Could you just shift it a tiny bit more towards the centre? Yes, just right! Ruth! Come and have a peek!'

'It's very nice,' Ruth admitted grudgingly. She didn't dare step too far into the room. It was bad enough seeing the vast expanse of double bed that seemed to be mocking her crumbling sensibilities from halfway behind her mother's back outside the bedroom.

'Are you excited?' Her mother turned to her and giggled.

'No, I am not!' Ruth said severely. 'I mean...I mean...'

'Yes, I *know* it won't be the first time, but there's something so *precious* about my baby girl, married and sharing a bed with her husband. I can still remember when you hated boys, for goodness' sake!'

Ruth belatedly wished that she had continued to pursue that path.

'Oh, Mum. Please!'

Claire affectionately gave her daughter a hug and they watched the delivery men depart with wildly different thoughts going through their heads.

The so-called divorce, Ruth was fast realising, coming after the so-called marriage, would hit her parents hard. Much harder now that they had met the so-called husband and had had a chance to like him. She sighed with a mixture of frustration and sheer worry.

'I know.' Her mother patted her arm and ushered her back into the house. 'You feel a bit misty-eyed as well, don't you?' They strolled into the kitchen while Claire continued to prattle on with whimsy about childhood and getting older.

'You wait until you have your own,' she said knowingly, as she filled the kettle and spooned coffee into two mugs. 'I only wish, you know, that your dad and I could have had a big wedding for you. Or at least had *something*.

This niggling, guilt-inducing line of conversation had reared its head soon after Ruth had arrived back with her news weeks previously, and she was disconcerted that it was surfacing once again.

'I mean, darling, I *do* understand. Franco had to dash away without any notice at all and you simply had to leap at the chance or risk missing it altogether, but still...'

'I know, Mum. If things could have been a bit different, then, well, you know I would have loved to have had a white wedding. A very *small* white wedding... But, you know, sometimes things just don't work out the way we expect them to...'

She relieved her mother of the mug of coffee and took a couple of sips, then headed for the larder and the biscuit tin. Disappointingly, the chocolate bourbons had all been eaten. She would have to have a word with her dad about that. Hadn't he promised to stay away from the biscuits?

She returned to the kitchen to find her mother waiting for her with an unnerving glint in her eye.

'Darling, I've had a wonderful idea.'

'Yes?' Ruth asked warily, edging back into her chair and making do with the custard creams.

'You know we were talking about how disappointed we both were that there was no white wedding...?'

Ruth hadn't realised that she had ever mentioned any such thing, but she nodded obligingly anyway.

'Well...' The smile on her mother's face made her look like a girl of sixteen. 'What about a *blessing*? Just something right here, in the vicarage. Something terribly informal. We could ask a few of the parishioners. You *know* how fond they all are of you...and now that Franco is going to be around for a little while...well, I'm *sure* he'd be delighted with the idea...!'

'Delighted with what idea?'

Both women swung around at the sound of Franco's voice from the kitchen doorway.

'No idea,' Ruth burst out. 'Mum was just...' She caught her mother's eye and lapsed into sulky silence.

'Come in here, Franco. You look exhausted. I'll make you a cup of coffee and tell you all about *my wonderful idea*!'

CHAPTER NINE

'How could you?' Ruth watched stormily as Franco strolled towards the ridiculously huge double bed and proceeded to test the mattress. He kicked off his shoes, rolled up the sleeves of his shirt and, after bouncing on the bed a few times, lay down with his legs crossed and his arms folded behind his head.

'Incredibly comfortable,' he informed her, ignoring the look of outrage on her face and allowing his eyes to roam lazily over her. 'Not too hard, not too soft. Goldilocks would have a field-day on this one. Even *with* the three bears towering over her, she'd still be inclined to stay put.'

She was, he thought delightedly, positively *vibrating* with dismay at the way he had grabbed her mother's idea and gone along with the concept, lock, stock and barrel. She obviously had not the slightest idea how delicious she looked, standing there in the doorway, hands on hips, body thrust belligerently forward, her blonde hair swinging across her face and her perfect mouth downturned. How could any sane man be expected to hold a normal conversation with a woman who was so immensely provocative without even realising it?

The pair of jeans, which fitted snugly on her frame, were too long, and had been roughly cuffed at the bottom where there was just a sliver of teasing, slender ankle peeping out before a pair of inappropriately fluffy bedroom slippers took over. The checked shirt, which might have looked unappealing on any other women, *radiated* sexuality on this one, and Franco indulged himself by staring at her, taking it all in, enjoying every minute of his inspection.

He could well imagine her breasts underneath, clad in one of those functional stretchy Lycra bras she seemed to prefer wearing, the kind that were designed to do nothing for a man's imagination except perhaps squash it. But gazing at her breasts contoured beneath the sporty elasticised fabric had brought him a thrill that no lacy bra on any woman had ever succeeded in doing in his life before. One very short meander down memory lane and he could conjure up the image without any difficulty at all.

'Are you going to say *anything* or are you just going to *lie there*?' Ruth spluttered, pink-faced.

'I'm just going to lie here,' he replied seriously, watching as her face went a shade brighter.

When he had first arrived at the vicarage, unannounced and seething with what he considered well-justified rage, he had expected no more than a brief but explosive showdown at the end of which he had planned on leaving with his mind well and truly satisfied. He had reluctantly but eventually given in to his insane desire to see her one last time and *find out why she had run out on him*, but he had had every intention of making sure that he left with the last word.

It still mystified him that she had managed to bewitch him right back into feeling those old, inconvenient feelings which he had spent weeks stuffing away in a cupboard labelled *soft*.

He couldn't look at her without feeling desire, and

he couldn't listen to a word she said without being utterly captivated by her contradictions.

'You could always come and lie next to me,' he suggested helpfully. He flicked an invisible speck of dust from his trousers and said casually, 'You can't avoid the bed, you know.' He patted the space next to him. 'I'll talk to you about it if you'd just relax a little.'

With a fuming, strangled sound, Ruth shut the bedroom door and then leant heavily against it.

You can't avoid the bed. Did he think that she imagined, for one minute, that she *could*? When it engulfed the entire room and made looking at anything else within those four small walls an impossibility?

'I am very relaxed,' Ruth informed him stiffly, and he grinned at her.

'If your fingers dig any harder into your sides, you'll rip your clothing.'

Ruth refused to see anything funny in his remark. She didn't know what game he was playing, whether he was inspired by some sick desire for revenge just because she had had the temerity to walk out on him, but she wasn't going to stand for it. Her hands might be tied, but that didn't mean that she was going to let him get away with murder.

'Just answer me,' she said through gritted teeth.

'When you calm down.' He swung his long legs over the side of the bed and stood up, stretching. Then he began to undo the buttons of his shirt.

'What are you doing?'

'What does it look like I'm doing?'

Ruth gulped. In many ways it would have been easier if she had never seen him naked before. As it was, her mind could provide her with all the tantalising and accurate details about his body, well muscled, hard and lithe. She had traced its contours with her fingers often enough to know how helpless the sight of it would make her feel. She shifted her eyes away and maintained a lofty silence.

'I'm going to have a bath,' he said mildly. 'The drive from London was a nightmare.' He stripped off his shirt, rummaged in one of the two suitcases he had lugged up with him, and extracted a white dressing gown of the expensive hotel variety.

She had never seen him in a dressing gown before. Nudity was something he was not uncomfortable with, and when they had been lovers he had enjoyed her watching his nakedness as much as she had enjoyed doing it.

'Care to come? I could soap you.' He threw her a long, slow smile. 'You've always enjoyed that.' His voice was low and husky, and in spite of herself she felt her body begin to stir at the memory.

Another fractional tilt of the head gave him the answer to that one, but, although she looked away, she could still see him out of the corner of her eye as he shrugged off the work shirt and then the trousers and finally his boxer shorts.

Oh, *God*. Ruth licked her lips. Every muscle in her body, every pore and vein and blood vessel seemed to be stretched to breaking point, and a fine film of perspiration had broken out over her entire body.

'Do you remember?' He took a couple of steps in her direction, and, with alarm, she realised that the dressing gown had still not been donned. He had it hooked over one shoulder.

'No!' Her head was now at a right angle, but the bedroom was so small that she couldn't help *but* see his magnificent body. Nor could she fail to notice his flagrant arousal.

'Of course you do,' he said in a silky persuasive voice. He was now standing close enough to her that if she reached out a couple of inches she would bump into him. 'You'd climb into the bath, luxuriate in the water and *I would...*'

'Ruth promptly covered her ears with her hands and squeezed her eyes tightly shut.

'I would...'

She felt his hands cover hers and gently prise them away from her ears.

'I would soap you all over, starting with your feet, massaging the soles so that you'd sink a little deeper into the water, and then...'

'I'm not interested!' Ruth said breathlessly. She couldn't help but hear him, but she refused to open her eyes and see him as well.

'Oh, yes, you are. I know you a damn sight better than you think and I know when your mouth is saying one thing and everything else is screaming something entirely different.' He leaned a little closer and spoke into her ear. 'You used to laugh because your legs would be unsteady when you finally stood up so that I could finish my job, so that I could work the soap into a foaming, warm lather and then I'd...'

'Shut up!'

'Are you getting turned on?'

'No, I'm not.'

'Then I'd soap your breasts, full, slippery breasts...your nipples would be hard and you'd have your head thrown back as if you were offering them to my mouth, holding them out to be suckled.'

He took one crucial step closer and his hard arousal pressed against her thighs.

Ruth was finding it remarkably easy to remember just how wobbly her legs had used to feel when she'd tried to stand up in that bath. Much the same as they were feeling right now. She pressed herself back against the door, breathing rapidly.

'And then,' he murmured into her ear, holding her head with his hand so that she couldn't escape him, 'I would work the soap over your stomach. Remember? Over your stomach and down to your thighs...'

'No. Stop. Please.'

'And between them. Slowly and thoroughly. Between your thighs, and then I would touch you where you were aching to be touched, and rub you there, and there would be no telling where your natural dampness and the bath water began... Are you wet for me now?' He laughed softly, and then flicked his tongue into her ear so that she moaned and squirmed at the same time. 'Can I feel? Find out if you're as turned on as I am?'

His voice was mesmerising. There was no other word for it. She had been hypnotised, or at least that was how she felt. He undid the button of her jeans and then pulled down the zip. From a great distance, she seemed to be watching all of this, and to be incapable of stopping it.

He pushed his hand beneath her underwear and then, what she had been waiting for, every nerve stretched to breaking point, his finger slid inexorably into her, rubbing against the dainty bud, now swollen with pleasure, circling and pressing it until she thought she might go mad with desire.

Stripped of sanity, she found herself shakily unbuttoning her shirt, easing her breasts out of her bra without bothering to unclasp it at the back, and she watched, fascinated, as his mouth found her engorged nipple and he began tugging at it, pulling it into his mouth while his tongue rasped against the tender, swollen bud.

'Enjoying this, darling?'

Ruth nodded. In a minute she would concentrate on the stupidity of her actions. Right now his mouth and fingers were doing crazy things to her nervous system, crazy things she thought she might be addicted to.

'Why fight what we feel for one another?' he whispered, straightening to kiss her while his fingers continued to play with her moist, feminine cavity. 'We still want one another. Why stop it? Why not just see where it leads?'

Ruth drowsily considered his question, and when she opened her eyes it was to find him looking at her urgently.

'Accept this,' he said. 'Let's enjoy one another.'

His words were like a gush of cold water over her. He wanted her to enjoy what they had, but even now she could feel her own enjoyment fading and her erotic oblivion being swiftly replaced by dawning horror that she had been so happy to jeopardise her peace of mind for the sake of a few moments of stolen pleasure. She pulled away sharply.

'Stop fighting me,' he said. 'Why fight? Why wage war when we can make love? Why struggle when we both want to give in?'

'Because giving in to what we felt for one another was what landed us in this mess.' She risked opening her eyes to look at him.

'Lying to your parents is what landed us in this mess.'

'And how would it have been any different otherwise?' Ruth demanded, finding her strength now that she wasn't having the ground yanked away from under her by the seductive lure of his voice with all its erotic fantasies. She had squirmed totally out of his grasp and was shakily redressing herself.

He clicked his tongue and stuck on the ubiquitous dressing gown.

'If you'd said something from the start...'

'How could I?' she asked hotly. 'Neither of us had planned on a baby. Are you telling me that you would have been over the moon if I'd sat you down and informed you that you were going to be a daddy?'

Yes. The tiny word crept into his head with shocking effect. He stared at her and his mind had gone completely and utterly blank. Blank but for that single admission that had stolen into his brain without giving the slightest forewarning of its intent.

Taking his silence for agreement, Ruth felt her anger gather momentum.

'You would have been horrified!' she said, hugging herself tightly as he pulled the robe around him and gazed down at her belligerently. 'You say that you know me better than I think. Well, *I* know *you* better than *you* think! You've lived your life this far without managing to be snagged by anyone and that's the way you like it. You've made no bones about that! Did you think that I was the sort of girl to push you into a role of responsibility you had neither courted nor wanted? Would you have appreciated the gesture?'

Ruth couldn't believe that she was raging at this man with a furious eloquence that she had never had at her command before. He had given her strength without even knowing. Just one more thing, she thought bitterly, to be lost in the rubble of their relationship, one more good thing to spend the rest of her days remembering.

Franco continued to stare at her in silence as he grappled with his own line of thought which, having taken root, now seemed to be growing at a frightening rate.

So this was what it felt like to have the shoe on the other foot. A ridiculous situation, of which he had zero experience, had come home to roost with a vengeance.

Ruth might well have done what she did for misguided but naïvely altruistic reasons. How ironic that he now found himself in the position of craving the one thing she didn't want. Stability, commitment. He couldn't bring himself to say the *Marriage* word, not even to himself.

'Well? *Well?* Are you going to answer me?' she pressed on bitterly. There was the glimmer of tears in the corners of her eyes and she wiped them away with an exasperated gesture.

'You make it sound as though I intend to swan through life as a bachelor so that I can die a lonely old man, because picking women up and dumping them is what I enjoy doing...'

'Let's be honest,' Ruth said painfully, looking away from him. 'Even if you *were* to get married, at some point in the future, later rather than sooner, then it wouldn't be to someone like me. Just because I'm a country bumpkin doesn't mean that I'm the village idiot as well. I *know* the kind of woman you would be attracted to, the kind of woman you would want by your side, and I don't fit the bill.' She gave a short, choked laugh. 'I'm not polished, I don't possess all those sophisticated little ways, I blush too much!'

'That's a load of nonsense. You...'

'Don't, Franco,' she said wearily. 'What's happened has happened. All we can do is accept it now, but if sleeping with you is part of your end of the deal, part of the deal for agreeing to keep my parents in the dark about the reality of the situation, then, thanks but no thanks.'

'How the hell can you talk about making love together as a *deal*?' He shook his head and raked his fingers through his hair. 'What kind of man do you think I am, for God's sake? The sort who would try and blackmail you into bed?'

'I didn't mean that,' Ruth objected, confused because her words had been misinterpreted somewhere along the way. There was nothing sleazy about Franco, but without thinking she had made him sound that way.

'Don't worry,' he said harshly, 'you can sleep peacefully in the bed tonight. I won't lay a finger on you. And in the morning I'll be gone.'

His words went straight to her heart like a sliver of glass.

'There's no need,' she began weakly.

'Correction. There's *every* need. And you needn't worry that I'll spill the beans to your parents. They, at any rate, deserve better than that. No, I'll do the vanishing act you were so desperate for me to do and then I shall make contact with you via a lawyer.

Know this, though—I will *not* vanish out of my child's life, and I don't care *how much* that will suit you. I *will* see the baby and you *will* accept maintenance for yourself and for the child. What you do with yours is your affair, but no child of mine will ever want for anything.

'Now—' he nodded to the door against which she seemed adhered as though with glue '—if you don't mind, I'll go and have my bath. Where you sleep is your concern, but I shall be sleeping on that bed. Take it or leave it.'

Ruth stood aside silently to let him pass, and when she heard the click of the bathroom door further down the corridor she felt her body sag, as though invisible strings holding it up had suddenly been severed.

Now that she was getting what she wanted, she realised what she had known all along. She didn't want it. She never had. She didn't want Franco to do a convenient vanishing act, and she didn't want her communications with him to be reduced to conversations between lawyers.

But there was a big difference between what she wanted, what she could have and what had been offered, and Ruth knew that, however tempting it was to snatch at the little she had on the off chance that it might lead to bigger, more substantial things, she would be a fool to do it.

She undressed and slipped into her nightie, the starched maiden aunt one, and then crept along the corridor to the unused bathroom, which was the size of a matchbox, and up a few winding stairs *en route* to the attic. There, she washed her face, brushed her teeth and then rested on the sink and stared at her reflection in the mirror.

Looking for changes in her body had become something of a nightly ritual. After she had recovered from the initial shock of her pregnancy, a deep feeling of satisfied pleasure had taken its place. She had become accustomed to inspecting her face and her body for any differences. Her breasts, she knew, had grown. She had never been flat-chested and now they were heavy, the nipples bigger and darker than before.

Her stomach was beginning to fill out too, though not obviously so. She just fitted into her clothes a little more snugly. Soon those small changes would become unmistakable, until her stomach would swell with her child, *their* child.

Knowing that Franco would not be around to witness any of those changes was like carrying a splinter around in her heart.

Knowing that he would share their child but not her life was an ache that seemed to have no end.

Worse than that was the knowledge that one day he would meet a woman with whom he wanted to build his life, and it would be inevitable that she, Ruth, would meet this woman, would know that the happiness *she* would never have belonged to someone else, and she would have to smile bravely through that knowledge even if she was weeping inside.

It was scant comfort to know that she was doing the right thing in standing firm against Franco. She had already paid dearly for giving in to temptation. She placed the flat of her hand against her stomach and stood very, very still, wondering if she could feel the baby move inside her. But it was too early yet, and, with a little sigh, she headed back towards the bedroom.

Evidence of Franco's decision to leave was strewn around the room. A pile of clothing lay on the bed and his two suitcases had been dragged out and opened. More clothes were crammed in, a creased bundle of shirts, trousers, underwear, ties and socks.

Ruth watched numbly as he continued to hurl more various items of clothing from bed to case, ignoring her in the process.

'There's no need for you to leave tonight,' she said weakly, and when he didn't bother to look at her, she repeated herself in a louder voice.

'But isn't that what you *want*?' Franco jeered, flinging some aftershave into the case with venomous precision. He was wearing a pair of khaki-coloured trousers and a shirt which had not been buttoned up and gaped to expose the muscular wall of his chest.

Yes, he admitted with vicious self-disgust, he had finally reached the bottom of the road. Here he was, self-control shot to hell, acting like a toddler. And *she* was to blame. She of the creamy hair and creamy skin and innocent, dreamy smile that could drive a man mad within seconds. She had reduced him to *this*. Pelting clothes into a suitcase glowering with rage and confusion and sheer, bloody *hurt*.

He looked at her, standing by the door, her face wearing an appalled expression, and a lifetime of knowing precisely what to say on precisely what occasion deserted him. He knew that if he opened his mouth he would not be able to hide his bewilderment at this strange turn of the tide.

'It's for the best,' she said miserably. 'But there's no need for you to...to be so dramatic... I mean...'

'Dramatic?' His voice was thick with an ominous tone of threat, and Ruth looked at him hesitantly. Of course she had said the wrong thing. Didn't she specialise in that? It was only natural that he would be furious at her refusal to go along with him. He was a sophisticated man of the world. He would be utterly perplexed at the moral inconsistency of a woman who could happily sleep with him until she got pregnant, and then wouldn't come within a mile of him.

'I d-didn't mean *dramatic...*' she stammered.

The accuracy of the description had cut to the quick. He *was*, he knew, being dramatic. Behaving like a complete ass. And the worst of it was that he just couldn't help himself. His hand was throwing items of clothing into the suitcase, the muscles in his face were contracting into an expression of glowering rage, his mouth appeared to have a will of its own and was spouting forth the sort of rubbish that he would have sneered at in someone else.

And where the hell was his brain in all of this? His brain was fine, thank you very much. His *brain* knew full well that he should just walk away from the situation and give her what she craved, namely his absence, even though her body might still want to be touched by his.

'Mum and Dad are going to wonder... I mean, we've... *you've* only just gone and bought...' She gestured towards the bed, which had been the source of this final, tragic showdown. 'What are they going to think?'

'It's time you stopped living for what your parents

want,' he said harshly, snapping shut the suitcases and buttoning up his shirt.

'I don't *live* for what my parents want.' Ruth took a deep breath and lashed out with unexpected vigour. 'I consider their feelings. That's something entirely different. Haven't *you* ever considered the feelings of someone else?'

There was a telling silence, then Ruth said slowly, 'You haven't, have you? You've always had what you wanted. You have money and charm and good looks and...and...everything's always gone your way. You've never *had* to stand back and think about other people because other people were always there, thinking about *you*.'

'That's a load of rubbish,' he countered uncomfortably, wondering how her description of him as having charm and good looks had managed to backfire into an insult.

'No, it's not. It's the truth.' She took a few steps into the room, stepping around the suitcases and heading for the small wooden rocking chair that was now jammed against the wall since the arrival of the double bed. She sat down and looked at him.

'That's why you're in such a rush to get out of here. You wanted to sleep with me and because I said no, you decided to clear out as fast as your legs could take you. Now that you won't be getting what you want, you no longer feel the need to impress Mum and Dad, or even to tell them to their face that you're leaving. You've washed your hands of the situation and you can't wait to clear out.'

'Listen to yourself!' His voice was confidently dismissive, but he still had to admit to himself that what she had said made sense, even if every single word was wildly off target. 'I'm doing what *you* want and you have the nerve to tell me that I'm being inconsiderate!'

'I'm asking you to wait until morning, at least. You've gone and told Mum and Dad that...' She could feel her eyes welling up again, and she gulped back the urge to cry. Hormones, pregnancy and a naturally soft nature were conspiring to turn her into a sodden, weeping mess. 'That a blessing would be a brilliant idea, and now, just when they will have gone to bed crowing with delight at the thought of it, planning what needs to be done, you're prepared to walk out without even saying goodbye!'

'I...' Now he felt like a cad. For once in his life he had been propelled by emotion, and he had come out of it looking like a cad. He shot her a seething, defensive look, but was finding it difficult to defend his stance.

'Not that I knew what possessed you to go along with the idea in the first place,' she swept on, caught on an unstoppable current of recrimination. 'Things are complicated enough without them being further complicated!'

'I...'

'Will you let me finish?' The ferocity of her command threw him for six, and he literally took a step backwards before looking at her narrowly, the amusement back in his eyes as he absorbed the quivering angel in front of him.

He wasn't going to let her go. He was *never* going to let her go. And if she didn't love him, then she would learn to. Because she was the only woman he had ever loved and the only one he ever would. He would use the physical hold he knew he had over her and he would work until her defences were broken.

The decision left him with a feeling of calm. Let her rant and rave; her fate was sealed. He was her fate just as she was his, and his pride was not going to stand in the way of something as big and overwhelming and wonderful as this.

'So now you just intend to walk away and leave *me* to pick up the pieces behind you...!'

'Well, there would be no pieces to pick up if it weren't for you in the first place...'

'There's no point harking on about what was done...'

'Why are you so against the idea of a blessing, anyway?' Franco asked, swerving away from the topic of his departure, which appeared more pointless and rash as the minutes ticked by.

'Because it doesn't seem *right*,' Ruth muttered, angling her body up to him.

'It's no less *right* than the fictitious marriage we're supposed to be enjoying!' he bit back with grim logic.

'You know what I mean,' Ruth was obliged to counteract stubbornly, and he shook his head in wonderment, as though thoroughly bemused by her illogic.

'No, I don't! I don't damn well know what you mean! And I'm sick to death and utterly fed up with all of this!' *Where was he going with this?*

He stalked across to the suitcase and began pelting clothes out, back onto the bed, where they collected into a hideously untidy mound. Her mouth had dropped open, which was mildly satisfying.

'I'm staying! Do you hear me? I'm not going anywhere? I'm in love with you and you'll damn well accept that and start loving me back if it's the last thing you do!'

As a declaration of devotion, he was forced to admit it left a great deal to be desired, but he was beyond caring.

'And will you stop looking at me as though I've turned into a three-headed alien? You're pregnant with *my* child...' even in the midst of his roaring anger he couldn't prevent a note of pride from creeping into his voice '...and if you think that you're going to selfishly waltz out of my life now, then you're wrong! We're man and wife—'

'But we're not *really*...' Ruth interrupted meekly.

'Well, we *will be*! We're getting married. We're going to be a family! Do you understand me?'

'Because you love me?' She gazed at him, adoring the sullen lines of his mouth and loving him for the strength she knew it must have taken for him to broadcast his feelings when he was uncertain of the response.

'Yes,' he muttered grimly.

'Adore me, even?'

A slow smile began to tug the corners of his mouth. 'Even that,' he agreed.

'Would worship be too big a word?'

'Not big enough...'

Ruth smiled. 'Ditto.'

CHAPTER TEN

RUTH felt as though she was swimming. Swimming up to the surface of the water, where she would be able to take a huge gulp of air and breathe again. That would have been very nice, were it not for the fact that she didn't want to regain consciousness. She couldn't quite think why, but she knew that floating around in her present dreamlike state was infinitely better than waking up to reality.

She opened her eyes tentatively to find Franco staring down at her. She was lying on a bed in a very small room with white walls and a television inappropriately set on brackets against the wall. Around her was a scrunched-up mass of white sheets. Fear and panic flooded her, and she felt the desire to cry well up inside her like an unstoppable tidal wave.

In the space of a few seconds everything, every emotion, every word and every thought, came back to her with nightmarish clarity.

She had been standing in the finished nursery at their newly bought London mews house. Her parents had been deeply impressed because all the decorating had been contracted out to professionals. Someone had come in and, in the space of a week, had turned the high-ceilinged room with the gorgeous bay window into a wonderful green and yellow nursery.

Of course Ruth had muttered about the expense, through sheer habit, and Franco had squashed her reluctance with raised eyebrows and an amused, teasing remark about the impossibility of climbing ladders and hanging wallpaper when her stomach was the size of a large beachball.

'It's decadent.' She had grinned back at him with a sigh. 'You're a very, very decadent man, and I'm surprised the local vicar gave you his blessing to be involved with me.'

'The local vicar,' he had murmured seductively, 'has no idea how deliciously decadent his daughter can be when the mood takes her. Or, for that matter, how often the mood *does* take her!'

At that point in time, with the sunshine streaming through the window and with only five weeks of her pregnancy left to go, there had been no clouds on the horizon.

No clouds, at least, until she had felt the rapid onset of contractions when none were yet due. She had made it to the telephone, even as her waters had broken, and had managed to get through to Emergency, but Franco had been at a meeting in the depths of Wiltshire and she had had to leave a breathless and urgent message with his secretary.

The worst thing she remembered were the ominous words, *The baby's showing signs of distress. We'll have to perform a Caesarean.* To her untrained ears that had sounded like a death sentence on her baby, and the anaesthetic delivered to knock her out had come as a blessing.

'Ruth...' Franco began, now leaning towards her, and she turned her head away and bit her lip.

'No, don't say it. Please don't say it.'

'You silly girl.' When he lifted his hand to stroke

her hair she could feel it trembling, and she looked at him. His face was haggard. He looked as though he hadn't slept for a week.

'The baby...' She found that she couldn't get the words out properly. The rest of the unfinished sentence stuck somewhere at the back of her throat and she had to rely on her pleading, tear-filled eyes to complete what her mouth could not say.

'Is in the Special Case Unit.' He smiled at her, and Ruth closed her eyes and felt her entire body go limp with relief. The relief, however, was short-lived. 'We had a girl, my darling, and she's beautiful.'

'Are you sure?' Ruth whispered. Was he lying? Was he lying because he felt that she was too weak for the truth? She looked straight into his eyes, anxiously trying to prise the truth out of him, and he kissed her on her forehead.

'I think I know enough to recognise the difference between a boy and a girl.'

'I know, but you *know* what I mean...'

'She's absolutely fine, Ruth. Small, but the doctors have said that there's no reason why we shouldn't be able to take her home in the next couple of weeks. She just needs a bit of feeding up, and they want to make sure that her lungs are functioning to full capacity before they let her go.' He kissed the corner of her mouth. 'They'll be in to tell you all this themselves in a little while, and as soon as you're up to it we'll go and have a peep at her.'

'Mum and Dad...?'

'Know, and are on their way down.' He exhaled a long, shaky breath, squeezed shut his eyes, and when he re-opened them they were suspiciously shiny.

'Don't ever scare me like that again, Ruthie,' he said unsteadily. 'I want to tell you this before the doctors arrive and I'm shooed out.

'When Caroline interrupted me in that meeting and told me that there had been a little hiccup and the baby was on its way, I think I felt my heart stop beating.' He laughed drily under his breath and looked at her.

'This may come as a shock—you *know* what a calm, placid, accepting person I am...' to which Ruth couldn't help but chuckle with tender denial '...but I was quite a boor with the driver, who stupidly seemed to attract every traffic jam and red light between Winchester and London and idiotically couldn't turn his car into a hovercraft.

'Then I was even more of a boor when I got here...demanding to be told what was going on...accosting every nurse on the ward for updates on how you were doing in the operating theatre...virtually asking for the surgeon's references to be shown to me...I'm fairly surprised that they treated me as indulgently as they did...'

'I've been in perfectly good hands,' Ruth chided, thrilled with his confession, though he hardly needed to tell her, because after all those months she was *totally secure* in her knowledge of how much this wonderful man improbably adored her. 'Now, tell me all about her. Does she have any hair?'

'Not much, I'm afraid. She's very tiny, but she has the loveliest long fingers.' He seemed to be struggling to find the right words and Ruth smiled at him.

By the time she was robed and walking, supported by Franco, with her parents behind them, to the Special Care ward where her daughter was, Ruth had heard enough of her little miracle of creation from Franco to write several books on the subject. Fatherhood, the one thing he had steadfastly avoided until he had found himself without option, appeared to have turned him into a doting, boringly proud dad.

'There she is,' he said proudly, pointing to a little sleeping beauty, and Ruth smiled and looked around at her parents.

'She looks just like you,' her mother said, smiling. 'Let's hope she's not as demanding!'

One year later...and as Ruth lay on the beach, with her head resting on Franco's shoulder and his arm thrown carelessly around her, she felt his free hand creep suggestively across the taut contours of her stomach.

'Are you *mad*?' She giggled and looked around her, but at a little after eleven in the night the beach was empty of people. The silvery moonlight made the surface of the tropical sea turn to glass and behind them the rustle of coconut trees was the only sound to be heard. That, and the steady lapping of ocean against shore.

'Why not? How many honeymoons do a couple have?'

'Depends how many times they get married,' Ruth said sensibly, and she smiled as his arm tightened around her.

'In our case, then. One honeymoon.' He nibbled her ear and blew into it, sending an erotic thrill through her. 'And we have ten long, lazy, Natasha-free days to enjoy it just how we want to, and if that includes making love on the beach at midnight, then why not?'

The free hand slipped beneath her shirt and found the full swell of her breast, unrestricted by a bra. He cupped the soft mound and then rubbed her nipple with the pad of his finger until it jutted into hard arousal. With a sigh of pleasure Ruth stretched out, raising her arms above her, all the better to enjoy the feel of his hands on her body.

He was right. Natasha was back in England, being looked after by her adoring grandparents, who, from virtually the minute she had arrived at the vicarage for a visit, were insisting on taking her to do the rounds of the parishioners.

And Natasha seemed to love the attention. She had left the hospital at two weeks, still small and hairless, and now, at the end of a year, possessed some very sturdy limbs, a headful of pale golden hair and cornflower-blue eyes that were fringed by the same dark lashes as her father's.

'But what if someone comes along?' Ruth whispered half-heartedly, revelling in the flash of Franco's possessive, hungry eyes. She sighed as he slowly began undoing the buttons of her shirt.

Even at this hour it was warm enough to be wearing only a short-sleeved shirt and a pair of shorts. Underneath them, the giant-sized beach spread was a scant but effective barrier against the pale sand, and as the last of the buttons on her shirt was undone Ruth wriggled sensuously, closing her eyes and waiting for that moment when she would feel the wetness of his mouth enclose her throbbing nipple.

She arched herself up a bit and shuddered as the moment arrived and his tongue flicked across the sensitive peaks, followed by his mouth as he began suckling hard on the protruding buds, taking them one at a time until she was lost in a world of sensation.

Her fingers curled into his dark hair and she moaned when he started tugging down her elasticised shorts. He knew her body so well, and yet it never failed to amaze her that he could still turn her on with the same deep, greedy need that she had felt the very first time he had laid a finger on her.

She dropped her knees to either side and his eager, determined fingers slipped beneath her briefs, unswervingly finding the little soft spot and the core of her femininity, gently rubbing it while her body responded with moist approval.

If a hundred spectators came along now, there would be nothing she could do to stop the waves of pleasure engulfing her and her need to go to the final place of fulfilment. He trailed his tongue along her stomach, which had fortunately tightened back into shape, although its contours were slightly more rounded and womanly than before, while his fingers continued to idly tease her pulsating womanhood.

Her underwear was damp when he finally removed it, so that he could press her thighs against the sand, spreading wide her legs and settling between them to enjoy the mysterious, intensely feminine dampness between.

Ruth moaned as his tongue slid through the furry, downy patch of hair, carving a path to that beating centre of excitement. She tilted her body upwards and rotated her hips while his mouth became greedier, enjoying her writhing body with the appetite of the gourmand feasting upon an exquisitely prepared meal.

Before she could reach the pinnacle of fulfilment,

however, Franco raised his head, allowing her frantic craving to abate, giving him time to slip off his shorts and guide his thick, hard arousal deep into her.

He moved slowly at first, enjoying the way she moved and wriggled, wanting him to speed up his tempo so that she could reach orgasm.

He teased her all the time about being a vicar's daughter, yet also being the most wanton, abandoned woman in bed he had ever known, but, however many positions they sampled, this was still the one he liked most. His body over hers. Like this, he could look down and feast his eyes on the vision of her breasts, bouncing as she twisted under him, the nipples larger and darker now than they had been before she became pregnant.

Sometimes he stilled them with his hands, loving the feel of their softness, enjoying the sensation of massaging them and kneading them until her nipples seemed even more engorged and swollen pushing upwards, offering themselves to his mouth.

Most of all, however, he just enjoyed watching her face, her eyes shut, her nostrils flaring as he brought her closer and faster to her climax.

It seemed as though he could never tire of this bewitching woman who had borne his child and who, with the flicker of an eye, could still turn his muscles to jelly.

Work, the thing he had lived and died for, had faded into a paltry second best to his wife and child. Meals out on a nightly basis had become an intrusion into what he wanted most to do—namely, get home as early as he could, in time to see something of his daughter. And then, when she had gone to sleep, to enjoy his wife's home-cooked food and the deeply relaxing, wonderfully satisfying conversations they had. No high-powered banter with clients could come close to watching her blush or giggle or just look at him with her wide grey eyes.

He felt the salty film of her perspiration mixing with his, and for a fleeting second he closed his eyes and pushed deep into her, opening them to gaze at her face as she emitted a long, satisfied groan and he felt his own life force seep out of him and flood her body.

Would it be ridiculous, he wondered, if he told her *thank you*?

One month later, and with Natasha sound asleep in her cot, Ruth curled her body into Franco's, drawing up her legs and resting her head against his chest. She could hear his heart beating in this position and there was something foolishly comforting about that.

His feet were stretched out on the table in front of them, and on the television a blonde presenter was winding up the news with a touching, sentimental story of some endangered animal or other in a zoo somewhere or other.

Ruth didn't really hear what was being said. She had been waiting for this moment all evening, enjoying the thrill of anticipation as they ate their dinner, chatted and touched and chatted and touched again, their minds and bodies perfectly in tune with one another.

'Oh, by the way,' she said, stretching and sitting up straight so that she could see his face, 'a bit of news.'

He smiled slowly at her. 'Seeing that you've left it

this late, I know it's got to be important. Not to do with the retreat, is it?'

That was their code name for the house they were buying in the country, not five miles away from the vicarage—somewhere they could escape to on the occasional weekend when they weren't seeing friends.

'Don't tell me that half-wit estate agent's screwed up.' He frowned, anticipating unwelcome news. The cottage, derelict though it was, had limitless potential, and if they lost it he would personally hang the little twit by the feet from the nearest available tree. He had done precious little to secure the deal in the first place.

'No, no, no,' Ruth said hastily, seeing the warning signs from her husband, who could still intimidate when he chose and whose appreciation of the estate agent handling the matter had been reduced to rubble when he'd caught the hapless boy sneaking furtive glances at his wife.

'What, then? Come back here, where you were sitting. I liked being able to put my hand just there, on your left breast.'

'In a minute,' Ruth told him, determined not to be side-tracked, even though the prospect of his hand caressing her breast was almost too tempting to resist. 'I want to see your face when I break this to you...'

'Break what?'

Ruth took a deep breath and said, in a pleased rush, 'You're going to be a father for a second time!' His reaction was everything she had hoped: surprise very quickly followed by delight. 'I *think*,' she added, 'that a certain night spent on a certain beach when a certain man couldn't keep his hands off me is to blame for that.'

'Oh, is that right?' he murmured softly, the strong, aggressive contours of his face softened by his smile. 'All I can say to that, Mrs Leoni, is that it worked…'

'What did?'

'Well…' He pulled her toward him and returned his hand to the place he wanted it to be, covering the mound of her breast, then he kissed the top of her head. 'My plan for Natasha to have a baby brother or sister…' He pulled down the straps of her vest-style tee shirt to expose the breast he had been caressing, soft and full, the big nipple ripe with expectation of the baby growing inside his wife.

'Does that mean…' Ruth lowered her eyes and smiled a secret smile '…that now your dastardly plan has succeeded there'll be no more rehearsals for that baby brother or sister?' She lay back against the arm of the sofa and pulled the vest down to her waist, watching as his eyes glittered in appreciation of her body.

'Typical female!' he growled, bending to nuzzle her soft skin. 'No logic at all…'

Ruth closed her eyes and sighed. How was it that her parents had never told her that heaven was something you could touch…?

Marion Lennox is a country girl, born on a south-east Australian dairy farm. She moved on – mostly because the cows just weren't interested in her stories! Married to a 'very special doctor', Marion writes for Medical Romance™ as well as Tender Romance™, where she used to write as Trisha David for a while. In her non-writing life, Marion cares for kids, cats, dogs, chooks and goldfish. She travels, she fights her rampant garden (she's losing) and her house dust (she's lost). After an early bout with breast cancer she's also reprioritised her life, figured out what's important and discovered the joys of deep baths, romance and chocolate. Preferably all at the same time!

**Watch out for Marion Lennox's latest medical drama: BRIDE BY ACCIDENT
On sale this month, in Medical Romance™!**

EMERGENCY WEDDING

by

Marion Lennox

CHAPTER ONE

WELCOME home banners? Confetti showers? Yellow ribbons tied to old oak trees?

Whale Beach had prepared none of the traditional welcome home displays for Dr Susie Ellis. What she received was a shower of condoms—two hundred or so, she thought, if she didn't count the ones rolling under the bus or scooting off the jetty to splash into the sea.

As a welcome it was spectacular, Susie decided. She smiled with delight, even as she realised it was accidental. The bus driver had hauled out a parcel from between the passengers' belongings. It had resisted, and then suddenly burst open in all directions.

Condoms were flying everywhere.

The cluster of Guides who'd alighted with Susie stared in amazement, and then burst into delighted adolescent giggles as they realised what they were seeing.

'I assume those are mine.'

The voice made Susie jump. It was deeply male and richly resonant, with a lilting trace of a Scottish accent. She turned to find a man climbing from a dusty red Range Rover. His expression was resigned, as if he was accustomed to Whale Beach postal services and this was nothing new.

The condoms were his?

Why on earth would he need so many? Susie's freckled nose crinkled in amusement as she assessed his chances of retrieving them. The chances weren't great. The Guides were swooping on the condoms with shrieks of joy, and their leader was snatching them back with cries of horror. The condoms were everywhere! Including...on her?

Susie put her fingers to her hair and there was a disc resting in her mop of blonde curls. She lifted it free, grinned and handed it over to the stranger.

Who was he? He might be a local, but she didn't know him. Maybe he'd arrived at Whale Beach after she'd left. Whoever he was, he was obviously very needful of condoms. A heap of condoms!

'I don't want mine,' she told him, pressing the foil-covered protection into his hand. 'It's a start, at least.'

He accepted her offering with a resigned and slightly crooked smile. He looked nice, Susie decided as their fingers touched. The stranger seemed thirtyish, or maybe a little older. He was seven or eight inches taller than Susie's five feet four, he was broad-shouldered but with a lean, well-muscled body and he was tanned and weathered in a way that made him look like he spent his life outdoors.

Their fingers kept touching and their eyes met.

He was, in fact, almost breathtakingly good-looking. With a tiny gasp she hauled her fingers back. What was she doing?

No, she definitely didn't recognise him. She might have been away from Whale Beach for four years, but she'd definitely have remembered this outstanding member of the male species.

How could she not? Even as she tried to keep her appraisal detached, she had to admit he was gorgeous!

She took him all in, approving his casual yet smart opennecked shirt and good-quality jeans. His crinkling jet black hair was as dark as Susie's riotous curls were blonde, and his deep grey eyes had laughter lines that sort of made you want to smile right back at him.

He was finding it hard to smile, and the laughter behind his eyes was fading. The man was clearly worried. He'd accepted Susie's condom offering without a word, seemingly unaware of her jolt of attraction, and he was now turning to the bus driver.

'Are the rest safe?'

'You mean there's more?' Susie asked incredulously, and the stranger shot her a withering look.

'The rest of the parcels are safe,' the bus driver told him, hauling extra packages free with considerably more care. Then he couldn't resist asking the obvious. 'They're not all full of condoms, are they, mate?'

'No.'

'There's another one stuck in your hair,' one of the Guides told Susie, and she blinked and foraged for more. Her curls were thick and tangled so they'd have held a good few, and she'd been in the direct line of package fire.

'You'd best give it to the man.' The bus driver grinned at Susie and his glance flickered downward. Which was nothing new. Advanced pregnancy seemed a universal attraction. 'It's a bit late for you to be needing these, love,' he told her.

It was indeed. Susie's smile didn't fade. She reached forward to retrieve her suitcase from the hold of the bus, but the driver lifted it down before she reached it. 'Don't you go carrying that yourself,' he told her, putting it at her feet in the expectation that someone else would help. 'Not in your condition.'

Susie shrugged at that. She had no choice. She might be seven and a half months pregnant, but for the last two years—or even before that—ever since Charlie's lymphoma had been diagnosed, Susie had been very much on her own.

She coped herself, or she didn't cope at all.

'I'm OK,' she told him. 'I've managed this from overseas and I'm on the home leg now. Is there a taxi in town?'

'Only Eddie's minibus.' The driver had stooped again and was collecting all the condoms within reach. He glanced up as the vehicle in question pulled up at the wharf. 'Here it is now, but I'd guess it's already been booked by the Guides.'

'It has.' The Guide leader sniffed and started shepherding her charges minibus-wards, trying to collect condoms from her charges as she went. She wasn't successful. Discs were being stuffed everywhere. For fifteen-year-old girls, this was precious booty indeed.

'The bus is taking us to the Scout camp three miles out of town,' she told Susie, clearly taking pity on her being left with these appalling males. 'I'll send it back for you, if you like.'

'That'd be kind.'

'Or maybe the man with the condoms could give you a lift.' The woman's tone said it was unlikely—he really was a species apart.

But maybe he could. The stranger looked up from where he'd been retrieving condoms from behind the bus's wheels, and he managed a smile. Once again it caught Susie's attention and it held. It was some smile!

'I'm sure I can,' he told her. 'If you don't mind waiting until we've collected these, and if you don't need to go too far, I can give you a lift anywhere locally.'

His smile deepened, and Susie took an almost unconscious step back. Whew! This was a smile to make a girl's heart do back flips.

This was ridiculous! She tossed a metaphorical bucket of cold water over herself and told herself to be sensible. Seven-and-a-half-months-pregnant women were in no position to be attracting strange men. She had no idea who he was—and the man was retrieving two hundred or so condoms!

'I don't think so,' she said cautiously, and she could see by his broadening smile that he guessed exactly what she was thinking.

'Hey, they're not all for me.'

He sounded wounded and she had to fight back laughter.

'That's...very reassuring,' she managed, trying to keep her face straight. The man was an engaging lunatic. 'Are you collecting them for your friends? Or do you just have one special friend to share them with?'

He chuckled. It was a rich, deep laugh that matched his smile beautifully, but he didn't answer her question. Maybe it didn't deserve an answer. 'Um...no. Look, I just have to collect the rest of the mail and then I'm free to take you wherever you want.'

'No,' she said, more firmly than she felt. One part of her wanted very much to accept his offer, but there was something about this man that she didn't trust.

It wasn't just the condoms. It was something about his gorgeous smile...

Charlie. Think of Charlie, she told herself firmly. She was a widow and the thoughts she was thinking seemed almost a betrayal.

But...despite Charlie she was thinking them.

'I'm tired after the bus trip,' she told him, and if she sounded scatty and ungrateful she couldn't help it. She motioned to the post-office-cum-café at the end of the wharf. Its windows looked out over the harbour to the mountain peaks beyond—a view Susie had missed for four long years and a view she'd love the chance to soak in again.

Blaise, the postmistress's golden Labrador, was wagging her tail from the top step. Susie was delighted to recognise her old friend, and also to see that the Labrador was heavily pregnant. Her sense of homecoming deepened.

'Hi, Blaise,' she said with pleasure. The greeting gave her time to gather her composure before she turned back to the stranger. 'Sitting here, waiting for the minibus, will be no hardship at all,' she told him, and received another of those blindingly gorgeous smiles for her pains.

'I guess not. It is fantastic.'

It was. Gandilong Peninsula—an Australian wilderness on Tasmania's east coast—would have to be the most beautiful place on earth, bar none. Susie was so glad to be home she was close to being overwhelmed, by emotion as well as condoms.

'At least let me carry your baggage.' He grinned, and before she could stop him he'd heaved her suitcase up the post office steps and set it beside the placid Blaise. Then he stood and looked down at her, his keen eyes assessing.

'You're sure there's nowhere I can drive you?' he asked, and she collected herself enough to give him a reassuring smile.

'I'm sure. Honestly. Blaise will keep me company.'

The man hesitated, his intelligent eyes taking in Susie's advanced pregnancy, her travel-stained maternity dress and battered suitcase, her weariness and her obvious solitude. It was uncommon for lone travellers to come here, much less heavily pregnant ones without obvious money, and his eyes narrowed in concern.

'You're staying in town?' he asked.

'Yes.'

'And you have somewhere organised to stay?'

She must be a local if she recognised the dog, but why was no one meeting her?

'Yes to that, too.'

So that was that. There was nothing else he could help her with. 'Then I guess I'll see you around.' But there was just the faintest trace of reluctance in his voice, as if he really would have liked the opportunity to assist.

Strangely, Susie was feeling the same. But she didn't need him, she told herself firmly. She didn't need anyone. The past awful years had taught her that.

'I guess you and your condom-bearing friends will be sure to see me at some time,' she told him. 'Whale Beach is hardly big enough to avoid people.'

He heard the inference. His face creased into laughter. 'Much as you'd like to,' he finished for her. 'It's OK, you have nothing to fear.'

'Because I'm in an interesting condition already?' she enquired blandly, touching her very pregnant abdomen. 'How kind. By the way, has it escaped your attention that the condoms that rolled to the other side of the bus are being pecked by seagulls? If I were you, I'd be checking for peck holes for the next few months.'

'Hell!' He left her then, and stalked around the bus. A flock of gulls rose and flew a few yards off to await their next opportunity. 'These aren't edible, dopes!'

'Good luck,' Susie called to him, lifting a hand in a farewell wave. 'Now and in the future. Peck holes can be disastrous.'

'Thank you.' He glared. And then he couldn't help himself. The grey eyes twinkled and he looked again pointedly at her stomach. 'I guess you'd know.'

'I sure do, though it wasn't a seagull that caused this.' If only he knew! 'But you're welcome,' she said cheerfully, and turned her back on the lot of them—Guides, bus driver and good-looking man with far too many condoms.

Good-looking males apart, she suddenly needed to be alone.

Because, welcome or not, she was so happy that she felt like hugging Blaise to her and shouting her joy to the world.

She'd made it. She was home.

CHAPTER TWO

Two hours later the minibus finally deposited Susie at her destination.

Whale Beach Medical Centre, Hospital and Nursing Home were all built as one. The house itself—Susie's home since childhood—was at the end of the long row of connecting whitewashed stone buildings. A verandah ran the entire length, with French windows opening alike from hospital wards, medical reception rooms and the living quarters of the doctor's residence.

It was a beautiful building—and it was home.

But still it was the medical centre. There were cars parked out the front. Clearly her father's former partner, Robert Fraser, was seeing patients and Susie didn't want to face anyone yet. She wanted to get her bearings, dump her gear and take a few deep breaths.

So she carried her suitcase around to where the house yard overlooked the creek meandering down to the sea. This was the doctor's private garden. Her private garden. Susie opened the gate and there was a child in a wheelchair—sitting under her tree!

Whatever Susie might have been expecting after four years' absence, it wasn't this. She pushed the gate wide and it lurched drunkenly on its hinges. That was OK. Robert, the elderly doctor who ministered to Whale Beach's medical needs, had his own home apart from the hospital, so she'd expected a neglected house, but she hadn't expected a child.

She walked cautiously forward, edging back into her territory. The child seemed asleep. Pale and over-thin, the boy was slumped forward with his face resting on pillows. Something was seriously wrong with him, Susie decided.

Something more than a temporary broken limb had immobilised him.

So what had put him in a wheelchair? Her professional curiosity was aroused. He was nine or ten years old, she guessed. He had deep black hair that curled into tendrils and badly needed a cut. Long black lashes fluttered down over his too-pale cheeks, and his jeans and sweater seemed too big for his lanky frame.

Diagnosis? Uncared for, maybe—but what else?

He wasn't paraplegic or quadriplegic, Susie thought, or if he was then the cause must be very recent. His legs still had muscle mass, but there was no plaster cast or brace to indicate a break.

So what was wrong with him? And what was he doing under her tree?

Her tree...

Susie's senses were pulling her everywhere. Distracted, she dropped her suitcase and looked up at the vast eucalyptus casting shade over the garden. The tree sprawled outward, leaning toward the sea. You could see for ever from its highest branches.

Long ago, Susie's father had threatened its removal so he could grow more vegetables, but after his tiny daughter had learned to climb Dr Ellis Senior hadn't stood a chance. The tree had stayed.

Now, looking up through its branches for the first time in years, Susie's emotions were close to overwhelming her. The child in the wheelchair momentarily forgotten, she placed a hand on her very pregnant middle and made her own unborn child a promise.

'You'll climb this, too,' she swore. 'That's why I brought you home, all the way from England. This is where you'll grow up and, despite everything, I know this is what your father would have wanted.'

That was enough! Any more and she'd start to weep, and the time for tears was long over. This was the time for action and for happiness—for setting down roots and getting on with the rest of her life. She closed her eyes, and when she opened them the child was watching her.

'Hello,' he said, and it was evident by his cautious tone that he regarded her presence as an unwanted intrusion.

'Hi.' She smiled, trying not to sound defensive. After all, this was her back yard.

'Can I help you?' The boy was being polite, but his face was wary. Oddly wary. This was a child who seemed afraid of shadows.

'I guess... I'm looking for Dr Fraser.'

'Both the doctors are inside.'

Both the doctors? Susie blinked, trying to make the pieces of the puzzle fit. Robert was the only doctor here, and that didn't explain the presence of the child.

'Is there a queue, then?' she asked cautiously. 'Is this why you're outside—waiting to be seen?' Maybe an anxious mother had pushed him around here for a little peace while she kept his place in the queue.

But it still seemed odd. The doctor's private garden was sacrosanct, and the locals knew it. The child's answer was more puzzling still.

'No. I live here.' His tone added an unspoken rider. You don't. So what are you doing here?

'You *live* here?'

'Yes.' He was about as welcoming as a wet blanket, and he might just have slept but his weariness was still obvious. He sounded exhausted. 'We do. This is private. You'll find the door to Reception around the front.'

'I... Yes. I know my way.' She moved to the verandah and the child's voice cut sharply across the tranquillity of the garden.

'I said Reception is around the front. That's a private entrance.'

'I know it is,' Susie said grimly, and pushed open the back

door. Enough was enough after all. 'I know it's private. After all, it's *my* house.'

Both doctors?

Susie's mind was racing. What on earth was happening? Since her father had died, there'd never been more than one doctor in this town, no matter how desperately Whale Beach needed more. The whole area was desperately short of doctors. This was growing stranger and stranger by the minute.

What was most curious was that there were male voices raised in anger, and the voices were coming from the centre of the building. To be specific, they were coming from the room Robert Fraser used as his surgery.

Susie took a deep breath and walked toward the voices, listening all the way. Outside, the child was bristling in anger, but even though a ramp had been newly built to accommodate his wheelchair, he made no move to follow.

Which was just as well, given the state of her emotions. This was still her house, she reminded herself. No one had permission to be in this section. The rest of the buildings contained the surgeries—one for her father while he'd been alive, and one for Robert. They contained waiting rooms, Reception and beyond them the wards of the small bush nursing hospital and nursing home, but the house itself should have been as she'd left it four years ago.

It wasn't. Someone had added the wheelchair ramps, and there were personal belongings she didn't recognise scattered everywhere. And on the kitchen table were boxes she did recognise.

The condom boxes?

She took everything in as she made her way through to the closed door of Robert's surgery, and she listened unashamedly to the voices as she went.

'Why didn't you tell me?'

It was a male voice—deep and rich and strongly masculine with just a hint of a Scottish lilt. She'd been right in recognising the condom boxes, then. Here was her friend from the bus, but the laughter she'd heard then had disappeared completely. What she heard was fury.

'I've made Jamie promises I can't keep,' the voice snapped. 'The Australian Medical Board will never approve my registration here now.'

'I'm sorry, Darcy.' This was another voice she recognised. Her father's partner was close to seventy, and it was Robert she was coming home to work with. Or…was it?

Robert was still talking. He sounded as if he was explaining—or trying to.

'Darcy, since Susie's father died, I've tried my best to find a new partner,' he was saying. 'No one's wanted to come, and I've been desperate to wind down. The practice really is too big for one doctor, the tourists are increasing and with this post-polio syndrome getting worse, you know I can't cope. I'm getting tired. Susie's always known she'd be more than welcome to work here, but she moved to England with her husband four years ago. He died two years back and she made no move to return. But now… Like it or not, this is her house and it's her surgery.'

'And she writes and says she'll be home any minute.'

'She has the right to be here.' Robert sounded distressed, and Susie's heart went out to him. He'd been under too much of a strain. Val had written that the polio he'd suffered from as a child was causing recurrent problems. She should have come home earlier, she thought bleakly, but it had been such a hard decision. What to do?

Unconsciously her hand crept to her stomach as she listened.

'Darcy, I'm sorry but I can't see what I can do for you,' Robert was saying. 'Your application for rural doctor status here was a bolt out of the blue. I was so grateful. But Susie—'

'Susie has precedence, and I'll never get registration now.' The stranger sounded sick as he heard the implacable note in Robert's voice. 'You know how important it is for me to get residence here, but the Australian government only appoints overseas doctors to areas of need. You had to talk hard to convince them you wanted to wind down. But now... With two doctors here—you and this Susie woman—I'll never be permitted to stay.'

'I'm afraid you won't.'

'So where does that leave Jamie and Muriel? And what about you?' The stranger sounded concerned as well as angry. 'With post-polio syndrome affecting you so badly, you need serious medical help here, Robert. Not someone who thinks half the medical income is her right. This woman's reputation around the town is hardly that of a hard-working doctor.'

'That's not fair.' Robert was on the defensive now, and Susie could understand it. Robert had always been one of her staunchest allies. 'The town doesn't know what Susie's like as a doctor. She hasn't been home for years, and then it wasn't to work. It was to be with her father. Whale Beach has never seen her as a practising doctor, but her qualifications are excellent.'

'They say she's a bit of fluff.' Darcy—whoever Darcy was—now sounded derisive. 'What is she? Twenty-seven? Twenty-eight? And she's already been through one husband.'

'That's hardly fair...'

He obviously wasn't in the mood to feel fair. 'Robert, since I've moved here I've heard one story after another about her, and all I'm hearing is fluff. They tell me she's known as the matchmaking medico, with half the young ones in town saying they owe their relationships to her.'

Out in the hall and still avidly listening, that made Susie smile. So Whale Beach still remembered her. Matchmaking medico? Hmm. Well, maybe she had been at that.

'I'm not disagreeing with you there.' Susie could hear the weary smile behind Robert's words. 'Our Susie's a breath of fresh air, but she does—or did—have a habit of poking her nose into other people's affairs. Maybe if we can think of a way to keep you both here, she'll get you married.'

'Oh, great.' The Scottish accent broadened in distaste. 'As if I need a wife...'

'Why have you never married?' Robert asked curiously, and Susie's left ear promptly flattened against the closed door. Any minute now she could be sprung by a patient or receptionist, and this was none of her business, but she wasn't leaving for the world. After all, this was her house and here was gossip—in her very own surgery!

'As if I have time for women.' Darcy gave a harsh and derisive laugh. 'I learned early to steer clear. My mother deserted us. She walked out when I was five and we never saw her again. My sister stuck around until I was thirteen and then she did the same. Like my mother, she went from one partner to another. The result's outside sitting in that wheelchair, and my sister doesn't give a damn about him. You're not married, are you?'

'No,' Robert said mildly. 'But only because—'

'Because you saw sense. Women! They're all the same. You get attached and they just mess with your life and leave. And here's another one coming to mess us up.'

'Just because your mother and your sister were fickle...'

'And my fiancée,' he said savagely. 'Despite my father's advice, I tried the love bit, but I was a fool. So from now on I want nothing to do with women. Ever!'

It was as good a cue as any. Oh, dear.

Susie took a deep breath, knocked lightly—and opened the door.

Whoa...

At the bus stop, the stranger had seemed good-looking and charismatic. Here, in the closer confines of the surgery with a white medical coat thrown casually over his outdoor clothes, the man was almost overwhelmingly attractive.

She recognised him at once, but if he recognised her he gave no sign. He gave her a blank, cursory assessment as something that might have crawled out of a piece of overripe cheese. His mind was obviously on far more important matters than interfering patients.

'This is a medical meeting,' he snapped, digging his hands into the pockets of his coat and turning away from her. 'Our receptionist is out the front.'

But Robert's reception wasn't so cold. The elderly doctor stared at Susie for a microsecond, and then the walking stick he was carrying was cast aside and he was across the room enveloping her in a vast, welcoming hug before she could say a word.

'Susie. Susie! Welcome home, girl. It's so good to see you. Let me look at you.'

He held her at arm's length and there could be no disguising the joy on the older man's face. It warmed Susie's heart, and it made the unknown Darcy take a step back and stare in confusion.

This was...Susie?

There could be no doubt. Robert was turning the woman to face him and his weary eyes were glowing with pride and with love.

'Darcy, let me introduce my god-daughter and the daughter of my very dearest friend. This is our Susie—or I should say, Dr Susie Ellis. Susie, this is Dr Darcy Hayden.'

She'd had more warning than Darcy. Susie was more collected—sort of. She managed a smile, she held out a hand in greeting, and after an infinitesimal pause Darcy took it.

He still looked stunned.

'*You're* Dr Ellis?' he asked incredulously, and she nodded politely. Warily.

'That's right.'

'I'm...' He took a deep breath, collecting himself. 'I'm pleased to meet you,' he managed. 'Again...'

I bet you are, Susie thought dryly, but she somehow kept her smile in place. His hand was strong and warm and sort of nice. Maybe he was nice, she thought. Just...not nice to her any more. Two hours ago he'd been concerned for her, but now she was in the way of his plans.

'Did you find all of your condoms?' she asked politely, and despite her wariness her eyes danced. 'Or do you need to be frugal for the next week or so?'

But his sense of humour had disappeared completely. 'The local shopkeeper refuses to stock them. They're for the pharmacy we're trying to set up,' he snapped. 'Or...we *were* trying to set up.'

'What do you mean by that? Is there a problem with my arrival?'

One thing Susie had learned over the last two years was that you didn't get anywhere by shilly-shallying. You stated what you wanted, you stated it over and over, and you didn't budge until you got it. Her hand crept to her stomach again. Here was the living proof of that.

'I couldn't help hearing your voices from the hall,' she said, and then watched as both men's eyes followed the protective curve of her hand. 'Robert, has my coming home caused trouble?'

'Nothing that can't be sorted,' Robert said uneasily, his eyes widening as he took in her condition, but Susie had turned again to face Darcy.

'Well?' she said—and waited.

'You're pregnant,' he said flatly.

'Well diagnosed.' A thirty-three-week pregnancy was a bit tricky to disguise. Susie's green eyes twinkled, her humour resurfacing as it mostly did. There wasn't much she couldn't bounce back from.

Not after the hand the last four years had dealt her.

'Yes, I am,' she said, and there wasn't the slightest hint of defensiveness in her voice. Why should there be? She was so proud of this pregnancy.

'And you're proposing to come here and work as a partner to Robert?' Her obvious pride in her pregnancy hadn't deflected him one bit. Darcy's voice was still incredulous, his anger breaking through.

'That was the plan,' she told him. 'But I gather there's a problem.'

'Robert needs a full-time partner!'

Her smile died. 'That's what I'm prepared to be.'

'In between breast-feeding and nappy changes! Ha!'

'Excuse me?' There was no mistaking his anger now—the blatant hostility. He was furious. But he didn't have a monopoly on anger. Susie took a step back and her green eyes flashed. Anger met anger head on. OK, there might be a problem, but she had some rights here, too. Like—this was her home!

But Darcy was giving no quarter. 'Robert needs a full-time medical partner,' he repeated, as if she were too stupid to understand without repeats. 'He's been advertising for a couple of years, and you must have known that. He has post-polio syndrome and he should be winding down. With me here he can do that. We can even expand the practice—like putting in a pharmacy so our patients don't have to travel thirty miles to get their medicines. But now, if I can't stay here, he's stuck with you!'

His disgust was starting to grate. Susie flushed, put her hands on her hips and glared. What gave him the right to judge?

'This is my home,' she said, in a voice so soft it was dangerous. 'The surgery belongs to me. Robert has never bought out the property from my inheritance. He's never wanted to.' She took a deep breath. 'I gather that's your son outside? Am I to assume you're living in my house?'

'Susie...'

Susie's eyes flew to Robert who was looking distinctly uneasy. 'I'm sorry, love, but it all got too complicated,' he told her. 'It seemed easier to let Darcy and Jamie live here, and I couldn't contact you. I've been trying for weeks. I wrote to your English address but it came back unopened.'

'So by just arriving out of the blue you're putting me out of a job and out of a place to live.' Darcy's face looked like thunder. 'Of all the—'

'Inconsiderate doctors?' Susie finished for him, flashing fire. 'That's hardly fair. Robert's been asking for years if I'd like to come home, so I wrote and told him I was coming. Then, when I get here, there's someone living in my house.'

'Your letter only arrived with today's mail,' Robert said unhappily, and Susie faltered in mid-fire. Surely not.

'I sent it three weeks ago.'

'From where?'

Uh-oh. Susie blinked, thinking it through. She'd been upset and frightened, and she'd fled to one of the remotest parts of Scotland while she'd come to a decision.

Maybe the postal system hadn't been all that crash hot, she thought ruefully. And added to Whale Beach's remote status...

'It arrived today, Susie,' Robert said again. He gave her a half-smile that told her he was deeply worried. 'We've only just read it.'

'Oh, heck.' She bit her lip and glanced sideways at Darcy Hayden's thundercloud of a face. 'I'm sorry, but I never dreamed you'd have found another doctor. I've been in Scotland, taking time to think things through. I...I came to a decision there.'

'About your future.' Robert's face softened. 'Susie, you should have told me you were pregnant.'

'I didn't want you worrying.'

There was a pregnant pause. A very pregnant pause. Robert was fighting valiantly to figure out a way to ask, but there wasn't an easy one. Finally he just asked it. He was a family doctor after all, and sometimes it was just easier to bring the hard question into the open.

'Is there a man on the scene?' he asked finally.

Her face tightened. 'No. Not since Charlie died.'

'Charlie being your husband,' Darcy said heavily, and Susie turned and gave him an old-fashioned look.

'Well guessed.'

'I thought he died two years ago?'

'He did.' Her chin tilted as she read the snap judgement in his eyes. 'So what are you saying? You've taken my house and my job, and now you now want to run me out of town with an S branded into my forehead as a scarlet woman?'

'Susie, that's unfair,' Robert said uneasily, and Susie took a deep breath and admitted that maybe it was. A little. A very little.

But he—Darcy or whoever he was—had some explaining to do, and it didn't help that he was looking at her pregnant bulge like it was the product of a scandalous affair.

'So tell me,' she said, forcing herself to count to ten and give the man a chance. OK, if they'd just received her letter this morning, then maybe they were forgiven for using her house. She had told Robert he could use it for emergencies if he ever needed to, and if Robert hadn't known she was coming and had finally found himself a partner...

Oh, heck. This was hard. She needed this job.

'Just tell me,' she said again, and met Darcy's steely eyes full on. 'Why are you living in my house—and why am I messing up your life plans to practise medicine in Whale Beach and sell condoms by the thousands?'

Darcy was forcing himself to count to ten as well. He needed this job. Hell, he'd never needed a job so much in his life. With his medical qualifications, jobs were normally his for the taking, but they weren't for the taking in this wilderness. Like it or not, he was stuck in this place, and this woman was definitely interfering with his plans.

It wouldn't be so bad if she was competent, he decided— if she could do the job—but this pregnant scatterbrain wasn't Whale Beach's answer to its medical needs. He was!

But he was living in her house. She owned the partnership and Robert would come down on her side. That was clear.

So... Talk her out of it, he thought desperately. Maybe even turn on a bit of charm. Tell her how needful he was.

He needed to be persuasive.

'I need to be here because of Jamie,' he told her, and Susie's watchful eyes grew thoughtful.

'Jamie's the little boy outside in the wheelchair?'

'That's the one.'

'And Jamie would be...your son?'

'No.' He was thinking fast as he spoke, trying to figure out the best way to present his case, but his hesitation had her exasperated.

'You need to be explicit here,' she told him. 'Otherwise we'll be here till Christmas.'

'Jamie's my nephew,' he told her. 'He's my sister's child. My sister... Well, Grace is no saint as far as motherhood goes. She abandoned Jamie with his paternal grandmother when Jamie was five, and now no one knows where she is. Muriel—Jamie's grandma—has been doing a first-class job of looking after Jamie, but a few months ago she had a stroke.'

'I see.' Susie didn't but she was prepared to listen. 'Muriel is...?'

'Muriel Barker,' Robert told her from the sidelines. These two were sparking off each other and Robert seemed an outsider—a worried outsider. 'Sam Barker was Jamie's dad before he was killed in a road smash a few years back.'

'I remember.' She did, too, thinking back to the vague rumours of a woman Sam had married and regretted. She also remembered Muriel's steely decision to take on their unloved child.

'Jamie's been pulled every which way. He has all sorts of problems, and now Muriel's in hospital with no long-term chances of taking care of him again.' It was Robert talking now, deeply worried. Trying to make Susie see Darcy's point of view. 'Two months ago, Social Services were saying Jamie needed to go into foster-care and Jamie was desperately unhappy. Apart from his grandma, the only relation he had was his Uncle Darcy who was working as a family doctor just outside Edinburgh. So I contacted Darcy and Darcy offered to take care of the child—back in Scotland.'

'That was good of you,' Susie retorted.

Darcy caught her note of disdain and the thundercloud on his face deepened.

'I happen to like the kid,' he snapped, and she nodded.

'Very uncle-like.'

'Shut up, Susie,' Robert said warningly, and she managed to give him a smile. It was a flash of the old Susie returning.

'Yeah, OK. So we have a concerned Uncle Darcy taking Jamie back to live in good old Scotland. What happened to that plan?'

'Jamie collapsed,' Darcy said, in a voice that took all the humour out of the situation. 'He was nervy as hell to begin with—with parents like his who could blame him? But with Muriel's stroke...'

'He came down with the flu and got pneumonia on top of it,' Robert said heavily. 'From then it's been one thing after another. But unspecific things. He's had swollen glands, he's been throwing temperatures for no good reason, he's getting weaker and weaker, and he sleeps. All the time.'

'We've run a battery of tests,' Darcy interrupted, and he turned to stare out the window, as if he could see beyond into the garden where his nephew was probably asleep again. From this window all you could see was the sea, the lovely bay where whales came in to give birth to their young, but Darcy wasn't seeing any whales. He was looking at a very personal nightmare. 'The paediatricians in Hobart have now classified it as CFS.'

'Chronic fatigue syndrome?'

'Yes.'

'How old is he?'

'Ten.'

Susie frowned. 'That's incredibly young to be suffering from CFS.'

'Young, but there have been instances as young as nine. And Jamie's been under incredible pressure. He's intellectually gifted, he's sensitive and he knew from the start that his parents didn't want him. His gran does want him, he loves her, and he's been desperately trying to take care of her alone because he didn't want her to go into a nursing home.'

'But she had to be admitted anyway, and Jamie's pneumonia triggered the CFS,' Robert added. 'He just didn't seem to get over it. His AST—his liver transaminase—stayed twice the upper limit of normal range, he's had constant sore throats and headaches, and finally he found it impossible to get out of bed. By the time Darcy arrived, Jamie's problems had compounded into a psychiatric disturbance, with him curled into a foetal position. He was almost unable to talk, with no spontaneous conversation at all. If you knew the time and effort it's taken for Darcy to get him back to this stage...'

'He's still far from well.'

'That's what I mean,' Darcy broke in. 'And to move him now... If I can care for him here then he can see his grandmother every day. He can wheel himself through the building to visit her whenever he wants. This place and Muriel are his only constants. Muriel won't shift from Whale Beach. To tear Jamie away without her—to take him back to Scotland with me—is impossible. Like it or not, the kid needs me.'

Susie blinked. This was looking unarguable. 'So you're prepared to work here?'

'Yes. I've been practising family medicine in Scotland, and I have no ties. I came out here, liked what I saw and decided the obvious solution was to care for Jamie here.'

'And you need to work.'

He sighed. 'I'm hardly old enough to retire. This is a long-term problem. I'm not poor but I'm not exactly rolling in money.'

'You can't just stay on a visitor's permit?' Susie was

clutching at straws here. The more she heard, the more she didn't like what she was hearing.

'This is long term and you know it,' Darcy said harshly. 'If you're any sort of doctor at all, you'll know CFS doesn't disappear overnight, and there's still the issue of tearing him away from his grandma. Muriel won't move. We've had enough trouble persuading her to stay in a nursing home, much less leave Whale Beach.'

'So you'll stay here until Jamie's better—or Muriel dies.'

'That was the plan,' he said harshly. 'With Robert's blessing, I'd decided to work here, and until you turned up it looked possible. Under the rural doctor scheme, overseas doctors can apply to practise in Australia, as long as they sign a contract to work for a minimum of two years in an under-doctored place.'

'Which this place was until today,' Robert said. He hesitated, watching Susie's face. 'Do you really want to work here, love? I mean, you'll have a baby to look after soon.'

She bit her lip. This was hard. Back in England it had seemed simple enough, but now, faced with Darcy's dilemma, things were no longer clear cut. 'I need to work,' she told them. 'Like you, Darcy, I can't afford not to earn a living, and here I have a home.' She closed her eyes. 'I'm sorry. If I'd thought—'

'Or let us know earlier,' Darcy said roughly. 'It would have helped.'

'It wouldn't have made any difference at all,' Robert told them. 'The problem's the same. There's hardly a rural community in this country that's not screaming for a doctor. Even though we can use two doctors—heaven knows, I was busy enough when your dad was here, Susie—there are other places where the need is greater. If there's a full-time doctor already working in Whale Bay, or two part-timers—you and me, Susie—then Darcy won't be given rural doctor status unless he moves elsewhere.'

'And Jamie's grandma is here.' Susie stated the irrefutable fact.

Silence. There was nothing to say.

'I guess I could retire completely,' Robert eventually said bleakly, and the two younger doctors stared at him.

'No,' Susie said. 'You don't want to, do you?'

'No, but—'

'But it wouldn't work anyway,' Darcy said shortly. 'You stated your need to wind down when we applied for my registration. As far as Immigration is concerned, I'm eventually expected to be the sole doctor here, and that's why they'll accept me. There are places up and down this coast with no doctor at all. If Dr Ellis here comes back to work, there's no chance of me getting registration to practise in Whale Beach, and there's no chance I'll be able to stay.'

'The whole thing's impossible.' Susie's voice was bleak. She was watching Darcy's face, and she didn't like what she saw. Or maybe she did—and that made the whole thing worse.

But Darcy was still looking at options. 'Look, how much useful medicine are you going to be able to do with a baby anyway?' he demanded. 'Why not take a year or so maternity leave? Most women do.'

Ha! Susie's stomach clenched in envy. Maternity leave? What a luxury! But it was a luxury for women with stable, wage-earning partners, or for women with savings that hadn't been eroded by years of illness-induced debt.

'Because I can't afford it,' she said through gritted teeth. 'I might own this house, but that's all I own. I'm broke.'

'You might have thought of that before you became pregnant.'

Her sympathy for the man's dilemma was fading fast. Any minute now she was going to slug this creep. 'Thanks for the suggestion,' she managed. 'It's almost eight months too late and I don't need it.'

'And you don't need me.' He sounded as angry as she was. 'You expect me just to move on.'

'I don't know what I expect,' she told him. 'Look, can we...?'

Then she paused. The door was opening, and a middle-aged woman appeared from the hall. It was Val, the receptionist who'd worked here since Susie was tiny. Susie started to smile, but Val's eyes registered Susie only for a microsecond. Clearly there were more important things on her mind.

'Oh, Susie, it's you.' But this was no welcome. Her face was shuttered in distress. 'Dr Fraser...Dr Hayden...'

'What is it, Val?' Darcy stepped forward, sensing trouble.

'Kerry Madden's just rung. The haystack's collapsed. Steve Madden and his children are trapped underneath.'

CHAPTER THREE

THE troubles Susie was causing might well no longer exist. Every doctor in the room moved into professional mode, and the change was instantaneous.

'Is there anyone but Kerry already at the stack?' Darcy's voice was curt and incisive, and Val winced.

'I doubt it. Kerry just screamed down the phone that they were all trapped and she needed help, and then she slammed the phone down. I assume she's alone.'

'Then contact the fire brigade,' Darcy told her. 'Get everyone you can there. The first thing is to get the hay lifted.'

'Try the pub, too,' Susie suggested. 'There are always people there.'

'I'll do that.' Robert was already moving to the phone. 'Val, you call the fire brigade and then ring every farm north of the Maddens' starting with the closest. Get every able-bodied person you can. I'll call the pub and the south farms, and I'll set up Theatre here so you can send patients back on need. I'll be here to receive them. Darcy, you and Susie get yourselves out there now. The Range Rover's got most of the gear in and it's only a two-seater.'

'But...' Darcy turned to Susie. 'Wouldn't it be more sensible for Susie to stay?'

'Susie no longer knows who's living where and who to phone,' Robert snapped. 'I'm damned sure Susie can practise medicine as well as me, or better, and it's best if there's a doctor here so if there's multiple injuries you can send minor things back to me and work on. You know that. So go. Don't just stand there, man. Go.'

Darcy made one last protest at Susie taking her place as a doctor. 'I don't know where—'

'Susie knows where the Maddens' place is. Val will take care of Jamie. Stop arguing. Move!'

They moved. Once a decision had been made, Darcy Hayden wasn't one to mess with trivia. Neither was Susie. She'd been trained in emergency medicine. She deferred to Darcy as he knew where equipment was, but she was right behind him, lifting saline bags and IV cradles, snapping open bags and checking drugs were where they were meant to be and gathering any other gear she could see that was clearly needed.

Finally she followed Darcy to the Range Rover with a speed that matched his.

Until a few weeks ago she'd been working in a busy casualty department in northern England and her pregnancy hadn't slowed her down a bit. She didn't falter until the back doors of the Range Rover were slammed shut, they were in the cabin and the Range Rover was roaring out of the surgery car park, Darcy's hand firmly blasting on the horn to warn oncoming traffic of their coming.

'How many kids do the Maddens have?' she said at last, as they turned onto the main road out of town and Darcy relaxed his horn blaring. 'When I was last here there were three but—'

'Five and another on the way,' Darcy said shortly. 'Kerry Madden had her three-year-old in for an earache three weeks ago. She's a sensible mother, but she's tired to death. The three-year-old and the one-year-old have been added since your departure. That makes five kids under twelve years old, and Kerry's pregnant again. And...'

'And?'

He'd paused. It was like he was talking to himself and had to be prodded to keep speaking aloud. Now he flashed her a look that said he'd almost forgotten she was there, but he shrugged and kept talking.

'Kerry's been ignoring this pregnancy. I only just managed

to check her blood pressure and listen to the baby's heart during the toddler's earache check. Her blood pressure was up then. Despite me asking her to have weekly checks, she hasn't been near me since. I've tried contacting her, but I can't get past her husband, and the man just won't listen. And now this! How the heck can this have happened?'

'Steve Madden's not the most intelligent farmer,' Susie told him. 'Or the most caring parent. Kerry was married at sixteen, and maybe he wasn't a particularly sensible choice. She does her best, but when I knew him Steve was almost thirty, he was drinking too much and Kerry was carrying all the load. If she's been busy with little ones... I'd be guessing he'll have pushed the kids to load the trailer, and they've been doing it unsupervised.'

'They'll have been loading from the bottom of the stack because it's easier,' Darcy said grimly. 'Hell.'

'It might not be so bad.' Susie was thinking it through. 'If there's only a few bales...' She paused and thought some more. 'No. Kerry's not one to panic, and she could have shifted a few bales herself. Especially if the kids were yelling from underneath, which you'd think they would be. Surely they can't all be desperately hurt.'

Darcy's grim face tightened even further. 'You think they'll be smothered?'

'If there were only a few bales they could fight their way out,' Susie said. 'Steve's a big man. So I guess we're expecting pressure fractures and internal injuries.' She lifted the cellphone from the console near the gear lever, and cast Darcy an enquiring look. The more she thought about this the more she didn't like it. 'Should I put the air ambulance on standby from Hobart in case we need an airlift?' she asked. 'We can always cancel if we don't need it.'

'Good idea.' He cast her a sideways glance of dawning respect, then waited as she dialled and listed requirements. As she finished, he frowned, clearly puzzled. 'You know the system?'

'I was brought up here, remember?' she said softly. 'My mother died when I was ten and after that I went everywhere with the two doctors. I was literally practising medicine before I went to medical school.'

'They were good friends—your father and Robert?' Darcy had eyes for nothing but the road, but even though their minds were already in emergency mode, there was time to talk of other things. The Madden farm was still three minutes away.

'They were.'

It was good to think of something other than the awfulness ahead. Years of working in Casualty still hadn't hardened her, but now Susie managed a smile, remembering. 'Neither doctor was what you might call a one-eyed medical man. My dad loved gardening and fishing, and Robert loved his painting. Neither was money-hungry. Apart from peak tourist season, they've practised here almost as part-time doctors, and they loved it.'

'We've become busier. The tourist season is practically year-round now, and when your dad died Robert was left alone. You were never tempted to come home?'

'I was...busy,' Susie told him cautiously. 'Robert told me he wouldn't mind working as a lone partner for a bit to save for his eventual retirement. He planned it so it'd be one last burst of hard work and then he'd quit. But then...well, my husband died, and after a while Val wrote and told me just how hard Robert was finding it. As you say, the tourist influx has added hugely to his workload, and now Robert's polio symptoms seem to be returning.'

'They have,' Darcy said grimly. 'It's a damnable disease. He suffered so much as a kid, and now to have symptoms coming back as he ages... It's not fair.'

'No,' Susie said bleakly and she thought of her Charlie. 'Life's not.'

That gained her another curious glance. There were things about Susie that Darcy didn't understand, but he couldn't afford to look too deep. He had things he had to defend. Like Jamie's future.

'So you came home,' he said flatly.

'Yes.'

He cast her another sideways look, assessing. 'But now I'm here. The problem's solved. Robert has help, so you can return to England with a clear conscience. I'd assume after years in England you have a life there?'

'It's not as easy as that.' Damn. It was so hard not to sound resentful. This had all seemed so straightforward—before Darcy.

'Why not?'

She flashed him a glance that said the thing was obvious. 'That's a stupid question. I need to work and who's going to take on a pregnant doctor? The hospital I was working in needs a full-time casualty officer. I can't stay as emergency specialist in a busy hospital and look after a baby at the same time. I'm broke and I need to work full time to support myself. If I keep working in England—or anywhere else in Australia, for that matter—I'll have to put my baby in child care. Here, I have a home and I can use...'

But he was only seeing what was affecting him. 'You're expecting to use Val for child-minding,' he said explosively.

She nodded, refusing to respond to his anger. 'Maybe. If she's willing. Much as you use Val for Jamie now, I'm guessing. Or if not Val, then I can find someone else who can come into the house while I work in the surgery. That's how my father cared for me after my mother died, and as I got older I went everywhere with him. The locals accepted it as normal. If they wanted Dad, they got me, too. It's a perfect set-up.'

'It is.' His hands clenched white on the steering-wheel, and she sighed.

'I'm sorry.' She was at that. She couldn't have been more sorry if she'd tried. He had his needs, but so did she, and they didn't mesh. If she stayed then he couldn't. It was as simple as that—and she couldn't leave.

'We'll talk about it after this,' he said grimly, and she nodded, but she could see no solution. One of them had to go. But the best thing to do was concentrate on medicine, which looked much the easier option at the moment.

'Take the next turn on the left,' she told him. 'The house is half a mile on the right and the gate to the haystack is another hundred yards past the letter box.'

'You know this country like the back of your hand.'

'I should,' she said softly and then added a rider. 'It's my home.'

Kerry Madden was waiting for them, and by the look on her face things were desperate. Her face reflected horror.

It also reflected exhaustion. Not only had she run back to the house to make the phone call, she'd also run the length of the paddock and somehow torn down the fence to allow vehicles through. And she'd done all this while carrying a hefty one-year-old.

Susie squeezed herself into the middle of the seat to make room. The back of the Range Rover was set up as an ambulance, so it was either that or climb over onto one of the stretchers. And Kerry needed attention. As Darcy steered the Range Rover onto the rutted ground between road and paddock, he paused momentarily to allow the woman to clamber aboard. She climbed in, then sagged against Susie in a state of absolute collapse.

'Put your head down,' Susie ordered as Darcy focussed on getting the vehicle to the haystack at the other end of the paddock. 'Now, Kerry.'

The woman was so exhausted she couldn't speak. Susie lifted the child from her arms, pressured Kerry's head between her knees and concentrated on keeping her conscious. The last thing they needed was for Kerry to faint.

Kerry Madden...

Susie had known this woman since childhood. They'd shared a desk at school; they'd been best friends for a while—but things had changed dramatically for both of them.

In her arms Susie held Kerry's one-year-old, and it didn't take a medical degree to tell that Kerry was almost as pregnant as Susie. And although they were the same age, Kerry seemed much older.

She looked worn from child-bearing, she was wearing ripped and stained khaki overalls, her blonde hair was badly in need of a cut and her work-stained hands were scratched and bleeding, as if she'd been trying to haul the haystack apart by herself.

And there were other differences. Worrying differences. Her hands were puffy, and her wedding ring looked far too tight. Looking further, Kerry's face was swollen and it wasn't just from crying. Her eyes were set back in cheeks that Susie was more accustomed to seeing in patients who'd been on steroids—not healthy young pregnant women.

There was more to be concerned about here than the accident, Susie thought, but the accident was all Kerry was worrying about.

'I can't find any of them,' she gasped while Susie still held her head down. Her face was ashen, she could hardly speak and her lip was bleeding from where she'd bitten it. 'None. Oh, God. None.' She took a searing breath, fighting for words to explain the unexplainable. 'Half the stack's come down.'

As Kerry fought to sit up again, Susie put her arm around the woman's shoulders and held her, hard. She willed her strength into Kerry as she stooped to talk with her. 'Take your time. Tell us what's happened.'

Another jagged breath. Kerry's fear was raw and almost palpable, and above her head Susie and Darcy exchanged concerned glances. There were medical needs right here. They'd have liked to have stopped now and attend to her, but there was no time.

'Come on, Kerry. You can do it.'

And she did. Somehow, although her voice was a thready whisper with no strength behind it at all, Kerry raised her head from her knees, gazed sightlessly though the windscreen and started to speak.

'Steve sent the children out this morning to load the trailer—like he has every day this week,' she whispered. 'It's school holidays, you see, and Steve said it was time they helped, even though I worried. I've been so tired with this pregnancy I haven't had time to go down and check like I normally do. But Steve said it was fine. Anyway, Steve took the truck to meet them a couple of hours ago. He attaches it to the trailer when they've finished loading, you see, and they go round the cows together. But then none of them came home for lunch.'

The child in Susie's arms stirred and fretted. Kerry reached out, and the woman's stained and scratched hands stroked the baby's hair in a gesture of instinctive comfort. Susie had an almost unbearable urge to do the same to her.

'Then...' Kerry forced herself to continue. 'Then I waited and waited, until Daniel woke...' she gestured to the baby '...and we walked over the paddocks to find out what was keeping them. And half the stack's fallen.'

Her breath sucked in at remembered horror. 'Oh, God... It was so high. They must have been pulling from underneath. The truck's there—it's still by the haystack—but the trailer hasn't got any hay on it and Steve's not there. Or he's underneath. He must be. And the keys...the keys must be with him. I had to run back to the house and it's so far...'

Her voice faltered and her words ended on a shattering sob. Susie's arm tightened around her shoulders, instilling what comfort she could.

'Hang on, Kerry,' she told her. 'Help's on the way. We'll have every adult in the district here within five minutes and the stack will be pulled apart before you know it. And the hay's not too heavy. Just think the best.'

'Oh...' She could barely take in what Susie was saying,

but somehow she thought that through. 'How? I only phoned the surgery before I ran back.'

'Val and Dr Fraser are phoning everyone they can think of to get them here.' Susie hesitated. The Range Rover was still lurching across the paddock, but already she could hear the screaming of the fire engine approaching from a distance. She glanced back and the road was filling with a stream of cars. 'Here comes the cavalry.'

Kerry glanced back, saw what Susie was talking about and for the first time her eyes seemed to focus. She turned back to Susie, her eyes widening. 'You mean it.' And then her eyes widened further. 'It's...it's Susie Ellis. Our Susie.' Finally she realised who she was talking to. Until now there hadn't been room in her terrified thoughts for recognition of her old friend. 'I didn't know you were home.'

'I always come home when I'm needed,' Susie told her, and her voice was filled with foreboding. 'Or maybe when I'm not needed. Let's just hope I'm not needed now.'

She wasn't—or not in the way she'd thought.

Within two minutes there were twenty vehicles surrounding the mass of collapsed hay, and there were more able-bodied men and women shifting hay than could possibly be needed to haul the stack apart. Susie was left on the sidelines.

The stack had collapsed at one end. One half was still standing, but the other was a vast, jumbled heap of broken bales. Grant Dobson, Whale Beach's fire chief, took charge. Darcy moved in to help haul bales, but before he did, he ordered Susie to stand back and wait with Kerry.

'Kerry's under enough pressure without this,' he told Susie in an undertone. 'Just look at her! It's my bet her blood pressure's sky-high. I was worried about her before this, and with the exertion she's undertaken she's risking this pregnancy. All the signs are of advanced pre-eclampsia. It'd be best if you could get her back to the house.'

Susie shook her head, knowing such a demand was impossible. There was no way she could make Kerry leave. It was all she could do to stop her throwing herself at the bales again.

'I'll stop her doing anything physical, but it's useless to try and get her away from here. She stays,' she told Darcy. She met his eyes directly, and the man had enough sense to accept what she said. Kerry was immovable.

'Then get my bag from the truck, check her blood pressure and make her sit. I don't want her going into shock.' He glanced at the woman's swollen face, and his expression tightened. 'Or worse.'

And he could see from Susie's face that she knew exactly what he was talking about. Susie wasn't stupid.

But Susie was frustrated. Kerry refused point-blank to leave or to sit, or even allow Susie to check her blood pressure. She stood like she was frozen, simply staring at the stack, watching as Grant and Darcy took charge.

'I want no more pressure from the top,' the fire chief was saying. 'No one climbs. We're taking out bales from the sides, and we're reinforcing as we go.' He frowned as his volunteers started work. 'I can't understand why no one's making noise from underneath. The hay's loosely piled, and there's no vast mass bearing down.'

'It's heavy enough,' Darcy said, giving Susie another silent message to keep Kerry clear—to move her so she couldn't listen—but Grant frowned again and continued.

'Yeah, it could crush a kid, but a bale falling against a man is another thing. It'd be unlucky if it completely crushed him, and if it moved sideways there'd be an airlock. And even if Steve was unlucky... We're talking five people here. And why is the trailer empty? If Steve came up here and found the kids buried then he wouldn't be underneath himself.'

'Kerry said he came up an hour or so after the kids.'

'Then the kids should have put a fair bit of hay on the trailer before he got here.' The fire chief was still thinking it through. 'The other possibility is that they all went around to feed the cows, came back to load for tomorrow and then got into trouble, but that doesn't sound like our Steve. Never do anything today that can't be put off until tomorrow is our Steve's motto in life.'

He shook his head, and motioned his people to work. He had no more time to waste on idle thought. 'OK. All we can do is dig, but be careful.'

'Watch for air locks,' Darcy ordered the volunteers. 'Move slowly, and act like it's a game of pick-up-sticks. You only move a bale if you're sure you're not causing more bales to move, and I mean that. Work in pairs and hold everything steady. I want no more damage than has already been caused. Go!'

They went. Practically the whole adult community of Whale Beach seemed to be there now, and within twenty minutes they'd shifted every bale until they reached the section of the stack that hadn't collapsed.

And they found no one. Not one body. Not one injury.

No one.

All that time, Susie had been standing on the sidelines, holding onto Kerry—or maybe Kerry had been holding onto her, and holding as if her life depended on it—but as the bales cleared to the section that was still neatly piled and the workers stood back, confused, Kerry's frozen control finally snapped. She broke into jagged, tearing sobs and fell to her knees. Susie knelt with her.

'Oh, God. Where are they? Where are they?' At the movement of every bale, Kerry had been waiting for the worst. As the last section had been checked she'd practically stopped breathing and now there was no explanation. No bodies. Just…nothing.

And then there was a yell, sounding faintly from the far side of the Maddens' land. Someone looked up, someone yelled a warning—and there was Steve Madden striding across the paddocks toward them.

He was walking as if there were nothing wrong in the entire world, and he was followed by four children. Susie stared, and then put her hands on Kerry's heaving shoulders, turning her to see.

'Kerry...'

But Kerry was past noticing. She was dry retching onto the ground. Susie waited until the worst had passed, and then lifted her chin and forced her eyes to where the trail of children was growing clearer all the time.

'Kerry, stop it. There's no need for tears. They're on their way to us right now. They're safe.'

The woman didn't move from where she was kneeling. She lifted a tear-stained face and stared at her approaching family, but she didn't make a sound.

Neither did anyone else.

Silence.

What could have been a cry of triumph from the searchers didn't turn out that way. From across the paddock the Madden kids were speeding up as their father led them back to the stack. They were clearly fascinated by the presence of the fire truck and the crowd, but every person who'd been involved in searching was staring straight at Kerry.

Kerry's swollen face was now blank and pale with shock, and her eyes were disbelieving. She didn't say a word, but with Susie's help she staggered to her feet. Darcy moved to her other side, his face mirroring Susie's concern.

'Dear God,' Kerry whispered. At her feet, one-year-old Daniel was cooing and murmuring and grabbing handfuls of loose straw, as if he didn't have a trouble in the world, but not so his mother. 'Dear God,' she repeated. 'They're...they're all here. Safe. My babies.'

'They're all safe, Kerry.'

But it was finally too much.

'I'll kill him,' she whispered, and then her legs sagged from under her, her eyes rolled back in her head, and if Darcy and Susie hadn't been holding her tight she would have ended up on the ground.

'I don't see what all the fuss is about.'

Steve Madden hadn't changed one bit. Not a bit. Susie remembered him as a charming, good-looking male who'd got more than one girl into trouble before he'd finally married Kerry. It seemed his sense of responsibility hadn't improved with his marriage. Now, even though his wife was semiconscious on the ground, he was busy explaining his actions to the fire chief, and his voice said he was astounded that all this fuss had been made.

He'd got flabbier over the years, Susie thought. He had the look of a man who spent too much time with the bottle and not enough time on hard physical exercise. He certainly didn't look like a farmer.

'I came over to help the kids and the stack collapsed just as I got here,' he said petulantly, noting the looks of accusation all around him. 'Lucky the kids weren't under it. So I thought, damn, it's going to take days to rebuild, and I'd worked enough this morning. So we fed the cows and I took the kids for a swim. The river was great. I knew as soon as I got back to the house Kerry'd be on about rebuilding the stack, so I thought we might as well enjoy ourselves before she started carping on.'

'Kerry'd be right. There's rain coming and the hay needs to be covered,' one of the local farmers said heavily. 'You're a fool, Madden. You always have been.'

'You can butt out of my business, McGregor.' Steve Madden's face flushed crimson. 'Look, if Kerry's gone overboard and panicked.... And now she's fainted. Well, that's a woman for you. Hell, she might have known I wouldn't be stuck under that lot. It'd take a bigger stack than this to kill me.'

'It could have killed you,' the fire chief said, his eyes contemptuous, and then he moved deliberately away to where Susie and Darcy were working on Kerry. 'Is she OK?' Like

Steve, he'd assumed she'd simply fainted, but this was much more than a faint.

'No,' Darcy said. Kerry hadn't lost consciousness completely, but her muscles had gone into spasm and she was gripping Darcy's hand like she was drowning. Susie was fitting a blood-pressure cuff over her arm as Darcy organised an oxygen mask. They'd worked in tandem since she'd collapsed, each anticipating the other's needs, and they were working fast. Darcy spoke roughly to the fire chief but his attention was totally on Kerry. He flashed an enquiring look at Susie and she shook her head. Instinctively he knew she was as worried as he was.

'A hundred and sixty, a hundred and ten,' she said, and he winced.

'Her blood pressure's sky-high—hell, we're moving into eclampsia territory here. This isn't a faint. She's fitting. If we can't get her blood pressure down we're risking a stroke.'

'Eclampsia?' The fire chief looked a question.

'High blood pressure. Dangerously high blood pressure. It can cause fitting or a stroke and that's just the start of it. Hell, if we don't get it down... Steve, I *told* you she should be having bed rest, and why on earth...? Grant, can you clear the way to the Range Rover and bring the stretcher across? And radio to the air ambulance. We already have them on standby from Hobart, but tell them we need them urgently and we need a neonatal team on board.'

'A neonatal team?' Steve's attention was finally caught. 'What—for the baby, you mean? No way. She's only six months gone.'

By his side his oldest child, a little girl of about eleven, was standing looking like her world was falling apart, but he ignored her completely.

'I warned you...' Darcy stated.

'She'll be all right as soon as she gets her breath back,' Steve interrupted uneasily. 'This is only a stupid faint. Hell, she might have known we'd be safe. Of all the damn fool things to think!'

'She thought it,' Darcy said heavily. 'But that's past. Let's just concentrate on keeping your wife and baby safe.'

'Safe! Hell, Kerry's not in any danger, is she?'

Susie looked around the crowd of volunteers and made a swift gesture to a woman she recognised. It was understood. The woman stepped in, lifting the little girl away from her father. 'Come on, love,' she said, 'Let the doctors look after your mummy.'

And with the child gone, Darcy could finally say what he wished. 'I told you weeks ago,' he snapped. 'Her blood pressure was rising then. I wanted weekly visits, and Kerry needed rest. I wanted her in hospital then for a complete check, but you wouldn't hear of it, and now you pull a stunt like this. I explained—'

'You didn't!'

'You wouldn't listen,' Darcy said heavily. 'But you're listening now.' He motioned to baby Daniel who was busy stuffing straw into his mouth, and then to the distressed little girl. 'I suggest you look after your son, Mr Madden. Look after all your children, in fact. Follow us into the hospital as soon as you can. We can't wait for you. Dr Ellis and I are going to need every bit of luck we can get—and then some—if we're to save your wife.'

Kerry had her second major convulsion in the back of the Range Rover and it was far worse than the first. From semi-consciousness, her body started jerking in rigid muscle spasms, and she slipped into complete oblivion almost immediately.

'I'm not surprised,' Darcy said heavily, pulling to the edge of the road as Susie rolled Kerry onto her side. One of the firemen had come with them and Kerry's small body was so swollen that it took their combined strength to roll her. 'I'm coming back in there,' Darcy said. 'Henry, take over at the wheel, and take it slow.'

Then he was in the back with Susie, organising equipment and fighting to keep Kerry still. The roads here were rough and unsealed, and injecting under such circumstances—and in such cramped conditions—was something Susie wouldn't have liked to try, but Darcy had obviously done it before.

'I should have gone out to see her,' he said, half to himself and half to Susie. 'Three weeks ago I was worrying about her blood pressure and now, with this swelling, she'll be lucky not to have a major stroke.' He was injecting intravenous diazepam, but his set face told Susie he knew the uselessness of what they were doing. They could do so little while they still had to worry about Kerry's baby. The diazepam dose he could give to a pregnant woman wasn't nearly enough.

And Kerry's baby was so far pre-term....

She should be down in Hobart right now.

'The raised blood pressure was only mild three weeks ago?' She was guessing, but Susie had seen enough of Darcy's caring to know he wouldn't have sent a woman with pre-eclampsia home.

'Yes.' His voice was rigid with anger and Susie could tell that some of that anger was directed at himself. 'Although, as I said, I couldn't do a complete check. Steve was waiting and she wouldn't stay for more than a couple of minutes. As I told you, she was more worried about her toddler than herself. I rang a couple of times and got Steve. I talked him through the pre-eclampsia threat—told him I was worried—but he assured me Kerry was fine. He was helping and she was getting plenty of rest. He can be...persuasive.'

'He's always been that.' The Range Rover had slowed to almost a crawl. The local police car was giving them an escort, its blue light flashing in front, but the need for speed was less than the need for immediate treatment. Darcy had located the vein and set up an intravenous line almost as easily as if they'd been in a casualty cubicle.

But Kerry was still rigid on the stretcher, her body arching into spasms and never losing its awful rigidity. Her convulsion was lasting way too long.

'How are you at emergency Caesars?' Darcy asked grimly, and Susie winced.

'How many weeks did you say?'

'Twenty-six.'

'Darcy, there's so little chance…'

'Of a viable baby? I agree. Not if we deliver it at Whale Beach, but unless the air ambulance is available right now—which it hardly ever is—then I don't think we have a choice. We'll lose Kerry if we don't get this baby out.'

'But—'

'Susie, the neonatal team will be here as soon as possible, and we'll have to depend on them to increase the baby's chances of survival. If we can keep it alive that long. We—you and I—though, can't think of that. If we wait then we lose both mother and baby. We go in now and concentrate on Kerry.'

'Darcy, I don't think I can.'

He cast her a hard, uncompromising look.

'Robert seems to think your medical skills are up to scratch. You can give an anaesthetic?'

'Yes, but not like this.' All Susie felt was panic. 'I've never given an anaesthetic for a woman as ill as this. I have general training. This is specialist anaesthetic territory.'

'And it's specialist obstetrician stuff. Unfortunately I don't have a specialist obstetrician and I don't have a specialist anaesthetist. I have you and we have Robert. If you can't do it then Robert must, and your hands don't shake as Robert's have started to do.'

Darcy fixed her with a look that allowed no argument. No matter what he thought of her as a person, he needed her now as a doctor, and everything else was put aside. 'Robert will have to be the one to cope with the baby if the neonate team doesn't arrive on time. We'll radio ahead and tell him to set up Theatre for emergency Caesar. As soon as we get back I'll telephone for specialist obstetric advice, but I don't think that advice will give us a choice.'

'Darcy, no.' But she knew the protest was futile.

'Welcome to the medical world of Whale Beach, Dr Ellis,' Darcy said grimly. 'This is what you wanted. This is what you've got!'

CHAPTER FOUR

SEVEN hours later, Susie finally had time to sit. Seven hours...

They'd been some of the longest hours she'd ever spent, she thought as she slumped into the armchair in the kitchen at the rear of the house. And they'd failed. Three doctors hadn't been enough.

It hadn't been for want of trying. Darcy was a fine doctor, she'd discovered. He'd been amazingly skilled at surgery and he was someone she'd be content to rely on in most emergencies, but this had been an emergency that had needed a city hospital, a full obstetric and neonatal team and luck thrown in for good measure.

It hadn't happened. The plane with help had been delayed for too long to wait. Darcy and Robert and Susie had pitted every ounce of their medical skills against the odds, but the odds had been too great.

The result? One Caesarean. One tiny baby boy who'd lived only minutes, despite their desperate attempts to save him, and one desperately ill woman who'd been transferred by air to Hobart, still convulsing.

Kerry would be lucky to live, Susie thought bleakly. At least now that she was no longer pregnant, the medical teams could concentrate solely on her survival. In the intensive care unit of Hobart's main hospital she had a chance but, dear heaven, at what cost?

Steve, still blustering but sagging around the edges, had gone with the air ambulance, accompanying the flying medical staff and Kerry to Hobart. Robert was coping with evening surgery and Darcy had returned to the farm where Kerry's parents were taking care of their grandchildren. His job was to take them the news, and try to explain the unexplainable.

Both jobs would be terrible, Susie thought grimly. Robert's and Darcy's. Every patient in the district would know about the tragedy by now, and Robert's job of answering the locals' questions would be almost as bad as Darcy's.

Sometimes being a doctor was the pits, Susie decided wearily, and ran her hand protectively over her own abdomen. Please, God, that such a nightmare not touch her...

'The baby died.'

She glanced up. Here, in the big, open-plan kitchen that had been her home for ever, Susie had slumped down in the armchair by the stove like one who was completely at home. She'd forgotten it was also home for ten-year-old Jamie.

'Yes, Jamie,' she said gently. 'We did everything we could, but sometimes everything's not enough. The baby was too little to be born, and it died.'

He nodded, with a look that was over-wise for his years. 'Uncle Darcy will be sad.'

'I guess a lot of people will be sad.' She watched as the small boy pushed his wheelchair across to the kitchen table. He was so serious. So...

Hardened, she thought suddenly. He was a child who expected the worst, and he expected it because the worst always happened. His mother abandoning him. His father dying. His grandmother having a stroke.

And now here was Susie, coming to tell him his uncle couldn't stay here with him. She knew full well what it meant. If Jamie wanted to stay with Darcy then he'd have to return to England and leave his grandmother. What sort of a choice was that for a small boy to make?

'Val says to tell you there's a casserole in the oven,' he told her. 'I've already had mine, but there's heaps for you and for Uncle Darcy when he gets home.'

'Thanks.' She wasn't hungry but, heavily conscious of the new little life within her—and how fragile it was—she forced herself to go through the motions. To spoon out a plateful of casserole and eat it while the small boy's eyes watched her every move.

'I've been to see Gran,' he said at last, and she nodded.

'Your gran's in the nursing home?'

'It's right next to the hospital,' he told her. 'I can wheel myself there from here. Gran likes seeing me a lot, and I go at least twice a day. It's easy from here.'

He paused then, as if he had something very important to say. And finally it came. 'I told Gran you'd come back,' he said tightly. 'And she said...she said if you'd come back to work then my uncle can't stay here and I'll have to go away.'

Oh, no. Susie thought back to what she remembered of Jamie's grandma. Muriel Barker had always been as sharp as a tack, and it seemed her stroke hadn't deprived her of any of her mental faculties.

'We need to sort that out,' she said. 'We'll talk about it over the next few days.'

'Gran says if you work here then the government won't let Uncle Darcy work here, too. Is that right?'

She swallowed, but there was no way out of this. 'Yes.'

'But you can't work and have a baby,' Jamie protested. 'You have to look after it. You can't be a doctor, too.'

'I can.' She sighed. 'Many women must work when their babies are tiny, and I'm one of them. I can't afford to do anything else, Jamie.'

'But if you work, what happened to Mrs Madden might happen to you.'

She smiled, trying to be as reassuring as she could—which wasn't very reassuring. 'I won't work that hard. I promise.'

His mouth turned mutinous. 'But it's true. Gran says if you work here then Uncle Darcy will have to leave, and they'll make me go with him. I asked Dr Fraser. He says the only reason they're letting my uncle stay in Australia—working here—is that Dr Fraser wants to retire and Whale Beach won't have a doctor without him.'

'Jamie—'

'Dr Fraser says Uncle Darcy might get a job further along the coast.' The child's words were increasingly desperate. 'But it's thirty miles at least to the next town. They'll make me stay with him. I know they will, and I know he won't bring me to see Gran every day. He won't have time.'

'Jamie, I can't—' But there were no counter-arguments.

'If my uncle goes, I'll stay here by myself,' he said furiously. 'You can't just come and kick us out.'

'Jamie, this is Susie's home.'

The voice from behind made Susie start. She'd been so intent on the small boy's fury that she hadn't heard Darcy enter. Now she turned to find him standing wearily at the door.

His face was haggard. What he'd had to face—explaining to the Madden children that there was no new baby, and explaining to Kerry's parents just what Kerry's chances were—must have been dreadful.

And now this! He'd come home to face Jamie being evicted from the home he'd pinned his hopes on.

The knowledge almost overwhelmed her. This big-hearted man who'd come half a world to give his nephew a home, who'd cradled a dying baby with such tenderness that Susie had wept—this man who'd taken on the responsibilities for the medicine of this town—was now being robbed of everything by her.

But there were other things on her mind as well. Dreadful things. 'Kerry?' she said softly, and waited with a hollow feeling in the pit of her stomach for the verdict.

'I've just been in touch with Hobart. She's stopped convulsing for the moment and there's no evidence of stroke, so that's our one piece of decent news for the day. It's early yet, though.'

Susie nodded. Eclampsia couldn't be controlled until the

baby was born, but even after the birth there were often days or weeks of danger.

'We can only hope. And Steve's with her?'

'The hospital staff told me when she finally regained consciousness Steve was nowhere to be found. Out, getting drunk, I expect.'

'Oh, no! Poor Kerry.'

'She should kick him out,' Darcy said savagely. 'The locals tell me it's her parents' farm—not his. I can't understand why she doesn't.'

'Maybe she loves him.' Susie gave a bleak, wintry little smile and then turned back to Jamie who'd been soaking in their conversation like a sponge. 'Like your uncle loves you, Jamie. Coming all the way from England to care for you.'

'My grandma loves me,' Jamie whispered. 'No one else does, and now I have to go away. Dr Fraser says this is your home and I can't stay here any more.'

It was too much. 'Jamie, I'm not sure it is my home any more,' she said softly, and she saw Darcy's eyes widen. 'When I decided to come home I didn't know your uncle was here. Maybe I need to do a rethink. For tonight, though, we're all very tired. I need to sleep and then maybe we need to make some decisions in the next few days. But for now let's not worry about the future.'

'I'm worrying.' Jamie glared.

'So are we all,' Susie told him. 'We need a solution, but for now, even more importantly, we need bed.'

Bed was fine. Bed was easy. It was sleep that wouldn't come. Susie lay in the darkness in the bedroom she'd slept in as a child and stared up at the ceiling for hour upon hour.

The baby's death weighed heavily on her. No matter how much she practised medicine, unnecessary deaths always left her feeling sick at heart, and it was even worse now that she could empathise so strongly with what Kerry had lost.

She'd take better care of her baby, she promised herself,

but the more she thought of her future and the care she could give to her little one, the more she didn't like what she was seeing.

But she had so few options left. She had no money and she had to work. She'd walked away from the home she'd been offered in England and the fury she'd left still reverberated in her ears. She couldn't go back now.

But...neither could she stay. How could she evict Darcy and Jamie from this town?

How could she not? The baby was stirring within her, and the knowledge that she was totally responsible for this new little life was threatening to overwhelm her. The thought of the afternoon's events—of one tiny baby struggling vainly for life in Darcy's caring hands—made her dilemma seem even worse.

She had to give her little one a future. She must. She'd gone into this pregnancy with her eyes wide open, but now things were such a mess.

Sleep was impossible. Finally, in desperation, she pushed back her covers, threw on her robe and slippers and made her way through the quiet house.

Darcy was sleeping in her parents' room. Jamie was in the little room beside it—that was sensible as it meant if he needed his uncle he only had to call. Blessedly it meant also that they'd left her room as it had been.

But Susie didn't want her bedroom now. She wanted a cup of tea and somewhere to think—anywhere where she wasn't reminded of Darcy and his problems.

She padded through to the reception area of the doctors' surgeries. This was peaceful enough. But it was dark and lonely, and beyond were the lights of the little hospital. There was another need added to her list. Company. Life! She only had to go through the door and she'd be back in a medical world. Back where she belonged.

She looked like an escaped patient herself, she thought ruefully, and then thought, What the heck. The staff on duty during the afternoon's drama had all been familiar faces. They all knew she was back home, and the hospital kitchen would be warm. And she'd been lonely for so long...

She pushed through the dividing door. It swung shut behind her, and then snapped open again. She turned—and collided with Darcy, barrelling through behind her.

Because she'd turned, they met head on. He grasped her by the shoulders or she would have fallen.

Unlike her, Darcy was fully dressed. He hadn't been to bed, she guessed. His eyes were dark with fatigue, and his face shuttered as he took in her appearance.

More problems, his look said, and as she looked up at him Susie's heart wrenched in sympathy. She knew instinctively that he'd been going over and over the events of the afternoon, asking himself the same stupid question.

What could they have done differently to affect the outcome?

He was a caring doctor, she told herself as she looked up at him. A good man. To come all this way and make the decision to live in such an out-of-the-way place as Whale Beach for an ailing nephew. She felt so sorry for him. And there was something else she felt.

What?

This was stupid, she told herself fiercely as she tried to suppress the strange emotions she was feeling. Why was she reacting like this to Darcy's problems? She had enough of her own, she knew, but the chemistry between the two of them—this thing she was feeling as he held her shoulders—was there, whether she liked it or not.

'What's wrong?' His harsh voice barked the demand as he automatically steadied her. She blinked up into his concerned face. Darcy was in doctor mode, and he was assuming she was in trouble.

Well, she'd asked for that, she guessed. She was pregnant, she was in pink spotty pyjamas and a blue spotty dressing-gown, and she was in the hospital. Her eyes creased into involuntary laughter. Maybe he was right to assume she was here as a patient.

But he was too tired to see the laughter. 'Susie, what is it?'

Heck, he had the capacity to throw her right off balance, in more ways than one. The caring in his voice, and the feel of his hands on her shoulders as he steadied her... It did strange things to her—things she wasn't sure how to cope with.

'Nothing,' she said, and her voice was surprisingly defensive. 'I thought I might make myself a cup of tea.'

'We do have a kitchen in the house.'

We. The word was weirdly intimate.

'I know,' she managed. 'I didn't want to wake you.'

'As you see...' He looked down at his fully dressed self and gave a rueful smile. 'I'm already awake. And Jamie won't stir. It's as much as I can do to wake him in the daytime.'

'You've been called back?' She pulled away from his hold and, suddenly aware that his hands were still on her shoulders, he also pulled back with a hastiness that said he should have done so earlier. If he'd thought of it.

Or if she hadn't felt so soft under his hands...

She knew Darcy had felt what she was feeling. She could read it on his face. Somehow Susie watched with detached interest as he hauled himself back into doctor mode, forcing his voice to be formal as he answered her question. What was it that she'd asked? Had he been called back?

'Yes.' He motioned to the beeper on his belt. 'A drip's packed up. Laura Hendy had her appendix out this morning. She's a fit little ten-year-old and will probably be OK without the extra fluids, but I figured, what the heck, I couldn't sleep anyway.'

'You operated here this morning?' That didn't make sense. Robert's hands were no longer steady enough to give an anaesthetic.

'Ian Lars is the closest doctor to Whale Beach,' Darcy told her. 'He practises at Stony Point sixty miles north. We have a deal. I travel for his minor surgery requirements and he travels for my anaesthetic needs. That way patients can stay in their own hospitals. He came up early this morning to help me with Laura.'

'And in emergencies?'

'You've seen today what happens in emergencies,' Darcy said flatly. 'But it's the best we can do.'

'You need two doctors.' She fell silent. 'You must! Is Robert so incapacitated that he can't operate?'

'Yes.'

'And you're on call all the time?' The set-up here was puzzling her.

'Yes,' Darcy said briefly. 'As you know, he lives apart from the hospital and he can't cope with unbroken sleep. Heaven knows, he's suffering more than he lets on.'

'From the after-effects of the polio?'

'It's a damnable thing,' Darcy told her. 'From what he lets on—which isn't much—he suffered enough as a kid. He tells me he spent years in calipers and now, in his late sixties, as he's contending with arthritis and general aging, back comes the polio to haunt him. He doesn't want to give up medicine altogether. He loves living in this town, but there's very little he can do apart from straight consultation.'

Susie bit her lip, and Darcy nodded, knowing exactly what she was thinking.

'It's too much for you to take on,' he told her. 'You never expected full-time practice, but that's what you'll be getting if you stay here. Robert wants to stay in touch but, as you saw this afternoon, he's only too ready to stand back and let someone else take over. He coped with this afternoon's dramas and he did evening surgery but now he's exhausted. It's been too much for him. He can't be on call, and you need to know that.'

'I suppose so.' She faltered and bit her lip again. This was too hard. What was she getting into? She desperately needed time to think this through, and she didn't have it. Decisions were being demanded of her now.

'You need to see your patient,' she told him. At least then she'd be alone to clear her head.

'Do you want to come with me to see Laura?' he asked unexpectedly, and as her eyes widened he smiled, and there was a trace of sympathy behind his grey eyes. 'At a guess, you're roaming around, looking for company and there's company waiting. Laura will be delighted.'

She looked a question at him, and he smiled again, breaking the tension. 'You look worried,' he told her, softening still more. 'I know I've made things impossibly hard for you. The feeling's mutual, but for now maybe we need to call a truce and get Laura sorted.'

'You don't mind if I come?' She looked down at her pyjama-clad figure and managed an uncertain smile. 'I'm hardly dressed in doctor mode.'

'You look just fine to me,' he said, and it surprised her how his assessing eyes had the capacity to make her blush. 'I don't know why I don't wear the same. We could make it standard wear for doctors on night duty. Spotty pyjamas. Very sensible.'

'It might be sensible but it'll hardly make Laura think I'm professionally competent.'

'I suspect what Laura needs isn't doctors but attention,' he told her. 'A pyjama-clad diversion is just what she needs.'

'It's not what you need, though.'

'Maybe I do,' he told her. He shook his head and the look of uncertainty deepened in his eyes. 'Heaven knows, this is one hell of a mess I've got myself into. I've not been awake working until now. I've been up pacing the floor, trying to thing of a solution. Of any solution. I was almost glad of the call to take my mind off it.'

Laura was delighted to see them. The ten-year-old was

sitting up in bed, receiving visitors with all the aplomb of a senior member of the monarchy. There was a nurse with her. The nurse rolled her eyes at Darcy as he entered, then looked curiously behind him to Susie, but Susie hadn't time to be introduced before Laura started talking.

'I just wiggled my arm a little bit, Dr Darcy, and the drip came loose,' the child announced, her blue eyes limpid with innocence. 'The bipper started bipping, and Nurse Carrie came and sighed and said she'd have to get you to replace it. Were you asleep?'

Her voice indicated she didn't mind if he had been. This was a much more satisfactory state of affairs than sleeping. Then, like the nurse, her eyes moved to Susie. Satisfaction faded and her voice became accusing. 'Ooh. I know who you are. You're Susie Ellis, Dr Ellis's grown-up doctor-daughter. My mum says you've come home to stay and you're making my Dr Darcy go away.' She glared straight at Susie with full ten-year-old indignation. 'And that means my friend Jamie has to go, too, and my mum thinks that's terrible.'

How fast did news travel around this district? Susie wondered grimly, but she dredged up a smile.

'Nothing's been decided other than I've come home,' she told Laura. 'I hope you don't mind if I help with your drip tonight.'

There was a dramatic sigh.

'I expect it'll be a good thing.' Laura lay back and put out her hand with a theatrical little flourish. Darcy lifted it and started lightly tapping for a vein. 'I expect I'll have to get used to you. A lady doctor.'

'There's nothing wrong with lady doctors,' Darcy told her. He found what he was looking for, the nurse handed him the syringe and he slipped the needle back where it was needed. Laura sighed again. This time her sigh wasn't quite so theatrical and a tiny tremor in her voice said that the pinprick had hurt. She really was a sick little girl, and it was the middle of the night.

'I know there's nothing wrong with lady doctors,' she whispered. 'But I like my Dr Darcy...'

So did Susie.

By the time they had Laura settled, leaving her with Nurse Carrie for company until she went back to sleep, the notion was firmly rooted in Susie's mind. She'd thought it already but here it was, spoken aloud.

I like Dr Darcy...

And he was skilled! This community had been blessed by finding itself a wonderful doctor, she thought, and Susie was under no illusions as to the service she could give to replace Darcy. Twenty-four-hour call, seven days a week? No. She couldn't do it. Not with a newborn baby to care for.

Yet if she stayed, Darcy would have to leave. She thought back to the times her father had pointed out the difficulties the small towns around them had in attracting doctors. Whale Beach was fortunate, but other towns weren't.

What had Darcy said? The closest practising doctor was sixty miles away. That meant there were at least three closer towns without doctors at all. There was no possibility the government would allow a foreign doctor to set up practice here if Susie intended to practise herself.

And if Whale Beach had no Dr Robert, and they replaced Dr Darcy with Susie...

It was starting to look untenable in more ways than one.

They emerged from the ward into the corridor and she found Darcy was looking down at her, a question in his dark eyes. 'Penny for your thoughts?'

'What?' She was caught off balance. 'I guess I wasn't thinking of anything.'

'Liar. You were thinking you can't do it.'

'I don't have much choice,' she said blankly. 'I must.'

Anger flared, surfacing through weariness, and he snapped. 'You could always try returning to England—maybe even to the father of your baby.'

Oh, right. Her eyes closed at that, the ever-present pain rising to the surface. What a stupid thing to say. As if she could. She opened her eyes again and found Darcy still watching her. The anger had gone, to be replaced with the instinctive sympathy she was growing accustomed to.

'I'm sorry,' he said softly. Damn him, she knew he'd seen her pain. 'That was a foolish thing to say when I don't know your circumstances.' Then his gaze grew more intent, seeing past the surface light-heartedness she'd so carefully acquired over these last awful years. 'Are you in real trouble, Susie?'

She gazed helplessly up at him and there was nothing to give him but the truth. 'I'm in all sorts of trouble,' she agreed. 'For both of us.' She hauled herself together and managed a wan smile. 'But it can wait for morning. You can go to bed now.'

'I wish.' He glanced toward the nurses' station, and the charge nurse was grimacing and beckoning him over. 'Ha. I thought so. This looks like more work. Never mind. You go get your cup of tea and go back to bed, Susie, and leave me to it.'

'But—'

She got no further before she was interrupted.

'Darcy, Muriel Barker needs you.' The charge nurse, a middle-aged woman Susie recognised as Lorna Touldbridge, a friend from years back, had emerged from behind the desk to cut across their conversation. She shot Susie a brief smile of recognition. 'Hi, Susie, love. Welcome home.' Then she turned back to Darcy and her eyes were troubled.

'Darcy, they've just rung across from the nursing home. Muriel's distressed, her blood pressure's sky-high and they're worrying about her stirring herself into another stroke. Apparently Jamie's told her what's happening and she's worrying herself sick.'

'Damn.'

Susie winced. Here was more trouble down to her. 'This is my fault,' Susie said grimly, and Darcy nodded.

'It is, but there's not much you can do about it. I should have made time and talked to Muriel myself tonight. It's my responsibility.'

He was responsible for Jamie's grandma, too? He had Muriel's health on his shoulders? Susie shot Darcy a look of deep concern. He'd been pulled from carefree bachelorhood to this? He had the weight of the world on his shoulders and here she was, causing him nothing but grief.

It was looking more and more as if her decision couldn't wait until morning, she thought bleakly. Susie wasn't having another stroke for Muriel laid to her account.

'Let me talk to her,' she said urgently, and Darcy shook his head.

'That'll only upset her more.'

'Darcy...' She laid a hand on his arm and let it rest. 'I know Muriel. I can reassure her.'

'You can't reassure her.' He gazed down at her hand resting on his white sleeve. Gently he lifted it away and let it drop. 'This is an insurmountable problem, Dr Ellis.'

'Maybe. But it's a problem of my making. I need to see her.'

'Susie—'

'Let me try.'

'I don't know.'

'Darcy, I'm a doctor,' she told him. 'I'm not about to cause a further rise in her blood pressure. If I didn't think I could do some good, I'd leave it to you. I promise.'

He gazed at her for a long, unseeing minute, and it was Lorna who broke the silence.

'Let her try,' she urged. 'The one thing our Susie is renowned for is solving other people's problems. She's been doing it since she was four.'

'There's nothing you can do here.'

'Let me try.'

* * *

Muriel was in her seventies. Susie remembered her as a fine-looking, big-boned woman, but now she seemed to have shrunk. The stroke had diminished her, and the news she'd had that afternoon had made matters infinitely worse. Her eyes were swollen from weeping. She lay huddled in her bed, and the look she gave Darcy as they entered was despairing.

And Susie couldn't bear it. She hadn't wanted to say the words so soon, but they came out anyway. As soon as she walked into the room and saw Muriel's distress, she knew she could leave it no longer.

'Muriel, I won't do this to you,' Susie told her, before the door had even closed behind them. She crossed to the bed and took the woman's leathery hands in hers. This woman had worked so hard all her life. She'd taken on the care of her grandson without a protest, she'd loved him to bits and it wasn't fair that she should be torn from him now. 'I don't know what the rumours have been, but you're not to worry. I won't take Darcy and Jamie away from you. I'll get a job down the coast and take myself off, but I will not tear you from your grandson.'

There was deathly silence in the room as the old lady took this in. There was silence, too, from Darcy. She heard his swift intake of startled breath—and then nothing.

'Do you mean it?' The woman's voice was a thread of a whisper, hope flaring as she gazed up at Susie. Her eyes said she knew exactly who Susie was, and she knew exactly what she was promising.

'I mean it.'

'Oh, if you only could…'

'I can.'

'Muriel, we need to talk this through,' Darcy said at last. He walked across to the bed and took the old lady's hands from Susie. 'You've been getting yourself into a state.'

'Yes, because I thought…' The woman's eyes were still on Susie. 'I should have known you wouldn't do this to us, Susie, love. You always were a kind child.'

'I'm not a child any more,' Susie told her, trying to cut the tension. She gazed pointedly down at the bulge beneath her spotted dressing-gown. 'As you can see.'

'I can see.' A troubled expression swept across the old woman's face again. 'Jamie said you need to be here. This is your home. It's not right that you can't come back.'

'I can come back. At weekends. On my holidays. I'll get a job down the coast. There's any number of towns needing a doctor, so stop worrying this instant.'

She picked up the blood-pressure cuff and turned enquiring eyes to Darcy. 'Do you want to play doctor here or shall I?'

'I think I'd better,' Darcy said grimly. He took the cuff from her and slipped it on Muriel's arm. 'Not that we need it. I suspect after what Susie's just said your blood pressure will go down all by itself.'

'*If* she means it,' the old lady said, doubt still in her eyes.

'Of course I mean it,' Susie said indignantly. 'Have you ever known me to tell lies, Muriel Barker?'

'No, child, I haven't.' Muriel sighed and lay back on her pillows. 'But it's time you stopped taking troubles of the world onto your shoulders. To leave your home with a little one on the way... It's time you thought of your future.'

'I'll do that,' Susie promised. She stooped and kissed the wrinkled old forehead and then slipped from the room before Darcy could say a word.

I'll do that...

How was she going to do that?

Susie made herself a mug of tea and took it out onto the back verandah of the house. She no longer wanted company. She was feeling almost as bleak as she'd felt in the weeks following Charlie's death.

All her plans. They'd been pointless. She'd been unrealistic. Thinking she could just walk back here and everything would be the same...

She sat down on the back step and gazed forlornly out

over the creek toward the sea beyond. A wallaby was nibbling the grass by the creek. While Susie stared, a tiny joey twisted and tumbled from her pouch, then started nibbling the grass between his mother's paws.

'She's taking better care of you than I can of my baby,' Susie said grimly, and fought hard to stop useless tears welling behind her eyes. She wasn't going to cry. She wasn't!

But at least the joey had a home, and a mother he could be with all the time.

'Mind if I join you?'

Darcy's voice was so soft that she didn't jump. She nodded soundlessly and he came to sit on the step beside her. Jamie's wheelchair ramp took up half the wide steps. What was left was a narrow strip just wide enough for both to fit, and Darcy's broad shoulders brushed the soft flannel of her gown as he settled beside her.

The warmth was somehow threatening, piercing the armour she'd so carefully built around herself over the last two years. She flinched and he felt it.

'Susie...'

'Leave it,' she said bleakly. 'There's nothing else to be said. You and Jamie can stay here. You must. So much depends on it.'

'And you?'

'Like I said, I'll get a job in a town along the coast.' She gave a rueful laugh as she thought of what lay ahead. 'There's no problem in getting a job. I'll charge you rent for this house and that'll pay for child care. See? I have it all sorted.'

'You had it all sorted.'

'I didn't. I should have let Robert know months ago that I was coming home.'

'Why didn't you?' His voice was soft and infinitely caring, and once again Susie felt the piercing of her armour. He sounded as if he cared—and no one did. She knew that now. The caring made her want to cry.

Crying would be stupid!

He was waiting for her to answer, and emotion achieved nothing. Talking achieved nothing either, but maybe he wouldn't condemn her so much if he knew.

'I thought...I thought somewhere else was home,' she told him.

'Somewhere in England?'

'Mmm.' She nodded. Out on the lawn the joey was growing braver, moving a good two feet from his mother. She concentrated fiercely on the two creatures, and tried desperately to block the feel of Darcy's sleeve against hers. His body against hers...

'This baby,' he probed, breaking the silence. 'Do you want to tell me about it?'

Why not? There was no secret.

'This baby is my husband's baby,' she said into the semi-darkness. 'Charlie's baby.'

'But—'

'From Charlie's frozen sperm.'

'I see.' And maybe he did. Maybe he knew the fight she'd undertaken to be inseminated with Charlie's sperm. Even if he didn't, his voice softened further, with a caring that was her undoing. 'Would you like to tell me about Charlie?'

Yes. She would. She'd been silent about Charlie for so long. There'd been sympathy for the first few months, but now it was as if he'd never existed. Except for her pregnancy...

'Charlie was a physician,' she said softly into the dark. 'A good one. He came to Australia six years ago to take a registrar job, but mostly just to see Australia. And to get away from his parents a bit. We met, we married and I followed him back to England. It was supposed to be happy ever after for everyone.'

'But?'

'But three months after our marriage we discovered he had

lymphoma.' She paused but there was no comment from Darcy. He knew as well as she did what such a diagnosis would have meant, and the fact that Charlie had died meant there were no questions to be asked.

She felt his concern, though. The warmth from his body seemed to intensify in the darkness, encouraging her to continue.

So she did.

'When Charlie first learned his diagnosis—before he had his first dose of chemotherapy—he had sperm frozen. We talked about it and decided it was only sensible if we were to have children after he recovered. Only, of course, he didn't recover. Then, when it was clear that he wouldn't make it, he asked if I'd still have the courage to have his child.'

'Oh, Susie…'

Darcy's words were a whisper of sympathy and the warmth she was feeling grew by the minute. Dissipating the bleakness of what she was saying.

'I couldn't do it straight away,' she told him. 'Charlie was right in doubting my courage. I wasn't brave enough. I missed him so dreadfully, and it was all I could do to keep putting one foot after another. We'd been living on his parents' estate in Yorkshire and working in a Leeds hospital, so I kept on working—only harder. I threw myself into my work with everything I had. But I couldn't forget how much he'd wanted a child to follow him…'

'So you want the baby for Charlie.'

'I want this baby for *me*,' she said fiercely, folding her hands over her stomach in a gesture of what seemed almost defiance. Out on the lawn the wallabies looked up, startled, and wallaby and joey instinctively moved closer together. Susie lowered her voice.

'I had to be sure, though. To have a baby, I needed security—a home—and, as I said, the one I had in England was part of Charlie's parents' estate. It seemed right at the time to bring Charlie's baby up in Charlie's part of the world.

So I talked it through with his parents, and to my surprise they were delighted.'

'Why to your surprise?'

'They didn't like me very much,' she admitted. 'They'd wanted an aristocratic English daughter-in-law and I was about as far from that as you could get. A yokel from down under. After Charlie died they treated me as if it was all my fault, so when I broached the idea of a baby I was stunned when they gave me their support.'

He thought that through. 'So what went wrong?'

'I had too much support,' she said bleakly. 'I had support, all right, but as soon as they were sure the pregnancy was well on its way and I wasn't likely to miscarry, I had so much overwhelming support that it scared me to death.'

'You need to explain that to me.'

No wonder Darcy was a good doctor, Susie decided, staring out into the dark. If he used this tone to his patients they'd tell him anything. They'd bare their souls to this gentle, sympathetic man, and she was no exception.

'Lord and Lady Fitzgerald suddenly realised they had an heir,' Susie said bleakly. 'Or heiress. It made no difference.'

'I still don't understand.'

'Neither do I,' Susie admitted. 'It was weird. Frightening. I knew they were strong people. Charlie had to fight to achieve independence, but their attitude to me and my baby was beyond anything he'd ever said about them. I can only think their son's death put them past reason. Anyway, they started laying down rules. My baby would be brought up as Charlie had been raised. I could live in our house as they'd promised—they wouldn't kick me out—as long as I obeyed the rules.'

'Rules?'

'I wasn't to interfere with the child's upbringing. I could work as much as I liked—as I said, Charlie and I had been working in a hospital in Leeds before his death—but the child would have a nanny chosen by them and would be brought up to inherit the estate. It seems that even though they disliked their son, the thought of the estate going to some distant cousin was dreadful.'

'But you're the baby's mother,' Darcy said thoughtfully. 'You have rights.'

'Yes, I have rights, but I don't have any money. Charlie was fiercely independent. We lived in a house on the estate because he loved the place and stood to inherit, but apart from that he had little to do with his parents. When he was ill they didn't help at all—they just wouldn't concede that he was dangerously ill—and by the time he died I was badly in debt. He badly wanted to die at home, you see, and he needed twenty-four-hour nursing. It cost heaps.'

'I can imagine.'

'I'd only just cleared those debts when I got pregnant. But I'd made the stupid, stupid mistake of assuming I was welcome to stay living in our house. I was wrong. I was only welcome as long as I agreed to their conditions.'

'And those conditions were unacceptable.'

'As you say.' Susie's voice was as cold as ice. 'I still had to work in Leeds, and according to the financial conditions they laid down I'd have had to pay rent so I'd have needed to work full time. I'd have seen less of my baby than I would have if I'd used a commercial crèche and I'd have had no say in its upbringing.'

'Oh, Susie…'

'I was alone, in a foreign country, pregnant and with these very powerful people threatening to take over my baby. I knew Charlie wanted his child to live where he'd lived, but I also knew Charlie would have hated his parents having control. They're so cold. I was so frightened.'

'So…'

'So a friend I worked with knew the trouble I was in, and he had a cottage in a remote part of northern Scotland. "Go sit by a loch and think about it," he said, so I did. And there I decided if I stayed in Charlie's country, the only alternative was for me to leave the area, get another job and have the baby cared for commercially while I worked to pay for that care.'

'Which is the same alternative you're facing now.'

'As you say. But at least it's *my* country. For me, it's home, even if I need to work thirty miles away.'

Silence. It stretched on and on in the still warm night, endless in its portent.

And then Darcy sighed.

'Susie, you need to stay here.'

'So do you.'

'If it was just me, you realise I'd walk away,' he told her. 'I never would have come here in the first place. But Muriel and Jamie have brought me here, and for their sakes I need to stay.'

'I know that.' He'd come half a world for the sake of one small boy, and Jamie wasn't even his son. How could Susie destroy that sort of commitment?

More silence. Out on the lawn, the joey tired of grass, slithered back into its mother's pouch and nestled down for the night. For some reason, the sight still made Susie want to cry. The wallaby's baby was safe, and her own baby wasn't. She'd made such plans for this baby, and now they were all useless.

Silence.

'The crazy thing is, this place needs two full-time doctors,' Darcy said at last. It was as if he were talking to himself. 'Robert deserves to be able to practise as little as he wishes, but with the increased tourist influx, even with me working full time, he's not able to back off. And there's no pharmacy. Patients have to order in drugs and it takes overnight to get them here. That was the story with the condoms. We hoped to set the pharmacy up, even though I knew we'd be stretched to capacity.'

'Oh.' The syllable sounded flat and hopeless, even to her.

'In fact, this place could use all of us.'

'The government will never agree to it,' Susie said.

'No. I had enough trouble convincing them Robert was desperate for help. Maybe if my two-year rural doctor visa had already come through...but it hasn't. I'm operating on temporary registration. My application for rural status still has to be processed and if you want to work we can't disguise you being here.'

'No.'

But suddenly something was whirring in the back of Susie's mind. Some germ of an idea...

'Susie, I'm sorry.'

'Don't be.' She cut him off, then rose and walked over to the trunk of her beloved gum tree. This idea she was having took some thinking through. Her mind was working in overdrive. Maybe it could work for both of them. If she had the courage...

Would Charlie mind?

No. He wouldn't. She knew that. Not if it meant his child was protected and loved as he'd want it to be.

So all she had to do was tell Darcy what she was thinking.

Whew! She took a deep breath and then another. Courage was something she'd never lacked, but this took maybe more courage than she'd ever needed in her life.

'There is one other way,' she said slowly.

'One other way of what?'

'Of getting you immigration status. Of you being permitted to work here. Of all of us being able to work here together.'

Darcy stared out at her in the moonlight. Blonde, with big eyes and diminutive, Susie looked almost ethereal—a fairy at the bottom of the garden.

A very pregnant fairy, wearing spotted pyjamas...

Despite himself he couldn't suppress a grin and she saw it. She put her hands on her hips and glared in indignation. 'There's no need to laugh,' she retorted. 'This is a very serious proposition, and it just could work.'

'How could it work?'

'You could marry me.'

CHAPTER FIVE

As a conversation-stopper, this was a winner. Darcy stared at Susie for a long, long moment, and then he stared some more.

'I have to assume you're joking,' he said at last.

'Why would I joke about something as important as this?'

'I don't...' His voice trailed off. The man looked like Susie had just thrown a bucket of ice water over him and he was only just resurfacing.

Well, then, she had to present her logic before he made it to the surface.

'If it was just for me I wouldn't think of it,' she said urgently. 'It's not. Maybe, if my logic is right, then it's a solution for all of us. For Jamie and Muriel and for Robert and for my unborn baby. And for you and me.'

'But you don't want to marry me.'

'Of course I don't.' The very idea was ridiculous.

Wasn't it?

'And I certainly don't want to marry you.'

His solidness steadied her. 'That's what's so perfect,' she said proudly. 'If I thought for one minute that you were interested in marriage for real then I wouldn't consider it. But...' she had the grace to blush '...I overheard you talking to Robert. You're not the least bit interested in marriage and I've already been married. I have no intention of remarrying for love, so we make a perfect pair.'

'Husband and wife,' he said faintly.

'Exactly.' She beamed. She was back in organisation mode now, and organisation was what she did best. 'Australian doctors can work wherever they want and, married to me, you'd qualify for citizenship. As far as immigration goes, it's wonderful. Our story's brilliant. We met in England through our common bond of the people we knew in Whale Beach. When Muriel fell ill, you came out to work here and look after Jamie, and I realised how much you meant to me. So I pined for you.'

'Pined?' His voice was disbelieving.

'Pined,' she said smugly. 'I'm very good at pining. I was wafting toward a decline so you rang me up and told me to come home, and as an aside you popped the question.'

'Oh, right.' He looked at her closely. 'You know, somehow I don't see Immigration swallowing the pining bit.'

'Why not?'

'Just a feeling.' The twerp actually grinned!

And maybe he had a point. Pining had never been her strong point—even when Charlie died. 'OK, I'll have refused to come home with you when you first asked,' she said equitably. 'Being a spirited lass with a good job and all. You can be the one who pined, and I can finally have felt so sorry for you that I just had to come. Anything for a quiet life. Don't you see? It's brilliant.'

'Sit,' he said suddenly, and he himself sat on the dilapidated garden seat under the tree. He motioned to the spot next to him and Susie had the sudden impression that this was how he'd humour a deranged patient.

'Hey, it's a good idea,' she said indignantly. 'It could work.'

'Tell me how it could work.' Once more, he was pacifying her.

'For a start, we could all stay in Whale Beach,' she told him. 'As my husband—as the legal spouse of an Australian citizen—you can live and work wherever you want. The Medical Board is starting to get tough with practice permits but they won't separate married couples. Especially when there are kids involved. And the more I see of this place, the more I figure we could use three doctors. You have Jamie to look after and you don't want to be run off your feet with work. I have my baby, and Robert has his health to consider. It could suit us all beautifully.'

He looked at her for a long, long minute, and his eyes widened. 'My God, you mean it!' he said incredulously.

'Of course I mean it.'

'Robert said you were a matchmaker but this takes the cake! You'd seriously marry me?'

She chuckled. 'Well, maybe not seriously, but at least legally. Yes.'

'Did you say we could all live here?'

'We must.' She was thinking things through as she spoke, but she knew there was no other solution. 'This house is big enough to hold us all, and immigration officials will want to check. In everyone's eyes we'll need to appear married. The only person who'll know anything different will be Robert, and I'm sure he'll support us. It's my guess he may even be delighted.'

There was a long, long pause. She looked uncertainly up at his hooded face. 'Darcy, it could work.'

'Yes, Susie, it could work.'

Her eyes creased in astonishment. 'You mean you agree?'

'No,' he said. 'I don't.'

'Why not?' She rose and put her hands on her hips, daring him with those luminescent green eyes. 'Darcy, it's brilliant.'

'It's loaded with potential disaster.'

'Like what?'

'Like who would you say was the father of your baby?'

That floored her. She stared down at him in astonishment. 'Why, Charlie, of course. I wouldn't want it any other way.'

'You'll tell that to Immigration?'

'Darcy, I'm not springing a paternity suit on you here. We met just after I got pregnant. We can work out something.'

He sighed. 'Susie...'

'What?'

'Go to bed.' He rose and put his hands on her shoulders, looking gravely down into her eyes. 'This isn't a split-second decision. We're talking marriage here. It involves all sorts of things, none of which you've properly thought through.'

He paused, and the feel of his hands on her shoulders sent warm shivers through the length of her body. He did the most amazing things to her, just by touching her.

She had to force her voice to work. Heaven knew, her mind wasn't working so something had to. 'But we need to make a decision,' she managed. 'The need is urgent.' Her voice had lost its sureness. There was a tremble behind her words that could have been weariness—or it could have been desperation.

Darcy heard it and his voice softened even further. 'We need to sleep on all of this.'

'You seriously think I can go to bed and sleep?'

'I think you need to try, or you'll tumble over with weariness,' he said softly. He put a hand to her chin and lifted her face so her eyes were meeting his. Then he bent and kissed her very lightly on the lips. 'You've had one hell of a day, Susie Ellis. I think this is about the most amazingly generous offer I've ever heard, but it involves all sorts of complications.'

'It's not just for you, you know,' she said, trying for asperity. 'I get something out of this, too. I can't work here on my own. It's taken me less than a day to realise that. Robert's too ill to be a full partner, and if I have a baby to care for then I can't work full time. I need a strong partner, and that partner's you. You're too good a doctor for me—or for Whale Beach—to give up.'

'Gee, thanks.'

She pulled back a little and—reluctantly—his hands released her.

'OK, we'll sleep on it,' she managed. 'Or we'll try. But don't write it off as impossible. It might just work.'

'It might at that,' he agreed gravely, and smiled. His smile in the moonlight was tender and warm, and for some stupid reason it almost made her weary knees buckle.

She looked at him for a long, long moment—and then she turned and fled as fast as her wobbly knees could take her.

Breakfast was very, very strained.

Jamie was at the table first. He was busy buttering a piece of toast; he looked up as Susie entered the room and his face shuttered down in pain.

'Go away,' he said.

'I'm not going to,' Susie told him. She was dressed in elastic-waisted jeans and a pale blue windcheater that reached almost to her knees. It didn't make her look like an efficient doctor—in fact, it made her look extremely pregnant and extremely cute. Despite himself, Jamie's attention was caught, and he left off his toast-buttering.

'When's your baby due?'

'In seven weeks.'

'Is it a girl baby or a boy baby?'

'I don't know. I'm not one for testing something that doesn't matter.'

'Don't you want to know?'

'Nope. I'm waiting to be introduced at the proper time.'

He seemed to approve of that. Then his remembered pain washed back and he went back to fierce toast-buttering. 'I won't be here to find out anyway.'

'You might be,' Susie said cautiously. Whatever happened, they seemed destined to see a bit of each other.

'You should be.'

Damn the man. Darcy had a habit of sneaking up on her like a ghost. Susie turned to find Darcy standing in the doorway, surveying them both.

'You might knock or something,' she muttered. 'You scared me.'

He smiled at that. 'Somehow I doubt if you scare that easily. And as for knocking... You're taking proprietary rights to your kitchen, then?'

She considered. 'Well, it is my kitchen.'

'It is.' He watched as she placed a piece of bread in the toaster. 'But that's my bread.'

She glowered. 'You want me to buy my own?'

'Not if you let me enter *your* kitchen.'

It was too much. The whole thing was ridiculous. She grinned. Her toast popped up, she buttered it and bit into it, and then waved magnanimously to the opposite chair. 'OK, Dr Hayden, you can come in. You can even share our breakfast table. The toast's very good.'

'Jamie and I pride ourselves on our toast,' he told her. 'Don't we, Jamie?'

But Jamie was looking suspiciously from one to the other. 'What's going on?' he asked, and for the first time the dragging fatigue had faded from the little boy's voice. 'Did you say...? Uncle Darcy, did you say I should still be here when Susie's baby is born?'

'It could be arranged.'

The boy laid down his toast and cocked his head on one side. 'How?'

'Susie might marry me.'

There was complete silence in the room for about two minutes while all present took this on board. Susie went on munching, her mind in overdrive. She was acute enough to know, though, that it was Jamie's reaction that mattered here. Darcy would be doing this for Jamie, so without his acceptance the plan was useless.

More than useless.

Marriage to Darcy...

For the first time, Susie took it on board as a real possibility. Last night it had been a spur-of-the-moment idea. Now, in the cold reality of morning, it seemed nothing but crazy.

But Jamie's first reaction wasn't that it was crazy. The child stared at them both for a long moment, and then decided he needed time to think about things. He wheeled his chair over to the sink and concentrated fiercely on making himself hot chocolate. It needed all his attention.

He did it while Susie tried hard to concentrate on something other than the man who'd just made this extraordinary proposal. Darcy sat down in silence, fed his bread into the toaster and waited for some reaction.

He didn't get one. In the end it was Darcy himself who had to force the issue. Who had to speak...

'Well?' he said. Jamie had his back to him and it was impossible for either adult to tell what he was thinking.

'Well, what?' Jamie was playing for time.

'What do you think of the idea?'

The boy turned his chair. His eyes went to Susie, then flitted to Darcy and then rested back on Susie again. 'You...you'd marry each other,' he said at last, and his intelligent mind had figured it out. 'You'd do it so we could all stay here?'

'That's right.'

Jamie's hesitation had given Susie time to get her emotions under control. This was a good idea, she told herself. It must be.

So act like it. Lighten the situation...

She twinkled at Jamie. 'I can tell you're amazed that someone would actually *want* to marry your uncle!'

'I'm not such an ogre,' Darcy started, but Jamie wasn't to be distracted by humour.

'When did you think this up?'

Darcy flashed an uncertain look at Susie, and she gave him an imperceptible nod. It was his call, her nod told him. He knew his nephew better than she did, and he'd know what to say. But she'd seen enough of the child to know that deceiving Jamie probably wasn't on the cards. He was too intelligent to be fobbed off with a story of an old romance.

So it was truth or nothing, she thought, and it seemed Darcy thought the same.

'We thought of it last night,' he admitted. 'But we can't say that to anyone but you. And maybe Robert and Muriel.'

'Why not?' Jamie was fascinated.

'Because Immigration won't let me stay unless Susie and I can convince them we've planned on marrying for ever.'

'You'll say that?'

'I won't lie unless I have to,' Darcy said seriously. 'But for you...'

'You mean you'll marry Susie so you get to stay here all the time. Just for me.'

'That about sums it up.' Darcy grinned down at his too-serious nephew. 'I know it's a sacrifice, but you don't need to feel incredibly grateful.'

'No.' Jamie, his face immeasurably thoughtful for one so young, turned to face Susie again. What he saw seemed to reassure him. There was no trace of a smile in his eyes. He was figuring the whole thing out for himself, and what he saw in Susie's face seemed to reassure him. 'It wouldn't be just for me,' he said at last. 'Marrying Susie would be OK for you, too. She's quite nice. And she's pretty. Even if she is fat.'

'Gee, thanks.' Susie's warm eyes sparkled and, amazingly, Jamie managed a smile in return. 'What a compliment!' she told him. 'You think I'd make your uncle a suitable wife?'

'I think you'd make a nice mother,' Jamie responded, and it was impossible for Susie to miss the note of wistfulness in his voice.

Whew!

Susie took a deep breath as more implications of what lay ahead unfolded. But if this was to work then she had to go all the way. From this moment, they had to live together as a family.

'I guess I sort of will be,' she told him, and intercepted a startled look from Darcy. 'Your uncle's your guardian,' she told him. 'If I were to marry him, I suppose that'd make me your guardianess.'

'That's like...like a mother?'

'That's right.' She flashed another glance at Darcy and saw he was thinking exactly what she was thinking, That there were implications all over the place here—for all of them.

Jamie was still into the mechanics of the whole operation. 'So this baby would be my sort of brother or sister.'

They were going way too fast, but there was no drawing back now. Not with those huge eyes watching every move. 'That's right,' Susie told him.

But Darcy was thinking fast. He could see the eagerness appearing on Jamie's face, and eagerness hadn't appeared on Jamie's face for a long, long time. He intended to make use of it.

'This is all conditional,' he said sternly, and Jamie turned his attention to his uncle. He flinched, as if he was about to have something snatched back from him.

'Conditional on what?'

'On you.'

'On me?'

'On you firstly acting like we're a family—because if we don't do that then Immigration won't let me stay.'

'I can do that,' Jamie said cautiously.

'And there's more.' Darcy had the undivided attention of both Susie and Jamie. Susie was as fascinated as Jamie was.

'It's also conditional on you agreeing to change doctors—and follow doctor's orders.' Darcy was pressing home his advantage for all he was worth, and Susie blinked.

'You mean...' Jamie was off balance. 'Not go to the doctor in Hobart?'

'Only occasionally from now on. I want your new doctor to be Susie.'

That had Susie's eyes widening. Whatever she'd been expecting, it hadn't been that.

'I'm not a paediatrician,' she told Darcy, and Darcy smiled at her.

'That's right. So Jamie will still need a paediatric check

every month or so, but the hands-on, day-to-day orders will come from you. As long as he agrees to obey them, we have a deal. We'll become a family.'

'And if I don't?' Jamie's chin tilted and Susie guessed there'd been run-ins already—this wasn't a child to submit to decrees with ease.

'I'm marrying Susie so we can get your health back,' Darcy said bluntly. 'That's a big thing. I won't do it unless you agree to follow medical orders. It's not worth it otherwise.'

'You mean you really don't want to marry Susie?'

'I don't want to marry anyone.'

Silence. Jamie thought about it for a little and then shook his head. 'I expect you do,' he said. 'Everyone does really. They just say they don't want to get married because they think it's sissy.'

Hmm. Susie watched Darcy's face. She was fascinated by what was going on here. The man looked confounded—almost as if he'd been caught out.

Sissy...

Nope, whatever else you could call Darcy Hayden, it wasn't sissy.

Darcy was knocked right off balance. Finally he took a deep breath and pulled himself together. 'Nevertheless, you'll follow orders, young Jamie.'

'What sort of orders?' Jamie eyed Susie with suspicion and Susie thought fast. What did Darcy expect here? It was some compliment he was paying her, she thought. Placing Jamie's health in her hands...

So turn into a doctor.

Jamie should be working toward a gradual return to health, she thought. Normality. That was mostly what was required. There were no magic cures for chronic fatigue syndrome. It was a disease that seemed to occur when the body's defence mechanisms had been put through too much, and patience and time and peacefulness seemed the only cure.

Normality. And normality meant for Jamie...a family.

A mother.

But how to put a mother's orders into the guise of a doctor's prescription?

'How long is it since you've been to school?' she asked curiously, and Jamie frowned and cast a suspicious look at his uncle.

'Answer Susie, Jamie,' Darcy said gently. 'She's the doctor here.'

Another dark look. Susie was obviously OK, but doctors weren't. He'd have had enough, Susie suspected. An overload of medical tests and diagnosis and treatments. 'Since I got pneumonia,' he said at last. 'About three months ago.'

'Hmm.' Susie looked at him assessingly, and her mind was in overdrive. 'Do you have school friends?'

'I did.' Jamie visibly shut off. 'I don't see them much any more.'

The child was growing increasingly isolated, Susie thought, and a glance at Darcy's face told her she was on the right track. The kids at school obviously liked him, though. Laura's reaction the night before had been defence of a friend.

So get those friends back...

'Well, as your doctor—'

He was still in anti-doctor mode. 'You don't look like a doctor.'

'I am.' She mock frowned at him and succeeded in drawing a reluctant grin. 'A fat one but a very stern one. As your doctor, I've decided we'll take a lunchtime constitutional together.'

'What's a consti...constitutional?'

'A brisk form of exercise,' she told him. 'Or actually not all that brisk. A sort of waddly form of exercise designed for pregnant mums and boys with CFS. What I figure is that every lunchtime we'll walk down to the school.'

'I can't walk.'

'There's the beauty of it,' she said gravely. 'You get to sit in the wheelchair and help push the wheels when I get tired, and I get to walk behind you and rest my tummy on your wheelchair handles. And every lunchtime we'll collect your school work for the day and say hi to your friends.'

'You mean go to school every day?'

'Just for a visit at first,' Susie said. 'You can stay for a while if you want, but—'

'I don't want.' His voice rose in panic and Susie nodded.

'No. That's fine. It's your decision when you go back. But we collect your school work, we say hi to your friends, we come home and you do a little bit of physiotherapy with me. I do a very nice back and leg rub. Then you do a couple of sessions of school work during the afternoon and next morning. Not for long. Say half an hour each. Then we take your work back to be corrected and collect the next lot.'

'And that's all?' Jamie was looking at her suspiciously.

'For the moment,' she said serenely. 'But I bet it'll help.'

'How will it help?'

Any medical treatment would be eyed with distrust, Susie thought, watching his face. He'd been through enough.

'It'll stop you falling behind with your school work so when this disease is cured—which it will be—you won't have to drop back a grade.'

He blinked. He clearly hadn't thought of dropping a grade. Susie could tell the very thought was appalling. 'I don't want to stay in grade four!' he said, stunned. 'I'm in grade five after Christmas.'

'Of course you are.' Susie approved. 'But when you get better—'

'I don't know if I will get better.'

'You will.' Susie rose and walked across to him, then stooped before his wheelchair and took both his hands in hers. Still Darcy had the sense to stay silent. 'Jamie, you have chronic fatigue syndrome. It's a disease that lots of people have had before you and lots of people will have again. And those people get better. You will get better, Jamie. It's just a matter of letting your body rest enough so it can recover at its own pace.'

He stared at her, his eyes enormous and full of mistrust. 'You promise?'

He must be so frightened, Susie thought, and wondered whether half the cause of his illness now was fear. To have his world crumbling around him, and then his body betraying him as well...

'I promise,' she told him. 'I swear.'

'When?'

'I'm not making promises on that one,' she told him. That'd be a stupid thing to do. 'Some people can take a long time to get better from CFS and some people get better very quickly. What I do think is that if you stay here, with Darcy and me and your grandma, you do the things we tell you to do and you stay in touch with your friends, then you won't get worse, and gradually we'll get you better.'

'You really mean it?'

'I really mean it.'

He stared at her for a long moment, and then he turned his chair so he faced Darcy head on. 'She's OK,' he said, and he was talking half to Darcy and half to himself.

Darcy grinned at his intentness. 'Yep. She's OK.'

'Can I go and tell Gran?'

'Before you do, Jamie, we need everyone to believe Susie and I met in England and decided to get married then,' Darcy told him urgently. 'Yesterday was so dreadful no one thought to gossip about Susie's return, but now they will. Can you help us here?'

He considered this with small-boy seriousness. 'You mean you want me to say you were all lovey-dovey from the start?' His face broke into a smile. 'Yuck.' But then his brow creased, still giving it serious thought. 'Yeah, I'll say it. But can I whisper the truth to Grandma? She'll help.'

'Of course you can.'

And suddenly everything was just fine with Jamie. 'Yes!' It was an exclamation of joy. He spun his wheelchair Grandma-wards. 'I'm going to see her right now,' he flung over his shoulder as he zoomed out of the room. 'And then I'm going to visit Laura in the kids' ward and tell her—and I'll make your romance sound so corny that even she'll believe it.'

Then Susie and Darcy were by themselves, and suddenly there was nothing to say.

The kettle started to boil. It whistled into the silence and then switched itself off. Still silence. What had they done?

'It seems we've organised a marriage,' Darcy said at last.

'We have.' She felt she was stepping on eggshells. 'What made you change your mind?'

'A sleepless night. The impossibility of any alternative.'

She looked doubtfully at his face. For her this seemed a reasonable option but for him... 'You know, you could put Jamie in foster-care and he'd probably survive,' she said slowly.

'I could do that.'

'So why don't you?' There weren't many men Susie could imagine doing what Darcy was doing—for a child who wasn't even his son. In fact, there wasn't one!

'I spent an incredibly lonely childhood,' he said softly. 'My mother and my sister didn't give a damn. The only thing that kept me sane was that my father loved me, and I can't bear for Jamie not even to have that.'

'So you'd come half a world and even marry a stranger for him to have that.'

He shrugged. 'It's no big deal.'

'I think it's a very big deal.'

She couldn't help herself. Darcy was sitting at the table and he was staring into space as if it didn't matter that he'd just committed himself to so much for one small boy. It was too much. Without thinking for one more second, Susie leaned over the table and she kissed him squarely on the lips. And something happened…

It was supposed to have been a kiss like the one he'd given her the night before—light and warm and caring. It was supposed to have been a kiss of appreciation.

But it was nothing of the kind.

In that moment when their lips met something changed. It was as if the air around them had suddenly received an electric charge. Susie's lips had intended to just lightly brush Darcy's, but instead…

Instead they locked onto his, as if they'd been charged with something she couldn't handle—magnet meeting metal and holding. There was some power here that she didn't understand in the least, but it held them tight against each other and wouldn't let them go.

It warmed them—it seared—from the toes up, and it locked their bodies together as if two beings were merging to become one.

It was a kiss, but it was so much more…

It was the beginning of something wonderful, Susie thought, and when it finally ended it had her sagging down into her chair and staring across the table in stunned amazement.

That wasn't meant to have happened. Neither of them had willed it.

But it had just been a kiss. Hadn't it?

No. Darcy was looking as blankly stunned as she felt, and she knew that he'd felt whatever it had been as strongly as she had. Wow!

She'd never felt like this with Charlie, she thought dazedly. Like she was being lifted from her own body and transformed into something else.

It must be her pregnancy, she thought desperately, searching for logic. It must be hormones or something. She dared another glance at Darcy and saw that he must be pregnant, too—or have the same hormones…

'Darcy, I didn't—'

And then another voice cut across the tension. 'Well, well, well. What do we have here?' They both spun like guilty teenagers and Robert was standing in the doorway.

It was such a relief! It was such a dissolution of tension that Susie almost laughed. But there was no laughter in Darcy's eyes. Instead, his face had become grim and intent, like his body had just betrayed him.

He stood, ignoring Susie completely and concentrating solely on the older doctor. It was as if every nerve in his body was concentrating on blocking the sensations of what had just happened.

It was Darcy who managed to speak first, and when he did his voice was as grim as someone announcing a funeral.

'I think you need to congratulate us, Robert,' he told the newcomer. 'You've just found yourself two partners instead of one—and you've just witnessed Susie's acceptance of my proposal of marriage.'

CHAPTER SIX

ROBERT thought the whole idea was fantastic—practical, workable and very, very funny.

'I told you she was a matchmaker,' he said, sitting down at the table and wiping his eyes. 'I went to bed last night feeling lousy as hell—partly because of what happened yesterday and partly because I'd put you in such a mess, boy. But I might have known our Susie would make it all right. It's fantastic!'

'It's not fantastic. It has major problems, but it'll serve the purpose,' Darcy retorted, still not looking at Susie.

'Yes, indeed.' The old doctor rubbed his hands together. 'It'll certainly serve the purpose. Whale Beach will have three doctors. Three!'

'Will we get away with it, do you think?' Susie asked doubtfully, and Robert smiled and smiled.

'Immigration won't question this, and I'd imagine the Medical Board will be delighted. This whole region has been a nightmare for them. With three doctors, Whale Beach will become a proper medical centre. We'll be able to expand. Instead of patients having to travel to other towns because I can't cope with everyone, we'll find patients travelling to us. It'll solve so many problems...'

'They'll ask why I applied for rural doctor status rather than stating that I was marrying,' Darcy pointed out.

'That's easy.' With such an enticement—two young doctors in the town—Robert was off and running in the invention stakes. 'You met early on when Susie went to England. I was worried about Jamie, I mentioned in my letters to Susie that Jamie had an uncle who worked near where she did, and she introduced herself so she could speak to you about my worries. Maybe you were at a medical conference together, and when she saw your name tag she stepped right up and introduced herself. That's probable. And it was love at first sight.' Robert beamed. 'Nothing could be more obvious.'

'But—'

'But, of course, Susie was married and then newly widowed.' Robert was allowing no interruption. He had it all sorted out in no time flat—and Susie was suddenly suspecting he'd thought of this marriage solution even before they'd thought of it themselves. 'So you were in love with Susie before you came out here to be with Jamie, but she was still getting over Charlie's death. She turned your proposal down. Then, after you left, she missed you so much—and you were living in the town she loved, and she was pregnant and alone…'

'Hey, this makes me sound pathetic,' Susie retorted, startled, and Robert grinned.

'That's right. A little pathos will go a long way in this touching tale. Now, if you can just make those big eyes fill with tears when you're talking to officialdom—and I know from past experience you can turn them on at will when you want something badly enough…'

'Robert. You're a—'

'A machiavellian schemer—just like you,' he told her approvingly. He beamed. 'Now, let's get this town's medical team organised.'

Which was why, by the end of the morning, Susie found her future mapped out and herself unpacking Darcy's precious condom boxes as well as the rest of his pharmaceutical supplies.

'Because until the baby comes we put you on light duties,' Robert had decreed. 'You're in charge of setting up the pharmacy.'

Darcy had said very little while Robert had planned, and Susie had simply been too stunned to argue. So now she sat surrounded by boxes of supplies and pharmacy paperwork, and she tried and tried to stop her head from spinning.

She was getting married!

Again.

The thought scared her to her socks, but then it became impossible to stop a frisson of excitement.

She'd enjoyed marriage. Because her mother had died early and she'd essentially been raised by her father and Robert, Susie was accustomed to male company. She didn't like living alone and marriage was the obvious solution. She'd met Charlie just as her father had died. Charlie had been a very good friend and their marriage had been built on trust and mutual respect.

And then there was sex...

Now, that was a problem. She frowned as she sorted tubes of cortisone creams into order. Sex...

With Charlie it had been lovely. They had been such good friends, and sex had been an extension of that friendship. Warm and comforting and safe.

It hadn't been exciting though, she remembered, and she'd always thought that somehow it could have been better. But he'd become ill so quickly that it had never happened. Still, even two years after Charlie's death, she ached for that aspect of married life, even if it never could be more exciting than she'd experienced already. The thought of spending the rest of her life celibate...

Whoa!

She sat back on her heels and blinked. What was she thinking here? This was a marriage of convenience, and the fact that she just had to look at Darcy Hayden and she was thinking about sex...

Well, she had to stop thinking about it, she told herself crossly. Concentrate on cortisone cream. Much more important than sex. If she got the percentages mixed up she'd have people losing skin all over the place, and Darcy and Robert would pack her off to England again so fast her feet wouldn't reach the ground.

Sex...

Darcy...

She sighed at the impossibility of separating the two—then looked up at the sound of approaching footsteps and there was Darcy looking straight down at her over the counter of their new little dispensary.

If he could read her thoughts... She blushed bright crimson, and as the colour swept all over her, she ducked her head and concentrated fiercely on percentages. One of the condoms she'd been packing was still lying on the floor. She stared down at it—and blushed some more.

Strangely, he didn't speak at once. She was aware of him watching her as she sorted tubes and blushed, but that was all he did. Watched.

'I'm getting it sorted,' she said at last, crossly. 'You don't need to check on me.'

'No.' He rounded the counter, knelt, lifted a pile of five-percenters and slotted them into their allocated place. 'I already have,' he told her.

'Checked on me?' Her eyes flew to his. They were a whole six inches apart and the heat in her face didn't abate one bit. 'W-What do you mean?'

'Last night, before I accepted your so kind proposal of marriage, I phoned the medical director of the hospital where you last worked.' His voice softened still further, making what he was saying weirdly intimate. 'His report was glowing. It seems we have us a fine doctor.'

Susie glared. 'But you had to check?'

'I had to check,' he said gravely. 'Of course. Maybe you should have, too. It's some commitment we're making.'

'Right.' Anger helped here, and her colour finally subsided. 'What about you, then? Are you a fine doctor?' But she knew. Unlike him, she hadn't felt the need to check, and the thought made her angrier still.

'Robert checked on me when I applied for a job.'

'I'm not Robert.' She glared, fuelling her temper. 'What sort of doctor are you? I mean, I know you can operate…'

'I'm a qualified surgeon,' he told her.

It didn't surprise her. The Caesarean he'd done had been perfect.

'But I thought you were in general practice.'

'I trained for surgery but I missed the people,' he told her. 'I liked being part of their lives. That's why I returned to general practice.'

'You like being part of their lives—because you don't want a life of your own?' It was a stab in the dark, but it hit a nerve. Darcy's face darkened.

'What do you mean by that?'

'Just that you don't want marriage. Or commitment.'

'What do you think I'm doing now?'

'Oh, you're marrying and committing,' she said. 'But not because you want to.' She was watching his face and she knew she was right. 'You're doing it because you think it's your bounden duty.'

He thought about that for a minute and then nodded. Agreeing. 'And you?' he asked as if her inquisition had given him the right to probe himself. 'You've been there before. So why did you marry your Charlie? I assume that wasn't duty.'

'Charlie and I were friends.' She managed a smile. 'He laughed at my jokes and I laughed at his.'

'And that's a good basis for a marriage?'

'The best,' she said firmly. 'So I married because I thought it might be fun. And…and it was.' For a bit. It was impossible to keep the note of sadness from creeping into her voice, and it was impossible for Darcy not to hear it.

'And it wasn't fun,' Darcy said, watching her face. He was still automatically sorting pharmacy supplies onto shelves. 'It was an appalling tragedy.'

'So that means your view's confirmed? Commitment leads to sadness?'

'For me it would.'

'That's your family history.' She nodded sagely. 'Yep, I can see that. Like varicose veins. Your mother had 'em, so therefore you will.'

'There's no reason to take this lightly.'

'No.' She managed a smile, and then struggled to her feet—no easy feat when one was almost eight months pregnant. Darcy hesitated for a fraction of a second—enough to let her know he was reluctant to make even this much contact after the kiss they'd experienced only hours ago. But finally he held out his hand and helped her to her feet.

And there it was again. The magnetism. The powerful warmth that almost melted them together and had Susie's colour mounting all over again. He was so...

Male!

She hadn't made love to a man for almost three long years, she thought suddenly, and now, desperately, she wanted to make love to this one. To Darcy. To her fiancé.

And pigs might fly before that happens, Susie told herself. What I need is a cold shower.

She couldn't have it. Instead she somehow had to block the feelings sweeping over her and get her face under control. 'Were you looking for me for something?' she managed. 'Other than to tell me my references are OK?'

'Yes.' He was still holding her hand, as if he didn't realise he was doing it, and it wasn't going to be Susie who pulled away. 'It's twelve o'clock. Lunchtime at school is in fifteen minutes. I phoned and told Jamie's teacher the plan, and I've just woken Jamie and told him we're ready to go.'

'We?' She blinked.

'For the first time I figured...' Yes, she thought with some satisfaction. He was right off balance, too. 'I figured we should go together. I mean, the aim is to present us as a family. Right?'

'Right.' She smiled at him and then looked down at their linked hands. 'Absolutely.'

He followed her gaze—and then hauled his hand back as if it burned.

'In public,' he said quickly, and her smile deepened.

'Of course. Where else?'

Medically the school trip was a huge therapeutic success, although Jamie was very, very nervous. In fact, if Darcy hadn't agreed to accompany them, Susie had the feeling she never would have got him there.

He hadn't been to school for months, and he'd cut himself off completely. Now he thought of himself as different—as an invalid—and the first contact would be the hardest.

But Susie knew she was right. She could still hear her old professor droning on and on.

'It's vitally important to treat chronic fatigue sufferers as if they have a condition that will get better. As soon as their carers start treating it as chronic—and the carer loses hope— you have an extra layer of depression to deal with and that depression may well be the thing that makes the syndrome last another year or more.'

So...

'This is just the beginning, Jamie,' she told him, walking beside him while Darcy pushed the wheelchair. 'You've reached rock bottom now. CFS doesn't get worse than this. What we need to do now is to slowly start the process of rehabilitation.'

Which started the minute they walked in the school gate. A cluster of children, just released from the classroom for lunch, saw them coming and crowded across to the gate to watch.

At first they stared in silence. Susie could feel Jamie cringe under their combined gaze, and she moved right into action. Bossy Susie at her best.

'OK, who's in grade five?' she asked, and a dozen hands shot up.

'Right, the rest of you clear off,' she told them. 'This is grade five business.' And all of a sudden it was. The grade-fivers, appealed to, reacted with authority and glared the rest of the onlookers away.

'Jamie's back,' Susie said to the remaining children. 'He's been dreadfully ill—as you can see—but he's on the way to recovery now.' Then she put on her helpless tone—the one that Darcy was starting to know. He cast her a suspicious look and she winked at him and turned back to the children. 'Now, who's Jamie's special friend?'

There was a fraction of a pause, and then half a dozen hands shot skyward. To be a friend to a kid in something as fascinating as a wheelchair seemed suddenly very desirable.

'Great,' Susie said. 'And I'd imagine the rest of you are his friends as well.' She gazed around her thoughtfully. 'You.' She pointed to the biggest boy with his hand up—a kid who had all the markings of the school tough guy about him. 'It's Tommy Guthrie, isn't it? It must be. You look just like your dad. Yikes, you've grown two feet since I last saw you.'

Tommy grinned. This obviously appealed, and he knew who Susie was. The whole town did by now. 'Yeah.' He lifted his arms and flexed his muscles. 'And I've grown crossways, too.'

'Are you strong enough to wheel Jamie in to meet his teacher? Miss Martin, isn't it?'

'Course.' His chest expanded a notch.

'You might need a couple of assistants to help you up the steps. Can you choose?'

'Mack and Fred,' Tommy said promptly, and Susie nodded.

'That's great.' She smiled around at the whole class of grade-fivers. 'And the rest of you... Can I trust you to make things easy for Jamie? Stop the other kids teasing him and stuff? Help with his wheelchair when he needs it?'

'Yeah.' The response was overwhelming.

And finally... 'Will you go with them now, Jamie?'

But Susie didn't need to ask. Tommy was already behind the wheelchair, Mack and Fred were at his side and Jamie was being reclaimed by his own. And his tentative smile said he thought maybe the idea was great.

'He's only allowed to stay for fifteen minutes,' Susie called as the procession moved importantly off. 'We'll wait here. Will you bring him back to us?'

'Too right,' Tommy said, and then was forced to pause as a small girl with red hair tugged Jamie's arm.

'If I stood on your wheelchair steps then they could push me, too.'

'We'll take turns,' another girl said, and Jamie disappeared, being pushed far faster than was safe, but in a welter of excited chatter and an overloaded wheelchair in the direction of Miss Martin.

'That,' Darcy said as the wheelchair rose precariously up the steps and disappeared into the building, 'was brilliant.'

'I'm a great organiser,' Susie said smugly. 'Robert told you that.'

'I can see.' He eyed her and there was a trace of doubt behind his smile. 'I'm beginning to wonder what on earth I'm letting myself in for.'

'A very organising wife,' she said serenely, and peeped a smile up at him. 'But don't worry. I won't organise you. Well, not very much.'

By the time they were due to be married, Darcy was starting to get a very clear idea of what Susie meant by 'not very much'.

It meant a lot.

She was simply the bossiest, most managing female he had ever set eyes on, he decided. They'd applied for a marriage licence. There was a minimum waiting period of four weeks and it took a little longer to make sure immigration and medical registration would be OK.

In those weeks Darcy had worked beside Susie as a doctor, he'd acted the devoted fiancé during immigration interviews, but as far as any other contact went he kept his distance.

Or he tried desperately to keep his distance. It was pretty much impossible when they lived in the same house, they practised medicine in the same hospital, they operated together, they discussed patients, they shared the same concern for Jamie...

They even ate at the same table. They discussed medicine, Jamie chattered about everything under the sun, but between Susie and Darcy there lay restraint.

Or maybe that wasn't true. It was certainly restraint on Darcy's side but it was consideration on Susie's. She knew he was feeling the pressure.

He was acting like a caged tiger, Susie thought as she watched the tension build, and she wondered more and more whether, when the time came to marry, he really would go through with it.

He had to. For Jamie's sake.

And medically he had to, for Whale Beach's sake.

In five short weeks the place had been transformed. The practice was working like a dream, with Robert only doing morning surgery, Darcy doing afternoons and Susie evenings. Sometimes they overlapped, but no matter how busy they were Robert was packed off at noon each day 'to paint, to do the physiotherapy exercises you've been set or to rest'. Susie herself had driven Robert to Hobart to be thoroughly medically assessed and was bossing him into acquiescence. 'Or else!'

In consequence, Robert's health was improving by the day, so much so that he was talking about doing more.

Their little pharmacy was running brilliantly. No longer did patients have to wait for much-needed medicines. Even the condom supply was decreasing, and medically the queues in the waiting rooms had disappeared. Already patients were coming from other towns where medical resources were stretched past their limits. Mothers were bringing their daughters from thirty miles away—'I'd be more comfortable with her seeing a lady doctor' or 'I've always hated the idea of having a man take a pap smear...'

Darcy and Susie were running two surgical sessions a week for planned operations, plus they were coping well with emergencies. Susie's anaesthetic training meshed beautifully with Darcy's surgical skills, and surgery cases which had previously been sent to Hobart were now being attended to in the town.

And Jamie was looking so much better. He was doing more and more, and his time spent sleeping was reducing by the day.

So there was no reason for Darcy to back out—was there?

He couldn't. They'd had to take on extra nurses and the town was buzzing about its wonderful new medical facilities.

As they were about the impending wedding.

'It's just so romantic.' Kerry Madden had come in for her first check-up since she'd been released from hospital in Hobart, and it was Susie she'd elected to see. 'Darcy's so nice,' she told her. 'You're so lucky to have waited.'

'You forget—I've been married before. I've hardly been pining on the shelf.' Susie was taking Kerry's blood pressure and giving an inward sigh of relief. The reading was close to normal. There seemed so few after-effects from her brush with death that Susie could hardly believe her luck. Medically Kerry seemed out of the woods.

Not psychologically, though. She'd lost her baby, the grief was still raw and dreadful, and she'd come near to death herself. It had been a life-changing experience, and now Susie sat back and surveyed her friend with concern. 'How are you coping?' she asked.

'What with?'

'With everything,' Susie said gently. 'With coming back to the farm. With the children and Steve. With the loss of your little one.'

For a moment she thought Kerry would say nothing—pretend things were OK. And then she took a deep breath and the floodgates opened.

'I'm not.' Kerry closed her eyes for a long moment, and then opened them and stared across the desk at Susie. 'I can't...I can't cope with Steve,' she admitted. 'He pretends nothing happened. He won't talk about our baby. You know we buried him as soon as I got back to Whale Beach. The undertakers had waited because I thought it was so important that I be here—but Steve wouldn't even come. He thought it was stupid. Forget it, he says, and he thinks I should get pregnant again straight away.'

'You mustn't do that,' Susie said urgently, startled into imperatives. 'You know that. Your body needs time to get over this battering.' She hesitated and then ploughed on. There was no easy way to say it, but it must be said. 'Kerry, you lost this baby from eclampsia. If you become pregnant again—especially straight away—then you risk exactly the same thing happening, and this time you might lose your own life as well as the baby's. You have five other children to consider. You mustn't.'

'I know.' Kerry gulped down a sob. 'The doctors in Hobart told me. But...Steve wants...'

'I would imagine that Steve wants you more than he wants another baby,' Susie said gently, and Kerry shook her head.

'N-no.'

'No?'

'He just wants a good time,' she blurted out. 'The farm where we live belongs to my parents and he keeps rubbing it in—that it's my farm. So he thinks I should do the work, despite the fact that the farm income supports all of us. It's an ongoing fight. My parents have their own place, but they won't deed the farm over to us because they don't trust Steve. And Steve hates it. But he won't take on any other job.

'Susie, I'm so tired, but I have to keep working because he keeps spending money. He gambles, he drinks far too much and he's at me and at me...' She took a deep breath and admitted her worst. 'He wants me for sex and nothing else.'

And there was only one thing to be said to that. 'Would you be happier without him?' Susie said gently, and Kerry flushed and stared across the desk at her. Her pale face lost even more of her colour, but then somehow her shoulders squared and she reached what Susie suspected was a conclusion that should have been reached a long time ago.

'Yes, I would,' she said at last, and her words were suddenly firm. And bitter. 'He's not faithful. And...and he hits me. I guess I've faced this all gradually over the years, only it's the first time I've ever admitted it to anyone else. He's nothing a husband should be. And I could cope on my own—I guess like you did when your husband died.' She looked at Susie, pleading with her with her eyes. 'I could cope—couldn't I?'

'I'll bet you could.'

'But...' Kerry faltered. 'How could I tell him?' She took a deep breath. 'If I ask him to leave...I daren't. He... When I say he hits me, I mean...he really hurts. He scares me—and the children.'

'So you'd like someone else to be with you when you tell him?'

'Yes.' There was no hesitation now. The decision had been made.

And there wasn't a social service department in this town, Susie thought reluctantly. Hmm. She looked down at her very pregnant self—she had three weeks to go—and thought she was hardly the person to cope with a man who could be violent.

'How about if we ask Darcy to be with you when you tell him?' she asked.

Kerry stared. 'You'll volunteer your husband? Won't he mind?'

That brought a grin. 'He's not my husband for another four days,' Susie said blithely. 'He's my medical partner, and I don't see why he shouldn't make himself useful.' Then, as Kerry gave a reluctant giggle, she raised her eyebrows and gestured at the intercom on her desk. She knew Darcy was in the next room. 'Shall I call him in to discuss it?'

Kerry took a deep breath, her laughter fading. Almost visibly she straightened her shoulders again. And came to a final decision. 'If I go home now, I'll be pregnant again in weeks,' she said. 'He thinks having kids makes him seem virile. If he catches me taking the Pill he'll bash me. So, yes, please. If Dr Hayden would…'

Dr Hayden would. Darcy came into the room at Susie's summons, he leaned against the wall and listened while Susie outlined the problem, and his face turned grim as she spoke.

He went straight to the nub of the matter. 'You say he hits you?'

'Yes.' Having gone so far, Kerry had passed the point where pride was keeping her silent. She turned her neck and pulled down her collar, and an ugly blue-green bruise was exposed for them to see. 'I'm still so tired.' She looked pleadingly at both of them as though she wasn't sure that they'd understand. 'The night before last I asked him if he'd milk the house cow, and then, when he said he wouldn't, Lisa— our eldest—told him he was lazy. So he hit Lisa, and then when I tried to stop him he hit me. It…it happens all the time. Mostly it's just me, but increasingly he's hitting Lisa and Sam, and the other kids will get it eventually.'

'And he hits hard.' Darcy fingered her bruise, tracing its edges. 'That's a nasty haematoma. Hell, Kerry. You could have him arrested for this.'

'That's not a bad one. He broke my arm once,' Kerry said diffidently. 'At least, I was sure it was broken but I wasn't game to come and see a doctor. Steve would have had a fit.

I just tied it up and kept going. And my fingers. He bends my hands back...'

'We'll take X-rays,' Darcy said firmly. 'Now. With evidence of old breaks, with that bruise on your neck and a signed statement by you, we'll get an on-the-spot intervention order to keep him away from the farm. We can contact Social Services in Devonport and they'll take it from there, organising access visits to the kids and so on, but that can wait. For now we get the police order, and then we'll break the news to Steve.'

'But...' Kerry faltered. 'Can I really ask him to leave?'

'The farm's in your parents' name, isn't it? I imagine your parents could ask you all to leave if they wished. Couldn't they?'

'Yes, but they wouldn't. They want the farm to be mine.'

'Would they support you in asking Steve to leave?'

That was obviously an easy question to answer. 'Yes. They hate him.'

'Then you're home and dry. And Steve's parents live close by,' Darcy told her. 'It's not as if he hasn't anywhere to go, and any number of people will testify that he's put nothing into your farm. He has no rights here apart from arranged access to his children.' He glanced again at her neck and his eyes darkened. There was no excuse for doing this to a woman. 'You're doing the right thing, Kerry.'

The weary woman looked at Darcy for a long minute. She looked at Susie and then back to Darcy.

'I need to do this,' she said at last.

'You do.'

'It just seems so...hopeless.' Her eyes blinked back tears. 'There's just nothing to look forward to any more. Nothing.'

'Yes, there is,' Susie said suddenly. She'd been thinking while Darcy had been doing his organising. What was needed here—seriously—was some light relief. 'What are you doing on Saturday?'

'Saturday?'

'It's our wedding day,' Susie confided. 'Darcy and I had thought we'd just pop down to Hobart and get married in a registry office—but if I can fix it in time, I've just changed my mind.'

'You've...' She had them both staring at her, but Susie wasn't to be stopped. She was in organisational mode again.

'What this town needs is a party,' she said. 'A proper wedding. And if we're having a proper wedding I need a matron of honour and a flower girl. Kerry, you were my best friend at school, and there's no one closer to me now. If I pay for the dresses, will you and Lisa do that for me?'

'Oh, Susie!' As a tonic it was amazing. Kerry even managed a smile. 'Really? And you want Lisa, too? She's been so miserable.'

'Of course I want Lisa.' Susie cast a sideways glance at Darcy to see how he was taking it, but he seemed too stunned to speak. Good. 'Jamie's being page-boy, and Robert will be Darcy's best man. We'll have a proper wedding ceremony in the little church on the headland, and then we'll organise a party to end all parties.'

'Hey, hang on a minute...' Darcy sounded stunned to the core but Susie fixed him with a look. She sent him a silent message and then she smiled again. This time at Darcy.

'Don't you think we need a party, darling?' she said sweetly. 'If I can arrange it?'

'I'll help,' Kerry said eagerly, and Susie looked at her and thought, Yes, this was the right thing to do. Some medicines didn't come in bottles. Sure, Kerry had enough to organise on her own behalf, but an offer of rekindling a friendship, and something to think about over the next few awful days— something to take the town's notice from her separation— was just what she needed.

And Darcy knew it. He couldn't refuse.

'OK,' he said finally. 'If you really want it.'

'I'm going to be the world's tubbiest bride,' Susie said cheerfully. 'But, yes—this is what I really want.'

CHAPTER SEVEN

IF THERE'S one thing small Australian towns were good at, it was organising celebrations, and on this occasion Whale Beach outdid itself.

Once the townsfolk learned what Susie wanted they came out in force. There'd been mutterings of disgust about the couple's intentions to marry in a Hobart registry office. Apparently the town thought this was just how things ought to happen, and they wouldn't be stopped by the lack of a bit of organisation. The fact that there were only three days left to organise was held to be no impediment at all.

'So we're having four hundred guests?' Darcy said incredulously, late on Friday afternoon.

He, Susie and their attendant nurse—Lorna Touldbridge—were painstakingly cleaning gravel from the elbows and forearms of Harry Blake. Harry, an enterprising eight-year-old with more courage than sense, had accepted a bet from his mates. He'd pushed his bike up to the top of Gandilong Bluff and had tried to ride to the bottom. It was a downhill distance of about half a mile by the gravel track—or about a hundred yards as the crow flew.

The crow might have flown but Henry couldn't, and neither had he been able to control his bike on such rough ground. The result was truly and bloodily spectacular. Luckily he'd been wearing thick cargo pants which had prevented major damage to his legs, and he'd thrown his arms up to protect his face. If he hadn't, they'd be transferring him to Hobart or even to the mainland for the attention of a plastic surgeon.

As it was, it was a job to be done under a general anaesthetic, and a couple of hours' intricate cleaning of every inch of exposed skin. Henry was going to be a very sore little boy for a long time. Darcy and Lorna cleaned as Susie kept careful watch of the child's breathing while she monitored the anaesthetic. The damage was too extensive to be done under a local anaesthetic, and the child was badly shocked, which made her job doubly tricky.

Still, there was time to talk, as there hardly had been since their decision to wed in public. Darcy had simply acquiesced. 'Anything to make Kerry's life more bearable,' he'd said, and little else, and he'd stayed as remote as he'd ever been.

But now...

'Four hundred guests?' Susie glanced up from her patient, her eyes widening as Darcy asked the question. She didn't know anything about four hundred guests. 'Where on earth did you get that number?'

'From me,' Lorna said in satisfaction. The middle-aged nurse was in her element—in fact, it seemed as if all of Whale Beach was enjoying this course of events very, very much. 'Last count was four hundred and fifteen. Kerry's mum told me this morning. She's taking the RSVPs.'

'But—'

'And if you knew how pleased Kerry's parents are with you, you wouldn't begrudge them the trouble,' Lorna said, casting an approving glance at the pair of them before she went back to tweezing embedded gravel from Henry's forefinger. 'Kerry got pregnant by Steve before she had enough sense to know he was rotten through and through, and her parents have been watching on the sidelines in increasing worry ever since.'

'She's lucky to have them,' Susie said, with a doubtful look at Darcy. Intent as he was on the job at hand, he was, it seemed, still taking the four hundred guest list on board.

'She is.' Lorna wasn't to be stopped. 'They moved in two minutes after the intervention order was served, and they've changed all the locks. They've employed a man to stay in the outbuildings at night—because they don't trust Steve an inch and he's so angry he's capable of anything. And now they're so delighted Kerry and Lisa are part of your wedding that they've taken it on themselves to move mountains. And they have everyone in Whale Beach right behind them.'

'It was just supposed to be a party on the beach,' Susie said weakly. 'With bring your own food...'

'Well, that wouldn't have been right,' Lorna said stoutly. She, too, took a peep at Darcy. She had the temerity to grin at the look of dismay on his face, and then she turned back to Susie. 'Kerry's mum is president of the local Country Women's Association. So they're catering.'

'But it'll cost a fortune!'

'Everyone who wants to come puts in,' Lorna said serenely. 'And so far I don't think there's a single occupant of this town who hasn't put in. Everyone wants to come.' Then she grimaced. 'Apart from Steve, that is, but we can ignore him. He deserves everything that he has coming to him, that one, and Kerry's mum told me this morning that Steve's own mum and dad have put their names down for the wedding. That's how much support he has.'

'It'll be hard for Steve to stay in Whale Beach under so much disapproval,' Darcy said, as if to thrust his mind from...how many? *Four hundred* guests?

'That's his lookout,' Lorna said stoutly. 'He's been knocking Kerry around for years and everyone knows it. Plus, he's got more than one girl into trouble—even after he was married. Because Kerry's put up with it the locals have kept it to themselves, but this wedding and you asking her to be your matron of honour—well, it's a celebration of more than just you two getting together.'

'I suppose so.' Darcy didn't sound the least bit sure.

'So you make sure you do us proud,' Lorna ordered. And then she looked sideways at the pair of them. Honestly, she thought. They looked so efficient and professional in their white coats but there were some areas where doctors were just hopeless. 'You know,' she ventured, 'Kerry discovered yesterday that Jamie didn't even have a dinner suit.'

'A dinner suit?' This time it was Susie who stared. 'Jamie?' Early in their relationship she'd taken the little boy shopping in Devonport. He now had a great new wardrobe, consisting mostly of surf gear which he'd decreed was cool, and she'd told him he could wear anything he liked to the wedding. He'd chosen a particularly garish surf shirt and cargo pants—like every other kid in the neighbourhood wore.

'He's a page-boy and he'll dress accordingly,' Lorna said sternly. 'Kerry's Lisa explained it to him—that it wouldn't be proper to wear anything else. Kerry's dad's driven to Devonport this morning to collect the hired suit. Oh, and the cake...'

'The cake?'

Both doctors were looking weak-kneed, and Lorna thought, Great. Kerry had asked her to let them know just how big this was going to be, so she'd chosen her time wisely to break the news, and they could hardly back out now.

There was little more to be said.

'Maybe we should concentrate on Harry,' she said blithely, going back to tweezing. 'Because he's on the guest list, too, and his mum's organised a wheelchair already.'

Which left them so organised there was nowhere for them to go but forward.

'It's going to be neat,' Jamie told them as Susie tucked him into bed that night. He was so much better now that her heart lightened every time she saw him. She and Darcy had worked as a team. There was almost always one of them with him, and when there wasn't he'd spend his time with his beloved gran.

There'd been no more infections. All it took now was confidence, Susie thought, and he'd be back on his feet. But for that confidence to build, there had to be security and love.

And Susie had so much love to give. She had it in buckets,

she thought, and she was aching to share. With her own wee one, with this little boy—and with his stubbornly unlovable uncle.

Susie had taken to coming into Jamie's bedroom after Darcy had said goodnight and giving the little boy a cuddle of her own. For the first couple of times he'd resisted, holding his thin frame rigid in her clasp, but now he snuggled into her just as if he liked it. Which, underneath his small-boy pride, he did. 'All my friends are coming,' he told her proudly.

'And you're wearing a dinner suit.' Susie smiled down at him and shook her head. 'I can't believe it.'

'Lisa said I had to.' He tried to sound disgusted but it didn't quite come off. 'But Lisa and Kerry said Uncle Darcy will be wearing one, too. He will be, won't he?' The child was suddenly anxious, and Susie frowned. She hadn't asked what Darcy intended wearing.

'I'm not sure,' she said tentatively. 'We'd better ask the man himself.' She rose and went out to the hall to call him, and then Darcy was in Jamie's room and the usual tension settled between the pair of them. It was as if he knew how much she wanted to broach the barricades—and he was intent on building them stronger.

OK. She wasn't doing any broaching now. She was just reassuring Jamie. 'Jamie wants to know if you're wearing a dinner suit like his,' she asked stiffly.

For a moment, Darcy didn't answer. He stood looking down at her as she settled again on the bed beside Jamie. They were quite a sight—his very pregnant intended bride and his pale little flannelette-clad nephew snuggled up beside her.

They were both looking at him with equal degrees of anxiety, and for the life of him he couldn't stop a smile. They looked so...

So right. He acknowledged it to himself, and as he did part of his tension slipped away. Susie had done Jamie nothing but good. She was sitting on his bed, the little boy was nestled into her side and he thought, I've given him a mother.

She'd made no promises about that, he thought, but it was clear all the same. Susie's body language was such that if anything threatened her little boy she'd have that threat for dinner—a mother dragon defending her own.

And Jamie was so different now. He was still confined to a wheelchair—it was almost as if it was a security blanket that he refused to release by practising walking on a frame—but he was so much more relaxed. He was putting on weight, and he was chattering and losing that hard-plated defence that held the world at bay.

There was more to medicine than medicine, Darcy thought, and his smile broadened. For Jamie, Susie was a tonic all on her own.

But they were both waiting for an answer. 'Does that smile mean you're planning on wearing jeans and an old T-shirt?' Susie said suspiciously, and he grinned.

'Kerry would kill me. Followed by Jamie. Nope. Kerry's given instructions all over the place, and I have mine. I'm wearing a penguin suit, ma'am, just like Jamie's. And what are you wearing, Dr Ellis?'

'That's for me to know and you to find out,' she said serenely. 'The only thing I can tell you is that it won't have a clinging waistline.'

'I can see that.' He looked down at her bulge and smiled again. 'You're getting very close. What if you go into labour tonight? That'd set the cat among the pigeons.'

'Pigs might fly,' she retorted. 'This baby knows its due date. That's in two weeks. Anyway, the way Kerry's organising things, she's probably organised a labour ward on the side. Just in case. Now, Jamie…'

'Mmm?' He was happy. Snuggled into his pillows, with Darcy and Susie laughing and relaxed, he looked for the first time since Susie had met him a child completely at peace with his world.

'You know what you have to do?'

'Lisa's told me,' he said. 'Lisa's got me organised.'

'We appear to be surrounded by a whole set of managing females,' Darcy told him, and stooped to kiss him lightly on the forehead. 'And, heaven help us, we can do nothing but what we're told.'

'We can't back out now.'

'No.' As Jamie slept, they'd walked silently out to the back verandah, each knowing almost instinctively what the other was thinking. This was a bigger production than either of them had ever envisaged.

'It's bigger than *Ben Hur*,' Darcy said slowly, and Susie looked uncertainly up at him in the moonlight and could only agree.

'Do you mind very much?'

'I can't mind,' he said heavily. 'It started out as a commitment to Jamie and now...'

'Now it's a commitment to the whole town,' Susie agreed. 'Scary, huh?'

'And what happens when Jamie's better, or when Muriel dies?'

'You'll want to pick him up and take him back to Scotland?'

'I could,' he said slowly, thinking the option through. 'He could adapt.'

'He's getting better by the day.'

'He is at that.' Darcy turned to her, and some of the tension faded. 'I have you to thank for that.'

'It's down to us both,' Susie told him. 'He's starting to be secure.'

'He has a mother and father and a grandmother.' The tension rolled back into Darcy's words. 'That's what he's feeling as if he has.'

'Mmm.'

'And if I take him away...' Darcy took a deep breath. 'No matter how cured he may seem, he may well revert.'

There was no doubting that. The doctor in her was forced to agree. As well as the part of her that was falling in love... 'I guess taking him back to Scotland would be a strain.'

'You know, this isn't looking like a temporary marriage,' Darcy said heavily.

'No.' Susie was no longer watching him. She'd turned and was looking out at the stars. 'It started out as an emergency marriage but long term...'

'Long term we may well be stuck with each other.' He sounded appalled and Susie winced.

'Jamie will grow up.'

'How long are we stuck together, then? Five years? Ten years? And the medical needs of the town won't have changed.'

Susie took a deep breath. 'OK,' she said softly. 'This is your last chance, but that chance is still available. Call the whole thing off and I'll walk away.'

'You'd do that?' His voice was impersonal and he, too, turned away—as if he needed to come to his decision without looking at her.

'I'd do that.' She bit her lip. It'd be dreadful—to dash so many hopes—but to trap a man into marriage... 'I'm not forcing you into this, Darcy,' she said firmly—more firmly than she felt. 'No matter how trapped you're feeling, I won't have you saying it's me doing the trapping.'

'But it is.'

'No.'

'It is. You see, I couldn't bear it if you walked away from here,' he told her, still with that strange, impersonal tone in his voice. 'I can't hurt you that much. You give and you give...'

This was crazy. 'You want *me* to call it off, then?' she said with asperity. 'Holy, heck! Darcy, to me this marriage seems a sensible solution. Not a deep, dark entrapment. It could also be fun.'

'*Fun?*'

'Yes.' Susie was infuriated with the man, and it helped. 'In case you hadn't noticed, this household isn't exactly lonely. We're making Jamie laugh. Jamie in turn is making us laugh, and together, medically and personally, we're achieving miracles. It's going to be a real pleasure watching Jamie improve and grow and become a loving, normal little boy. Oh, and by the way, I think we need a puppy.'

'A puppy?' Darcy said faintly, totally bemused, and Susie grinned.

'That's right. A puppy. Jamie needs something to be dependent on him. It's time he was out of that chair, and I think a puppy would help.'

'Oh, yeah?' he half jeered at her. 'And who'd exercise it and feed it and care for it?' She could see what he was thinking. More responsibility. It was coming at him from every direction.

She was still infuriated. 'We would,' Susie snapped. 'Jamie and me. This isn't more of your entrapment, Darcy Hayden. Puppies are great.' Then she softened a little, seeing the look of uncertainty wash across his face. 'You know, you could just enjoy it. I'm not like your mother or your sister. I'm here to stay. Now, if that makes you feel like running, then maybe you take after them—but *I* certainly don't. So…'

'So?'

'So you can get yourself married and become part of a family and enjoy it, or you can feel stuck for the rest of your life. Either way, once you've gone through with it I refuse to feel responsible. And that's all I'm going to say,' she retorted. 'Now, if you don't mind, I promised I'd drop in on Muriel before I go to bed—you know Lorna's offered to bring her to the ceremony tomorrow—and then I have a gentleman who needs catheterising. And—' she gave him a cheeky grin '—he asked specifically for me.'

'I can't imagine why,' Darcy retorted dryly, and Susie's twinkle deepened.

'Some people think I'm desirable,' she retorted. 'Just because you don't...'

He did.

That was the whole trouble, Darcy acknowledged to himself as he lay sleepless in bed later that night. Almost nine months pregnant, bossy and organising and always under his feet, Susie was starting to seem the most desirable woman he could imagine.

Why? How could he possibly be attracted to her?

It must be because he wasn't dating any other women, he decided. Back home in the UK, working in a major hospital in Edinburgh and then a smaller town within easy commuting distance of the city, he had rarely been without a partner. He'd moved on fast enough, but that had been no problem. Most of the women he'd dated he'd never had to see again.

But here, even before Susie had arrived, it had been difficult to be lightly attracted to a local woman. This was a tiny community. One date would have raised expectations he'd had no intention of fulfilling.

And now those expectations would be fulfilled tenfold. As of tomorrow he'd be married, and dating would be a thing of the past. He'd seen enough of the condemnation the community placed on Steve Madden to know that playing around wasn't an option.

Which left him permanently with Susie.

Who was gorgeous.

No!

It would be so easy, he thought, rolling over and thumping his pillow for the thirtieth time that night, to allow himself to be seduced by the prospect of family. Of love...

But love didn't last. It was a fantasy that destroyed people's lives. His mother and his sister had hurt Darcy beyond endurance. He'd watched his father break his heart, and he'd learned that loving meant exposure to unendurable pain.

Susie herself must know it, he acknowledged, otherwise this marriage would be impossible. She'd buried a husband, and she'd not be likely to expose herself to that sort of anguish again. So the arrangement must be formal. Unsentimental and non-sexual. A business arrangement only.

An emergency wedding that might well need to last for ever.

The problem with two doctors marrying, and the town's third doctor acting as best man, was that it left no room for emergencies. The wedding was timed for eleven. At ten-thirty a carload of kids rolled down the bluff a mile out of town and ended up in Casualty, with a combination of minor and not-so-minor injuries between them.

Which meant there was nothing for it but for the town's three doctors—plus Ian Lars, the doctor from Stony Point who'd decided this ceremony was worth celebrating—to take off their wedding finery, pin a notice to the church door and reschedule everything for three in the afternoon.

The wedding guests took it in their stride. These were local kids after all, and they were related or known to all. The Country Women's Association rescheduled their wedding lunch and called it wedding dinner, hot beef and turkey became cold collation, Kerry took Jamie and Lisa to the beach—'because they're bursting with excitement and Jamie'll make himself sick if he isn't kept occupied'—and the doctors got on with what they had to do.

Which, as far as Susie was concerned, wasn't much. The kids, in combination, had been extraordinarily lucky. She gave the anaesthetic for the repair of a punctured lung—which took an hour and was less complicated than they'd feared—she stitched one set of lacerations, but then she was put firmly out of the surgery by Robert, Ian and Darcy.

'You'll be fast asleep by the time you're married if you don't go and have a snooze,' Robert told her, in a voice that was sounding more and more like the confident Dr Robert of old. 'You're almost at term, my dear. Look after yourself.'

And with Darcy backing him up, and Ian sighing and saying he might have known this would happen but he'd take charge of the recovering teenagers while the actual ceremony was performed, there was little else she could do. So she retired to the bedroom she'd slept in as a child. She attempted to rest and failed, and then she sat and stared out the window.

And tried to think of Charlie.

His photograph was on her bedside table. She lifted it onto her knees and then sat and looked at it for a very long time.

She was doing this for him, she told herself. It was Charlie who had so desperately wanted this baby, and in marrying Darcy she was keeping Charlie's little one safe. So there was no way this marriage could be seen as a betrayal of her first love.

She was marrying for the sake of Charlie's child.

So why did it seem as if it was for herself?

A marriage of convenience couldn't work, she told herself, and the knowledge seared into her mind and stayed. They were kidding themselves. No contract to live in the same house for years—to share parenting as well as working side by side as doctors—could ever last the distance. Something would have to give.

There was a light knock and Kerry entered. She was dressed in a soft peach, strapless dress and she looked lovely. After her horrors of the last few weeks she looked almost serene and Susie thought that, at least for Kerry, this wedding arrangement was brilliant.

But how about for the bride and groom?

'It's time to dress again,' Kerry told her. 'The other doctors told me they'd sent you to rest, and I figured that was stupid. How could you rest? I thought you might be getting really nervous by now.'

'I am at that.' Susie gave the photograph a last glance and Kerry followed her glance.

'Is that your last husband?'

Your last husband. It sounded so...final. She flinched and Kerry saw it.

'I'm sorry,' she said softly. 'You must have loved him very much.'

'Yes.' Susie stared down at the laughing face of someone she hardly knew any more. They'd had so little time together before illness had struck...

Had she loved Charlie? It had faded so far into the past now that she couldn't tell. They'd been friends and then she'd nursed him to the end and promised to bear his child...

'What are you thinking?' Kerry asked quietly, watching Susie's face, and she saw her friend's mouth tighten in pain.

'I'm thinking.' She took a deep breath. 'I'm thinking it's time I put Charlie away,' she said. 'I loved him once, and part of me...part of who I am now is because of Charlie. But he wouldn't want me to spend the rest of my life in mourning. In fact, he'd be the first one to tell me to make the most of the rest of my life.' She took a deep breath. 'And to love again.'

And that was that. Carefully she opened her bedside drawer and placed the frame carefully away. Life was for now. Life was for moving on.

Life was...Darcy.

'I'm not going to waste a second of this marriage,' she said softly. 'I feel like I've been given another chance.'

'Because you love Darcy?'

Soon she'd be formally asked that question, Susie thought. Soon she'd be standing in front of every person in Whale Beach and they'd be waiting for her response.

And she thought of Darcy. Darcy as she'd last seen him, his medical coat stained, and his eyes filled with concern. He'd been taking a hysterical teenager's hands into his and holding her tight as she'd lain on the stretcher.

'No one's been killed,' he'd said in a voice that had resonated with reassurance. It had sounded throughout casualty, reaching the other injured kids and giving them the same message. 'You've just given yourselves a hell of a fright but there's no permanent damage. You, Helen, have broken your leg, which means you'll be wearing a cast for a few weeks, but that's no cause for hysterics. You've all been very, very lucky. Now, I have a wedding to attend, as I'm sure you all know, so let's cut the histrionics and get on with treating you.'

Let's get on...

Darcy gave himself to everyone, Susie thought. He'd given up his job, his country—everything—to keep Jamie safe. He'd even agreed to marry her!

How could she not love a man like that? Even if he was incapable of loving her back.

'Yes,' she said at last to Kerry's still unanswered question, and she knew she was right. 'I love him very much.' She closed her bedside drawer with a final snap, placing Charlie's memories firmly where they belonged. In the past.

Those memories wouldn't stop her putting everything she had into this marriage, she thought, and if that meant laying her pride on the line and loving Darcy to bits, even if it was unreturned, then that's just what she'd do.

This might be an emergency wedding—but Susie was playing for keeps.

And finally she was there.

She wasn't everyone's ideal bride, Darcy thought in wonder as he watched her pause at the far end of the aisle. Her pregnancy was almost full term; there was no way of disguising it, and she hadn't even tried.

She'd driven to Hobart to choose her dress—'something pretty, but sensible and practical that I can take in afterwards'—but at the last minute practicality had deserted her. The shop assistant had asked what the dress was for, and when she'd been told she'd gone all misty-eyed.

'Oh, but you can't be practical. Not at a time like this. And look what we have!'

Susie had looked—and was hooked.

The dress was almost white, but the gorgeous shot silk was shadowed with soft apricot, the colour appearing and disappearing as the dress swirled in lovely folds around her. It had tiny shoestring shoulder-straps and a sweetheart neckline, and it was gathered under her breasts and then allowed to fall in luxurious swirling folds down to the floor.

It was meant to be her dress, the shop assistant had declared, and now, as he watched Susie walk steadily along the aisle toward him, Darcy could only agree. She looked fair and vulnerable and lovely. The wispy trailing bouquet of white roses and baby's breath and the single row of her mother's pearls around her neck were her only ornaments.

She wore no veil. Her curls fell softly onto her bare shoulders. Her eyes were calm and serene, and she walked toward him with a tiny smile on her lips.

She looked almost as if she loved him and it was enough to take a man's breath away.

Dimly Darcy was aware of Jamie wheeling himself before her, the ring resting on a satin pillow on his knees. And Kerry and Lisa were her attendants, smiling broadly enough to take away their own heartache.

He was aware of them—but mostly he was aware of Susie.

What had he thought she'd look like? he wondered. Whatever it had been, it wasn't this. This embodiment of womanhood. This vision of serene and utter loveliness was...his bride?

She was looking up at him and smiling, waiting for him to respond. The whole church was waiting for him to respond.

And finally he managed. Susie reached his side, she handed her bouquet to Kerry and then she tucked her hand into his.

'With this ring I thee wed…' The words floated into his head before the vicar had a chance to open his mouth.

He was about to say the words he'd vowed never to say, he thought dazedly, and when he'd made this decision he'd thought he could do it and stay heart-whole and fancy-free.

But she was so lovely, and she was looking up at him with just the faintest trace of anxiety in her gorgeous green eyes.

She was doing this for him, he thought. She could have forced him to leave town. She hadn't wanted to wed again.

Susie, the brave heart…

She was still smiling—and she was waiting.

And so, at last, he smiled, and she smiled right back at him. Trust me, her smile said. I'm trusting you. I'm placing my future in your hands, to do with as you will.

As he was. They were in uncharted territory here, but there was nothing for them now but to go forward. The whole community was waiting.

'Shall we get married, then?' he whispered, and her eyes lit up with relief.

'I think we should,' she murmured. 'Now that we've come this far.' She twinkled up at him, and for the life of him he couldn't help but respond. He chuckled, and the hand holding hers tightened and held.

And then there was nothing else to do.

They turned to the vicar and were made one.

CHAPTER EIGHT

THE party afterwards would be talked of locally for years. It went on and on into the night, the entire town assembling on the beach. The local band struck up and seemed ready to play until dawn, the food was so abundant there'd be leftovers to fill Whale Beach households for weeks, and the night was moonlit and perfect.

And Darcy and Susie hardly saw each other. Once the dancing began, the bride and groom were parted as they were partnered in turn by every avid dancer in the district.

Susie was whirled from one set of male arms to another. The locals loved her, and they were desperately happy at this solution to the town's needs. She was congratulated over and over, her eyes danced with the music and she hugged everyone in turn and thanked them for providing this party to end all parties.

It was wonderful, but it couldn't last for ever. It was Darcy who realised how she was feeling, and came to his bride's assistance. He simply removed the local lad who was currently holding her, took her hand in his and turned and signalled to the band to hush.

'My wife...' There was a general roar of approval at that, but he kept on. 'My wife, as you may have noticed, is just a little bit pregnant.' Laughter. 'And Jamie is weary, too.' He smiled across at the little boy and his smile said that Jamie was with them. One of them. Part of this new, wonderful family. 'So we'd like to thank you all for doing this for us—for giving us this celebration—and I hope you'll keep the celebrations up through the night on our behalf, but now it's time for us to go home.'

'But I'm not coming with you.' It was Jamie. He'd been

sitting on the sidelines, but his mates had been with him for most of the night, taking turns to shove his wheelchair along the sand wherever he wanted to go. And, as ten-year-old boys would die rather than dance, there'd been no problem with him feeling left out.

And now he sounded definite—yet content.

'You're not?' Darcy frowned. He was still holding Susie's hand, and his touch made her feel secure and very, very blessed. If only it was for real...

'Kerry says I should stay with her for two nights,' Jamie was saying. His eyes danced. For a child with CFS he was holding up extraordinarily well. 'Kerry says you need to have a honeymoon, and people have honeymoons all by themselves. And she also says kids think honeymoons are really, really boring. People just stay in bed all day.'

Susie blinked—and then blushed to the roots of her curls as the townsfolk laughed around her.

'Yeah, you get off on your honeymoon, the pair of you. If you don't get on with it soon, there'll be a baby in bed beside you,' someone called, and the crowd burst into even more approving laughter.

Then Kerry burst in. 'It's OK, isn't it? Taking Jamie home with me? Mum and Dad have said they'll stay with me and help.' Their matron of honour was trying not to laugh, but she was anxious. Very anxious. Had she done the right thing?

And standing in the moonlight, holding his new wife's hand, Darcy couldn't bring himself to say they didn't need—didn't want—a honeymoon. The whole town had arranged this—had wanted this—and, besides, if immigration officials were to be placated, they'd have to see a marriage.

'Of course it's OK. Thank you very much,' he said gravely. 'If it's OK with you, Jamie.'

'It's OK,' Jamie said smugly. 'Kerry says that it's what I have to do to have a family.' But then he frowned. 'Though I don't know what you'll do without me. Bed sounds boring.'

And as the locals laughed again, Susie stooped and kissed

him soundly. 'We'll miss you, that's what we'll do,' she told him.

'Yeah, but I'll be back Monday,' he said. 'And then none of us will have to go away again. Ever.'

Susie cast an uncertain glance at her new husband, and his face was inscrutable.

'No,' she said. 'We won't.'

'That's all right, then.'

But it was only weeks since Kerry had lost the baby and Susie looked doubtfully at her matron of honour. 'Kerry, you're exhausted. You shouldn't be taking on more.'

But even that had been arranged. 'I told you, my mum and dad are coming to stay to help,' Kerry said smugly. 'See? This town has it all fixed.'

'And all we can do is to go along with it.'

'I suppose so.' It was later still and they were being driven home. Kerry had taken the children home to bed, but the bride and groom had been held up for an hour more while the wedding guests had organised the traditional send-off. They'd formed a ring and had sung chorus upon chorus of 'Auld Lang Syne' while each guest said goodbye. As if they were leaving!

It was nonsense, but still it was traditional, and the locals would have it no other way.

Now their bridal transport—the local newsagent driving his precious model-T Ford bedecked with bridal ribbons and trailing a clatter of tin cans—was taking them back to their house. Alone in the back seat, there was so little and so much that had to be said.

'I'm not all that happy about Jamie,' Darcy said quietly, staring straight ahead into the night. As if he didn't wish to look at his new bride.

OK, Susie decided carefully. If he wanted to talk about Jamie rather than the wedding, she'd go along with it. 'Why not?'

'It's too soon for him to be staying away.' Darcy frowned. 'You didn't see him at his worst, but he's come so far. I don't want a relapse.'

'He wants to go.'

'I know. We couldn't refuse. As you say, all we can do is go along with it and hope it's not a disaster.'

A disaster...

Was he talking about Jamie or their wedding? Susie looked at his closed face, and she knew with absolute certainty that he was talking of both.

And then they were home.

At least the ceremony was over, Darcy thought. That had to be the worst. He walked up the verandah steps, then frowned as Susie gripped the rail. Hell. She really was exhausted.

'Getting married two weeks before a baby's due is hardly what I'd recommend as your doctor,' he said, and she managed an uncertain smile.

'You're my husband now—not my doctor,' she retorted. 'Robert says I'm fine, and so I am.'

'You're not. You're totally done in.'

'I'm OK. Honestly.' But there was just enough dogged determination in her voice to make him know better. He knew exhaustion when he heard it, and he heard it now.

He might not be her doctor—but he *was* her husband.

Right, then. There was a marital precedent for what he was about to do, if not a medical one. What was a man—a husband—to do?

What was expected, of course! So with one easy movement he swept her into his arms and cradled her against his chest, her lovely bridal gown streaming out behind. Lying in his arms, she felt soft and yielding and very, very lovely, and his gut kicked in recognition of...

Of what?

Of something he had to ignore!

Susie gasped in his hold, but he managed to ignore that,

too. Striding forward, he kicked the door open and carried his bride inside.

'Put...put me down.' It was all she could think of to say, and then, as he placed her on her feet and her heart thumped back into place, she gazed around their home and received another shock. The tension faded as surprise took over. 'What the...?'

What, indeed?

To mark their wedding, the community had moved mountains. During the ceremony and afterwards, while the bridal couple had danced obliviously on the beach, people must have slipped away. They must have done it in shifts, Susie thought dazedly, otherwise their absence would have been noticed.

'I don't believe this,' she whispered. The kitchen was festooned with white helium balloons—hundreds of them floating every which way. And the walls...

They'd been...painted?

The paint was hardly dry. The colour scheme hadn't been changed, but everything was clean and lovely. Dull drapes, stained from years of neglect, had now been replaced with new. The wooden table had been scrubbed and polished until it shone, as had the Baltic pine floorboards, and there were gay new cushions tied onto every chair.

Susie and her new husband could only stare. The smell of new paint and beeswax had their senses reeling.

A card stood on the table. It was large and white—the size of a glossy magazine—and it had a single golden wedding band embossed on the cover. Nothing else.

Stunned, Darcy lifted it, flipped it open and read it aloud.

'"You've given Whale Beach a medical team fit for a city,"' he read. '"In return, Whale Beach gives you a home fit for a marriage. Bless you both."'

And there were signatures. Looking over her new husband's shoulder, Susie saw that there was a signature from almost every inhabitant of Whale Beach.

'It's the town's wedding gift,' Susie whispered, gazing around the kitchen in awe. 'Oh, Darcy, it's lovely.'

But Darcy's face was more than bemused.

'A home,' he repeated. 'Not a kitchen. The card says a *home*. Shall we see what they've done everywhere else?' And without waiting for his bride to follow, he strode out to inspect the other rooms.

They, too, had been changed. 'Good grief.' Darcy reached the door of the sitting room and stopped dead.

'They must have planned this from the day we announced we were getting married,' Susie said, awed, as she looked at the gorgeous hand-sewn cushions in their newly painted sitting room. 'And how they did it...'

'They had just twelve hours.' Darcy was moving again. He hauled open Jamie's bedroom door and sighed with relief. It had been repainted, but essentially unchanged. 'At least they've had the sense to leave the bedrooms be.'

'N-no, they haven't.' While Darcy had checked Jamie's room, Susie had checked her own. She was standing in her bedroom doorway. Or what had been her bedroom.

The local women had had a field day here. Susie's bed was gone. Everything she knew was gone. The room had been painted out in a soft pastel yellow. New yellow curtains hung from the windows, emblazoned with tiny white teddy bears. In the centre of the room was the focus—the most gorgeous crib Susie had ever seen. The ceiling was hung with mobiles. There were piles of baby clothes on a new set of shelves.

It was just lovely. But...

'But where do they think I'm going to sleep?' Susie muttered, and she felt herself flush all over. Help!

'They've heaved all your stuff into the spare room. Everything.' After one swift look at the nursery, Darcy had gone on to find the spare room packed with so much stuff they couldn't make it all out. His amazement was fast being replaced by anger. 'Did you know about this?'

'No!'

He was hardly listening. 'It's stupid. As if they expect us to sleep together.' He was striding toward his bedroom—her parents' old room—and his voice was full of anger. 'Even if we wanted to, the bed's only comfortable if you sleep right in the middle. I don't know how your parents—'

And then he threw the bedroom door wide and his words were cut short.

'Oh...'

Susie, coming up behind him, saw what he saw.

And it was all just too much. She couldn't be angry in the face of a gesture like this, and her sense of the ridiculous surfaced to overwhelm her.

Her parents' ancient bed had disappeared. Instead, there was a bed to bedazzle. It was king-sized. It was made up with gorgeous red satin sheets—emblazed with hearts, for heaven's sake! And it had mounds and mounds of heart-shaped pillows scattered all over it. A soft white quilt was folded at the base of the bed—as if anyone could really want to sleep in a bed like this—and it, too, was embossed with silken hearts. And above their heads floated more helium balloons, this time red and white, all heart-shaped and painted with tiny Cupids pointing arrows straight down at the bed.

Susie choked back laughter but it bubbled to the surface regardless. It was too much. The thought of her friends sneaking away in relays while they were being married—heaving furniture, painting like madmen, carting cushion upon dazzling cushion...

'You *did* know!' Darcy's face was rigid, and his words were an accusation. He was feeling like he'd been placed in a trap and the sides were edging in on him. He stared down at the bed, and the thought of Susie in it...

The knowledge slammed home like a bullet. He wanted her!

No! His only reaction had to be anger. It was his only defence. 'You knew they were doing this!'

'I swear I didn't.' But it was hard for her to get the words out. Despite Darcy's fury, she couldn't stop herself. Choking with laughter, she sank onto the amazing bed.

And that made everything worse. The bed was armed. Susie hadn't noticed it, but there'd been rice paper carefully stretched across the ceiling. A fine thread had been attached to the mattress, and Susie's weight was enough to drag it down. The thread snapped, whatever was holding up the rice paper was no longer doing its job and it fell.

Releasing what it held in place.

A shower of confetti floated down over them both. It wisped down over Susie, laughing helplessly on the sumptuous bed, and on Darcy, who was standing stunned and furious beside her.

'Of all the...'

He was almost beyond anger. She was so beautiful and he wanted her so much—and he hadn't planned any of this! His nicely controlled world was spinning out of control.

He'd sworn never to become emotionally involved. Sure, he'd done the right thing by Jamie, but he hadn't expected to find himself loving the kid. And now he'd organised a sensible marriage and his wife had turned out to be a fruitcake.

An incredibly desirable fruitcake!

On the bed, Susie stared helplessly up at him, and put her hands out in a gesture of entreaty. She was trying hopelessly to stop laughing.

'Oh, Darcy, we might have known they'd do something.'

'Might we?'

Her laughter faded into uncertainty. 'Darcy, we're the local doctors. We're important to the community. They had to have some input...'

'Into our lives?' He looked around the room in disgust and her laughter died completely. He had to get out of there.

Away from her! 'OK, if you think it's funny, you sleep here. I'll do a fast check to make sure there's no problems in the hospital and tell Ian he can go home. Then I'll organise some bedding in the living room.'

But Susie sobered at that. His anger was enough to sober anyone. 'Then we'll have to fix the spare room,' she told him, calmer now. 'There's no way I'm sleeping in this crazy bedroom by myself.'

By myself...

It had been the wrong thing to say. The wrong thing to infer. As soon as the words were out she regretted them with all her heart.

'We're not sleeping together!' Darcy's words were snapping and hard.

She flushed to the roots of her hair. 'I wasn't inferring that we should.'

'I don't know what you were inferring,' he said wearily, raking his fingers through his thatch of dark hair. 'I'm too tired to think, but this is all nonsense. For tonight, though... Look, get some sleep and then—'

But he didn't finish his sentence. There was an urgent peal from the front doorbell, followed by a series of frantic knocks. Whoever was out there wanted them in a hurry, and there was only one reason for that. Honeymoon or not, this was the doctor's residence.

And Darcy switched into doctor mode just like that. Susie barely had time to get to her feet before Darcy had reached the front door. She entered the hall in time to see him fling it wide.

Kerry was there, and she was carrying Jamie.

Jamie was in trouble. The child was choking and gasping, his face was streaming with sweat and tears, and he was breathing way too fast. As Susie reached them, Darcy was already lifting the child from Kerry's arms. Exhausted, Kerry sagged to her knees.

'He...he just started choking,' she managed as Susie

stooped over her. She had barely enough strength left to whisper, 'No. Don't worry about me. Jamie...'

But Susie was checking Kerry first. There were two patients here and Kerry looked dreadful.

'I'd just put them to bed,' Kerry managed. 'Dad's gone back to their place and Mum's staying the night with me—to help. I left Jamie in the room next to me and I heard him. He said his chest hurt and he couldn't breathe. I was so scared. I just lifted him up and ran to the car...'

'Put your head between your knees.' Bride or not, like Darcy, Susie was right back in doctor mode. Heavens, carrying a ten-year-old so soon after what Kerry had been through was the worst thing Susie could think of.

'I'm...I'm fine.' Kerry was pleading. 'Look after Jamie.'

Only now did Susie flash a look at Jamie. Triage, drilled into every doctor at medical school, taught her to prioritise—if there were multiple casualties and multiple doctors then each doctor should check on individual patients. Only turn your attention to another after ensuring the condition you're checking is non-life-threatening.

And that's what Susie needed to do here. Even though Kerry clearly thought of Jamie as the patient, she was ill herself.

But now, satisfied that Kerry was recovering her breath and not about to pass out, Susie turned to see what was wrong with Jamie. Darcy had laid him on the floor and was ripping his shirt open at the collar. The child was frantically fighting for air and his eyed were terrified.

'I'll get oxygen.' Susie rose to fetch it, but Darcy shook his head. His fingers were holding the little boy's wrist, and the fear that had suffused his face when he'd first opened the door had eased.

'No. I think a paper bag.'

Susie's eyes flew to Darcy's face—and then back to Jamie. A paper bag.

Hyperventilation, then?

It made sense, she thought swiftly. Hyperventilation was mostly caused by a panic attack. Staying in a strange house might well have caused it.

Damn, they never should have agreed to it, she thought bleakly, but at least he'd be OK. This would cause no long-term damage. They just needed to calm him down, and breathing into a paper bag was the best way to force his breathing to slow. She flew through to the kitchen and grabbed what she needed, and by the time she arrived back, Darcy had Jamie in his arms and was holding hard. Reassurance was the first priority.

'Jamie, you're just having a panic attack,' he told him firmly. 'That's all this is. The excitement of the wedding and staying away from home has made your breathing speed up. So that's all that's wrong. I promise. It's called hyperventilation and it's not dangerous. The fast breathing makes your chest hurt. You must slow it down.'

He signalled Susie with his eyes as she stooped before him. 'Susie's here. She's putting a paper bag against your mouth and I want you to breathe into it. Slowly. I want you to breathe so the bag blows up and deflates again.'

His grip tightened on his nephew's shoulders. 'I know you can hear me, Jamie.' It was a stern order, harsh enough to make Susie blink. 'So do it. Now. Breathe. Wait. Then breathe again.'

Jamie's eyes flew wildly to his uncle's as Susie held the bag against his lips. There was nothing for her to do but reiterate his uncle's orders.

'Do it, Jamie,' she said.

'Your chest will stop hurting as soon as you slow your breathing,' Darcy told him strongly. 'Come on, Jamie. Breathe. Wait. Breathe…'

And slowly, slowly, the awful choking subsided and the little boy's rigid frame relaxed. The paper bag held against his mouth expanded and contracted, expanded and contracted, and it slowed with each breath.

Susie let her own breath out with a sigh of relief.

They'd been stupid to think it'd be OK for Jamie to stay with Kerry, she thought bitterly. But Jamie had wanted to so much. Kerry's parents had promised they'd stay to help, and he'd seemed so much better...

'He's OK,' Darcy said into the stillness. 'Jamie, you're fine.'

Susie glanced again at Kerry. The girl was shocked to the core. Wordlessly, she took herself through to the surgery, grabbed her doctor's bag and headed back.

Things might be improving for Jamie, but the priorities had changed again. She knelt beside Kerry and took the blood-pressure cuff from her bag. Darcy intervened.

'Let me.' His concern sounded in his voice, and it wasn't concern for Kerry or Jamie. He was prioritising, too. Hell, Susie was exhausted herself. She glanced up at him, and before she could protest he'd handed Jamie into her arms.

'Sit down and take him and let me see to Kerry,' he said. 'Jamie, you don't mind being cuddled by Susie, do you?'

Of course he didn't.

And Susie didn't mind herself. She sat down against the wall and gathered the little boy into her arms, and it was all she could do not to burst into tears over his head.

She'd only known this child for such a short time, and he'd wrapped himself around her heart like a hairy worm. He and his uncle both.

But at least she could cuddle Jamie.

'Oh, Jamie, you scared us silly.'

He'd scared himself silly. She could see that in his eyes, and in the way his fragile body trembled in her arms.

'Did you hear your uncle tell you what's happened to you? It's called hyperventilation,' she told him. 'It's quite common and it doesn't do any damage. It was just too much excitement so soon after being ill.'

It probably hadn't been the excitement, she thought. It would have been a proper panic attack—being left in a dark room in a strange house, and having no secure base.

He had a secure base now, though, she thought, and as the thought hit her, her own doubts faded. However much Darcy hated it, for now and for ever, they'd provided him with a family. And that family would exist even if it meant Darcy sleeping in the red satin sheets, she decided. He'd do it if she had to knock him out to get him there.

Meanwhile, Darcy, unaware of his wife's resolutions, was examining a protesting Kerry.

'Your blood pressure's sky-high,' he growled. 'For heaven's sake, woman, what were you doing, carrying him?'

'I thought he'd die.'

'We left him with you because your mum and dad promised to stay as well.' Darcy was clearly puzzled. 'Your dad's strong enough to lift him. Why didn't he bring him here?'

'Dad had to go home.'

'Why?' There were things going on here that Darcy didn't understand. Kerry's white face still reflected fear, but she could see for herself now that Jamie was fine. So what else was wrong?

'Steve,' she whispered.

'Steve?'

'He phoned just after we'd brought the children home from the wedding,' she said. 'And he said such things. He threatened me, physically threatened, but I said Mum and Dad were with me so he wouldn't dare. Then he laughed and said if they were away then he'd torch their place. He'd burn it to the ground. So Dad rang the police and went around there.'

'Leaving you with the children.'

'Mum was still with me, and we thought the children were asleep. But then Jamie woke and Mum has a bad back and I had to bring him here. And now I don't know what Steve is doing.' She put her face in her hands and her body heaved in distress. Darcy caught her shoulders and held her.

'If your dad's told the police what's happening, there's nothing Steve can do,' he told her strongly. 'You're not to worry. I'll ring the police sergeant myself—just as soon as we get you to bed.'

'Bed...' She gazed wildly up at him. 'Me? No!'

'Your blood pressure's right up again and I'm not risking another convulsion,' Darcy told her. 'I'll ring your mother and tell her, but you're staying here tonight.'

'I...I won't stay in hospital. I can't. Mum will panic. And she can't cope.'

But Darcy wasn't taking no for an answer and Susie wondered just what Kerry's blood pressure was to make him take such a firm decision. It must be dangerously high.

'Your mother's a sensible woman,' Darcy was saying. 'She won't want you driving back to the farm tonight any more than we do. We'll organise the district nurse to give her a hand in the morning, but I'd imagine by then the police will have called Steve's bluff and your father will be there again to help her.'

She cringed, and Susie winced. The last thing they wanted was to further upset her. 'Hospital. No!' She was practically in tears. 'Lisa will freak out. I've only just convinced her I'm going to live as it is.'

'Then stay with us,' Susie said promptly. 'You're not going home tonight, but we can tell Lisa that you've stayed to help us look after Jamie.' Jamie was almost asleep in her arms, but he nestled closer at that, and gave a weary smile. It seemed OK with him.

It still wasn't OK with Kerry, but she was beginning to be convinced. She looked doubtfully at both of them. 'There's no spare beds.'

'Well, well, well!' The tension suddenly broke as Darcy's attention shifted. 'There's no spare beds... Now, how do you know that, Mrs Madden?'

And, in spite of the evening's trauma, a little colour crept back into Kerry's cheeks and the trace of a smile appeared. 'Uh-oh!'

'You wouldn't have had anything to do with the transformation of this house?'

'Who, me?' Her innocent act didn't fool anyone, and Darcy chuckled. It was as much as Susie could do not to stare. Fifteen minutes ago he'd been furious, and now he was responding with...laughter?

'OK.' The gleam was still in his eyes as he went on to part two of his plan. 'We agree you're staying here, and because of you and your accomplices...'

'Accomplices?'

'Accomplices,' he said definitely. 'Partners in crime. If you're partly responsible for a confetti-laden, heart-covered bed, then you get to sleep in it.'

Both women were goggling now.

'You've already got your pyjamas on,' he said. And Kerry had—she'd simply run out the door with Jamie and not thought about what she was wearing. Darcy flashed a quick glance at Susie and then looked away again. She looked stunning—still in her gorgeous bridal attire, crouched with Jamie nestled against her breast. His mouth twisted, but somehow he made himself continue.

'My...my wife is nine months pregnant,' he told Kerry—as if she didn't know. 'She's exhausted, and the bed's totally wasted on us tonight. Therefore I'll sleep in the living room on the settee which you've so kindly left us, and you and Susie will sleep together in your beautifully prepared wedding bed.'

'I couldn't.'

'You could.' He flashed a warning glance at Susie but Susie was there before him, and he could tell she knew what the advantages of his plan were. Kerry had been badly frightened and was exhausted. Her blood pressure was up past safety point, and she needed to be monitored. OK, she wouldn't go to hospital, so let her sleep beside Susie. That way Susie could monitor her beautifully. If she started fitting, her rigid convulsions would wake Susie at once.

It made sense.

'The locals would kill me,' Kerry said doubtfully. 'After all this trouble...'

After all this trouble, Susie's plans for Darcy would have to be put on hold, the bride thought sadly. Her husband's logic was unarguable.

'After all this trouble you're not going to cause us more,' Susie said sternly. 'No one has to know where you sleep. We'll give you a sedative to settle you, and then you'll sleep where you're told. That's an order. And as for us...'

'You don't want me.'

Susie peeped a look at Darcy and she managed a twinkle. Regardless of his anger, she still had plans.

'There'll be all the time in the world for Darcy and I to play in our big new bed,' Susie said. She kissed the top of Jamie's head and held him tight—and then carefully avoided looking at Darcy as her voice firmed.

'After all, we intend to stay married for a very long time.'

CHAPTER NINE

DARCY gave Kerry a sedative. She telephoned her mother who was relieved to hear she was staying put. She listened as Darcy contacted the police, and was reassured that Steve had been located. He was now sleeping off his blustering threats and drunkenness in a police cell. Only then did she allow exhaustion to hit her.

Susie barely had time to give her a thorough medical check before she slept. At six weeks post-Caesarean she shouldn't have been lifting anything heavier than a newborn, but she'd carried Jamie regardless. Thankfully she seemed to have suffered no long-term damage. As Susie gave a relieved sigh, regardless of satin sheets, crimson hearts and confetti, Kerry slept.

Thank heaven, Susie thought, looking ruefully down at her friend. She shouldn't have let her do this wedding organisation.

But then she thought of Kerry's beaming face at the wedding, and she remembered Jamie's enjoyment. It had been a risk worth taking. Both of them had gained from today, even if it had ended in drama.

Kerry seemed fine—but what about Jamie?

She couldn't sleep until she knew he was settled. Leaving her friend soundly sleeping in the bridal bed, she made her way back through the house. Jamie was nestled in his bed, with Darcy sitting beside him.

One glance told her things were OK. Jamie's breathing was back to normal. His colour had returned to a healthy pink and he was speaking seriously to his uncle. Darcy was still in his dinner suit, minus jacket and tie. He looked...

It didn't matter how he looked, Susie told herself hastily.

The things she intended for Darcy would have to wait. Concentrate on Jamie.

'I've spoiled your wedding,' he was saying, and Susie's heart wrenched at the thought.

'How could you have done that?' She stooped to give him a kiss, somehow managing to avoid touching the man beside him. 'We had a lovely wedding. The best. Didn't you enjoy it?'

'Yes, but...'

'But what?'

'But I got sick again and interrupted you.'

'That was after our wedding.' She grinned. 'Your little drama didn't stop us being legally married. The whole thing went without a hitch. Didn't it, Darcy?'

'Yes. Of course.' But Darcy wasn't looking at her. He was concentrating only on Jamie.

Jamie thought about this and decided Susie's words had merit. OK, he hadn't spoiled their wedding, but... 'I've spoiled your honeymoon, then,' he said sadly. 'By getting sick.'

'You spoiled nothing.' Susie wasn't having a bar of this self-chastisement. It was the last thing Jamie needed. 'Your uncle and I were just standing around in our wedding clothes wondering what to do next. I think we felt silly as bride and groom. We make much better doctors. Isn't that right, Darcy?'

'I...' He sounded confused.

He *was* confused. She was too close. Her gorgeous dress was brushing his arm and she was...

'Of course it's right,' she swept on. 'We can't keep on being a bride and groom for ever. So you saved us from a quandary.' She looked contemplatively down at uncle and nephew as Darcy's arms held Jamie tight. The sight made her feel warm all over—but how much did she long to be a part of it?

Concentrate on Jamie...

'You turned us back into doctors simply by showing us an interesting symptom,' she told him. 'Hyperventilation is a very interesting medical phenomenon, and Darcy and I were very interested indeed.'

'Were you really?' Jamie looked confused at that, but a little bit hopeful, and Susie's smile broadened.

'I've never cured hyperventilation with a paper bag before,' she said thoughtfully. 'My textbooks told me how to do it but you're the first patient I've ever practised on. So, you see, I've had a very interesting medical time—as well as a very interesting wedding. All in all, it's been a most satisfactory day.'

Jamie gave this his serious attention. 'I guess saving me was more interesting than being in bed,' he conceded finally, and at last Darcy relaxed enough to chuckle.

'Yes, indeed,' he told him. 'But that's not saying you were at the point of death or that you should try it again. Our Dr Ellis has had her learning experience. She's turned back into a doctor, we're back to normal, so now can we all, please, go to sleep?'

'She still looks like a bride,' Jamie muttered, and Darcy somehow kept his smile straight.

'She does a good job of camouflage. She might look like a bride but underneath the lace she's all white coat, starch and penicillin. And bossy!'

'Really?' The little boy was smiling and Susie relaxed. Great.

'Really,' she said. 'You have no idea how bossy I can get when I don't get my own way. So co-operate now, or I'll have to do something really, really drastic.' She fought for a threat of sufficient magnitude. 'Like...taking the racing wheels off your wheelchair.'

He gave that the attention it deserved, and he grinned, but there was another worry behind his weary eyes. 'I don't have to go back to Kerry's,' he asked anxiously. 'I mean, it was nice there, and when Lisa said I should let you have a honeymoon I thought it'd be great. I thought I wanted to but it was...'

'It was too soon.' Susie nodded. 'You're absolutely right. Your uncle and I both thought so, but you and Kerry and Lisa were so excited we let it be. You'll find we're much sterner from now on.'

'Really?'

'Really.' She cast a doubtful look at Darcy, but then forced her voice to be firm. 'From now on, this is your home. This is where you belong. With me and with Darcy.'

'Because you're my mother and my father now,' Jamie said in sleepy satisfaction. 'And there's me and there's Grandma. There's four of us.'

'And a new baby any time now,' Darcy said, and only Susie heard the note of strain in his voice. 'A proper family...'

'That's what we need to be.'

With Jamie safely asleep, they'd made their way to the kitchen. Susie filled the kettle. OK, she was exhausted, but there were things to be said. Things to be sorted...

'What?' Darcy sounded abstracted, like he intended heading for bed and leaving her behind.

'A family.'

'I know that.'

'So you're going to have to stop flinching every time we're referred to as a family.'

'I don't flinch.'

'You do flinch,' she said soundly. 'Watch.' And before he knew what she was about, she leaned over the table and kissed him lightly on the lips.

He flinched.

She stood back and her eyes narrowed in thought. 'Married couples don't do that,' she said, trying hard to keep it light. 'They kiss back.'

His face shuttered down. 'In case you'd forgotten, this is a marriage of convenience.'

'Not in the town's eyes. Not even in Jamie's eyes now.' She frowned, then turned to pour cups of tea. She didn't need tea, but it gave her something to look at that wasn't Darcy.

The man she loved...

'Jamie needs security if he's to get well,' she told him, trying hard to keep the note of strain from her voice. 'You already know that. He should be on his feet by now, but he won't try. He's clinging to his wheelchair like a security blanket. He collapsed tonight because he wasn't secure. Darcy, he's desperate for a family. For the whole bit. For a mother and a father who love him. And who love each other.'

'I don't—'

'You don't love me?' She turned then and faced him, placing her hands quietly behind her back. Her face was white with fatigue but this needed to be said, and there was no other time to say it. 'I know you don't love me, Darcy, but you're going to have to show affection or this whole damned house of cards will come tumbling down.' She took a deep breath. 'I'm not that bad—am I?'

'No!' He took a deep breath and searched her face. 'You're saying that you can do this?'

'Do what?'

'Love me.'

There. The words were out in the open, like an open wound just waiting to cause pain. And they would, one way or another. Because the time for prevarication was past. Susie was in this with everything she had.

With her whole heart.

'I guess I do,' she said, and the world held its breath.

'You *love* me?' He sounded incredulous.

This wasn't a great start!

'It must be something I inherited from my parents,' she said, trying hard to keep her voice light. 'An ability to love. I seem to do it all the time. I loved my mum and dad, I loved

Charlie, I love Jamie to bits, I love Robert, and I've been watching you for these last few weeks and—'

'You can't!' It was said with such revulsion that Susie backed a step.

'Why can't I?' She pondered. 'I think it's like the chickenpox,' she said at last. 'You catch it and then you're stuck. Like it or not.'

'I don't want it.'

'No?'

'No. Chickenpox only lasts a couple of weeks—thank God—and I never asked for any sort of commitment.'

'I know that.' She somehow made her face expressionless. 'You didn't. But I can't help what I feel, Darcy, and I thought you ought to know what you're stuck with. For more than two weeks. Like it or not, you have that commitment and it's up to you to do with it as you will. I'll ask for nothing from you. But I'm telling you, any time you change your mind and decide you want me as a proper wife—as *your* wife— I'm ready and waiting.'

'Susie, this is ridiculous.'

'It is, isn't it?' she said, and she couldn't quite keep the note of bitterness from entering her voice. 'Like getting married and going to sleep on the settee. Alone. But needs must and I accept it. For tonight.'

'For ever.'

'For however long it takes.' She filled the teacups and handed him one. 'Now, drink your tea and then get on with what has to be done.'

'What has to be done?' he asked warily.

'You were going to check this morning's car-crash victims and make sure that Ian has gone home,' she reminded him gently. 'You were going to turn into a doctor again.'

'Oh, yes.'

'It's easier being a doctor than a husband,' she said thoughtfully. 'But I guess you'll grow accustomed to your new role. In time.'

* * *

The teenagers were fine. Ian had allowed two of them to go home, and the other two were sleeping soundly. The boy with the punctured lung was the worst injured but his breathing was deep and even, and there seemed no problem. Darcy was leaning over his bed with his stethoscope when he heard halting footsteps behind him. He turned to find Robert watching him from the doorway.

'He's all right. Pulse is steady, breathing's sound. Ian's had him specialled but I've just reduced the checks to fifteen minutes. They've been damned lucky.'

'They have.' Darcy turned around to face the elderly doctor. 'I thought Ian was looking after things until I took over.'

'Which left Stony Point without a doctor tonight. No. As soon as the bride and groom left, I cut along here and sent him home.' Relieved of his huge workload, Robert was growing more and more responsible by the minute. Any time now he'd be kicking Darcy out and taking over the reins again. Darcy smiled and Robert saw it.

'What's so funny?'

'I was just thinking how much your health has improved. You hardly need two more doctors.'

'Which is just as well if Susie's ready to drop her bundle.' The old doctor rubbed his hands as if he could hardly wait. 'Now that's one confinement you will wake me up for.'

'You need your sleep.'

'Nonsense. These damned exercises and new pills Susie's bossing me into have done me the world of good.'

'Which explains why you're here?'

'With three doctors we don't need an out-of-town medico. I'm keeping an eye on the place tonight.'

'There's no need.'

'Of course there's a need,' Robert was grinning. 'You go on back to that wonderful bed of yours.'

So Robert, too, had been in on the plans. Darcy's face darkened.

The older man was looking at him as if he were an interesting specimen. 'Didn't you like your surprise?'

'Susie did. She thought it was funny.'

'And you?' Robert's face was still thoughtful. 'You don't approve?'

'It's a marriage of convenience,' Darcy burst out. 'How the hell—?'

'How the hell are you going to tell her you don't want her?' The older man pursed his lips. 'I can see that must be hard. When *she* wants *you*.'

That statement took Darcy's breath away. He stepped out into the corridor without a word, and Robert followed.

'You knew!' Darcy said at last.

'Knew what?'

'That Susie's imagining she's in love with me.'

'I'd be a fool not to. It's as plain as the nose on your face.'

'No.'

'Yes. That's why you had no trouble with Immigration. Smelling of roses, the pair of you.'

'Robert, I'm not—'

'Darcy, you are,' Robert said gently before he could finish. 'Of course you are. You're just too damned scared to admit it.'

The whole town was conniving against him.

Robert went home at last, which gave Darcy the run of the hospital. He was tired, but he didn't feel like sleeping. He made his way to the children's ward. Harry was there, still suffering from his bike escapade. His mother had brought him to the wedding ceremony in a borrowed wheelchair, but he'd come straight back in afterwards. The wounds were extensive, he lived on a farm that was none too clean and no one wanted to risk infection.

Darcy expected Harry to be asleep, but the little boy's eyes opened as his doctor entered and he managed a smile.

'It was a cool wedding, Dr Hayden.'

Cool... As a compliment from a ten-year-old, it couldn't be beaten, and Darcy smiled in return. 'Thanks, Harry.' He crossed to the bed and lifted the child's wrist, feeling his pulse. It was a bit too fast for his liking. 'Are you hurting?'

'Just a little bit,' Harry admitted. 'The nurse gave me some pills but...'

'But maybe after the events of this afternoon you need something stronger. If you can cope with a pinprick of a needle, I'll give you something that'll help you sleep.'

'That'd be good.'

He was a brave kid, Darcy thought as he called the nurse and prepared the injection. Maybe too brave. Catapulting down gravel bluffs on none-too-steady bicycles was taking things too far.

Funny... That was exactly how he was feeling, Darcy thought. Like things were careering around him and he was way out of control.

Medicine! Concentrate on medicine!

Three minutes later the injection had been given. Harry didn't whimper as Darcy gave him a mild dose of morphine, and he snuggled down without complaint.

'It'll work in minutes,' Darcy told him, ruffling his hair. 'And tomorrow you'll feel better. By Monday I expect you'll be able to go home.'

'Yeah.'

'Do you want the nurse to stay until you go to sleep?'

'I'd rather you did,' the little boy said pointedly.

Darcy considered it and thought, Why not? After all, all he had to go home to was a settee. So he dismissed the nurse, hauled up a chair and proceeded to wait him out.

He didn't need to wait long. Harry was exhausted and as the drug took effect his eyes fluttered closed.

'Thanks for staying,' he whispered as he drifted into sleep. 'And, Dr Hayden?'

'Mmm?'

'My mum says, preggers or not, our Dr Susie was the prettiest bride she's ever seen. And I think so, too.'

Muriel agreed.

With Harry safely asleep, Darcy tried to think of something else he could do to put off trying to sleep. Check the nursing home, he told himself. In case Robert or Ian had left anything undone.

The only one awake was Muriel and she greeted him with pleasure.

'It was just the loveliest wedding,' she told him. 'Gorgeous!'

'Just because it gave you what you so desperately want...' But he smiled as he said it, and Muriel smiled back.

'If I thought you were doing it just for Jamie and me then I'd feel dreadful,' she told him. 'But she really is lovely.'

'Yes, she is.'

'And it'll be no problem pretending to the authorities that you're marrying for love,' she said sleepily. 'Any fool can see that it's just around the corner.'

'That's ridiculous.' Or was it? 'Anyway, I'm not here to discuss my love life.' Trying to distract himself, he checked Muriel's chart. Her obs were beautifully normal.

'As you'd expect,' Muriel told him. 'You think I intend dying now?'

'I suspect not.' He managed a grin. She'd live for ever, he thought, and as long as Muriel lived Jamie would want to be here.

What had he let himself in for? Indefinite marriage?

'There's no way I'm off to meet my maker now,' she was saying. 'Not when everything's so beautifully settled. Tomorrow they're moving me into a room in the hostel section—around the back, overlooking the creek. Jamie'll be able to run along the verandah and visit me any time he wants.'

But then the satisfied look faded and she frowned. "That

is, he'll be able to do that when he can run. He will run again, won't he, Darcy?'

'He will.' Darcy touched her wrinkled hand in a gesture of reassurance, pushing his own uncertainties aside in the need to reassure her. 'He hasn't thrown a temperature for weeks. His liver transaminase levels are almost back to normal. From now on it's just a matter of convincing him that the world can be trusted.'

'It can at that.' Muriel sighed happily and lay back on her pillows, content. 'If you knew the weight you've taken off my shoulders... Giving him a mum and a dad.'

'We never—'

But her fantasy wasn't to be interrupted. 'You are, you know. Any minute now he's going to want to call you that, if he hasn't already. And Susie will agree. She's the loveliest lass. You think that, don't you, boy?' Her hand grasped his and there was a trace of anxiety surfacing again. 'I'm not imagining it. You're nutty on her.'

And she was another who knew the truth. 'Muriel, you know this wedding is a matter of convenience.'

'But you think she's lovely?'

There was nothing to say to that but the honest answer. Darcy replaced Muriel's chart on the end of the bed, and he sighed.

'Yes, Muriel. I think she's lovely.'

'Excellent,' Muriel said contentedly. 'My family...'

And how was he to find sleep after that?

'There's dogs everywhere!'

Darcy opened his eyes. Jamie was beside him in his wheelchair and a glance at his watch told him it was ten o'clock. He practically yelped.

'There's three dogs,' Jamie announced.

This wasn't making sense. Darcy threw back the covers from his roughly made settee and concentrated on his nephew. It must have been almost dawn before he'd finally slept and, of course, the alarm was in his...in Susie's bedroom.

'*What* did you say?'

'I said there's dogs in the kitchen,' Jamie said patiently. He had the air of a child supremely in charge of his world. 'Three puppies, actually. There's one for you, there's one for me and there's one for Susie. The black one's mine and I'm calling him Buck.'

'Jamie!'

But Jamie was gone, spinning his wheelchair and heading for the kitchen. 'Come and see,' he shouted. 'Three puppies. Just for us.'

Darcy showered and dressed in record time. Still feeling like he was half-asleep, he emerged to find that there were indeed three puppies in the kitchen.

And so was his new bride, her friend Kerry and his nephew. The three of them were crouched on the kitchen floor and puppies were crawling everywhere. They were about two months old—three fat Labrador puppies—two golden and one black.

They were all very, very cute.

'Where,' Darcy said carefully, stopping in the doorway to avoid standing on a pup, 'did these all come from?'

Susie looked up. She was casually dressed again, in her maternity jeans and enormous windcheater, but she still looked just as gorgeous as she had yesterday. Her hair was tousled, she had no make-up on but she made his heart jolt within his chest. It was crazy, but it felt almost as if his heart hadn't really been operating without her.

'There's been a bit of a mix-up,' she said. Her green eyes twinkled and she picked up the closest puppy and hugged it. 'Now, all we have to do is to decide which one goes back.'

'Which *one*?' Darcy stared. 'Wherever they come from, they can *all* go back.'

'We can't do that,' Susie explained. 'No, Dopey, don't

step in your milk. It's for drinking. You'll offend the townsfolk. Hold him, Kerry.'

'What have the townsfolk got to do with it?'

'It's part of the honeymoon package,' Susie explained, refusing to let him get more than a word in edgeways. 'Everyone knows I love dogs, and the postmistress's Labrador had pups just as I arrived back in town. It seems she put one aside for me first thing. As a gift.'

'And then I did the same,' Kerry confessed. She smiled shyly at Darcy, almost as if she expected to be kicked. What had Steve done to her? 'I sort of rang her and said I'd like to give a puppy to you and Susie as my own personal wedding present.' She lifted Dopey and cradled him, milky paws and all. 'He makes a gorgeous gift, don't you think? Though I couldn't imagine how to wrap him.'

'And then there was me,' Susie said, flashing a twinkling smile up at her brand-new husband. 'I sort of thought I'd like to give one to Jamie. So I rang and told Mrs Roebottom to keep one, and I told her today'd be a good day to give it to him.'

'And she never said.' Kerry was laughing openly now. 'She took Susie's and my money without a blink and half an hour ago she turned up with three puppies.' She chortled. 'So you have one each. This place will be almost as chaotic as mine.'

'We're *not* keeping them.'

'Which one will you give back?' Susie was hugging one puppy, Jamie was trying to cling to another and Kerry was holding Dopey and gazing up at him with eyes that were far too anxious. 'Maybe we can't. Three people—three puppies,' Susie said happily as she saw the trace of uncertainty in his eyes and knew she'd won. 'We'll be able to walk them together.'

'Susie, Labradors live for fifteen years.'

'Maybe longer.' She tilted her chin and met his look head on. She knew exactly what he was thinking.

'I don't want a puppy!'

'We're not giving them back.'

'Susie, this is ridiculous.'

'It is, isn't it?' she agreed calmly. 'But Jamie and I have had a family vote. The puppies stay.'

'A family vote?'

'Yes.' She twinkled. 'The family vote is two against one and you're outgunned. Maybe when this baby's born it'll be sensible and level-headed and like cats instead of dogs, but until that time majority rules.' She pushed herself awkwardly to her feet and handed Darcy a pup. 'So meet Dopey. Dopey, meet your daddy. He's your latest responsibility, my love. Get used to it.'

CHAPTER TEN

HE NEVER would.

For the next few days Darcy worked in a haze as he came to terms with the fact that he was finally, irrevocably married.

He couldn't forget it for a moment. Even at work it was always there.

The townsfolk thought this marriage was the best invention since sliced bread and they let him know it at every opportunity. Every patient he saw asked about his wife, asked when their...*their*...baby was due, and asked about Jamie and the puppies. They thought the set-up was perfect.

So did Immigration. Three days after their marriage, an official appeared for a spot check. He arrived at lunchtime. Jamie wheeled to the door and let him in, Darcy was kneeling persuading Dopey to drink—well, Dopey had been deemed his puppy and he wasn't gaining weight like his brother and sister—and Susie was serving up lasagne. She greeted the official with cheerful good humour, served out an extra helping and let the meal go on as planned.

Darcy might have been quiet, but between Susie and Jamie and puppies the meal passed in a riot of laughter and chaos. Eventually the official rose to leave and he shook Darcy by the hand.

'There's no problem with this at all,' he said warmly, looking down at the puppy chewing his shoelace. 'Did you say there were more puppies in the litter?'

'The postmistress has one left,' Jamie told him.

'Then I think I'll collect it on my way home.' The official beamed. 'My daughter's been at me for a dog and I've never seen the need, but looking at you people and how much you're giving...' He sighed. 'I just wish all my immigration checks were as happy as this one.'

'Which means we've done it.' Darcy returned after seeing him out to find Susie hugging Jamie in delight. 'That's the last of our obstacles.'

'So we can be a family for ever.'

'Yes.' But then she looked up at Darcy and knew there was one more obstacle to overcome.

Her husband needed to fall in love...

And he wouldn't.

Every night Darcy made up the bed on the settee and lay in the darkness and swore. He'd been dragged into this whether he liked it or not, and he didn't have the foggiest idea where to go from here.

Let go, an insidious voice whispered in the back of his head. You have all the love you need. Susie and Jamie are forming something you can be part of.

But he couldn't take that final step. The bleakness of his childhood held him back, like a tangible chain stopping him from taking that last step forward.

A small tongue crept out and licked his face and Darcy poked Dopey's nose back under the quilt.

'You're not supposed to be here.' Why had Susie allocated him the runt of the litter? he thought bitterly. Dopey needed extra feeding, extra attention, extra love. He was supposed to be sleeping with his brother and sister, but he cried in the night and each evening after he knew Susie and Jamie slept, Darcy threw back his covers and retrieved the little fellow from his basket.

And gave him what he wanted.

Love?

'Labradors live for fifteen years,' he told the darkness. 'I can't take three Labradors back to Scotland. Maybe I'll just take you.'

Another lick, and then Dopey settled himself to sleep against his chest.

Just take Dopey?

And leave Susie and Jamie and Muriel and Buck and Crater...

Hell!

Susie's baby was overdue.

'You're sure of your dates?'

'Of course I'm sure.' Susie was indignant. 'One thing IVF does is make you sure of your dates. I can name the time I met the test tube, right down to the nearest minute.'

'Then you are overdue.'

'Only four days.' She raised her eyebrows at him. 'Hardly enough for alarm—or induction, Dr Darcy, so don't look at me with drips in your eyes.'

'You wouldn't like to go to Hobart and have the baby?'

'No, I would not.' They were treating a farmer who'd rolled his tractor. He'd had a crash bar fitted so what could have been a major tragedy had ended as one fractured ankle. Susie had anaesthetised while Darcy had set it, but as she rose from her stool she winced and Darcy saw it.

'That wasn't a contraction?'

'That wasn't a contraction.' Her humour was fading with the advancement of her pregnancy. 'I'll tell you when I have a contraction.' She thought about it and decided to admit, doctor or not, that she was as nervous as any first time mother. 'In fact, I suspect I'll tell the whole world when I have my first contraction.' She gave a rueful smile. 'I have an awful feeling that I'll yell.'

'Yelling's permitted. Have you been practising your breathing?'

She sighed. 'Yes, I've been practising my breathing. Sir! As my partner, you should be doing the exercises, too.'

He wasn't amused. 'I know how to breathe, but, Susie, you shouldn't be working.'

'I'm not sick. I can still give an anaesthetic. One fractured ankle wasn't worth asking Ian to come for.'

'No.' It had been simple enough, and yet he was still worried. 'Susie, how about if you just look after the pharmacy from now on?'

'And do no medicine at all?' She shook her head, her blonde curls swinging in the way he loved.

He *liked*, Darcy corrected himself. He liked.

'There's still Jamie to look after,' he told her. 'There's some medicine for you.'

'Jamie's back at school in the afternoons now.'

'But he needs—'

'Medicine? Doctors?' Susie shrugged. 'I don't think so. To tell you the truth, I don't know what he needs.' While she talked she was watching Edward Harrow's chest. The big farmer choked and coughed. She lifted the intubation tube away and his breathing dropped straight into regular rhythm. 'Very nice,' she said approvingly, 'I'll bet he's not even sick. That was the lightest anaesthetic I've tried.'

'You're learning.'

As a compliment it wasn't much, but still she flushed with pleasure. 'I've been reading up,' she admitted. 'But I still don't match the level of surgery you're capable of. Now I've realised how much I need anaesthesia, I wouldn't mind doing a short intensive training session. That is, after that baby's born.' She peeped a smile at him. 'If you can cope with all the babies on your own.'

'What—leave me with your baby?' He was appalled.

'I meant the puppies and Jamie.' She grinned at the look of horror that had washed over his face. 'I won't saddle you with a breast-feeding baby, Dr Hayden.'

'Thank God for that. But, Susie…'

'I know.' Her laughter faded as she checked again on her patient. 'You're still worried about Jamie. Me, too. He's losing muscle mass all the time. It's time he was out of that damned chair. But I can't make him try.'

'Neither of us can.'

Susie nodded. 'I've been on to the paediatrician in Hobart and he says we just have to give him time. But, meanwhile, every day he's in the chair he's growing weaker. He should be out climbing trees, doing all the things a boy his age is capable of.'

'He's not capable.' Darcy adjusted the backslab on the farmer's foot, strapping it so the leg was immobile, then watched the process of Edward surfacing to consciousness. He wasn't quite there yet.

'He's not confident.' Susie sighed and put a hand to a back she had to admit was aching. 'That's all he needs. Confidence. And trust.'

'Surely he should trust us?'

'We're not really a family,' Susie said softly, watching her dials instead of her sort-of husband's face. 'Of all the townsfolk, Jamie's the only one who knows our marriage is really a sham.'

'It isn't a sham. It was a legal wedding.'

'You tell that to your nephew, then,' Susie said stoutly. 'He sees how you behave. Say it as if you believe it. And then try saying it to me.'

Damn.

Darcy worked on throughout the day, but Susie's words kept ringing in his ears.

They were ridiculous.

They were blackmail, he thought. She was pressuring him to love her, and he couldn't love on demand.

He couldn't love at all.

But he did love Jamie, he decided. His sister had brought her tiny son home when he'd been a toddler, and Darcy had fallen so hard that when Jamie had needed him he'd dropped everything and come half a world to help.

And, despite himself, he had to concede that if he could have waved a wand and got rid of Dopey the Dog he wouldn't have done it. The puppy seemed to sense that Darcy was his special person and he followed him everywhere.

So, yes, he loved Dopey.

But Susie?

Susie was the limit. The line he wouldn't cross. She was a bossy, organising, matchmaking medico, and she was living with him because he had no choice. That was all.

Why wouldn't she go to Hobart to have this baby?

But why should she? And why was he worrying? There were no complications, Robert had assured him, and she was only four days overdue. But a man couldn't help worrying. After all, she was his wife.

Even if his love extended to Jamie and Dopey, and that was the end of it!

The week stretched on.

Five days overdue.

Six...

The whole town was holding its breath. Everyone was anxious, it seemed, except Susie.

'I'll deliver when I'm good and ready,' she told the other two doctors. 'I have a feeling my baby's much quieter in than out, so if you're looking at induction you can go find someone else to practise on.'

'You're looking tired, Susie,' Robert told her roughly. 'You shouldn't be doing anything.'

'I'm hardly doing anything. One piddly little surgery and anaesthetics when I'm needed. I'm bored. I want to start a young mother clinic.'

'What?'

'I've been reading about them and we had them in England,' she told the men. 'In the cities there are special prenatal clinics for very young mums. We have more than our share of teenage pregnancies at Whale Beach. I reckon I could do something useful.'

'Later,' Darcy told her uneasily. 'For now you go and put your feet up.'

'My feet are fine where they are. My blood pressure's fine, my baby's heartbeat is strong and there's nothing to worry about.'

And there was nothing Darcy could say to change her mind.

Kerry came in to see her that afternoon, still subdued but coming to terms with all that had happened over the past few weeks.

'You're going really well,' Susie told her. 'Apart from the emotional upheaval you must still be going through.' She looked down at her very pregnant stomach and grimaced. 'I'm sorry, Kerry. It must be hard for you to see me like this.'

'No.' Kerry shook her head. 'It's not. I'm not saying I don't ache for my little one but, if anything, you having this baby will make it easier. When I get desperate I can come in here and give it a cuddle and, heaven knows, there are cuddles enough needed at home.'

'The kids are having trouble adjusting to life without Steve?'

'The littlies miss him,' she admitted. 'He was great with them when they were tiny. Playing with them, I mean. He didn't do any of the work but he was fun. It was only as they got older that he didn't like them. But Lisa and Sam are more settled now he's gone. They were both afraid of him.'

'And you?'

'I should have split with him years ago.' She hesitated. 'I...I'm still afraid of him, though. His parents haven't been supportive of him, and he's very angry.'

'He wouldn't dare come near you. The police are watching him.'

'I know. But he's refusing access visits and...well, he's so angry I don't know how it's going to find an outlet.'

'Well, let's just hope he gets into a brawl at the pub,' Susie said roundly. 'Or gets a job where he can vent his spleen on physical work. You have enough to worry about without fretting over him. OK, Kerry, let's check your blood pressure and then you can go check our three puppies.'

Sunday. Still no baby. Darcy was practically climbing the walls.

'Tomorrow I'll induce you.'

'You're not coming near me.'

'I'll get Robert to induce you, then.'

'If Robert says I need to be induced then I agree,' she said serenely. 'Meanwhile, you keep out of it.'

'I wish Robert was here now.'

'For heaven's sake!' It was Sunday afternoon, the hospital was quiet, there were no scheduled clinics and Robert and one of his mates had gone into the bush on a painting expedition. 'He told us where he was, he has his cellphone with him and he'll be back by five o'clock. It's two now. I'm hardly likely to do anything dramatic in three hours.'

'I don't like it.'

'Darcy, if you don't stop clucking I'm going to throw something at you,' Susie said savagely. In truth, this waiting was getting to her, too—plus the fact that she had to be so near to this man all the time and his worry without love was driving her nuts. 'Go and make Jamie practise his walking.'

'You know that's hopeless.'

'Then toilet-train your puppy. He's the worst of the lot of them. Do anything!' She glared. 'Just stop looking at me like I'm an unexploded bomb. Keep away from me, Darcy Hayden, or I might go off!'

'I wish you would.'

'Go!'

* * *

In the end he did have something to do, and it was almost a relief when it happened. The police sergeant rang, looking for him.

'Darcy, we've got a car crash down at Storm Rocks. It's just been rung in. Someone's trapped in the car.'

'Who is it?'

'I don't know. Whoever rang just said they needed assistance because someone was hurt, and hung up before I could get details. There's no farms down that way so I can't find anything out until I get there. But you may well be needed. Will you come?'

Darcy cast an uneasy glance at Susie but she was outside, throwing balls for the puppies. 'Of course I'll come.' Why wouldn't he? 'Fine.'

'See you there, then.'

'Do you want me to come, too?' Susie asked a few minutes later.

'No.' Darcy wasn't happy about leaving his wife, but it was only two hours until Robert was due back. She was showing no signs of labour. 'Val's not here for Jamie, and it sounds like a single vehicle accident. It could be nothing, but it'll take me half an hour to get there and back.'

'Plus the time you're there.' She wrinkled her nose. 'As long as it's nothing serious.'

'I hope it's not.' He stooped and ruffled Jamie's hair and bestowed a pat on his beloved Dopey. 'I have my cellphone, Susie. Ring if you need me. You guys behave yourselves.'

'You should kiss Susie goodbye,' Jamie said thoughtfully, and Darcy grimaced.

He didn't. But, heaven knew, he wanted to.

Five minutes after Darcy left, the phone went again. Susie struggled inside—she struggled everywhere these days—and lifted it, and then frowned as she listened to a voice she didn't recognise.

'Doc…' It sounded muffled and faint, but urgent. 'Is that the doctor?'

'This is Dr Ellis.' She put on her best professional voice and listened intently. She could hardly hear.

'I...I'm having a fight breathing.' The voice stopped as if he was having trouble finding strength to go on. 'Asthma,' he blurted out at last. 'I used the pump but...' The voice trailed off.

'Where are you?' She snapped the command, trying to rouse someone she suspected was drifting toward unconsciousness.

'The Verity farm. I'm looking after it while they're away. I'm... I'm...'

The line went dead.

Hell!

Salbutamol, oxygen, adrenalin...what else did she need for an acute asthma attack?

An assistant, but there wasn't a nurse to spare. She also needed Val to look after Jamie, but she rang Val's home and there was no reply.

Her mind was racing, all the time aware of how quickly asthma could kill. She had to go. The hospital car was available, but what about Jamie?

Should she send him over to the hospital? His grandmother had been taken for a drive for the afternoon by an old friend. He'd hate to sit in the hospital like a patient.

She used to go with her father, she thought, no matter how urgent the call. Why not Jamie?

'Jamie, we have an urgent case out at the Verity farm,' she called. 'Will you come with me in case I need a hand?'

He hesitated for all of two seconds. His eyes lit up like candles.

'You mean a medical emergency? Great. Let's go.'

The Verity farm was about as far into the back of beyond as any farm was likely to be.

'The Veritys have gone overseas to visit their daughter in New York,' Jamie told her importantly as they drove. He was intent on his new role as medical assistant and was racking his brains for information. 'I wonder who's looking after the place. I didn't think anyone was.'

'I don't know who he is, but he sounded sick.'

'With asthma?' He sounded doubtful.

'Asthma can be a pretty frightening illness,' she told him. 'Especially when you're on your own.'

'I guess.' He eyed her sideways. 'Can I really help?'

'Maybe you should stay outside while I find out what's wrong, and then you can come in.' They'd thrown his wheelchair into the back of the car, but she didn't want him coming in if the man had died. As he well might have, by the sound of him.

He understood. Jamie was one wise child. 'So you want me to stay outside and make myself scarce until you call— in case it's yucky or in case whoever it is hates kids.'

'Got it in one.' She grinned at him. 'You'll make a great medical assistant.'

His small face grew more serious still. 'I hope so.'

Only it wasn't an asthma attack.

Susie knocked on the front door and received no answer. Jamie was pushing his chair out of the car as she knocked. He'd become adept at climbing into the wheelchair himself so she left him to it. Now she gave him a 'stay back' wave, tried the door and found it was unlocked, and went on inside.

The first room was the kitchen. No one. Then the living room. No one there either. Finally the front bedroom. She opened the bedroom door, and Steve Madden grabbed her from behind.

Steve...

She screamed but it was cut off fast and became a muffled gasp as his fingers clapped hard down over her mouth.

'Shut up, bitch, or I'll hurt you.'

'What—?'

But her words were cut off again. A rag was being tied around her face, cutting into her mouth.

'Your fancy doctor of a husband took away my family,' Steve said savagely, and in his voice there was a hatred that was almost implacable. 'Kerry never would have kicked me out if it wasn't for him. She wouldn't have had the guts. So now it's *my* turn to take away *his* family.'

Oh, God, he meant to kill her! Susie struggled wildly in his grasp but she was no match for him. He was big, she was much, much smaller and she was nine months pregnant into the bargain.

'You needn't fight. I'm not planning on killing you just yet. This won't be quick.' He was hauling her wrists together now, and the rope he was using hurt. He was a little bit drunk, she thought, but not drunk enough. 'I'm suffering and so will you,' he told her. 'And so will he when he finds out what happened to you. Eventually...'

He had something planned.

'It'll be nice and slow,' he said, roping her wrists into a knot that cut. 'I've thought it all out. No one comes here. The Veritys aren't due back for months and the chasms in the cliffs are deep enough for my purpose.'

Susie's terrified mind switched from the pain in her wrists and the threats Steve was making. Suddenly all she could think of was Jamie.

Steve didn't know he was here. Please, let him not come in. Please, let him not call out! But Steve didn't know of his presence. Yet.

'We'll take this. I don't want anything to do with you found in the house.' He lifted her doctor's bag, and then paused and opened it. Her cellphone was on top. 'You won't be needing this where you're going. Or your car keys.' He slipped them into his top pocket and he smiled. His smile was pure evil. 'It'd never do if you could call for help—now, would it?'

He pushed her before him out the back door and, blessedly, miraculously, Jamie was nowhere to be seen. Susie stumbled in front of him as he pushed her out behind the house and toward the sea. It was useless to resist. All she'd do was hurt herself—or induce labour. Either way, she had to be passive. For now.

She'd never been so frightened in her life, and ten minutes later, when she saw what was before her, she was doubly so.

Dear God...

The chasm slashed into an outreach of the rocky peninsula, about five hundred yards from the house. To Susie's terrified gaze, it was shaped like a huge grave, maybe twenty feet deep, and it had steep, smooth sides of granite.

For one dreadful minute she thought he intended to push her over the edge, but he looked at her appalled face and he smirked.

'No. You're not getting out of it that easily. I want you to suffer for longer than a couple of seconds while you fall.' He untied the gag from her face. 'I don't want you choking either. That'd be too quick. I want it to be slow. You can yell all you like from down there, and no one will hear you. The sounds of the sea will block everything. You can yell until you die and then your husband will know what it is not to have a family.'

She caught her breath and tried desperately to stay calm. To stay in medical mode. 'Steve, don't do this,' she whispered. 'I know things are bad, but I can help you.'

'Don't call me Steve.' He must be on drugs, Susie thought as she saw the glazing of his eyes and the pinpricks of pupils. His hatred was beyond reason, and she knew he was almost beyond hearing.

They were now at the very edge of the chasm, and she was sick with fear. Beside them was a coil of thick rope which he'd obviously left here some time before. Swiftly, as if he was afraid of being followed, he looped one end of the rope through the knot holding her wrists together. He tested it for strength and then he nodded, satisfied.

'OK,' he snarled. 'Now it's time for you to go where you belong. Sit down and slide over the edge.'

She couldn't. She stared at him in horror but his face was implacable.

'I'll lower you slowly or I'll push you,' he said indifferently. 'If it's any comfort I badly want you alive. For a while. I want whoever finally finds you to know you've suffered for a very long time. So I'll lower you slowly but I can be persuaded otherwise very easily. So get over the side, or I'll push you!'

And, with one final look at his face, she went.

It was the most terrifying thing she'd ever done. Hooked by the wrists, she dangled helplessly, unable to find any sort of foothold in the smooth rock.

Even for Steve it was an effort not to drop her but, mad or not, the man was doggedly intent on fulfilling his plans. Slowly he lowered her, while her arms screamed in agony and her mind screamed that any moment he'd let go.

He didn't. She bumped down, her back thumping in and out against the rocky sides. Finally her feet hit solid rock.

Now what? Susie gazed about her in horror. The chasm was maybe twenty feet long and eight feet wide, and on all sides the rock walls rose smoothly to twenty feet above her. One gap broke the rock wall, and that gap led straight down to the sea, a sheer drop of fifty feet to rocks and crashing waves underneath. And underfoot there was rock and more rock. Not a vestige of vegetation. Nothing.

Her vision of an open grave grew even stronger.

Finally she looked up. Steve was staring down at his prisoner, and his face was twisted into an expression of evil satisfaction.

'I've got a present for you,' he said, and his smile was almost pleasant.

He lifted his end of the rope high into the air—and threw it down on top of her.

'Suffer,' he said. And then, as an afterthought, he tossed down her doctor's bag, which smashed open and scattered its contents over the rocks.

'That's what I think of your medicine,' he said.
And then he walked away.

Jamie.

For the first minutes after Steve left her all she could think of was Jamie.

He'd be by the car. He'd be waiting. Steve had her car keys. He'd go back to the car and move it. Of course, that's what he'd do. And Jamie would be there.

Steve had set this up to hurt Darcy by killing his wife. Blessedly he hadn't included Jamie in his plan, but if Jamie was there she was under no illusion as to what would happen.

She couldn't call out to warn him. To call out to Jamie might let Steve know he was here, and who knew how long the man would stay nearby?

Dear God…

She found a scalpel from her bag and spent a frustrating and painful twenty minutes loosening her wrists. Finally she did it, but it was of no help at all.

God help Jamie…

CHAPTER ELEVEN

'WHERE are they?'

Darcy sounded deeply worried. Robert was back at the hospital, Lorna was with him, Val had come over, and they were all facing a very junior nurse in the hospital foyer.

'All she said was that she was going out to an asthma case and she was taking Jamie.' The young nurse was defensive in the face of Darcy's anxiety. 'She said she'd take her cellphone with her.'

'It's turned off.'

'She wouldn't have turned it off,' Lorna said. 'She knows the rules about being a country doctor.'

They all did. The golden rule was to stay in contact at all times.

'But my call to a car accident was a false alarm,' Darcy said slowly, thinking it through and not liking it. 'There was no accident. It was a hoax.'

'You think Susie's call was a hoax, too?' Lorna was also looking worried.

'I don't know.' Darcy raked his fingers through his hair. 'Asthma, you said? Wasn't there anything more than that?'

'It was in the middle of visiting hours and everyone wanted me to do flowers.' The young nurse was practically in tears. 'Maybe she said where she was going, but I didn't hear.'

'Great!'

'Maybe there's something wrong with her phone.' Robert was trying to calm things down. 'The battery could well be flat and she's not receiving.'

'It's been too long.'

'Then maybe she took Jamie for a drive after seeing her

patient. If she hasn't figured there's something wrong with her phone then she wouldn't know we'd be worried.' Robert glanced at his watch. 'It's only five. It's hardly time for her to think we'd be worrying.'

'But—'

'It's just because she's so pregnant.' Robert placed a comforting hand on Darcy's shoulder. 'Darcy, calm down. You're acting like every other expectant father.'

'Then why was my call a false alarm?' he said stubbornly. 'Why would someone call the police and report an accident if not to get me out of the way?'

'Now you're being paranoid,' Robert told him. 'Kids make false calls all the time.'

'Sergeant Browning said the caller was an adult male.'

The phone rang in the nurses' station. Lorna left them to answer it.

'Are you sure you can't remember where she said she was going?' Darcy was practically pleading with the young nurse but she shook her head in distress.

'I'm so sorry. I just can't...'

'Look, I'm sure we're worrying about nothing,' Robert said, but then paused as, behind them, Lorna replaced the receiver. He could tell by her face that something was wrong. 'Lorna?' He turned to face her. They all did. 'What is it?'

'I don't—'

'Just say it,' Robert said roughly, and his face was now as tightly worried as Darcy's.

'Oh, Robert!'

'Lorna!'

She caught herself. 'That was the Devonport police,' she managed finally, and she sounded sick. 'There was an accident about an hour ago just outside Devonport. A car ran off the road and hit a tree. According to the identification they found in his wallet, the driver's Steve Madden, but the car he was driving is registered to the hospital.' She took a deep breath. 'They described it and it fits. It's the car Susie was driving.'

'Susie?' The words sounded as if they were dragged from Darcy's lips, and it was almost a groan. 'Was she in the car? And Jamie?'

Lorna closed her eyes, and then somehow found the courage to go on. 'There's no sign of either of them,' she told them. 'They weren't in the car. Steve's unconscious, and by the sound of his injuries it might be quite some time—if ever—before anyone's able to talk to him.'

Susie's back hurt.

It didn't feel bruised. The pain was more than that. She must have wrenched it as Steve lowered her down the cliff face, she thought, because it stabbed like it was on fire.

But she had other things to think about than her back. Like…how was she going to get out of here?

She glanced at her watch for the thousandth time. It was two hours since Steve had dumped her here. She'd explored every inch of her prison and there was no way out.

But overriding every other concern were her thoughts of Jamie.

'Susie?'

The call was so faint that she thought she must be dreaming. She'd been sitting on a rock, but now she jumped to her feet and then winced as the pain in her back struck home again.

'Susie!'

'Jamie!' Blessedly it was Jamie. His worried face was peering over the edge of the cliff, and he sounded as if he couldn't believe it was really her.

'Jamie, don't come closer. You'll fall.'

'I'm lying on my tummy,' he said with injured dignity, and then his voice quavered with relief. 'I thought he'd thrown you over the cliff. I thought you were dead.'

'Well, I'm not…'

'I heard you scream,' he said. 'So I hid, and I hid for ages because I'm scared of Mr Madden, but then after he drove away in our car I came looking for you.'

'In your wheelchair!'

'I found out that I can walk if I hold onto things,' he said, still in that small, scared voice. 'And I crawled a bit. It took me ages to find you.'

'Oh, Jamie…' What he'd been through, to make it this far…

What now? She was fighting to gather her wits—to think of what was best. What they desperately needed was a phone.

'We need to phone for help. Jamie, can you manage to get back to the house and phone?'

'I tried that,' he told her, still slightly affronted that she was doubting his intelligence. 'After Mr Madden drove away I went into the house. The phone's dead. The Veritys must have had it disconnected while they're away.'

Impasse.

Now what? The Verity farm was a good four miles from the main road, and the house was accessed via a rough farm track. Even if Jamie could somehow walk a little, he'd never make it that far. He could use his wheelchair, but if it tipped, or if Steve got rid of the car and came back to gloat…

There was nothing for it. She had to get out of here by herself.

'Jamie, there's a rope down here,' she told him, trying to ignore the messages her back was giving her. She'd been able to do this as a girl, so why not now? 'Steve threw it down on top of me. If I tie an end to a rock and throw it up, do you think you could tie the other end to a tree? Really, really tightly?'

'I'm Cub Scouts,' Jamie said indignantly. 'Course I can. Reef knot or clover hitch?'

'A clover hitch, I reckon,' Susie said, sighing in relief. Bless all Scouts… 'But find a good strong tree.'

'I'm not stupid.' He was still peering anxiously down at

her. 'You think you can climb up the rope? You're pretty fat.'

'Remind me to cross ice cream off my shopping list,' she said dourly. 'Watch your mouth.'

'But you *are* fat.'

'Jamie!'

'And you'll never be able to throw the rope up this high.'

'Stand back and watch me,' Susie said. 'I wasn't Whale Beach junior discus-throwing champion for nothing. Sampson Susie, that's what they called me.'

Sampson Susie did it but it was a Herculean effort. On the third try, the end of the rope landed near where Jamie lay. He took it and spent a good three minutes securing it to a tree. Finally, the rope attached to his satisfaction, he returned to peer anxiously over the edge.

'It's tight enough now for you to climb. If you can.'

But he was right to doubt her. She couldn't climb anywhere.

The back pains she'd been so studiously ignoring were now threatening to overwhelm her. Her rock-throwing had been the last straw. Now she was sitting with her back against a rock and she was concentrating on her breathing like her life depended on it.

'Susie!' Jamie stared down at her, and he sounded terrified.

She couldn't answer him. The pain was overwhelming. How long ago was it since the last wave of pain? A minute?

Dear God!

The pain receded then—just a little—and she opened her eyes, just in time to see Jamie slithering down the rope toward her.

'No!' He was her last link with life, and he was trapping himself, too. 'Jamie, no!'

It was too late. He was slithering the last few feet, his wrists twisted into the rope to slow his decent as if he'd done this millions of times before.

And then he was by her side.

* * *

'What's he done with them?'

Back at the hospital Darcy was sick with dread. He was pacing as he waited for the police sergeant to arrive, and he was listening to no one. 'He's mad. He's violent and the locals say he's high on drugs. He could have done anything.'

'I'm sure he wouldn't,' Robert said uneasily, though he didn't believe it for one moment.

'Oh, God, where are they?'

'Jamie, you know I'm having my baby?'

'I figured that.' The small boy had crawled over to where she lay. His face was fierce with concentration and worry, and his mind was totally focussed. How could he be only ten years old? 'Tell me what to do.'

He sounded about twenty instead of ten, Susie thought wildly, and she gave an almost hysterical giggle. Then the next contraction rolled in and she found she was gripping Jamie's hand like she was drowning. Ten years old or not, she needed him.

'Just be here for me,' she said.

'I can do that.' He looked down at their linked hands and his wise little face tightened with responsibility. 'I won't leave you alone. But when the baby arrives, tell me what to do, Susie.'

He was a ten-year-old obstetrician but he was all that she had.

'In my bag,' she said between gasps. 'Steve threw it down. There's sterile dressings. Just...just spread them under me so the baby has something clean to be born onto.'

'I can do that.' He started to haul off his windcheater. 'I'll put this under it so it'll be soft.'

'No.' She shook her head, trying desperately to focus on something other than the pain. 'Keep your windcheater on so we have something warm to wrap the baby with.'

He thought that through and found it acceptable. 'OK. Anything else?'

It was a normal birth, Susie thought wildly. A normal presentation. Nothing could go wrong. Unless...

She waited until the next contraction passed and then made herself keep talking. 'Find some scissors, too,' she told him. 'And there's twine. We might need that. Jamie, the only thing that could go wrong is if the baby's born with the cord around its neck. Listen...listen while I tell you what to do.'

Darkness fell over the hospital, but there was no hint of sleep. Every able-bodied person in the district was searching.

But they didn't know what they were looking for.

'He could have put them out of the car anywhere between here and Devonport,' the sergeant said heavily.

Or pushed them over a cliff, Darcy thought. Or buried them. Or...

He was going mad!

'She's nine months pregnant,' Darcy said into the stillness. 'Surely he wouldn't hurt her. Surely...'

It was Susie who was uppermost in Darcy's thoughts, Robert decided as he watched his younger partner. He'd married Susie to protect Jamie, yet now he was crazy with fear for Susie—the wife he hadn't wanted.

So Robert decided he'd just test him.

'I guess this is one way of getting rid of all your responsibilities,' he said softly—and waited for the reaction.

It came. Darcy turned to him with such a look of blazing fury that Robert took an instinctive step back.

'You think I *want* to get rid of Susie?'

'You didn't want to marry her.'

And then Darcy acknowledged to himself what subconsciously he'd known from the moment he'd clapped eyes on her.

'Oh, God, Robert, I love her,' he said bleakly. 'I love Jamie, but Susie's my *wife*. My love. She's my life.'

* * *

Nothing and nothing and nothing.

'I'm going out of my mind,' Darcy said. 'Is there no news from Devonport?'

'Steve's deteriorated,' Robert told him. 'They think he's overdosed and that's why he's crashed. They doubt he'll wake.'

'What the *hell* has he done with them?'

Charlotte Louise was born by moonlight. She was born with the cord around her neck, but Susie had explained things clearly. Jamie felt it as the head emerged, and luckily it was loose enough to deal with easily. Without a fuss and with the concentration of someone who knew the world rested entirely on his young shoulders, Jamie slipped the cord carefully, very carefully, over the baby's head. Then he delivered the shoulders and let the little one slide onto his neatly prepared bed of dressings.

After that, the birth was blessedly normal.

Following Susie's whispered instructions—which were difficult to hear when Charlotte was making her presence felt in no uncertain terms—Jamie cut and tied the cord. Then he wrapped the baby carefully in his windcheater and handed her to her mother as though she were the most precious thing in the world.

And as if he was the most experienced obstetrician.

Finally he cleared up as best he could, sat down on hard rock—and burst into tears.

Susie was so exhausted she was almost past speech, but she had to speak now. Jamie had wedged her soft leather doctor's bag under her head as a makeshift pillow. She held her daughter tight in one arm, and with the other she reached out and pulled Jamie to lie beside her.

'Well done, Jamie...'

'We did it,' he quavered, and she hugged him tighter.

'*You* did it,' she told him. 'And now I have two kids. My

two wonderful, wonderful kids. You're the best there is, Jamie.'

His tears dried and he nestled closer. And thought about it. Comforted and safe, the small boy was allowed to emerge from the serious adult who'd just delivered a baby.

'That,' he announced in a voice that barely wobbled, 'was the yuckiest, blurkiest, most disgusting thing I've ever done. Yuck, yuck and double yuck!

'And you did it brilliantly,' Susie said through her own tears, looking at the downy head of her perfect little daughter. 'Oh, Jamie, what would I have done without you?'

'Died?' he said hopefully, and despite all her trauma and her exhaustion Susie managed to chuckle. Jamie's chest was expanding by the minute, and his small-boy ghoulishness was wonderful after the despair of the last few hours.

'I guess maybe I would have,' she told him, because that was what he clearly expected.

He nestled closer, profoundly pleased, but also profoundly weary. It had been some day for a small boy recovering from CFS. 'What'll we do now?' he asked.

She wasn't up to making plans. They'd have to wait. 'I don't know about you,' she whispered, holding him close, 'but, Jamie, I'm afraid I don't have a choice. I'm going to sleep.'

And when Susie woke it was dawn. Jamie was already awake and he had it all organised. He really was the most intelligent child.

'I've been thinking.'

She blinked. 'Yes?'

'Yes.' He was all concentration. 'And I have a plan. There are always firespotters looking over the whole district in the summer. All we need to do is light a fire to attract their attention.'

She thought it through and found a flaw. 'We can't light a fire down here.' It was bare rock.

'So I'll climb up the rope and go back to the house.'

'Jamie, you can't.'

'Yes, I can.' He flexed his muscles—Superman personified. 'See. I'm strong. My arms have been getting stronger and stronger from pushing my wheelchair. And they taught us at Cubs how to go hand over hand so fast you don't fall.' He hesitated and thought some more. 'I'll take my shoes off and throw them up to the top so I can use my toes to help, too. Then I'll put them on again when I reach the top.'

This from a child who'd been wheelchair-bound?

'Jamie—'

'And then I'll find something at the Veritys' farm to light.' He frowned, thinking it through some more. 'It'll have to be something big to attract the firespotters' attention, but I don't think I should set the house on fire. Do you?'

'No,' Susie said faintly. 'I don't.'

'But they won't come if they just think it's a barbecue. It'll have to be something like a shed. Something away from the house.' He brightened. 'Maybe they'll have a woodstack.'

She shouldn't let him do it, Susie thought wildly. He was so young.

But what choice did they have? There was no water down here, and nothing to eat. They were both dry and hungry now, and it was only going to get worse. Soon neither of them would have the strength to climb the rope.

'Jamie, if you're sure you know how to light a fire safely…'

'Of course I'm sure. They've taught us lots of stuff at Cubs.' He grinned. 'I can even rub two sticks together if I have to.'

'Oh, Jamie!'

'But I bet I can find some matches and paper in the house. Now, you're not to worry.' He was sounding more adult every minute. 'It might take me a while to get there, and even longer to light the fire, but I bet I can do it.'

* * *

Ten o'clock.

Eleven.

Nothing.

Darcy was going out of his mind.

'Sir?'

Casualty had been turned into a makeshift search headquarters. The boy who entered was in his late teens, and he looked as if he wasn't sure whether he should be there.

'Ben?' The police sergeant looked up as the boy entered. 'What's up?'

Ben fidgeted, still unsure. He was in dirt-stained jeans and a ripped windcheater, and he was almost backing out of the door as he spoke. It was as if he was sure he was wasting their time.

'You know I'm on firespotting duties over the university break?'

'Yes.' The policeman frowned. 'There's no real fire danger today, though. It's mild and there's no wind.'

'No, but I was still up in the tower. It's my job.' He gave a rueful smile. 'I've just been relieved. I know the fire brigade are all involved in the search and the guy who relieved me said we shouldn't worry you with this, but...'

'But what, boy?'

'There's a fire,' he told him. 'It's only a little one, like someone burning a heap of rubbish. It's mostly smoke and it's not moving. It started an hour ago and already it's dying down. Normally we'd send someone out to remind people fire restrictions are in force, but today, with...with all the drama we wouldn't bother. But it's belching a heap of smoke—and it's coming from the Veritys' place.'

'So?' Darcy was so sick with fear that this interruption seemed stupid.

But the police sergeant had focussed.

'You might have something, Ben,' he said slowly. He turned to Darcy. 'The Veritys have been away for months,' he told him. 'Their place is deserted—and it's about the most remote farm in the district. If someone was stuck out there and the phone was out...'

'It is out, sir,' Ben said diffidently. 'I tried it when I came down from the tower, but the operator says the line's been disconnected while they're away. That's what I was wondering. If the Veritys are away, who lit the fire?'

'What are we waiting for?' Darcy was striding out the door before anyone else moved, and the others were left to follow.

The cavalry arrived to find Jamie sitting on the Verity farm gate, waiting for them.

Jamie...

Darcy was out of the leading police car almost before it stopped, gathering his nephew to him in an all-enveloping hug. He shoved his face in the boy's hair and his heart almost stopped, right there and then. 'Jamie, are you OK?'

'Yep.' Jamie was grinning into his uncle's sweater. It had taken longer than expected, but his plan had finally worked. 'I'm not in my wheelchair,' he said proudly.

'I can see that.' The others were out of the cars now—the fire chief, the police sergeant, State Emergency Services officers... Before their eyes, what had been a small wooden outbuilding was a now burnt-out shell. It still poured out black smoke. Jamie had cleared the surroundings, filled the shed with a heap of old tyres and had then set it alight. The residual smoke was black and putrid.

But Darcy only had eyes for Jamie.

'Susie...' he said, and his voice cracked with fear.

But the little boy's grin widened still.

'They're OK, too.'

'They?'

'Susie and our baby,' he told them happily. 'It's a girl. Susie's going to call her Charlie, and I delivered her all by myself!'

Still Susie and Charlotte Louise waited.

Jamie...

Darcy…

They were entwined in her heart, she thought as she dozed and worried and dozed and worried through the long, long morning.

Jamie and Darcy. The two men in her life.

Where was Jamie? She was so frightened for him that she felt sick. Jamie, lighting a fire. Jamie, burnt…

Dear God, she loved him so much. If anything happened to him she couldn't bear it.

It was time for bargaining, she thought. When she and Darcy had married there had been another option they hadn't considered. She was considering it now.

She loved Jamie. She loved Darcy but he didn't love her. Therefore…

Therefore if Jamie was all right then she'd care for him. She'd look after him as her own—and she'd let Darcy go.

'I promise,' she whispered. 'I can cope on my own. I can!'

As if in immediate response to her promise, there was a yell from the top of the cliff and she looked up.

They were both there.

Jamie and Darcy.

Her loves.

CHAPTER TWELVE

DARCY didn't get Susie alone for the rest of the day.

The SES officers reached her first, lowering a stretcher and a team of their men. Then Robert pulled rank and was lowered as well.

'I'm her doctor, and I'm not completely incapacitated,' he growled, so it was Robert who reached her and hugged her first. He reassured her about Jamie and examined her new little daughter.

She gripped his hand and said, 'Darcy.'

He winked and said, 'That husband of yours has been going quietly crazy. It won't hurt to play hard to get for a bit. Let's leave him to sweat.'

She thought that through, but she remembered her promise. She loved him so much, she thought. But she loved Jamie, and Jamie was safe. If Darcy wanted to go...

And then the world moved in. SES men strapped her to the stretcher, and another strapped Charlotte in a cradle against his chest. Then mother and child were carefully inched to the top of the cliff where they were surrounded by joyous well-wishers.

And Darcy.

There was so much he wanted to say, but in the presence of others he could say nothing. He could only watch as she hugged her tiny baby and looked up at him with eyes that were over-bright from exhaustion and relief.

'You look after Jamie,' Robert told him, twinkling at his frustration, and he did. He needed to.

The little boy was covered in scratches and bruises. He was filthy, exhausted and dehydrated, but he was so pleased that he could hardly contain himself. Darcy cleaned him, anointed his scratches, fed him and tucked him into bed. Surrounded by praise and by puppies, the world was his oyster.

'I did it,' he said over and over again. 'I saved them.'

If ever there was a magic psychological cure for a recovering CFS patient, this was it, Darcy thought wonderingly as he tucked his nephew safely under the covers and restrained a pup from licking his face. Jamie had been an unwanted child for so long, and now he was loved and he was secure and he'd earned his place firmly in the ranks of the town's heroes. Darcy looked at the wheelchair sitting beside Jamie's bed, and thought they might just as well throw it away right now.

'I walked,' Jamie said, following Darcy's train of sight. 'I had to. My legs felt really, really wobbly but I walked.'

'You did.' Darcy gathered him to him and hugged him hard. And then he said what had to be said.

'Jamie, you know when I came here one of the kids taunted you and said you should be grateful. That if I hadn't come you'd be a foster-kid?'

Jamie's tired eyes took in his uncle's face. 'Yeah.' He remembered. Kids had the capacity to be cruel, and Lorna had overheard this taunt and passed it on to Darcy. 'I suppose... I suppose he was right,' he said doubtfully.

'No. He wasn't right,' Darcy said strongly. 'It's me who's the lucky one. Not you. If I hadn't come here, I'd never have met Susie. I'd never have had a great kid like you and I'd never have had you around to save my whole family.'

'Your whole family?'

'Susie and Charlotte Louise and you. My whole wonderful family.'

Jamie was tired but he was still game. 'But you don't love Susie.'

'Whoever told you that?'

'You did,' Jamie retorted. 'It's just a marriage so you get to stay here.'

'Maybe it was at the start,' Darcy admitted. 'Maybe it was when I was stupid. But no longer. Now it's a marriage because I love you all very, very much.' He looked down at the squirming puppies and he grinned. 'Even Crater and Buck and Dopey.'

'Have you told Susie that?'

'No,' he admitted, laying Jamie back down on the pillows and watching his eyelids sink toward sleep. 'But as soon as I can tear Lorna and Robert away from her, I intend to do just that.'

Midnight.

She should be asleep, Darcy thought. She probably was. But Lorna and Robert had finally left, the wards were silent and there was no one about. He could just see...

He pushed open the door of the maternity ward and stepped inside, closing the door silently beside him.

Yes, Susie was asleep. The crib was by her side and her daughter snoozed peacefully beside her.

What he had to say could wait. He had all the time in the world, he thought, and there was no way he'd wake her.

He'd pull a chair over to her bed and just watch. For however long it took.

Susie was dreaming and he was there. Darcy.

It was the loveliest dream. There were no rocks, no pain, no threats. Jamie was safe, her little daughter was asleep beside her and the man she loved was by her side.

She opened her eyes, and there he was. Her dream was real.

'Darcy.'

He didn't say a word. For a long, long moment there was silence between them, and then, almost shyly, Susie reached out and took his hand in hers.

'Thank you for coming,' she said, and her voice was absurdly formal.

Hell, where to start?

'Susie—'

'No.' She shook her head and it was enough to stop his initial urge to lean forward and gather her into his arms. He hesitated, and the feel of his hand beneath her fingers sent warmth right through him.

He'd been such a fool. To have this for the taking—and to not take it...

'Love...' It was the faintest of whispers, as if the word was dragged out of him. All the uncertainty in the world was in that word, and Susie misread it.

'I'm not your love.' There was the hint of bleakness in her voice but she steeled herself to keep it back. She'd had such a long time to think things through. All that dreadful morning.

'Darcy, we've been stupid,' she managed.

He'd been stupid. How on earth could she think she'd been anything of the kind? He shook his head. 'Why?'

'Because we don't need to be married.'

How had she figured that one out? The pronouncement took his breath away.

'Why ever not?'

'Because I love Jamie.'

This conversation wasn't going the way he planned. Darcy shook his head again, clearing cobwebs. In truth, he hadn't slept at all the night before, and he was probably more exhausted than she was. Nothing was making sense. 'Susie, I don't understand. I'm sorry.'

'I'm sorry, too,' she said sadly, pulling her hand from his. 'For not seeing it before. But it's the solution to everything. I love Jamie so much. You can't believe how wonderful he was. He can stay here with me. It's as simple as that. I have Robert and Muriel and Val and the whole town to help me care for my two children and my three puppies. We can cope. And you can go back to your beloved Scotland.'

It was as simple as that.

She was granting him his freedom, he thought numbly. He could walk away from all the ties that he'd never wanted.

He could simply walk away.

No!

'But Dopey would pine.' As a gut reaction it was ridiculous, but at least it made her smile.

'You could take him, too. Mind, you'd have to toilet train him to get him on the plane.'

But he was back on track. 'I have a better idea,' he told her, and his voice was so shaky that she could hardly hear him. His hand reached out and gripped hers again. He held her tight, and the terror of the last twenty-four hours came sweeping back. 'If you'll listen.'

'But you—'

'Susie!' It was a curt command and she blinked.

'Yes?'

'Stop organising and shut up for a minute,' he told her.

'But—'

'Or I'll do something drastic,' he warned.

She eyed him sideways, liking the tone of his voice. 'Like what?'

He thought of the direst possible threat, and he just knew that brain needles or enemas or even wheelchair racing wheels didn't cut it here.

'Like kiss you?' he said—and waited.

'Fate worse than death,' she retorted, and then she really heard what he'd said and she gasped. 'You mean, if I don't shut up, I'll get kissed?'

'That's the plan,' he told her.

'But—'

'That's it! You asked for it.' He lifted her into his arms and he did just that.

For a very long time.

And when they finally pulled apart—only inches but enough to get their breath back—things had changed. The world had changed. Susie's eyes were glowing with a million stars. She was lying back on her pillows, her gorgeous curls were splayed out over the white linen and Darcy was looking down at her with all the love in the world, right there in his eyes.

He hardly had to say what was in his heart—but he did all the same.

'I love you, Susie Ellis Hayden,' he told her, and the world righted on its axis—exactly as it was meant to be.

'You...you're just saying that because you've had a shock.' She was still intent on letting him off the hook if he wanted, but he was hooked tight, and it was the most desirable hook he'd ever felt. This woman was his wife. His beloved Susie.

'We had to have an emergency wedding,' he told her.

'Yes, and—'

'And then I stuffed it up by imagining it could only be a marriage of convenience. But, Susie, losing you...'

'Hush.' She put a finger on his lips to stop the tremor. 'I'm safe. We're all safe.'

'We're safe, but I don't want a marriage of convenience,' he told her. 'I want a real one. Starting right now.'

There was joy bubbling within her—a joy so great she thought she'd burst with happiness.

'You mean...me and you? For ever?'

'And Jamie and Charlie Louise and Dopey and Buck and Crater,' he said, and he peeped down at his infant daughter and liked what he saw. 'She's beautiful,' he said in satisfaction. 'Just like her mother. You produce the most gorgeous babies, my love. How do you feel about having another? Not right away, but in a year or two. When we've house-trained this lot.'

'You can't mean it,' she said, but she knew he did. How could she doubt it? This was her happy-ever-after, and it was happening right now. 'You can't really want us. Not for ever.'

'Certainly for ever,' Darcy said sternly, turning back to take her into his arms. 'Certainly for ever, my love. From this moment on, consider yourself properly married.'

'But—'

'No buts.' There was no room for them anyway. No doubts. No buts. Nothing. 'We might have had an emergency wedding, my beautiful Susie, but it was no marriage. From now on, though…this is an emergency marriage. Starting right now!'

MILLS & BOON®

Live the emotion

Her Latin Lover's Revenge

When only seduction will settle the score!

In November 2005, By Request brings back three favourite romances by our bestselling Mills & Boon authors:

Don Joaquin's Revenge by Lynne Graham
A Sicilian Seduction by Michelle Reid
Lazaro's Revenge by Jane Porter

Don't miss these passionate stories!

On sale 4th November 2005

Available at most branches of WHSmith, Tesco, ASDA, Borders, Eason, Sainsbury's and most bookshops

Visit www.millsandboon.co.uk

More drama and emotion for your money!

SPECIAL EDITION™
Extra

First Born

USA TODAY Bestselling Award-Winning Author

LINDSAY McKENNA

presents an emotional, dramatic tale in her bestselling series Morgan's Mercenaries.

Jason Trayhern was a skilled fighter pilot going into combat with a new partner. And she was just too...*female*.

If they hoped to see a future, together or apart, they needed to survive this dangerous mission first!

'When it comes to action and romance, nobody does it better than McKenna.'
—*Romantic Times*

Available at most branches of WHSmith, Tesco, ASDA, Borders, Eason, Sainsbury's and most bookshops

Visit www.silhouette.co.uk

MILLS & BOON

Live the emotion

Tender romance™

WIFE AND MOTHER FOREVER by *Lucy Gordon*
(The Rinucci Brothers)

Evie Wharton is a free spirit – the complete opposite to millionaire single dad Justine Dane – but she wants to help his troubled son. Evie soon discovers that behind Justin's dark demeanour hides a painful past. Can she help Justin face his demons and show him how to love again?

CHRISTMAS GIFT: A FAMILY by *Barbara Hannay*

Happy with his life as a wealthy bachelor, Hugh Strickland is stunned to discover he has a daughter – he's absolutely terrified! Luckily Jo Berry gives him a hand with the little girl – soon it seems that the ideal solution would be to give each other the perfect Christmas gift: a family…

MISTLETOE MARRIAGE by *Jessica Hart*

This Christmas Sophie Beckwith must face the ex who dumped her and then married her sister! Only one person can help: her best friend Bram. Bram used to be engaged to Sophie's sister, and now, determined to show the lovebirds that they've moved on, he has a plan: he's proposed to Sophie!

TAKING ON THE BOSS by *Darcy Maguire*
(Office Gossip)

Tahlia has tried so hard to prove herself at work – but Case Darrington has stolen her promotion! And it doesn't help that he makes her go gooey inside whenever she looks at him! She wants to prove that it should be *her* sitting in Case's chair, but that means getting up-close-and-personal with her new boss…

On sale 4th November 2005

Available at most branches of WHSmith, Tesco, ASDA, Borders, Eason, Sainsbury's and most bookshops

Visit www.millsandboon.co.uk

MILLS & BOON®

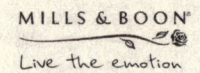

Live the emotion

Modern
romance™

THE DISOBEDIENT VIRGIN by Sandra Marton

Catarina Mendes has been dictated to all her life. Now, with her twenty-first birthday, comes freedom – but it's freedom at a price. Jake Ramirez has become her guardian. He must find a man for her to marry. But Jake is so overwhelmed by her beauty that he is tempted to keep Cat for himself...

A SCANDALOUS MARRIAGE by Miranda Lee

Sydney entrepreneur Mike Stone has a month to get married – or he'll lose a business deal worth billions. Natalie Fairlane, owner of the *Wives Wanted* introduction agency, is appalled by his proposition! But the exorbitant fee Mike is offering for a temporary wife is *very* tempting...!

SLEEPING WITH A STRANGER by Anne Mather

Helen Shaw's holiday on the island of Santos should be relaxing. But then she sees Greek tycoon Milos Stephanides. Years ago they had an affair – until, discovering he was untruthful, Helen left him. Now she has something to hide from Milos...

AT THE ITALIAN'S COMMAND by Cathy Williams

Millionaire businessman Rafael Loro is used to beautiful women who agree to his every whim – until he employs dowdy but determined Sophie Frey! Sophie drives him crazy! But once he succeeds in bedding her, his thoughts of seduction turn into a need to possess her...

On sale 4th November 2005

Available at most branches of WHSmith, Tesco, ASDA, Borders, Eason, Sainsbury's and most bookshops

Visit www.millsandboon.co.uk

MILLS & BOON®
Live the emotion

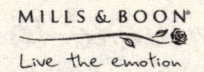

1005/01b

Modern
romance™

PRINCE'S PLEASURE *by Carole Mortimer*

Reporter Tyler Harwood is ecstatic when she gets the chance to interview handsome Hollywood actor Zak Prince. Zak finds working with this stunning brunette fun! But someone is out to make mischief from their growing closeness – and soon candid pictures appear in the press...

HIS ONE-NIGHT MISTRESS *by Sandra Field*

Lia knew that billionaire businessman Seth could destroy her glittering career. But he was so attractive that she succumbed to him – for one night! Eight years on, when he sees Lia in the papers, Seth finds that he has a love-child, and is determined to get her back!

THE ROYAL BABY BARGAIN *by Robyn Donald*

Prince Caelan Bagaton has found the woman who kidnapped his nephew and now he is going to exact his revenge... For Abby Metcalfe, the only way to continue taking care of the child is to agree to Caelan's demands – and that means marriage!

BACK IN HER HUSBAND'S BED *by Melanie Milburne*

Seeing Xavier Knightly, the man she divorced five years ago, changes Carli Gresham's life. Their marriage may be dead, but their desire is alive – and three months later Carli tells Xavier a shocking secret! But by wanting her to love him again Xavier faces the biggest battle of his life...

Don't miss out!
On sale 4th November 2005

Available at most branches of WHSmith, Tesco, ASDA, Borders, Eason, Sainsbury's and most bookshops

Visit www.millsandboon.co.uk

Look forward to all these wonderful books this Christmas

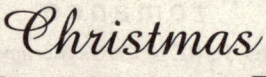

Introducing a very special holiday collection

Inside you'll find

Roses for Christmas *by Betty Neels*
Eleanor finds herself working with the forceful Fulk van Hensum from her childhood – and sees that he hasn't changed. So why does his engagement to another woman upset her so much?

Once Burned *by Margaret Way*
Celine Langton ends her relationship with Guy Harcourt thinking he deserves someone more sophisticated. But why can't she give back his ring?

A Suitable Husband *by Jessica Steele*
When Jermaine begins working with Lukas Tavinor, she realises he's the kind of man she's always dreamed of marrying. Does it matter that her sister feels the same way?

On sale Friday 7th October 2005

To be or not to be…his mistress!

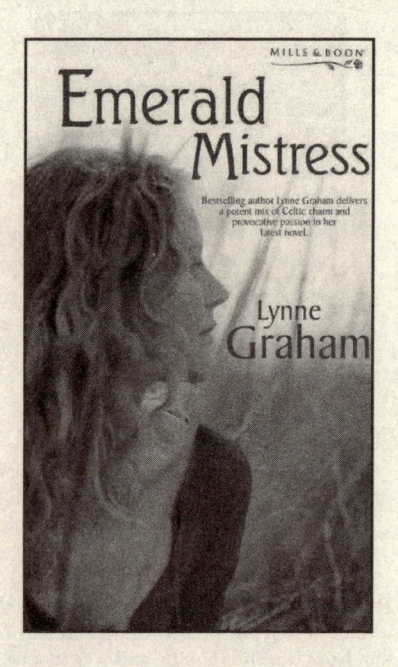

Emerald Mistress

Bestselling author Lynne Graham delivers a potent mix of Celtic charm and provocative passion in her latest novel.

Lynne Graham

When Harriet's world crashes down, the unexpected legacy of a cottage in Ireland seems like the perfect escape – until she discovers that the man who cost Harriet her job is entitled to half her inheritance! Rafael's solution is to make her his mistress – while Harriet's is to resist this sexy neighbour…if she can.

On sale Friday 7th October 2005

Available at most branches of WHSmith, Tesco, ASDA, Borders, Eason, Sainsbury's and most bookshops

2 FULL LENGTH BOOKS FOR £5.99

No.1 *New York Times* bestselling author

NORA ROBERTS

"The most successful novelist on Planet Earth."
—Washington Post

MYSTERIOUS

THIS MAGIC MOMENT and *THE RIGHT PATH*

On sale 18th November 2005

Available at most branches of WHSmith, Tesco, ASDA, Martins, Borders, Eason, Sainsbury's and all good paperback bookshops.

Christmas is magical – when you share it with someone special

SHENANDOAH CHRISTMAS by Lynnette Kent

After his wife dies, Ben Tremaine doesn't think the holidays will ever be festive again for his children – or him. But when Caitlyn Gregory arrives and puts smiles on their faces, he starts to wonder if Christmas wishes can come true after all.

THE CHRISTMAS WIFE by Sherryl Lewis

A single father has enough trouble juggling career, home and family – let alone the attraction he feels for a former high school classmate. But perhaps a trip down memory lane is just what he needs to make this Christmas the best – and most romantic – ever.

On sale 21st October 2005

MILLS & BOON

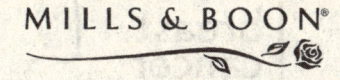

BCC/AD b

During the month of October Harlequin Mills & Boon will donate 10p from the sale of every Modern Romance™ series book to help Breast Cancer Campaign in *researching the cure*.

Breast Cancer Campaign's scientific projects look at improving diagnosis and treatment of breast cancer, better understanding how it develops and ultimately either curing the disease or preventing it.

Do your part to help

Visit www.breastcancercampaign.org

And make a donation today.

breast cancer CAMPAIGN

researching the cure

Breast Cancer Campaign is a company limited by guarantee registered in England and Wales. Company No. 05074725. Charity registration No. 299758.
Breast Cancer Campaign, Clifton Centre, 110 Clifton Street, London EC2A 4HT.
Tel: 020 7749 3700 Fax: 020 7749 3701 www.breastcancercampaign.org

BCC/AD a

breast cancer CAMPAIGN

researching the cure

The facts you need to know:

- **One woman in nine** in the United Kingdom will develop breast cancer during her lifetime.

- Each year **40,700** women are newly diagnosed with breast cancer and around **12,800** women will die from the disease. However, survival rates are improving, with on average 77 per cent of women still alive five years later.

- **Men can also suffer from breast cancer**, although currently they make up less than one per cent of all new cases of the disease.

Britain has one of the highest breast cancer death rates in the world. Breast Cancer Campaign wants to understand why and do something about it. Statistics cannot begin to describe the impact that breast cancer has on the lives of those women who are affected by it and on their families and friends.